Taken for a Fool

A Caroline Spencer Novel

Leslyn Amthor Spinelli

Printed in the United States of America
First Printing, November 2016
Door Creek Press
P.O. Box 17383
Minneapolis, MN 55417

www.LeslynAmthorSpinelli.com

Cover photograph © Claire Ogunsola
Author photograph © Claire Ogunsola

ISBN 13: 9780998112404
ISBN: 0998112402

Also by Leslyn Amthor Spinelli

Taken for Granted

Taken by Surprise

For Gianna
God is gracious

CHAPTER ONE

The P word interrupted my reverie and, truth be told, scared the bejesus out of me.

Sitting at our out-of-the-way table at Louisianne's in downtown Middleton, Wisconsin, late that Friday evening, I felt completely content. Over companionable conversation in the sparsely occupied restaurant, Dominic and I had shared a leisurely dinner of pecan crab cakes, shrimp etouffée, and blackened catfish. Lulled by the jazzy piano version of "Iko-Iko" wafting from the barroom and a bottle of Pecina Rioja, I'd been mesmerized by the warmth of Dominic's hand on mine, his mellow voice, and his eyes. Those soulful ebony eyes that had drawn me to him a few months earlier as I'd come out of my grieving widow's fog.

He can't be asking me to marry him. It's too soon! Reading my alarmed expression, a flush of embarrassment crept up Dominic's neck and face. He reached for his empty water glass and scanned the dining room in vain for the waitress. Instead, he took a swig of wine. "Oh, man, what a bad choice of words," he said. "I didn't mean *that* kind of proposal, Caroline. We're not ready to take that leap."

Dominic Marquez had been a good friend during the two years since my husband David's death in a car accident. A private investigator with unmatched determination, he'd uncovered evidence that resulted in a three-million-dollar insurance settlement, ensuring the financial security of my four children and me. I'd long suspected he was in love with me. But I had never felt pressured to move beyond friendship.

One night, several weeks earlier, I had found myself sitting next to Dominic on the couch, holding hands. Later, we'd hugged goodbye. A brief kiss sealed our next goodbye and a longer, though still-chaste, kiss sealed the next. With each baby step toward intimacy, I'd felt like an adolescent—nervous, excited, and a tinge guilty. Was this okay? My body had responded with an emphatic "yes," but my mind was still married to David.

Now, I couldn't find words to ease the awkwardness. But Dominic regained his composure. He pushed aside our slice of Key lime pie and leaned across the table to stroke my cheek.

"Breathe," he said.

I inhaled the air-conditioned air deeply a few times. "Okay," I said, after my heartbeat resumed its normal pace.

He shifted a bit in his chair, then cleared his throat. "What I should've said was, 'I have a *suggestion*.' This evening makes me believe that we've moved two or three steps past friendship. It's not my imagination, is it?" His eyes, with their lush black Spanish lashes, were downcast, as if he couldn't bear to watch me say "no."

"It's not your imagination," I said quickly. "We have."

I glanced at the plain gold wedding band David had given me more than fifteen years earlier, still on my left hand. I remembered our wedding day, when I'd choked up while repeating the "till death do us part" vow. I remembered grinning as we exited the church to The Beatles' "When I'm Sixty-Four." I closed my eyes. *Oh, David, we never had the opportunity to talk about this. Is it all right with you that I move on?*

Dominic touched my ring gently and waited in silence until I finally looked up and nodded.

"Well, I for one am rather anxious to see where those steps might lead," he said. "Are you?"

"Anxious is a pretty good way to describe it. It's been almost twenty years since I've been in a new relationship. I'm not sure I'll know what to do."

"I guess the question is, do you want to give it a try?"

My eyes stung with tears. "Yes."

Dominic took a clean linen napkin from the vacant table next to us and pressed it into my hand. "Go ahead and cry. I understand why this is hard for you," he said, with a smile that beckoned to me through the flood of tears, melting away my uncertainties.

After a few moments, I sniffled, blotted my cheeks, and set the napkin aside. I took his hand. "Tell me about this proposal."

He grinned. "Well… I hoped you'd agree to a romantic getaway in Chicago next weekend. I called Abby and Glenda yesterday—"

"Dominic!" I said, dropping his hand in mock horror. "You told my mother-in-law and my best friend before you asked *me?*"

"I did," he said, flushing and looking down at his lap. "I wanted to have plans in place in hopes you'd say 'yes.'"

I slid the dessert plate back in front of us. "And since I said 'yes,' how 'bout we have some celebratory pie while you tell me more?"

We each took a bite. The smooth, tangy morsel melted in my mouth and slid down my throat. "Oh. My. God," I said, "If your getaway plans are half as good as this pie, we'll never want to come home."

"Amen."

We savored the rest in silence, signaled the waitress for coffee, and sat back to talk. I knew Abby—who doubled as our live-in nanny/housekeeper/cook—liked Dominic, but I couldn't imagine their conversation about his proposed tryst. After all, she was David's mother. Would she resent Dominic for wanting to step into David's place? I wiped my mouth and set aside my napkin. "Tell me what you said to Abby. How did she respond?"

Dominic chuckled. "I was so nervous about it that I called Glenda first for advice. You know Glenda—she whooped with excitement. She told me Abby would be fine with it and said to tell her she'd help with the kids. That gave me enough courage to make the second call." He paused for a sip of coffee.

"C'mon," I said. "Finish the story."

"Okay, okay. Seems my call woke both Abby and the baby up from naps. Abby was kind of disorientated at first. I told her I was going to invite you to go away with me next weekend, but beforehand I wanted to make sure it was okay with her—adding that Glenda had promised to help with the kids. Then that shrill noise from Abby's hearing aid rang in my ear and I realized she hadn't heard a word I'd said. So, I repeated my pitch, getting more nervous with every word." He took another sip of coffee.

"And?"

He waited a beat, clearly enjoying my suspense. "I think her exact words were, 'It's about time!' She called back ten minutes later to tell me she'd talked to Julia, who was ecstatic about the whole thing, too. They're planning a weekend full of activities for all the kids."

Unexpectedly touched by David's mom's and his sister, Julia's, approval, I felt a lump in my throat. "Thank you," I whispered to the universe.

We left the restaurant hand in hand. The stifling heat of the summer day had dissipated. "Do you mind if we take a little stroll?" he asked.

"If you don't mind lending me your jacket," I said, nodding toward the sport coat he carried. "The breeze feels chilly, and I left my shawl in the car."

He stopped to wrap the jacket around my shoulders, gazing into my eyes, then enveloped me in his arms. "I'm so glad you said 'yes,' Caroline."

"To the stroll?" I teased.

"Hush," he said, and nuzzled my neck. The warmth of his skin, the musky scent of his cologne, the stubble on his cheek, and the breathlessness in his voice awakened a longing I hadn't felt in years.

Minutes later I heard someone yell, "Get a room!" and looked across the street to see a trio of drunken college-aged boys in bright red UW Badger T-shirts.

"Thanks for the suggestion," Dominic yelled back, with a grin. He turned to me. "Wait until you hear about the room I reserved for next weekend."

In the car, with eyes on the road and both hands on the wheel, he told me his plans. "I got a great deal on a luxury room at the InterContinental Hotel on Michigan Avenue," he said. "King-sized bed, marble bathroom, bathrobes… the works." He paused and shook his head. "I'm sorry. If you think that's moving too quickly, I can get us separate rooms."

I laughed. "Wouldn't that defeat the purpose of a romantic getaway?"

"I was hoping you'd see it that way," he said, with the briefest glance in my direction.

I found his fastidious driving habits endearing and smiled to myself. "What else do you have planned?"

"I got tickets for the late show at Second City on Saturday night—I remembered you said you love going there. I want you to pick the restaurant for dinner, maybe someplace on Navy Pier if the weather's good? We can go to the Lincoln Park Zoo, hang out at the lakefront… whatever you want.

"Going anywhere without a passel of kids sounds wonderful to me."

"There's one more thing I wanted to run by you," he said, when we stopped at a light on Monroe Street. "Would you mind having a light lunch with my mother and Dani on Saturday—nothing that would spoil dinner. We could park the car at Mom's on the North Side and take the 'L' to the hotel afterward.

"If you don't want to, I'd completely understand," he added, hastily.

"I wouldn't mind. I'd love to meet your mom."

"Good, because she's already got the menu planned— and she's a fantastic cook."

"You're telling me your mother and your sister are in on this, too?" I asked, bending sideways to nudge his shoulder with mine. "Who *doesn't* know?"

He laughed. "I don't think Abby has told your kids yet."

A few minutes later, he parked in front of my house. "I wish I had a pickup truck with a bench seat," he said, tenderly stroking my cheek.

"It's probably good you don't," I said, with sincere regret. "I'd love to extend this wonderful evening, but I need to relieve Abby." I shrugged off his sport coat and gathered my things while Dominic got out to open my door.

He leaned against the car and pulled me close. We shared a long, slow kiss that dizzied me with desire. "Do you want to come in?" I managed to croak.

Dominic glanced toward the house. "I'm not sure that's wise," he said. "Someone's awake."

I turned and saw my twelve-year-old daughter, Lily, looking out her second-floor bedroom window with a furrowed brow and a stone-cold expression.

Headed to Chicago the following Saturday, our plan began to go south—figuratively—during a blinding rainstorm on the Kennedy Expressway. The heavy traffic set my nerves on edge and pulled to the forefront my fear of dying in an accident and orphaning my children. On high alert for hazards, Dominic gripped the wheel of his ten-year-old Buick Regal so tightly that his olive-skinned knuckles showed white. But it was the phone call that set things off.

The shrill ringtone and simultaneous vibration from Dominic's iPhone, rattling in the console cup holder, made us both jump. Dominic had a strict personal rule against using cell phones while driving. I wondered with irritation why he hadn't powered it off.

I glanced at the screen. "Your mom," I said. "Do you want me to answer it?"

I had neither met nor spoken to his mother in the whole time I'd known Dominic. It had been almost two decades since I'd had a new boyfriend whose mother needed introductions. *I'm too old for this!*

"You don't need to answer it," he said. "We should be there in under an hour—we're almost to O'Hare. Whatever it is can wait until then."

Five minutes later, the phone rang once more.

"Mom again?" he asked.

"Uh-huh."

"Put it on speaker, please." I noticed the vein in his temple throbbing as he stared through the windshield wipers. "What is it, Mom?" he asked with unmasked irritation when the call connected.

"It's me—Dani," I heard his sister say. "My phone's charging so I'm using hers. Something weird is going on with Mom. I wanted to give you guys a heads-up."

I'd met Dominic's older sister, Dani, twice. The first time Dominic brought her by my house in Madison, baby Lucy had cried incessantly from an undiagnosed ear infection. The second time, the three of us had met for dinner at State Street Brats—sans kids. I'd liked the way Dani piled the relish and mustard on her brat and ate with pleasure. She'd consumed three Miller Lites without expressing guilt about having one too many. This was a smart, down-to-earth woman with whom I had immediately connected.

"Hi, Dani, we're on speakerphone," I said. "Please tell me your mom hasn't decided she doesn't want to meet me, after all."

"Hey, Caroline," she replied. "It's not that, but I'm not sure what's up."

I took a sip of the coffee we'd bought at the Starbucks drive-thru in Rockford, spilling some on my beige silk pants when Dominic braked abruptly. I let out an involuntary, "*Shit!*"

He handed me a napkin from the console. "Dani," he said, "it's pouring rain and traffic is horrific. Just tell us what you called about."

"Okay—don't get testy. I got to Mom's about an hour ago, just as the mailman was leaving. I handed Mom the mail and went to the kitchen to get some coffee. When I got back to the living room, she was crying but refused to say why. She told me to call and tell you not to come, then went into her room and locked the door."

"¡Dios mío! Esto no tiene ningún sentido."

"I *know* it doesn't make any sense, Dominic," Dani said. "This was way more abrupt than any mood swing she's ever had, and I have no idea what brought it on. I convinced her it would be unspeakably rude to cancel lunch. So, she's in the kitchen now, finishing the meal. I'm out on the porch and intend to stay here 'til you arrive. Hurry up, okay?"

"We'll be there as soon as we can," he said, and nodded for me to disconnect.

He tapped his fingers on the steering wheel, apparently lost in thought. I fidgeted in my seat and finally—giving in to the temptation I'd been resisting for miles—reached for the brown paper lunch bag Abby had handed me before we left. "It's a few of my chocolate-chip-oatmeal cookies," she'd said, "—in case you get hungry on the road." I opened the bag and saw a piece of paper torn from a spiral notebook. Abby had written, "Have a wonderful trip!" and my four-year-old twins had added smiley faces and signed their names with blue and green crayons. I grinned and popped a cookie into my mouth. I didn't fully taste it but was gratified, just the same.

"Want a cookie?" I asked Dominic.

He shook his head.

The stop-and-start, bumper-to-bumper traffic and Dominic's silence counteracted my calming breaths, but during our forty-five-minute crawl to the Addison Street exit, at least the rain stopped. "Look," I said, pointing out the windshield, "a rainbow. Maybe it's a good omen."

He gave me half a smile. "I'm not a big believer in omens."

But he did come out of his funk and point out some sights on the North-Side cross-town thoroughfare. "That's the sandwich shop where I had my first job." A few blocks further east, "That huge brick building is Lane Tech, where I went to high school."

Dominic took a left on Leavitt Street and a right onto West Waveland Avenue. "Here it is," he said, with subdued pride. "My neighborhood."

I could only imagine how pretty this residential neighborhood was in bright sunshine. The narrow, tree-lined street with modest, early twentieth-century, one- and two-family homes—most with front porches, colorful flowerbeds, and immaculately kept lawns—was beyond inviting and made me forget for a moment the coming introductions in Alejandra Marquez's apartment.

He nodded toward a brownstone two-flat. "That's it—the one with all the crockery flower pots on the porch." He pulled into a parking spot a half-block down the street. "Let's take our bags with us so we don't have to come back to the car after lunch," Dominic said. "The 'L' stop is the other direction."

"How old were you when you moved here?" I asked, as I pulled my wheeled overnight bag from the trunk.

"Ten. We'd lived in Evanston until then, but after my dad died we couldn't afford to stay there. My uncle owned this place and rented the first floor to us. About fifteen years ago, Mom bought the building. It was a working-class neighborhood then—I guess it still is, though perhaps a bit more gentrified. She rents out the upstairs, which easily covers the mortgage."

The rain had freshened things up; the summer air smelled of honeysuckle and clean concrete. We nodded to an elderly man sweeping shallow puddles from his front steps with a weathered broom. Dominic rested his hand lightly on my shoulder as we approached his childhood home. As promised, Dani waited on the front porch, seated on a wooden bench painted with gleaming, dark-red enamel. She turned to exhale one last stream of cigarette smoke, then stubbed out the butt in a huge, potted begonia. She stood to hug us.

The siblings—both lean and muscular—shared the same flawless olive complexion, dark eyes, and lustrous, dark brown hair. I felt mousy next to them, with my faded blond hair, prone-to-freckles skin, and the extra five pounds I hadn't been able to shed since Lucy's birth. Wearing no makeup, a faded yellow sundress, and Teva sandals, Dani managed to look like she'd stepped off the cover of *Mademoiselle* magazine, though a slight tremor in her hand hinted at underlying stress. She was several inches shorter than Dominic's six feet and her face was slightly more angular, but they both had a dimple in the left cheek when they smiled.

"I see you're still driving that old-lady car," Dani said, with a grin.

"Scoff if you want, but that car is my secret to successful surveillance—nobody expects to be tailed by a Buick," Dominic said. He nodded toward the pack of cigarettes on the porch railing. "I thought you quit."

"I was down to one a day—until today," she said, collapsing back onto the bench. "I just finished next Saturday's ration."

Dominic chuckled for half a second. "Have a seat, Caroline," he said, leaning against the railing. "I need a little more information before we head inside."

Dani scooted over to make room for me. She ran her hands quickly through her hair twice, and then a third time more slowly. "Okay… Mom had been cooking up a storm. She was dressed to the nines and even had on a little makeup. I went to the kitchen to grab a cup of coffee and glance at the newspaper and by the time I came out, she was going into her room."

"You said she was crying."

"Uh-huh. Almost sobbing, actually. Her face was blotchy and she was trying to wipe away tears with the hem of her apron. I said, 'What's wrong?' but she didn't respond. She dropped some papers on the floor in the doorway to her room and I bent to pick 'em up for her, but she yelled, 'No! Leave me alone.' She snatched up the papers, went in her room, and locked the door."

Dani reached for another cigarette, then stopped herself. "So… I'm trying to talk to her through the door. She won't tell me what's upset her, just that now she 'can never make it right.' That's when she said I should call and tell you not to come."

"Can never make *what* right?" Dominic asked, sharply.

"I don't know!" Dani snapped back.

He hung his head. "Sorry. I can't imagine what she could she have gotten in the mail that upset her like that."

"Maybe medical test results?" I asked.

Dani shook her head. "Other than some acid reflux, Mom's fine."

"What about Aunt Luz?" Dominic asked.

"Her cancer's responding to the chemo," Dani said. "I know Mom's pretty worried, but no one would send medical information about Luz to Mom."

"How 'bout financial statements?" I asked.

Dominic touched my shoulder. "Mom's only debt is her mortgage, and that's almost paid off. She doesn't have a lot of money, but what she has is invested in conservative mutual funds with a reliable broker—whom she had me investigate to verify he's no Bernie Madoff. She pays off her Discover card balance in full every month and watches the statements like a hawk to make sure her identity hasn't been stolen. If she got a report reflecting major losses or fraudulent charges she'd be on the phone to the police, not hiding in her room."

We didn't speak for a few moments. A tantalizing aroma wafted from the open window next to me, and I heard strains of classical guitar music coming from the recesses of the apartment.

Dominic stood and extended his hands to help Dani and me from the bench. "We might as well get this over with," he said.

Chapter Two

Dominic held open the door and I followed Dani into their mother's apartment—and what felt like a completely different world. The parquet floor of the entryway led into a living room with stark white walls, crowded with ornate iron lamps and light fixtures and heavy, earth-toned furniture and draperies. If we hadn't walked in from a front porch in Middle America, I would have sworn I'd been transported to Seville.

Dani turned to me. "Wow, huh?"

I nodded.

"Imagine what it was like for us as kids—living in a frickin' Spanish museum," she said. "Mom never wanted us to forget our roots. We weren't even allowed to speak English at home unless we had Anglo company."

Dominic shuddered. "She promised not to lapse into Spanish over lunch," he said to his sister. "I'll go get her. You two can have a seat."

I sat in an upholstered chair with elaborately carved, dark wooden arms and legs—the word *sturdy* came to mind. I found it more comfortable than it looked but couldn't imagine relaxing in it. Dani collapsed onto one end of a gold brocade sofa and rested her feet on the massive coffee table. "I'm glad you came," she said with a sigh. "I hope this goes well."

Before I could respond, I heard Dominic's voice from the back of the apartment. "You're upset about something, Mom. You need to tell me what."

"¡No! No es cuenta de tu."

"Yes, it *is* my business. You invited Caroline and me for lunch and now you've gone into one of your moods for reasons you won't explain."

"Hablaremos de eso otro día," I heard her say with a tone of authority.

"Okay, Mom," Dominic replied, more quietly. "Now, please come meet her."

"She said, 'We'll talk about it another day,'" Dani translated for me. "But I'm not sure he'll let it rest."

I wiped my clammy palms on my slacks and stood as Dominic and his mother entered the room. A slender woman—perhaps five-four—she walked with a regal but weary gait, holding onto his arm as if to steady herself. "Mom, this is Caroline Spencer," he said. "Caroline, my mother—Alejandra Marquez."

I extended my hand. "It's nice to meet you, Mrs. Marquez."

She stared at me vacantly until Dominic nudged her. "Thank you for coming," she replied, briefly shaking my hand. "Excuse me while I put lunch on the table. Ayúdame, por favor, Daniela."

Dani sighed and got to her feet. "I'll help you, Mom. But remember: no Spanish today."

"She doesn't look well," I whispered to Dominic as his mother and Dani left the room. "Maybe we shouldn't stay."

"That would make it worse. I promise we'll leave as soon as we're done eating."

Dwarfed by its furnishings, the small dining room contained a formally-laid table with lighted candles, an antique sideboard and curio cabinet, and four upholstered, straight-backed chairs. "Please sit," Dani called from the adjacent kitchen. "Lunch is served."

When Dominic, Alejandra, and I were seated, Dani came through the swinging door bearing a white crockery platter. "Berejenas con miel—eggplant fritters with honey—fresh from the oven. Make way, the platter's hot," she said. Then, "For heaven's sake, Mom, move the candles or I'll burn myself putting this on the table."

Dominic popped up and moved the candles to the sideboard, extinguishing them with his thumb and fore-finger. "Never mind, Mom. They looked lovely when we sat down."

Alejandra bit her lip and looked down at her lap. We passed our plates to Dani, who dished up the fritters.

"These are wonderful, Mrs. Marquez," I said, after the first bite.

She nodded but didn't reply.

"It's a traditional Andalusian dish," Dani said, "like everything she's serving today. That's the region in Spain where Mom grew up."

"I've actually been to Andalusia," I said, "on a choir trip when I was in high school. We stayed in Seville. Did you live near there, Mrs. Marquez?"

"No," she said, focused on her plate.

Dominic exchanged a nervous glance with Dani. "Mom lived in a small town outside of Málaga," he said, "—until she married Dad. As I think I told you, he was a professor at the University of Barcelona."

"Uh-huh," I said. "Economics, right?"

"Yes," Dani said. "Which put him at odds with Generalissimo Franco. Dad was eventually granted political asylum here, when I was five years old and Dominic was a baby. He got a job at Northwestern University and—though he appreciated his Spanish roots—never looked back."

"After Dani and I were in school full-time," Dominic said, "Mom went to UIC and got her degree. She taught Spanish at Lake View High School and just retired a few years ago."

We finished our appetizers in silence, punctuated by the clinking of cutlery on china plates. When we declined more fritters, Alejandra set her napkin aside and got up to clear the appetizer plates. "Pardon me while I go finish the soup," she said. "The fideos—I mean vermicelli—takes a few minutes to cook."

"Soup?" I whispered to Dominic and Dani. "I thought we were invited for a *light* lunch."

Dani shrugged. "Everything's relative."

The savory sopa de pollo—chicken soup with vermicelli and prosciutto, topped with chopped, hard-boiled eggs—was among the best soups I'd ever tasted. Alejandra didn't partake of it, though, instead remaining in the kitchen to prepare the next course.

Dani took our empty soup bowls to the kitchen and ushered her mother back to the table. "Tell Caroline about our entrée while I go get it," she said. The heavenly aroma of roasted garlic floated from the kitchen when the door swung open.

Alejandra sighed. She put her napkin on her lap and smoothed it several times, making no eye contact with us. "It's a simple dish: scrambled eggs with asparagus and shrimp, cooked in olive oil and topped with parsley. I hope you like it."

"If it tastes half as good as it smells, I'll love it," I said. And, indeed, I did. Though anxious to escape the tension at the table, I told myself to eat slowly and savor each bite.

Dani finished her meal first, leaned back in her chair, and gazed around the room. "Mom," she said, "how come you're not wearing your anniversary ring? I've never seen you take it off."

Alejandra finally looked up from her plate. "¿Disculpe?"

"I said, 'Why aren't you wearing your anniversary ring?'"

"It's at the jewelers being repaired."

"What happened to it?" Dani asked.

"What difference does it make?" Alejandra replied, shooting her daughter a dark look.

"Just curious. No need to get defensive."

Alejandra wiped her lips with her napkin, stood up, and said, "If everyone's finished, I'll serve dessert. Coffee? Tea?"

"Oh, Mom," Dominic said, as he touched my knee under the table. "We really don't need dessert."

"What, pray tell, am I supposed to do with a pan of flan if you don't eat it?" she asked, blinking back tears.

"Small pieces then, please," he said, with equanimity. "And I don't care for coffee or tea. Caroline?"

"No, thank you," I said, pushing my empty plate away. "May I help you clear the table, Mrs. Marquez?"

"There's so little room in this damn dining room. Daniela can get out more easily," she said, and headed again for the kitchen.

"¡Jesucristo!" Dani muttered, standing to take our plates. "Can this day get any more effed up?"

The answer quickly became apparent. Dani returned with a stoneware pitcher, refilled our water glasses, and slumped into her chair. "This mood seems worse than usual," she said, sotto voce, to her brother.

Alejandra came through the swinging door a moment later, carrying a silver tray of plated flan. "Escuché eso, Daniela," she said.

"I don't care if you heard me," Dani replied. "You're being rude, especially to Caroline. And speak English."

Alejandra handed us each a plate containing a large slice of caramel-topped flan and set a miniscule piece at her own spot. "I hope it came out okay," she said with a sullen look.

"It always does, Mom," Dominic replied.

I took a bite. The smooth, delicate custard tasted delectable on my tongue but displeased my stomach, already struggling with stress and too much food. I couldn't imagine eating it all. "This is delicious, Mrs. Marquez," I said.

"Thank you," she said, without a glance in my direction.

I ate another small bite, put down my spoon, and tried to calm myself. The windowless dining room walls felt like they were closing in, and my ears began to ring. *It's not a panic attack*, I told myself. *Just a touch of anxiety.* I pushed back my chair and stood. "I need to use the bathroom."

Alejandra's chair blocked my exit, and she seemed not to have heard or seen me. "Mom," Dani said, "get up and let Caroline out."

"Oh, lo siento," Alejandra replied, as she stood and moved her chair with exaggerated effort. Dani rolled her eyes.

The breeze through the bathroom window and the tap water I splashed on my face restored my equilibrium. I couldn't help feeling disappointed at Dominic's failure to stand up to his mother. Dani had been the one to remind her to speak English and to mind her manners, while he'd kowtowed to her sullen mood.

Though my stomach had quickly settled, I probably stayed in the bathroom for ten minutes—longer than courtesy allows—before finger-combing my hair and opening the door. I took a few steps down the short hallway toward the dining room and paused to listen.

"…What did you get in the mail today that upset you?" Dani asked.

"I don't know what you're talking about," Alejandra replied.

"Was it a statement from your broker?" Dominic asked. "I've told you a hundred times that your investments are fine—they're in conservative funds. Ups and downs are to be expected. If those fluctuations are going to send you into tailspins, you need to let me monitor the account."

I heard the clatter of plates and cutlery. "Get out of here, both of you!" Alejandra shouted. "And mind your own business."

I headed to the living room, unsure whether to sit. Dani joined me a few moments later. "Up for a walk?" she asked.

"Dominic and I planned to head to the hotel right after lunch," I said, with a glance at the carved mahogany grandfather clock in the corner—unable to ignore its baritone ticking. "It's already 2:30."

"I know. But he's the one who suggested you and I go out and get some air. He's gonna stay and try to get to the bottom of this."

My heart sank. "I guess it's better than sitting here."

She grabbed her purse from an end table and yelled toward the kitchen, "We're leaving, Dom. Call or text when you want us to come back."

I swallowed another wave of disappointment.

She lit a cigarette when we hit the sidewalk. "I could really use a cold beer. How 'bout you?"

I could really use a chilled glass of Pinto Grigio in our luxurious bed at the InterContinental—both before and after getting to know your brother in the Biblical sense.

She looked at me as though she'd heard my lament. "I know it's not what you had in mind."

"True. But a beer *would* taste good."

The mile-long trek to D'Agostino's Pizzeria, a few blocks west of Wrigley Field, helped burn off some nervous energy, particularly since Dani walked faster than anyone I'd ever known. It helped, too, that our pace wasn't conducive to conversation. She held open the door for me, and I tried to be nonchalant as I caught my breath. A wave of refrigerated air raised goose bumps on my bare arms.

"This place has been here for years," she said, waving to the carryout counterman who called her by name. "Dominic and I grew up on their pizza, and I worked here when I was seventeen."

We went around a corner and approached the ancient bar, where two middle-aged men—one wearing a Cubs hat and the other wearing a faded Cubs T-shirt—sat staring at a NASCAR race on TV. Otherwise, the place was deserted. "It'll pick up when the game comes on," Dani said. "The Cubbies play the D'backs in Arizona at 5:00. They've got a good IPA here—is that okay with you?"

I nodded.

"How 'bout we sit on the patio?"

We settled into two wrought-iron armchairs, and my goose bumps receded as quickly as they'd come. The hefty bartender—surprisingly fleet of foot—delivered a pitcher of beer and two frosted mugs. Dani lit a cigarette while I poured.

The cold beer, with its distinctive hoppy flavor, tasted every bit as good as it appeared. I took two, long, thirst-quenching sips, then wiped the corner of my mouth with a napkin from the table's dispenser. "Good choice," I said, "though I'm not sure I'll be much help drinking a pitcher."

"After the scene at Mom's, I'm thinking *one* pitcher won't be enough."

I couldn't conjure up an appropriate response. We sipped in silence for a while.

"May I?" I asked Dani, nodding toward the pack of cigarettes sitting on the table. "I quit the habit more than fifteen years ago but still occasionally indulge."

She grinned conspiratorially. "Be my guest, but don't tell Dominic."

I inhaled deeply. The lightheadedness brought on by the infrequent use of nicotine, combined with a slight beer buzz, felt heavenly. I relaxed for the first time all day.

Dani poured herself a second beer. "I'm really sorry for the way my mom acted. I should've listened when she said to tell you not to come. But Dominic wouldn't have abided her canceling lunch."

"Yet he abided the monkey wrench she threw into his plans with me…"

Without a word, she lit another cigarette and exhaled slowly. *Oh, shit. I just criticized both her brother and mother—she has every right to take offense.*

She waited a beat then spoke quietly, without a trace of rancor, "Dom's the designated worrier for our mom. Sometimes he gets wacked out about it."

"Designated worrier?"

"Yeah. When our dad was dying—he'd had stomach cancer for a couple years and the treatments didn't work— he had Mom bring us to the hospital to say our goodbyes. Dad's pretty doped up. He takes Dominic's hand and says, 'From now on, you'll be the man of the house. I'm counting on you to take care of your mother and sister.' Dom nods his head up and down like a bobblehead toy and says, 'I will, Dad. I promise.' I'm fifteen at the time and having none of his sexist nonsense, so I say, 'I can take care of myself,' and storm out of the room without saying goodbye."

I nodded, picturing ten-year-old Dominic making such a promise to his father and his angry, teenaged sister leaving the bedside in a huff.

"I stayed pissed for the next three years and took care of myself by spending most of my time with friends and moving out as soon as I graduated from high school. Dominic lived out his promise to take care of Mom, despite the toll it took on him."

"What—" My question drowned in the wake of a fire truck rushing up Southport Avenue. "What kind of toll?" I asked when the siren faded.

"Emotional mostly, but she was physically abusive a time or two."

I stifled a gasp.

"When we were growing up—even when Dad was alive—the atmosphere in our household was dictated by Mom's moods. Usually she was a driven woman, cooking up a storm and cleaning 'til the whole house sparkled, attending college with straight As, helping with our school projects. You didn't dare stand in the way of her agenda. As long as you went along, she was a joy to be around: upbeat, funny. We loved those days. But sometimes she'd get testy and yell at us or throw things, and even my dad couldn't calm her down. Worst of all—maybe once or twice a year—she'd go into a deep depression. Wouldn't come out of her room for days, called in sick to college or work, wouldn't eat. Dad said it was stress and she just needed time to recharge her batteries."

Dani paused to top off her glass. "More?" she asked.

"Sure."

She set down the pitcher and continued. "Back then, people—especially hard-headed people like my father—weren't likely to admit a family member needed psychiatric help. It wouldn't do for a renowned economist to have a skeleton pushing to get out of the closet. So, we all toughed it out. She got worse after Dad died, though, and Dominic worried incessantly. He tried to be the perfect kid, but even that wasn't enough to ward off her moods."

"And no one helped? Not even your Aunt Luz?"

She shook her head. "After Luz's husband set us up in the brownstone, Mom didn't speak to her for several years. You'd have thought she'd be grateful, but Mom was convinced they were gouging her for rent. In retrospect, I think Mom was just pushing Luz away so she wouldn't realize how sick she was." The sound of a rubber bike horn emanated from Dani's phone. "My daughter. Hold on." She picked it up and began typing.

I reached for another cigarette, striking the match three times before managing to light it, and sank back against my chair. *Why couldn't it have been Dominic texting her?* My own phone sat impotently on the table.

"My kids are with their dad this weekend," Dani said, when she finished the text. "I'd hoped to meet some friends for dinner tonight and to get in a round of golf tomorrow, but guess *that's* not gonna happen.

"I'll cut to the chase: Mom is bipolar—what used to be called manic-depressive—though it took years to figure it out. During my first abnormal psych class in college, I realized something was seriously wrong with her, and the next time she slipped into depression, I got her committed for evaluation. The psychiatrist put her on antidepressants and agreed to release her if she complied with outpatient treatment. Mom took the meds as prescribed and willingly went to talk therapy. Within a few months, things were on a pretty even keel."

"But?"

Dani hung her head. "Then she complained about side effects from the medication—particularly weight gain—and they switched her to one that happened to induce mania. The first major episode seemed to go on forever, and she was *so* hateful to Dominic. One day she hit him with a lamp."

"He never told me any of this."

"It got uglier. She almost lost her job for flying off the handle at a student. She went through three different psychiatrists and God knows how many talk therapists over the course of four or five years. Dominic even lived with Aunt Luz one summer while Mom went to some holistic healer in Arizona. I finally threatened to have her committed for electroshock therapy unless she saw the psychiatrist my graduate advisor recommended. He correctly diagnosed her, put her on lithium to stabilize her moods, and life got better for all of us. And after two years at city college, Dominic felt comfortable going away to the university."

The waiter interrupted her. Without consulting me, Dani ordered another pitcher and two appetizers, then stared at the city bus stopped beside us for a traffic light, apparently lost in thought.

I checked my phone—no messages. I shifted in my seat. "It's almost 5:00. Should we text Dominic?"

"Go ahead," Dani said absently. "I need to use the restroom." I watched her navigate around three, now-occupied tables, mumbling "excuse me" as she bumped into two of them.

I typed the text: "We r @ Dag's pizza. R u ready for us to come back?" I stared at the screen—Dominic usually replied quickly to messages. Nothing. Seeds of anxiety began to take root in my brain, fed by a flood of discouragement. *For God's sake, Dominic, answer the frickin' text.*

The waiter brought our beer and appetizers—bruschetta and toasted ravioli—before Dani returned. He nodded at my almost-empty glass and moved to refill it. I shook my head. "Not yet, thanks." Though not the least bit hungry, I needed food in my stomach to keep my wits about me. I stabbed a cheese-filled ravioli with my fork, dipped it in marinara, and popped it in my mouth.

"Good?" Dani asked, as she sat down.

I nodded and moved a few more to my plate.

"Any word from Dom?"

"Nope."

"That's not a good sign. We'll head back after we eat—I ran into some friends inside and they'll gladly finish the beer for us." She poured us each another glass and divvied up the appetizers.

After a few bites, she resumed her story. "Mom's gone off her meds several times over the last twenty years. That's pretty typical for folks diagnosed with BD. They miss the mania—or in Mom's case, the hypomania, which is a little less drastic and never psychotic. And after being on the meds for a while, patients tend to forget how awful the depressive episodes were."

"What happens when she goes off the meds?"

"Sometimes she's okay for a while and we don't notice, but eventually she becomes too depressed to hide it. Before Dominic moved to Madison three years ago, he'd stop by every day to check on her and assess her moods— though she refused to let him monitor her medications.

He was constantly voicing his suspicions, and frankly, I think he was getting a little paranoid about things. Mom finally blew up and told him to get a life. I agreed with her, and I promised him I'd carry the vigilance baton. It makes more sense anyway, me being a psychiatric social worker and all."

Dani ate a bite of bruschetta and took hold of her beer mug, tapping the handle with her forefinger, apparently weighing her next words. Finally, she looked up at me. "I gotta be honest with you. I suspect Mom went off her meds again several months ago. I asked her one time and she wouldn't answer. Said something new-agey like 'I'm in an excellent space right now. Stop worrying.'"

"What made you suspect?"

"Lately, she's been gone for whole afternoons at a time—on days when she's not scheduled to do volunteer work or anything—and is vague when I ask about it. Plus, it's not just the anniversary ring that's missing. Dad acquired a small painting by the famous Spanish artist Joan Miró some years before we moved here. It was hanging in Mom's living room until recently. I noticed a couple weeks ago it was gone and asked her about it. She claims she's having it appraised, but I'm not so sure. And she started cooking and cleaning the minute she found out you and Dominic were coming to visit, which I initially thought was cute and normal. Now that I think about it, it feels more like hypomania."

"Did you tell Dominic you think she's off her meds?"

"No. I didn't want to worry him."

So you tell me *and let* me *be the one to decide whether or not to worry* him? *Thanks a lot.*

I pushed aside my beer and half-eaten appetizers and reached for my purse. "Let's pay and head out. I need to talk with your brother."

"You're right. It's time to go."

Dani summoned an Uber car to take us back to Alejandra's brownstone, and then dialed Dominic. She listened for a moment and hung up in frustration. "Straight to voicemail. So much for your romantic weekend."

I glanced at my own phone—6:00—and said a silent prayer that he'd been able to talk sense into his mother, that our evening could be salvaged. We had a few hours before we'd lose our reservation at the InterContinental and five hours until the show at Second City.

"I'm not sure how romantic it was destined to be," I said, my cheeks flushing with embarrassment. "Good chance it'd be awkward as hell. I haven't dated since 1998."

"Believe me, it's like riding a bike," she said, with half a grin as we climbed into the car.

My unease grew; we hit every red light on Addison Street and Dani picked at the skin on her chapped lower lip.

She let out a sigh when the driver stopped in front of her mother's apartment. "Might as well see what we're dealing with," she said. She got out of the car and tripped over the curb, landing on her knees and sending the contents of her purse flying. "Fuck, fuck, fuck!"

I mumbled thanks to the driver and went around the car to help. She brushed the dirt off her legs and stood tentatively while I picked up her belongings. "You okay?"

Dani nodded and headed for the front door, entering without knocking. I followed a few steps behind.

Dominic sat on the living room sofa, elbows on knees and head in hands. He didn't look up when we walked in. The Cubs game—the graphics showing the score tied in the bottom of the third inning—played, sans volume, on a small, flat-screen TV. His cell phone lay within easy reach on the end table beside him.

"What the hell, Dom?" Dani asked. "Why didn't you answer our text, or call?"

He barely raised his head. "I turned off my phone. One of my clients was texting incessantly and driving me nuts. I told you I'd call when you should come back."

I sat down beside him, and Dani sank into an ancient, brown-leather, wing-backed chair. "After you left, Mom went back into her room and locked the door," he said, with a tone of defeat. "I decided to leave her alone for a while. When I knocked and tried again—maybe an hour and a half ago—she asked why I was being so disrespectful and ignoring her request for privacy. I said, 'Fine, Mama, I'll wait until you're ready to come out and talk.'"

"Did it sound like she was crying?" I asked.

He shook his head. "Not really. More like she was just tired."

"And she hasn't come out to use the bathroom?" Dani asked. "It's been hours."

"No."

Dani stared down at her lap.

I took Dominic's hand. "You need to tell him, Dani," I said, trying for a quiet but assertive tone.

"Tell me what?" he asked.

As Dani relayed her suspicion that Alejandra had discontinued her mood-stabilizing medication, Dominic's face grew stony. "I didn't see the sense in both of us worrying," she concluded. "I'm sorry."

He waited a beat, then pulled his hand from mine, stood up, and stormed toward the closed bedroom door adjacent to the living room. "You know this puts her at a greater risk for suicide, Dani! How could you not tell me?" He pounded on the door, calling, "Mom! Open up."

No response.

Dominic took a step backward, raised his right leg, and kicked the door. The doorframe splintered, but the lock held. He threw his weight against the door, and this time it opened, banging against the wall with a reverberating thud. He barged into his mother's room. Dani and I joined him a moment later. Alejandra lay awkwardly on top of the burgundy brocade bedspread, motionless, her head tilted to one side and her mouth open.

Dani screamed, "Mom!"

Dominic pulled his mother to a seated position and shook her limp body. "She's barely breathing. Wake up, Mom! C'mon—wake up!"

I saw an open prescription bottle on the bedside table. "Dominic, Dani—" I said, pointing. "She may have taken those pills."

"Call 9-1-1," he yelled at me. "There's a landline in the kitchen. Dani, see if you can get a pulse."

My fingers trembled as I punched the number into the clunky beige phone—so old the numbers were almost worn off its keys—and waited what seemed an eternity for the dispatcher. "Her pulse is weak," Dani called from the bedroom. "We can't wake her up!" I relayed the information with as much calm as I could muster. *Why did we stay at D'Agonstino's so long? What were we thinking?*

The ambulance arrived ten minutes later. Two EMTs, a stocky black woman and a muscle-bound Hispanic man, wasted no time on pleasantries. They quickly assessed the situation and lifted Alejandra onto a gurney—a bit roughly, I thought. The woman sealed the pill bottle in a plastic bag and stuffed it into her pocket while her partner secured an oxygen mask on Alejandra's face and a blood pressure cuff on her arm. "Do you have a preferred hospital?" she asked.

"Thorek," Dani replied, grabbing her mom's purse off the dresser. "I'll bring her medical cards."

"One of you can ride with us," the man called over his shoulder as he pushed the gurney toward the front door.

"You're in no condition to drive, Dani," Dominic said, reaching in his pocket and pulling out his car keys. "You ride along with Mom. I'll meet you at the E.R."

Should I wait here? Should I go with you?

Before I could open my mouth, they all rushed out the door. I stood alone—abandoned—in the living room, leaning against the doorjamb. As the siren sounded and the ambulance roared away, I noticed Dominic's cell phone, still powered off, sitting on the table where he'd left it.

CHAPTER THREE

Angry tears streaming down my face, I flopped onto Alejandra's sofa, silently cursing its uninviting character. Dani was right—who'd want to live in a frickin' museum? The grandfather clock taunted me with its incessant ticking. Ticking away precious minutes of what should have been a blissful weekend.

I replayed the last half hour in my mind and realized Dominic hadn't uttered one word to me after barking orders to call the ambulance. Yet he'd had the wherewithal to notice Dani shouldn't be driving. *Guess that tells you where his priorities lie. Oh, give the man a break—his mother's mentally ill and might not make it. Or might be brain damaged if she lives.*

But it suddenly became perfectly clear: I could not spend one more minute in this stifling apartment waiting for God knows what and for God knows how long. I rummaged through my purse to find paper and pen and scrawled a note, "Gone to hotel – C," which I left on the table with Dominic's cell phone. I grabbed my overnight bag, shut the door behind me, and headed for the "L" stop.

I'd lived in Chicago in my twenties and visited many times since, so had no fear of its mass transit system. I could've hailed a cab on Addison Street, but there'd be at least another hour of daylight and I decided I could use the seven-block walk to depressurize.

I pulled my bag down Addison, lulled by the rhythmic sound of its wheels clunking over the sidewalk cracks, still crying but glad to be moving. No one noticed my tears. Three people, engrossed in their cell phones, waited at a bus stop as I walked past, and a woman walking an overweight dachshund moved aside to let me by, without a glance at my face. The street traffic was noisy and brisk, the smell of diesel fuel permeating the night air.

I navigated the turnstile at the "L" stop smoothly enough to aggravate only one patron behind me, and lugged my bag up the steps to the platform only a tad breathlessly. I found a single seat at the back of the train car and crumpled into it, mentally and physically exhausted. A teenaged white kid sitting in front of me smelled vaguely of marijuana, and rap music leaked from his earbuds as he nodded to the beat.

I sat for a moment and realized what I needed most— with the possible exception of another beer—was an objective opinion. I pulled out my iPhone and texted Glenda, "Can u talk?"

The phone rang in response. "Hey, I'm surprised to hear from you!" my best friend said. "How's the weekend going?

"I'm on the 'L' headed downtown," I said in a loud voice—trying to drown out the unkempt toothless man talking to himself across the aisle. "I feel like I've fallen down a rabbit hole and need some advice from above ground."

She paused. "*I'm* on the train, not *we're* on the train? Why are you going downtown alone? Where's Dominic?"

I told her the story and cringed when I noticed the toothless man staring at me with pity in his eyes.

"Well, Dominic must've had his head up his ass to leave without saying goodbye. That brings him down a notch or two in my book," my friend said.

In mine, too, I thought.

"What's your plan?" Glenda asked.

"I'm going to check into the InterContinental, take a swim, and then enjoy a hot shower."

"Dominic *does* plan to join you this evening?"

"I guess it depends on what happens at the hospital," I said. "Any word from my family?"

"Since you asked…" she said, then paused.

"What?"

"Jake and I were over at your house earlier. Lily told him you and Dominic went to Chicago for the weekend. Jake starts singing, 'Caroline and Dominic, sittin' in a tree…!'—you know how aggravating ten-year-old boys can be. Lily stormed from the room. I'm not sure she's ready for you two to be romantically involved."

My right temple throbbed. "That makes at least two of us," I said with a wave of bitterness. "I gotta go, Glen—I need to transfer at Belmont. Thanks for listening."

I boarded another train at the Belmont station, sat next to the window, and peevishly stowed my carry-on on the seat beside me. *If the car fills up I'll move it to my lap, but not until then.* It was a relief to spend the rest of the ride focused on unemotional logistics. When the train passed the Armitage station and proceeded underground, I studied the map on my phone and decided to get off at Grand Avenue. I emerged from the subway tunnel, took a moment to get my bearings, and found the Michigan Avenue hotel without difficulty.

I pulled back my shoulders, raised my head high, and strode into the InterContinental's majestic lobby. *I belong here. I'm a millionaire!* I told myself, even though my seven-figure insurance settlement had been committed to paying off my mortgage and kids' educations. And even though *Dominic* had gotten us the room—at a deeply discounted internet rate.

"I'm checking in," I told the young, Asian woman at the desk. "Caroline Spencer."

She tapped her computer keys and shook her head. "I'm sorry, Ms. Spencer, but I don't see a reservation in your name."

"My… er, boyfriend… Dominic Marquez, told me he made the reservation in *both* our names, since I needed my family to be able to reach me in an emergency."

"How do you spell his name?"

I told her as I reached into my purse for my wallet. "Here's my driver's license," I said, trying to remain calm. "And I'll happily give you a credit card for the incidentals."

"Ma'am, I found the reservation, but your name isn't included. I'm sorry—I can't release the room to anyone but Mr. Marquez."

I bristled at the term "ma'am," but almost lost it at "I'm sorry." I pulled my credential case from the side pocket of my purse and slammed it on the marble counter. "I'm an assistant US attorney from Madison, Wisconsin, as you can see from this ID," I said—too loudly, based on the alarm on the clerk's face. "I'm trustworthy. Now, I'm not one to make waves, but if you can't check me in, I'll need to speak with the manager."

"If we could reach Mr. Marquez by phone—"

"Mr. Marquez is at the Thorek Hospital emergency room with his mother, who's in grave condition. So, no, he can't be reached. Please call your manager."

She nodded and made a whispered phone call. I paced back and forth in front of the counter for five minutes until the manager—a middle-aged, black man in an impeccably tailored silk suit—appeared.

"My apologies, Ms. Spencer," he said, reaching over the counter to shake my hand. "We inadvertently left your name off the reservation record which was sent to the front desk. And I'm very sorry to hear about Mr. Marquez's mother. To compensate for the confusion, may we offer you a complimentary upgrade to a suite?"

Hell, yes! I wanted to yell, but I nodded demurely, my knees still quivering from pent-up emotion. "Thank you, we'd appreciate it."

I fumbled through my purse for the crumpled five-dollar bill I'd found there earlier. I couldn't wheel my own luggage to a *suite*, and the bellman needed a tip. "Is your pool still open?" I asked the manager.

He smiled and nodded. "Yes, ma'am, until 10:00."

I had the pool to myself and had just finished swimming ten laps—alternating the sidestroke with freestyle—when I heard my phone ringing. I hoisted myself onto the deck and reached the chaise longue where I'd left it, just as the ringing ceased. Moments later, the voice message signal dinged.

"Hi. It's me," Dominic's message began. "I forgot my phone at Mom's apartment so I'm using Dani's. Just wanted to make sure you made it to the hotel and that the room's all right. Uh… Things are a little better here—it looks like Mom accidentally took too many sleeping pills. We're still at the hospital, but she's awake and talking and they'll probably release her soon. But Dani and I don't believe we should leave Mom alone tonight, and we've got some family decisions to make tomorrow morning. Uh… Call me when you get this."

Wrapped in a thick hotel robe, I sunk onto the lounge chair to consider my response. I didn't want to overreact.

Keep it light, I decided as I dialed. "Hey!" I said, with contrived cheerfulness, when Dominic picked up. "I got your message. Made it safely to the hotel and already swam a half mile in the pool!"

"No trouble checking in?"

Take the high road. "Only a little snafu, for which we got a free upgrade to a suite."

"How is it?"

"Amazing," I said, truthfully. "It's got a king-sized bed with a heavenly, pillow-top mattress, a nice sofa, easy chairs, and two flat-screen TVs. I haven't dared to open the minibar 'cause I'm sure everything in it is expensive and sinful. This is the nicest place I've stayed… in years." *Since my honeymoon.*

"I'm glad," he said quietly. "What time's checkout?"

Are you kidding me? I just managed to get checked in and you're asking about checkout.

"I think the guest folder said noon," I said.

"Good. I'll call or text you in the morning. Let's plan on a late lunch. Someplace nice."

"Okay." *Like lunch at "someplace nice" is gonna make up for a ruined weekend.*

"Caroline, I'm really sorry. This isn't how I hoped the weekend would go. Have a good night," he said. "I—"

"You too," I said quickly, and hung up. I'd sensed he'd been getting ready to say he loved me, which I wasn't ready to hear. *Then why am I so disappointed about spending the night alone?*

I'd planned on a shower, but the oversized, Italian marble tub looked too inviting to pass up. After a long soak, inhaling the exquisite scent of the hotel's Agraria lemon verbena bath salts and gel, I wrapped myself in what would have been Dominic's bathrobe and padded out to the minibar.

One glass of wine led to another, and when I got up to dress for dinner, my gait was decidedly crooked. I reached for the room service menu, instead, and chose a less-than-heart-healthy meal of oven-roasted mac 'n' cheese with a slice of Eli's cheesecake for dessert.

By the time the waiter arrived, I'd replayed Dominic's phone call in my head at least ten times, and tears of frustration stung my eyes. *Buck up, Buttercup. So what if he has family decisions to make? This is no big deal.* I poured the last minibar bottle of wine into my glass and sat down at the desk to eat, once again determined to fully appreciate every bite. I removed the lid from the entrée and ate with relish.

But the pièce de résistance—Eli's Totally Turtle cheese-cake, my favorite—finally brought a smile to my face.

I wiped my mouth with a plush hotel towel and sat back, palate and stomach satisfied. *At least the evening wasn't a total bust.*

Chapter Four

I woke at 9:00 the next morning, disoriented by my surroundings and sluggish from too much wine. I'd anticipated sharing the opulence and quiet of the hotel room with Dominic; now, the opulence felt cold, and the quiet screamed lonely.

I dressed in yesterday's clothes, wrinkles be damned, grabbed my purse and headed for the Starbucks downstairs. The ten-person line moved at a snail's pace, and I wanted to strangle the middle-aged woman in front of me—dressed in a leopard-print jumpsuit—whose order the barista simply couldn't understand.

A cup of house blend and cinnamon scone in hand, I found a table in the back corner and settled in to connect to the world. I clicked on my Facebook page and couldn't help but grin at the cover photo: my four kids nestled under a fleece blanket on the living room couch, giggling with abandon while Lily read a story. I sipped the coffee, lost in thought, reflecting on my life with David. How he would have cherished our growing family…

I hadn't been physically attracted to David when we'd met at his sister, Julia's, wedding. He was tall and muscular, but fair skin, carrot-red hair, and hazel-green eyes weren't my thing, and he danced like a dork. Nevertheless, I enjoyed talking with him and found his throaty chuckle and positive attitude infectious. After the wedding, we'd kept in almost-daily contact, mostly by phone, and he moved to Madison to join the police force when he finished his hitch as a Navy SEAL. By the time we married, I was head-over-heels in love with him—red hair, ambiguously-colored eyes, and all.

Twelve years ago—after a dicey ectopic pregnancy—we'd adopted Lily, the product of my college friend, Kate Daniels', affair with a Moroccan doctor. Seven years later, after two failed in-vitro pregnancies, we'd adopted Amy and Luke. The twins were the offspring of a Mexican father and an Anglo mother. So, our first three, brown-skinned kids bore no physical resemblance to David nor me. Yet, they were the children of our hearts.

David had been an incredible, hands-on father and our primary childcare provider at the time of the accident that took his life. His mother, Abby, moved in and took over that role before any of us knew I was pregnant with our fourth child. Lucy, born seven months after her dad's death, was a volatile redhead—much like her namesake from *I Love Lucy*. Eventually, though, the name Lucy—one more "L" in our family—became too much.

We were visiting my parents, shortly after Lucy learned to walk. My father looked up to see her standing perilously close to the backyard koi pond. "Lily… Luke… Lucy!" he yelled, as he ran toward her.

"It's too confusing," he complained, when he brought my wailing toddler inside. He snuggled Lucy on his lap. "Oh, sweet girl, what can we call you?" She smiled up at him with David's eyes, red curls bobbing as he bounced her on his knee. "What about 'Red'?

Lucy nodded and cried, "Red!"

"It's her favorite color," I said.

"All the more reason," my dad replied.

And so, Lucy had become Red.

All four children were healthy, smart, and, for the most part, well-adjusted. We made it a point to watch videos and pore through photo albums to keep David real to them. I knew Lily still missed her father, though she rarely spoke of him and often declined to participate in our memory fests. I worried about her, and not just because she opposed my growing closeness with Dominic.

I'd been so anxious to have a getaway from my kids, and now I missed them. I called home.

Abby picked up. "I didn't expect to hear from you," she said, with a chuckle. "Shouldn't you and Dominic be having a romantic breakfast in bed?"

"Yeah, well, he needed to handle something with his mother. I'm at Starbucks with a pretty good internet connection. I'd like to FaceTime with the kids. Is Lily around?"

"No. She spent the night at Marissa's. Can we FaceTime on your laptop? Lily left it on the dining room table."

Lily wasn't supposed to use my computer without permission, but I decided to let that slide. "Yeah. See if it's turned on. Just flip up the screen."

"Hold on a minute," she said, and I heard the phone clunk onto a table. "Yep, it's on," she said, when she returned.

"Okay. I'm gonna hang up. When you hear the computer ringing, click the 'accept' button."

I placed the video call and waited while it rang on their end—six times, seven, eight. Finally, Amy's smiling face, smeared with jelly and toast crumbs, magically appeared on my screen. "Hi, Mommy!" she said, with delight. Then I saw Abby, a bemused look on her face, walk up behind Amy. The top of Luke's head—hair askew—popped in and out of the picture.

"Where's Red?"

"She was pulling at her ear last night and started crying during dinner," Abby said, "so we went over to Urgent Care around 7:00. The doctor confirmed my guess—a pretty wicked ear infection. She stopped fussing after one dose of antibiotics, but I decided to let her sleep in this morning."

"Oh, Abby. I'm sorry you had to deal with that."

"No biggie. I called Glenda and she came over and watched the twins while I was gone. It only took a couple of hours."

So, Glenda was at my house when I texted her from the train. Why didn't she say something? I hate it when she tries to insulate me, as if I were some helpless kid.

I saw Luke and Amy, still in their PJs, trotting away from the dining room table. "They were engrossed in *Finding Nemo* when you called," Abby said, "and I think I forgot to put it on pause. I'll have them come back if you want to talk some more."

"That's okay," I said, a hollowness creeping into the pit of my stomach.

"You sound kinda down. Did everything go okay yesterday?"

I sighed. "In a word, no." I told her about the beyond-awkward day and mega-disappointing evening.

Abby listened intently, occasionally asking questions, while sipping tea from a chipped mug bearing the inscription World's Best Grandma. When I finished, she paused to take another sip before responding. "Have you heard from Dominic this morning?"

I blinked back tears. "No."

"Maybe you should call him. It's after 10:00—surely you wouldn't wake him."

"I'm not sure what I'd say. I'm pissed and hurt and lonely. The last thing I want to do is sound pathetic."

"You could tell him you're pissed and hurt and lonely without sounding pathetic."

"Not without a whole lot more energy than I have right now. Thanks for listening, though," I said. "It helped to commiserate with someone. I'll see you this evening."

I decided to send Lily a text, "Hi kiddo! R u enjoying the weekend? Call if u want."

Though reluctant to let her have a cell phone, I'd caved and bought her one for her twelfth birthday four months earlier. So far, she hadn't abused the closely-monitored privilege.

She responded a minute later, "Going 2 mall w/ Marissa. Call u later. K?"

CHAPTER FIVE

I finished my scone and first cup of coffee and stood in line for a second, debating whether to actually call Lily. The word *pathetic* kept coming back to me. I headed for the gift shop, instead. Within ten minutes, I'd selected a Cubs hat for Luke, a Hello Kitty wallet for Amy, a stuffed bear for Red, and a leather-bound journal embossed with butterflies for Lily. Armed with my purchases, I boarded the elevator to my suite.

I was just stepping from a deliciously hot massage shower when I heard Dominic's voice outside the bathroom door. "Don't be nervous. I knocked and there was no answer, so I went downstairs and got a key. I got us a late checkout, too."

Waiting for my heart to resume its usual rhythm—can you *really* avoid being nervous when you hear an unexpected voice in your hotel room?—I toweled off, used the remains of that glorious citrus body lotion, and ran my fingers through my wet hair.

When I emerged, Dominic was sitting at the end of the bed, shoulders slumped. I could hardly hide my alarm when

I saw his face: dark circles under downcast eyes, unshaven cheeks, uncombed hair. He had on the same clothes he'd worn the day before—now looking like he'd slept in them.

"Bad news?" I asked.

Dominic stood awkwardly, as if he hadn't the right to sit on the bed, and shook his head. "I don't know. The hospital released Mom around midnight, and we were up talking with Dani until 2:30. We tried to get her to commit to counseling but she refused, though she did agree to get back on the mood stabilizer. Then, even though we hadn't gotten much sleep, Mom insisted this morning that we all go to Mass. She cried through it, made the sign of the cross about fifty extra times, and told me and Dani to leave right after the service so she could meet with the priest. Said she wanted to walk home and clear her head. I asked her if she planned to hurt or kill herself. She said 'no,' she was trying to make things right, not condemn herself to hell for all of eternity. Pretty upbeat farewell greeting, wouldn't you say?"

He wrapped me in his arms, burying his face against my neck. "I'm so worried about her," he said, "and have no idea how to handle it."

I did what felt right: I began stroking his hair. "We'll figure it out," I murmured.

I don't know how long we stood holding one another, but I didn't want it to end. I craved his warmth. I drank in his vulnerability. I reveled in his musky scent and the stubble of his day-old beard gently scratching my skin.

Eventually, Dominic raised his head and stroked my cheek. "Oh, my god," he said. "You smell amazing. You are so beautiful... I want you so much."

"And I want *you* so much," I said, stepping back to untie my robe.

I lay beside him afterward, my head resting on his chest. I hadn't thought to close the drapes the previous night, and now sunlight filtered through the sheer window coverings, bathing us in soft warmth. The sheets and down comforter remained where we'd tossed them at the foot of the bed. Within minutes, Dominic's rhythmic breathing turned to gentle snoring, and I was doubly glad he'd asked for a late checkout.

Dani'd been right: having sex *was* like riding a bicycle. But making love with Dominic was like riding a much different bike than the one I'd been used to. David had been a considerate but urgent lover. Dominic was more present— grateful and tuned-in to every touch, every caress, every connection. *Like going from a racing bike to a beach cruiser*, I thought with a grin. *And I sure did enjoy today's cruise.*

I must've drifted off to sleep, too. The insistent vibration of my cell phone on the nightstand startled me awake. I grabbed for it and dropped it on the floor, shattering our reverie.

Lily. I glanced at the clock. A few minutes past twelve.

"Good afternoon, sweetheart," I said to my daughter.

"What'd you want?"

I swallowed an expletive and willed myself to remain cool. "It's customary, Lily, to start a conversation with a greeting. And I'm not fond of your tone. So, let's start over. Okay?"

A sigh. "Hello, Mom," she said, her voice laced with sass. "I just called to ask why you texted me."

"I texted you to say 'hello' and to invite you to call if you wanted to talk. That's all."

"Okay."

Keep it light. "Did you and Marissa have a nice sleepover?"

"Yeah. We stayed up pretty late. Her mom dropped us at the mall, and we just finished lunch at the food court." She paused as though she wanted to tell me something more but thought better of it. "Did you and Dominic sleep in the same hotel room?" she abruptly asked.

Taken aback, I stammered, then lied, "No… He stayed at his mother's house and I stayed at a hotel."

"When'll you be home?"

"Before you kids go to bed tonight."

"I'll let Grandma know. Bye." She hung up before I could respond.

I stared at the phone as if it could portend the meaning of the uncomfortable call. Dominic gently took it from my hand and laid it on the table on his side of the bed. "We'll figure it out. Lily. My mom. We'll figure it out together. It hasn't turned out the way we planned, but one very good thing's come out of this weekend," he said, with a smile.

He kissed me and traced my jawline with the tip of his finger, sending exquisite shivers throughout my body.

"Let's skip breakfast," I said.

Our second time was more delicious than the first. Slower, gentler, more satisfying. The afterglow of our lovemaking erased the dark circles under Dominic's eyes and eased my angst about Lily.

I'd gladly have spent the day in that glorious bed. But checkout time approached and my stomach rumbled audibly. "I'm famished," I said "How 'bout some lunch?"

"There's a Corner Bakery close to where I parked. Does that sound okay?"

"Perfect."

We stowed our bags in the trunk of Dominic's car and found a table on the restaurant's shaded patio. While we ate our tomato basil soup and sandwiches—tomato and mozzarella for me, chicken pesto for Dominic—I purposely kept the conversation light. When we pushed aside our plates, though, I forged ahead.

"I was thinking... maybe we should go visit your Aunt Luz. Sounds like she and your mom are pretty close. She might have some clues about what was in the mail."

"That *is* a good idea, but I don't want to upset her—what with her chemo and all."

"We'll take her some candy or flowers or whatever you think might cheer her up and tell her you wanted to introduce her to your new girlfriend. Then, in the course of the conversation, we mention that your mom seemed 'a little upset' about something she got in the mail, enough that she accidentally took too many sleeping pills, but is fine now... and ask if Luz has any ideas what it might be."

His eyes gleamed. "Does that mean you are my girlfriend?"

"You don't think I'm the kind of girl who makes love with just anyone, do you?" I asked, grinning back.

"So you *are* my girlfriend!"

"Yeah, but let's not tell Lily just yet. And let's talk about her after we see your aunt."

Did his smile just fade when I mentioned Lily? I willed the thought from my mind.

I stifled a "wow" when we walked into the lobby of Dominic's aunt's Lake Shore Drive apartment building. The three-story, glassed-in atrium held lush tropical plants, marble floors, fountains, and a sleek, granite-topped concierge desk. The concierge, a statuesque Latina wearing an impeccably-tailored, navy suit, checked her computer to make sure Luz had authorized us to come up, then graciously directed us to the elevator.

"Luz's late husband was an engineering professor at Northwestern when my dad began teaching there. Later, though, he went into private industry. He did very well," Dominic said, as the elevator made its ascent.

A small woman with thick, white hair and deep, brown eyes, Luz waited for us at the door. "Dominic, how good to see you," she said, as she reached up to cup his face in her hands. She turned to me and extended her hand. "You must be Caroline. I am honored to meet you."

"It's my pleasure, Mrs. Olson," I said, covering her small hand in mine.

"Please, call me Luz. And do come in."

Dominic handed her the vase full of brightly-colored, fresh flowers we'd bought from a florist in the Drake Hotel shopping arcade—pricey but worth every penny. Aunt Luz beamed as she sniffed the bouquet. She set it on an antique oaken table in the foyer, then turned to me again. "Dominic is the sweetest of all my nieces and nephews!"

Though the apartment's architecture was modern, the living room furnishings were overstuffed, comfortable, and colorful. Luz ushered us in and settled herself in a huge, red-and-orange-upholstered club chair. She kicked off her shoes and tucked her legs up under her. "I'm having some ginger tea," she said, motioning to a mug on the table next to her. "There's more in the kitchen, or beer in the fridge if you prefer. Would you mind serving, Dominic? I'm afraid this last round of chemo has left me with little energy."

"I'd be happy to," he said, as he stood up. "A beer sounds wonderful. Caroline?"

"Beer is fine, thanks."

When he'd left the room, Luz turned to me conspiratorially, eyes twinkling. "He's a keeper, don't you think?"

I laughed. "He's definitely a great guy."

Dominic returned with two bottles of Stella Artois and two tall, crystal glasses. He set the glasses and bottles on the coffee table and sat down beside me. "How are you feeling, Aunt Luz?" he asked.

She inclined her head. "A bit drained—and it troubles me to look in the mirror and see someone listless staring back. I'm afraid I'm a still a bit vain; I snuck in and applied a little mascara and lipstick when you called to say you were coming! I was thrilled to learn this particular chemo won't cause me to lose my hair. And though it's a hideous way to do it, I'm happy to say I've lost fifteen pounds. Guess there was a reason I kept the extra weight on all these years."

Dominic paused from pouring the beer. "You need to keep eating to keep your strength up," he said, with concern, "and you did *not* need to lose weight. In fact, you might want to consider getting a prescription for medical marijuana to counteract the nausea."

"I'll have you know I already got some," Luz replied, with a titter. "I don't smoke it, though, since this is a smoke-free building. I buy it in lollipop form."

Dominic did a double take. "Well, you go, girl!"

"Does it help?" I asked.

She shrugged. "A little bit. I was able to force down half a milkshake this morning."

We chatted for a while about her children and grand-children, and I dutifully took down a photo album from the shelf so she could show me who was who. One photograph, taken a few years earlier, showed Luz and her sister, Alejandra, arm in arm in front of the Lincoln Memorial in Washington, D.C. Both were tanned and smiling.

"Luz," I said, quietly, "Dominic and Dani are worried about their mother. She apparently got something in the mail yesterday that upset her so much she accidentally took too many sleeping pills. Do you have any idea what it might be?"

Dominic glanced at me warily. Luz took a sip of tea and stared into space. *Now you've blown it,* I thought.

Finally, Luz spoke. "I believe she's worried about money."

"What makes you say that?" Dominic asked, an edge to his voice.

"Because of the fortune teller."

"Fortune teller?" he echoed.

"Yes. A while back, a neighbor told me about this remarkable woman who'd done a reading for her. I asked Alejandra if she'd go with me—on a lark, you know. She agreed. The young woman, Barbara something-or-other, told us lots of things she couldn't possibly have known unless she had psychic abilities. She told Alejandra that money issues were like a dark cloud over her head."

Dominic raised an eyebrow. "You don't really believe all that hocus pocus?"

"Barbara also told me I had a health problem that needed immediate attention. Two weeks later, my cancer was diagnosed," Luz replied. "So, yes, I really do believe it."

Dominic sat speechless.

"Have you been back to see this fortune teller?" I asked.

Luz shook her head. "I don't really care to know my future if what it holds is bad. If Alejandra ever went back, she didn't tell me."

"Do you have any other reason to suspect my mother's having money problems?" Dominic asked.

"Well…" Luz rubbed her forehead, took two sips of tea, and finally looked up at him. "Alejandra hasn't been wearing her anniversary ring—you know, that beautiful diamond ring your father had made for her. Several weeks ago, I asked her where it was, and she said she'd taken it to the jeweler to have it repaired. But she still didn't have it on when she went with me for chemo on Friday. Maybe she's in need of money and sold it?"

Dominic fidgeted in his seat, crossed his leg, and began scratching his ankle. I got the sense he wanted to ask a zillion more questions but didn't know where to start. I turned to him and said pointedly, "You know, we promised your aunt we'd only stay a little while. I think it's time for us to get on the road, don't you?"

"Yeah," he mumbled. "Caroline's right, Aunt Luz. Can we do anything for you before we leave?"

"No, dear. I'm all set."

Dominic took the empty bottles and Luz's mug to the kitchen. Luz looked at me and whispered, "He worries too much about my sister."

Dominic returned and approached Luz to give her a hug. "We can let ourselves out."

"I won't argue with you," she said, leaning back against the cushions. "Thank you so much for the visit and the lovely flowers. It was delightful to meet you, Caroline."

I bent down to give her a kiss on the cheek. "It was great to meet you, too."

I took Dominic's arm while we waited for the elevator.

"Maybe you should talk with your mom's priest."

"I doubt he'd violate her confidence."

"Then maybe we should visit the fortune teller," I said, facetiously. "Or do they take an oath of secrecy?"

My joke fell flat.

CHAPTER SIX

During our ride back to Madison, I thought about our morning's love-making. My body felt deliciously satisfied. Grounded. Relaxed. Connected.

I grinned as I remembered Dominic's glowing face when I'd called myself his girlfriend.

But.

I glanced over at Dominic, trying to read his thoughts. Apparently sensing my scrutiny, he turned and reached for my hand. "What?" he asked.

"Just thinking about our weekend. I'm trying to savor the wonderful parts—which were *really* wonderful, by the way—and put the rest on the back burner." I paused, hoping he'd fill me in on his thoughts.

"And how's it working? The back-burner part, I mean."

Before I could respond, a car zipped past us in the left lane and then cut back in front of us with only inches to spare. My heart jumped. Dominic let go of my hand, gripped the steering wheel, and laid on the horn. "Hijo de puta!" he yelled. "I'm sorry, Caroline. That idiot could've made your kids orphans. Do you mind if we get off the interstate?"

My racing pulse precluded a verbal response. I shook my head.

Thankfully, we encountered no speed demons on U.S. Hwy. 12. But I did feel my blood pressure rise each time we came upon a slowpoke driver or a crawling farm implement. I wanted to be home before Luke and Amy's eight o'clock bedtime, and this route was decidedly longer.

The dashboard clock read 6:30 when Dominic pulled into the Culver's restaurant in Fort Atkinson. "I need a break and a bite," he said.

While he ordered our food, I found a table and called home. Voicemail. We had a cardinal rule in our house: no answering the phone during dinner. But I still felt a tinge of disappointment. I left a message: "Hi, Abby. We took an alternate route but should be home around 8:30. Let the twins stay up 'til I get there, okay? See you soon."

"I'm sorry I've been on edge," Dominic said, when he joined me at the table. "The situation with my mom, and that close call on the interstate, threw me off. Plus, I didn't get much sleep last night."

The waiter delivered our tray of butter burgers, fries, and Diet Cokes, and I waited until he left to respond. "Lily's call has me a little off-kilter, too. I'm not sure how to handle her almost-teenage angst."

"Maybe it has less to do with her age and more to do with not approving of me," he said, looking down at his food.

"She's always adored you, and it's been two years since David died. It's not like we're rushing into anything."

"It might feel like it to Lily."

"So what do we do?"

"Didn't you tell me once that Lily was seeing a grief counselor?"

I nodded. "She was. But she never really connected with her. When she asked to quit, I let her."

"Maybe you should try again."

"Maybe…" I knew, intellectually, that grief doesn't have a finite end point. But the idea of reopening barely-healed wounds gave me a headache.

We finished our meal in silence.

"What are you going to do about your mom?" I asked, when we were on the road again.

"I haven't a clue."

It was dusk when we parked at the curb in front of my house. My four-year-old twins ran to the front door and pressed their hands against the glass of its storm window, making happy fingerprints.

"Do you want me to come in?" Dominic asked.

"No, I think it'll be best if I do this alone." I leaned over and kissed him quickly. "Call me tomorrow, okay?"

Abby, Red on her hip, unlocked the front door and I entered to the warmest-imaginable welcome. Red practically jumped from Abby's arms into mine and plunked a slobbery kiss on my cheek. "Mommy, you're home!" Amy cried, bouncing up and down, while Luke pulled on my T-shirt, babbling, "You gotta hear what Red did today… so funny… can we get the dog?"

"Let's go in the living room," I said to them. "Can you bring that shopping bag, Luke? There's something in there for you." I hoped my gifts would be a sufficient distraction from the dog question, which I fully intended to ignore.

The kids loved their presents. Luke put on his Cubs hat and ran to look at himself in the hallway mirror, while Amy went to find coins for her wallet. When both returned with gleeful smiles, Red told them proudly that she'd named the stuffed bear "Susan." I savored their hugs and thanks for a moment before asking Abby the obvious question. "Where's Lily?"

"She said she was tired and went to bed early," Abby said. "After she came home from the mall, she spent the afternoon at the pool with Marissa. I think she had a bit too much sun."

Her wavering tone tipped me off, but I'd have known, anyway, that Abby was lying. Even if Lily had climbed Mount Everest, she wouldn't be asleep before 9:00.

"Well, let's get the rest of you kiddos to bed," I said, rising. "You're in your PJs, so I'm assuming you've had baths."

All three nodded.

"Have you brushed your teeth?"

Luke and Red nodded. Amy shook her head. "I'm the one telling the truth," she said proudly, as I led them upstairs.

Once the littles were tucked in, I trudged down the hall to Lily's room. In retrospect, I realized, things hadn't been right with Lily for a while, but I'd been ignoring the signs. It was like seeing a co-worker every day for six months and not noticing—until looking at before-and-after pictures— that they'd gained twenty pounds.

I knocked tentatively, then opened her door. She sat cross-legged on the bed, listening through earbuds to music on her phone, flipping through a magazine. Two, still-packaged tubes of lip gloss lay near her feet. She wore a pair of three-inch, silver, hoop earrings I'd never seen before.

"Good shopping trip?" I asked.

Lily nodded but continued to look at her magazine.

I glanced around the room. It had saddened me when, the previous winter, she'd insisted on painting the walls gray and replacing her little-girl décor with more sophisticated items she'd seen on Pinterest. But I had to admire her bedspread, throw pillows, and pink-and-purple DIY artwork—she seemed to have a flair for decorating. Thankfully, Grover, the raggedy, floppy-eared, stuffed dog she'd had since she was born, lay steadfastly on her pillow.

I wheeled her computer chair over and sat down. "Tell me about your weekend," I said.

"It was fine."

"Lily, I think we need to talk."

"Leave me alone," she said—way too loudly to be considered polite—then turned her back and buried her face in a pillow.

"Not until you tell me what's wrong." I walked to the opposite side of the bed and moved her by the shoulders to face me, pulling the pillow away from her face.

"I'm just tired."

"I want the truth, Lily."

"What are you? A human frickin' lie detector?" she said, wrenching away from my grip.

Keep it calm, I told myself. "We'll talk about your choice of words another time. Right now, the truth. And I'm guessing it has something to do with me and Dominic."

Silence.

"Are you upset that I'm seeing Dominic?"

"You go off on a fancy weekend and leave me and Grandma here to take care of those little brats. The only one who behaves is Amy."

"Except for work, I haven't been away without you kids since your dad died. And a big part of your generous allowance is based on helping with the littles, who I know are challenging, by the way."

She didn't respond.

"You haven't answered my question: are you upset about my seeing Dominic?"

"I just don't think Dad would like it, that's all. Now can you please leave me alone?"

I sighed. *You can't expect to get any more from her right now,* I told myself.

"Okay. We'll talk more about this when we've both had some rest."

I kissed the top of her head. "G'night, sweetheart. I love you."

"Whatever."

I found Abby in the living room, rocking in her glider at a furious pace. An untouched mug of black tea sat on the table beside her.

"Don't tell me you're upset with me, too."

A puzzled look crossed her face. "Why would I be upset with you?"

"For abandoning you and Lily with the three little hellions while I went to Chicago."

"Good heavens. You have every right to a getaway," she said, and I detected no hint of deception. But then again, I wasn't a human *frickin'* lie detector.

Rocking more slowly, Abby pushed the mute button on the television remote and added, "Lily didn't seem to mind helping with the kids while you were gone. Did she say she was upset?"

"Uh-huh."

She resumed her fast-paced ride in the chair and stared vacantly at the muted TV.

"Abby, you seem bothered by *something*—you're rocking a mile a minute and haven't touched your tea."

I was sure she was on the verge of telling me something substantive before thinking better of it. "No, I'm fine," she said. "Just a little keyed up. And, in time, Lily will come around to accepting Dominic."

I stifled my own *whatever* and swallowed my frustration. "I hope you're right," I said.

Abby clicked off the TV. "I think I'll head home," she said, somewhat abruptly and with a half-smile.

"Home" was her newly-remodeled apartment in our basement. When we'd purchased the four-bedroom house just prior to David's death, we'd planned to turn the exposed basement into a home office for his security consulting business. Those plans died with him, though, and the basement went virtually unused for almost two years. Abby had slept in the smallest upstairs bedroom, and Amy and Luke shared a room. As a newborn, Lucy slept in my room but we'd moved her in with the twins when she graduated from the bassinet to a crib. Three weeks earlier, the contractor had finally finished the renovations. We'd all breathed sighs of relief at having more privacy.

Still, it felt a little weird when she left each night. As if she were an employee. Tonight, it felt weirder than usual. We hadn't really finished our conversation.

"Sleep well," I told her, as she moved toward the door.

"You, too."

"And, Abby…"

She stopped and looked back.

"…good night."

CHAPTER SEVEN

When I left for work Monday morning, Lily was still in bed, snoring softly and hugging Grover, obviously relishing the freedom to sleep in that summer allowed. I'd spent a good hour during my Sunday-night sleeplessness thinking of things to say to her—ways to reopen the lines of communication—with no good strategy emerging.

On the way to my office, I dropped Amy and Luke off at Franklin School for their Madison School & Community Recreation day camp. This was "construction" week at camp. Luke, in particular, was going to be in seventh heaven amid the massive piles of LEGOs and other building blocks. Outfitted with the requisite plastic hard hat, fished that morning from his bedroom toy bin, he ran through the front door and bounded over to hug his teacher's leg, almost knocking her down. Amy moved more slowly but, wearing her own plastic, yellow hard hat, grinned from ear to ear as she showed her best friend the new Hello Kitty wallet.

Another camper's father, a for-real construction worker whom I'd met a few times, nodded from the opposite side of the room. Luke joined the group of kids surrounding him, all clamoring to see his tool belt. I felt a lump of sadness in my throat—Luke would never have the pleasure of introducing David to his peers, something that Lily had always enjoyed immensely.

A couple of extra-strength Tylenol tablets won the skirmish with my tension-and-too-little-sleep headache, and my day went smoothly enough. I finished my painstaking research and wrote an appellate brief defending Judge Coburn's sentence in a violent bank robbery case. Around lunchtime, Dominic texted me three smiling emoji, thanking me for a "splendid" weekend. In the afternoon, I met with an FBI agent about a pending embezzlement case.

I was almost out my office door at 5:15 when my boss showed up, carrying a three-inch-thick accordion file. A shorter, middle-aged version of my cinematic hero, Atticus Finch, George Cooper wore obviously off-the-rack clothes that were several seasons old. And he always seemed in need of a haircut. Despite his fashion and grooming shortcomings, he was the smartest lawyer I'd ever known, though he never flaunted his knowledge.

"Can you spare five minutes?" he asked.

"Sure." I sighed a hopefully inaudible sigh and set my vintage Coach briefcase on the floor. I motioned to the two upholstered armchairs opposite my desk. "Let's have a seat."

George put the file on my desk and sat down, leaning his chair back on two legs. I scooted my chair around to face him more directly. "Do you ever fall over?" I asked.

He chuckled. "Not since eighth-grade, when a growth spurt threw me off balance. This always drove my mother crazy—and I suspect I made a habit of it to spite her."

I laughed. "So, what's in the file?"

"The appellate case Lauren is supposed to be arguing before the Seventh Circuit in Chicago on Friday morning."

"*Supposed to be* arguing?"

"Yeah. She had a court trial set for this afternoon in front of Judge Coburn. Coburn rescheduled the trial for Friday and he's unwilling to move it. So—I need to either reassign someone to handle Lauren's trial here or send someone to Chicago to handle her appellate argument."

"And you think I could get up to speed on the appeal by Friday?"

"Absolutely." He paused, glancing at a photo of the kids on my desk. "Could you swing overnight child care for Thursday? You'd have to check in with the court clerk in Chicago by 9:15 Friday morning."

I always cringed when my work schedule threatened to impinge on my family time. I'd taken this job as a federal prosecutor just before David died, counting on his presence as a stay-at-home dad and assured by George Cooper that the workload would be tolerable. I could manage an occasional overnight, but I'd just gotten back from my getaway weekend with Dominic. Still, I didn't want my co-workers to think I was avoiding my fair share of the load.

"Hang on and I'll check."

George stared out the window while I called Abby.

"No problem," she said, when I asked if she could handle the kids alone on Thursday night. "You know my calendar's usually open, and there's nothing on it this week."

I nodded to George, who exhaled in relief.

As I drove through Regent Street's stop-and-start traffic on the way home, my stomach grew queasy. *Maybe the chicken salad I had for lunch was bad. Or maybe it's this beastly humidity.* By the time I pulled in the driveway, though, I'd concluded it was nerves: I wasn't looking forward to another run-in with Lily. *I should've thought to ask Abby about Lily's mood when I had her on the phone.*

Abby and my kids, plus Glenda's son, Jake, were on the screened-in back porch. Red sat on Abby's lap looking at *Dr. Seuss's ABC*. Lily and Jake were involved in an animated game of *Candy Land* with the twins. Judging by his grin, Luke was winning. Half-empty—or, perhaps, half-full—cups of lemonade and stray popcorn kernels littered the picnic table.

"Look at the Lukester," Jake said. "He's kicking our butts!"

Amy and Luke giggled at the word butts, and I couldn't help but laugh. But Lily—who'd been smiling before she saw me—adopted a stony expression and popped up off the bench, knocking her knee against the table in the process. She limped away muttering, "I'm so tired of his cheating."

The littles' happy moods continued throughout the evening, and, determined not to let Lily bring me down, I tucked them in with a smile on my face.

Lily was in her room when I finished, her door ajar. Moving closer, I realized she was on the phone. I paused to listen.

"Yeah, he's really cute," I heard her say. "…Oh, Marissa, you should totally go for it! …Okay—text me, like, when you can."

I knocked.

No answer.

I knocked again, louder this time.

"What?"

I pushed the door open and saw her pulling out her earbuds. *Pretending she didn't hear me the first time.* "Watch your attitude, please," I said, leaning against the doorframe. "I'd like to talk with you."

Her shrug screamed "Whatever!" and I felt the muscles in my neck tense. She set the phone on the table alongside her tattered copy of *Harry Potter and the Sorcerer's Stone* and sat forward on the bed. She wouldn't meet my eyes and picked up the phone again the instant it signaled an incoming text.

I forged ahead. "I was really upset about our conversation last night. I thought you were disrespectful."

"Sorry," she said, without an ounce of sincerity. She proceeded to reply to the text.

I waited 'til she quit typing. "Lily, are you jealous of Dominic?"

Still no eye contact. "I don't know what you mean."

"I mean, are you jealous that he's taking up time I could be spending with you?"

She shook her head.

"But you don't like him, is that it?"

Lily fidgeted and began twisting a strand of hair around her index finger. She didn't reply.

"All right," I said, with calm I didn't feel. "Let's try another topic: what'd you do today?"

"Nothin' much. Went to the mall."

"You've been spending a lot of time at the mall lately."

No answer. Even my pregnant pause didn't induce her to speak.

Finally, I walked over to the bed and kissed the top of her head. She squirmed. "I love you, Lily, and I'm not gonna let you push me away."

No response.

I wandered back downstairs and into the kitchen. I grabbed a cold Pabst, left over from my dad's visit a couple weeks earlier, then curled up in my overstuffed, living room chair.

Unsettled by my conversation with Lily, I chose a sure-fire method of tuning out: playing *Words with Friends* on my iPhone. I'd just laid down a favorite word—S-U-Q, for 37 points—when the phone vibrated with a call. Dominic.

"Hey," I said. "I was going to call you."

"I'm in Chicago."

"Chicago?"

"It's sort of a long story. Do you have time?"

"Yeah, I was just playing *Words*."

"Well, I decided to investigate a little more. I drove down this morning—while Mom was doing volunteer work at the nursing home. It didn't take me long to find what she'd gotten in the mail on Saturday," he said, his voice steeped with disheartenment. "The papers were right on top of her middle desk drawer."

"You went into her apartment when she wasn't there?"

"I needed know what's going on" he replied, tersely. "The papers were from the bank—threatening foreclosure on the two-flat. She's three months behind on the mortgage."

"Oh, Dominic. I'm sorry. Did you talk with her about it?"

"Not yet. I decided to try to find out where her money's going, first. Her checkbook wasn't there, and she keeps all her financial records online. I couldn't find or figure out the passwords on her computer."

"Maybe she's gambling?" I asked.

"That's Dani's guess. A couple of Mom's friends like to go to the racetrack and casinos, and she goes along sometimes. Maybe more often than she admits."

"What do you plan to do next?"

"I just met with a former co-worker, Emma. She's a really savvy P.I. and agreed to follow Mom for a few days. I'll stay here with Dani and do what I can while Emma's handling the surveillance."

"More snooping in the house?" I asked, half-kidding.

"Well, that's the rest of the story. When she got home this afternoon, Mom called me, all upset and yelling that Dani had been in the house without permission."

"How did she know someone had been in?"

"She says she put a piece of brown thread in-between the drawer and the desk, and she could tell that it had been disturbed."

"What did she say when you told her it was you, and not Dani?"

He paused a moment. "I haven't told her yet. I want to wait until I know more about what's going on. Dani's not very happy about it, but she agreed I'll be in a better position to investigate if Mom doesn't suspect me."

"This sounds just icky, Dominic. Wouldn't it be simpler to talk to her?"

"You saw how she acted on Saturday—she's not about to volunteer any information. Furthermore, she told me she's having someone change her locks tomorrow morning and doesn't intend to give Dani nor me a key."

Can't say I blame her.

"Anyway," he continued, "I just wanted you to know I'll be staying here for several more days."

"Okay."

"I'll keep you posted."

"Okay. Good luck."

"Thanks. G'night."

I replayed the phone conversation in my mind. The only time he had inquired about me was when he asked if I had time for his long story. Not one question about how I was doing. Or how the kids were doing. Or whether Lily was any more accepting of our being romantically involved.

Why didn't I tell him that I'd be in Chicago on Thursday night?

Chapter Eight

A voicemail from Dominic—which he'd left at 5:00 a.m.—greeted me when I got to work on Tuesday morning. "It's me. I didn't want to call your cell for fear of waking you. I owe you an apology for last night: I was so wrapped up in my own problem that I didn't even ask about you and the kids. Please call me." He closed with a little smooching noise, which instantly brought a grin to my face.

I dialed his number and grinned even wider when he answered on the first ring. "What's with the smooch thing?" I asked. "Are we in eighth-grade or something?"

He laughed. "What do you have against a little romance?"

"As a matter of fact, not a thing," I replied. I told him about my unexpected trip to Chicago, and we made plans to spend Thursday night together.

I checked into the iconic Palmer House Hilton Hotel in Chicago's Loop late Thursday afternoon. I'd stayed there before, but the two-story, gilded lobby with marble-topped tables, velvet furnishings, and ceiling murals still amazed me. And I couldn't help but smile as I remembered George

Cooper saying the brownie had been invented there as a special dessert for folks attending the 1893 Chicago World's Fair. George loved the Palmer House, in particular its reasonable government room rates.

I hurried to my room—dark and dated but spacious and impeccably clean—and hung up the gray, Calvin Klein pantsuit I would wear in court the next morning. I stood before the wood-framed, full-length mirror. Though a tad wrinkled from the drive, the black slacks and red silk blouse I'd worn to work that morning were comfortable, slenderizing, and suitable for dinner in the city. I'd already ditched my work pumps for sandals. After a quick application of lipstick, I headed down to the hotel's Lockwood Restaurant, which Dominic had chosen for its high marks on TripAdvisor and, more importantly, for its proximity to my room.

In the seconds it took for my eyes to adjust to the darkened barroom—half-filled with people in business attire sipping beer, wine, and unadorned cocktails—I looked around with a tinge of anxiety. While stopped at a traffic jam on the interstate, I'd texted Dominic to say I'd be late, so I knew he'd be waiting. Perhaps it was the residual adrenaline that had kept me alert in the nerve-wracking traffic. Or, perhaps it was my resentment of fate for stealing forty-five minutes of precious time with him.

My stomach lurched when I saw him sitting at a corner table, engrossed in conversation with a strikingly beautiful, blonde woman. Younger than me—probably about thirty—she wore her shoulder-length hair pinned up, but a few strands had conveniently fallen loose around her face. Designer jeans that fit like a glove. Vivid pink sweater emphasizing breasts that plenty of people would pay to have. Leather gladiator sandals with four-inch heels. Exaggerated gestures with long, slender hands.

I fleetingly thought of leaving, but my fight reflex prevailed. I finger-combed my hair, raised my head, forced a smile, and strode toward them, trying to project confidence I didn't feel.

Dominic spotted me first, his smiling eyes and that dimple erasing my every insecurity. He stood, hugged me, and nuzzled my neck. "I'm sorry traffic was so awful," he murmured. "Did you park at O'Hare?"

I nodded. "Then I couldn't get the fare machine to take my credit card and some spooky guy insisted I use his to take the train downtown... thankfully, he got off two stops before me."

"You're here now, and that's all that matters." I drank in the earthy scent of his shaving gel—Michael Kors for Men—lightheaded with desire, wanting nothing more than to head back upstairs with him. Too quickly, he released me from his embrace.

"Caroline," he said, as he pulled out a chair for me, "this is Emma Martin, the investigator who's been helping with my mother."

She extended her hand. "Nice to meet you."

I shook it, amazed at her silky skin. "You, too."

Dominic hailed the waiter. "What would you like, Caroline?"

I inclined my head toward his beer glass. "What're you having?"

"It's called Revolution Anti Hero—a local IPA. Try a sip."

My fingers touched his as he handed me the glass—a little connection that brought a smile to my face. I tasted the beer. "Good—I'll have one, too."

Emma looked up at the waiter. "Another maple Manhattan, please."

Dominic handed me an appetizer plate and nodded toward the platter of cheese and charcuterie. "Try the sausage on the left," he said. "And you'll love the grilled sourdough."

I spread some spicy mustard on the bread, added a slice of sausage, and took a bite. It *was* delicious.

Dominic ate a pickle from the platter and took another sip of beer before answering my unspoken question: *What's she doing here?* "Caroline, there've been some interesting developments today, so I asked Emma to come fill us in. Em, why don't you start over from the beginning?"

She paused a moment to pin up an errant strand of hair, revealing diamond earrings that had to have cost more than my minivan, and flashed him a smile full of perfect white teeth. "Sure," she said, then turned to me. "Dom and I decided our first step was to find out whether Alejandra's money problems were gambling-related."

Dom? I struggled to hide my irritation.

"And, bingo—no pun intended," Emma said, inclining her head in mock humility, "I found out her church seniors' group had a casino trip scheduled for 11:00 on Tuesday. I followed the bus to Harrah's in Joliet and watched Alejandra the whole time they were there. She and a couple of friends headed straight from the bus to the lunch buffet. Alejandra eventually played some slot machines but mostly walked around, people-watching. There was nothing to support our initial theory that she's addicted to gambling."

"Maybe she realized you were following her," I said.

"No," Emma replied, with a hearty chuckle.

Her confidence rankled me, especially when I noticed Dominic looking at her with obvious admiration. "Emma is the best P.I. I've ever seen. Notice that bag on the chair next to her?" he asked, nodding toward a large, buttery-soft, tan leather bag.

"Uh-huh."

"She's got two wigs, three pairs of glasses, several scarves, and a change of clothing in there. I've known her for five years, but we could pass on the street and I wouldn't recognize her if she didn't want to be recognized."

Emma gave him an "Aw, shucks!" look that curdled the beer in my stomach.

"Uh… if we're going to have dinner, maybe we should order now," I said, glancing around for the waiter.

"Oh, yes. Good idea," Dominic said. "Emma, will you stay and eat with us?"

"Sure."

Disappointed by Dominic's invitation and too distracted to study the menu, I selected what George Cooper had recommended: the pasta chitarra. Dominic ordered duck breast in ginger jus and a bottle of Chilean cabernet for the table. Emma looked up at the waiter with a coquettish smile. "I'll just have the carrot soup and another of these," she said, tapping her Manhattan glass.

"Em, why don't you finish the update while we're waiting for our food?" Dominic said. He turned to me.

"She learned something yesterday that might be worth pursuing."

"Oh?" I asked.

Emma opened her mouth to respond, but a telegraph tone emanated from her phone. She raised an index finger as if to say *hold on a minute* and began to answer the message—deftly typing with the edges of her French-manicured thumbs.

Dominic whispered to me, "Excuse me while I go use the restroom," and left the table. I nibbled at my appetizer and squirmed in my chair until the waiter brought our wine. I nodded my assent after tasting it and sipped with gratitude.

Dominic came back, laid a warm hand on my shoulder, and asked about my hotel room. "There's not much of an outdoor view, but the bed seems very comfortable," I said, in a teasing voice. Still typing, Emma got up and finished her message leaning against the marble pillar in the corner of our dining area.

"Can we get back to the matter at hand?" she asked, when she returned.

Irritated at her patronizing tone, I didn't respond.

"So… Alejandra left her place around noon yesterday," Emma began, then looked up in annoyance when our waiter approached bearing the tray with our food.

"Please be careful," the waiter told us, "these plates are very hot."

A mélange of mouthwatering aromas drifted up from the table, and I lifted my fork to taste a black truffle mushroom from my pasta. "Wow," I said to Dominic. "This is amazing."

He swallowed a bite of his entrée and grinned at me. "This is, too."

"As I was saying," Emma said, "Alejandra took the 'L' to the Armitage Avenue station. From there she walked several blocks west to a storefront with a neon Psychic Readings sign in the window. She knocked, stood there for a few minutes, and someone—it looked like a teenaged girl—answered the door."

Despite myself, her narrative compelled me to pay attention.

"There was a coffee shop across the street where I could sit and watch the storefront," Emma said. "Alejandra was in there close to two hours."

"Two *hours*?" I asked. Dominic, too, looked surprised.

She nodded, took a miniscule spoonful of soup, and another sip of her drink. "Finally, she came out with the young woman, they hugged, and Alejandra headed back toward the 'L' stop. I followed her on foot, staying a couple of paces behind her for half a block. Then I came up and walked along beside her. I said, 'Excuse me, but I couldn't help noticing you walked out of that psychic reader place. I've passed by it several times; it never looks open.' She smiled a little and said, 'Oh, you have to make an appointment, and there's usually a wait for the first visit. Sometimes up to a month. But I highly recommend her. Barbara is amazing. She's helped me so much.'"

"'Barbara,'" I said, glancing at Dominic. "That's the name your Aunt Luz gave us."

He nodded and turned to Emma. "And Mom got you an appointment for today?"

"Yep. She graciously offered to call Barbara and tell her she had a friend who'd like a reading. I took her up on it, and, lo and behold, there was an opening at 2:00 this afternoon."

Uncrossing her legs and leaning forward, she swallowed the last of her Manhattan and pushed the glass aside.

"As I was telling Dom when you came in," Emma said, turning to me, "I went back to the coffee shop around 1:00 today to reconnoiter the psychic's place before my appointment. Around 1:30, the young woman who'd hugged Alejandra yesterday left. I managed to get a couple pretty clear pictures of her." Emma took a digital camera from her bag, quickly located the photos, and handed it to Dominic.

He held the camera so I could see the screen and flicked through several photos. I had to admit the shots were good. The petite woman, probably in her twenties, had shoulder-length blond hair pulled back from her face with a purple-print headband. She wore jeans, a plain black sweater, and high-heeled wedged sandals, and carried a leopard-print shoulder bag. "These pictures are excellent," Dominic said. "We'll need prints, of course."

Emma grinned. "Ready for pick-up at the CVS up the street."

"I should've known," he replied.

"Anyway," she continued, "the girl didn't come back before 2:00, and another woman answered the door. I offered my hand and said, 'Thanks for getting me in so quickly, Barbara.' She told me Barbara had gone to take care of her sick child. Said her name was Sonia, and she would be doing the reading."

"Height, weight, hair, eye color?" Dominic asked.

Emma didn't miss a beat. "I'm guessing she's about fifty-five years old, five feet four, a hundred and seventy pounds, dark brown hair and eyes. She could probably pass for Italian or Greek, but she spoke with an accent I couldn't place.

"She led me to a little area that was divided from the rest of the storefront by brocade draperies. There was an altar-like set-up against the wall, with several lighted candles, a fancy Bible on an easel, and a praying-hands statue. A table with two chairs facing each other. She told me the fee would be twenty-five bucks for a half-hour session and I needed to pay upfront. I asked if she could change a fifty, and she said she'd look. She finally came back with a ten, two crumpled fives, three ones, and two bucks in change. This doesn't look like a booming business."

"Yet, Alejandra told you it's tough to get in," I said.

Emma shrugged and continued. "Sonia started with a deck of ancient Tarot cards but said they weren't giving her clear signals and she'd prefer to hold my hands. She reached across the table and held my hands loosely with her eyes closed. Finally, she opened her eyes, said she sensed I was suffering from a significant loss, and asked if that was the case. C'mon! What adult hasn't suffered from *some* sort of significant loss? I played along and told her the truth: that I'd just ended a long-term relationship."

Dominic glanced her way. "Did you and Paul break up?"

Emma folded her napkin and placed it alongside her half-empty soup bowl. "Yeah, I filed for divorce last month."

"I'm sorry," he said.

She nodded but didn't answer.

Without thinking, I reached over and grasped Dominic's hand. "Remember we have plans, Dominic? Could we get on with the rest of the story?" I turned to Emma. "Did Sonia do or say anything that would shed light on what's going on with Alejandra?"

She took no noticeable offense at my abruptly changing the subject. "Unfortunately, no. After she finished the reading—which was as hazy as the sky over Beijing—I reminded her that my friend, Alejandra, had recommended I see Barbara. I asked if I could make another appointment, this time with *her*. Sonia said Barbara's child was in a hospital out of town and she wouldn't be back any time soon."

"What does your gut tell you, Em?" Dominic asked. "Is this psychic thing with Barbara a dead end?"

Emma leaned forward, resting a hand above her cleavage. "I consider myself a pretty good judge of character…"

Yeah, you're obviously a human frickin' lie detector!

"…and I'm quite sure Sonia is just a small-time charlatan. My guess is that Barbara is, too. I suspect Alejandra and her sister went to see Barbara on a lark and she told them some things that rang true. It's just harmless hocus-pocus—nothing sinister."

I felt my phone vibrate and stood to extricate it from my pocket. "Excuse me," I said, walking several steps away from the table to answer the call. Lily.

"Hey! What's up, pumpkin?" I asked.

"You were supposed to text me when you got to Chicago," she said in an icy voice.

"Oh, honey. I'm sorry. It slipped my mind."

Clearly not appeased, she persisted. "How could you forget?"

I didn't want to lie, but neither did I want to fuel the fire. "I've been practicing my oral argument for tomorrow," I said, the deceit almost tripping on my tongue. "It always makes me nervous if I'm not super-prepared."

Silence.

"Lily, can I talk to your grandmother for a minute, please?"

"She's down in her apartment with the other kids. They wanted to sleep at her place," Lily said, with derision.

"You're upstairs alone?"

"Marissa's here. Grandma gave us money to order a pizza and said we could have our own sleepover."

Without asking for my input? With a kid I don't even know?

I heard the doorbell ring in the background. "Gotta go, Mom. The pizza's here..." She hung up.

My temples throbbed with anger. *Two twelve-year-old girls answering the door by themselves—without an adult in evidence! What in God's name were you thinking, Abby?*

I dialed Abby's apartment. Amy answered—something I never allowed. Swallowing my reflexive admonishment, I chatted with her for a minute before my mother-in-law got on the line.

"I just talked with Lily," I said, without masking the urgency in my voice. "I'm not comfortable that she and Marissa are up there alone—and opening the door to some strange pizza-delivery guy."

"It's not *some strange delivery guy*—Glenda's son, Trey, is doing the deliveries tonight," Abby replied, clearly puzzled at my tone. "And I think the girls are old enough and responsible enough to be trusted."

"How well do you know this Marissa?" I persisted.

"She's been over here several times and seems like a good kid. They just moved here from Seattle in April—the mother works at Epic—and she was in Lily's class. I met her mom when she brought her over tonight. We chatted a bit. She mentioned she was a Girl Scout leader in Seattle and that she's started teaching Sunday school here. I think she's got a pretty good handle on kids."

"And she knows you and the littles will be sleeping in your apartment downstairs?"

"Of course. But if it'd make you feel better, we could move upstairs. Red's out cold in the sleeping bag next to my bed, but I can wake her…"

Yeah… then I'd be the unreasonable helicopter mom. The one who's not around often enough to know her own kid's new BFF but still wants to be in control of her social life.

"Never mind, Abby," I said, with a sigh. "If you and Marissa's mom are fine with it, I guess it's okay."

"I'll run up and check on them a time or two."

"Good. Okay, then… have a good night. I'll be home before dinner tomorrow."

"G'night, Caroline."

I straightened my shoulders, took a calming breath, and walked back toward the table, where Dominic and Emma were again absorbed in conversation. "…I really don't think the psychic is worth pursuing," she said. "And, from watching her at the casino and talking with her briefly on the street, it doesn't look like your mom's spending her money on drugs or alcohol. Maybe compulsive shopping?

QVC and those other cable channels have reeled in plenty of people. Or she may be hitting the malls. You know, bipolar folks often suffer from compulsions."

I looked at Dominic. *She knows your mom's bipolar, and I just found out a few days ago?*

"Yes. Well…" he said, running his fingers through his hair. "I'll talk with Dani and see if she can suggest a way to look into that."

With Dominic's hand resting on the small of my back, we walked Emma out the Monroe Street entrance and waited with her until her Uber car arrived—in under two minutes. "I'll talk with you soon, Dom," she said, leaning in to give him a kiss on the cheek. She extended her hand to me. "Nice to meet you, Caroline."

I nodded and exhaled an evening's worth of tension as her car sped away.

It was 9:00 before Dominic and I got to my room. "I've gotta get out of these clothes," I said. I kicked off my sandals near the doorway and left a trail of clothing on the floor as I headed to the bathroom. "And a hot shower would feel heavenly. Join me?"

"I'll be right there," he said, with a grin. "I just need to check this phone message first."

I laughed when I stepped into the miniscule tub: *this is gonna be a* very *romantic shower!* The first few minutes under the piping hot water felt marvelous, but my laughter faded the longer I stood there by myself. When the water failed to drain and pooled around my ankles, I reached for a towel—far smaller and less luxurious than those at the InterContinental—wrapped myself in it, and came out of the bathroom.

Dominic stood at the window with his back to me, talking on the phone. "Yeah. I'll be there in about half an hour," I heard him say, before he hung up and turned around.

"Oh, Madre de Dios…" he said, unable to meet my gaze.

"Was that your mom?"

He shook his head. "It was Dani. Caroline, all this cloak and dagger stuff is getting us nowhere. I need to talk directly with my mother, tell her I know about the letter from the bank, and ask her what's going on. And I'm not going to be any good to you until I get that done. I'm sorry…"

I sank onto the edge of the bed, my knees weak with disappointment. "I understand." *That's a lie: I don't understand, but go. Just go!*

"You have to be in court tomorrow at 9:15, right?"

"Uh-huh."

"I'll try to be back before you head over there," he said, while fumbling through his wallet. "But—here—take my fare card in case I don't make it."

He gave me a chaste kiss, and I heard the door clicking shut behind him before I could find the words to reply.

Hot tears stung my eyes as I pulled back the covers and climbed under the cool sheets. Alone.

CHAPTER NINE

Wrestling with anger, disappointment, and guilt, it had taken me hours after Dominic left to fall asleep. When I answered my eight o'clock wake-up call, my head throbbed and my stomach churned. I snarled at the hotel's robo-operator and—with difficulty—resisted the temptation to phone George Cooper and beg for a reprieve from my court appearance.

Half a tube of concealer couldn't hide the purple circles under my eyes, and four Tums failed to calm my stomach. But after rehearsing my legal argument in front of the bathroom mirror, I emerged confident I could make it through the morning.

Wheeling the classic carry-on bag Abby had found on Overstock.com, briefcase slung over my shoulder, I left the hotel in plenty of time to stop at the Monadnock Building coffee shop, kitty-corner from the courthouse. During the three-block walk, my pumps rubbed the nagging begin-nings of a blister on my right heel. Navigating the shop's close confines with luggage, coffee, and a muffin proved challenging, but I found a spot at a slightly-tipsy table and gratefully sat. I hung my suit jacket on the back of my chair and settled down, determined to enjoy—or at least taste—breakfast.

I leaned over to take my phone out of the briefcase at my feet, just as a businessman in a pin-striped suit bumped the table, spilling my coffee down the front of my cream-colored blouse. "I'm so sorry," he said, handing me his napkin and looking around for others he could grab from nearby patrons. Fighting back tears, I blotted helplessly at the eight-inch stain while he mopped up the table. *Great, just great—I'm gonna appear in federal court looking like I've been shot in the chest with a brown paintball.*

The businessman reached into his breast pocket, extracted a sumptuous leather wallet, and thrust a fifty-dollar bill into my hand. "To cover the dry cleaning bill," he said. "And again, my sincere apologies."

"It's okay," I mumbled, too flustered to decline the money. *And it's not okay!* I thought as he left the coffee shop. *What in God's name do I do now?*

My iPhone, now sitting amidst a pile of soggy paper napkins, signaled an incoming text from Dominic—the "bamboo" tone he'd shown me how to set up a few weeks ago. I glanced at the screen: "Sorry, I'm still tied up…" the text began. *Of course you are.* Without opening the text, I switched off the ringer, shoved the phone into my jacket pocket, and headed for the door.

Panic rose in my throat when I saw the number of people waiting in the marble-floored lobby of the Everett M. Dirksen U.S. Courthouse. I glanced at my watch: 9:05. Though my credentials would allow me to bypass the metal detector, I had ten minutes to clear security, ride the elevator to the twenty-seventh floor, and check in with the clerk's office.

I made it—breathlessly—with a minute to spare. "Rough morning?" the smiling woman at the counter asked, eying my blouse.

"The understatement of the century," I replied, with half a grin.

"I'm not sure whether you saw the updated docket, but three cases in front of you were taken off. You're up second, at about 9:40, so I doubt you'll have time to wash and dry that spot. Maybe hold a legal pad higher than usual?"

No way I'm doing that. I've got five minutes to change. I limped down the deserted hallway—favoring my blistered right foot—into the accessible stall in the closest restroom, and rummaged through my suitcase for yesterday's blouse. *Better rumpled than wet.* I swallowed three more Tums and made for the courtroom.

The opposing counsel, Jason Bittner, gave a slight wave when I walked in. He'd gotten a haircut since I'd seen him two days earlier, as evidenced by the half-inch tan line above his crisp, white shirt collar. He slid over on the bench to make room for me then rested his hands firmly on his knees as if to ground himself. He'd confessed to me once how nervous he became during oral arguments. "You'll do fine," I whispered to him, then took three calming breaths myself. Five minutes later, our case was called.

I'd argued before three-judge panels at the Court of Appeals on two previous occasions. Contrary to her reputation for civility, the one female judge on today's panel scowled through most of my presentation. Her questions seemed calculated to unnerve. Strangely, rather than alarming me, she made me more determined and focused, and I saw glimmers of amusement in the other judges' eyes. The thirty-minute proceeding passed in a flash.

"You nailed it," Jason said, as we left the courtroom. "I predict they'll rule unanimously in your favor." A federal defender, appointed to represent indigent clients, Jason was a good lawyer whom I liked and respected.

"Thanks, but the cards were clearly stacked in my favor," I said, truthfully. "You did a great job with the hand you were dealt. Are you heading back to Madison?"

"Nah. Amanda and kids came with me and we're going to the planetarium and the Shedd. Catch you later."

I retrieved my overnight bag from under the bench where I'd stowed it and hobbled out of the courtroom. A utilitarian, vinyl-covered bench in the entry area of the ladies' room beckoned, though I cringed at its slightly sticky surface when I collapsed onto it and freed my feet from their bondage. Leaning back against the wall, I slid the phone from my pocket and switched on the ringer.

Another text from Dominic—sent at 9:30—awaited me: "Please, please forgive me? Meet me at the Lincoln Park Zoo (Gateway Pavilion) at noon? I'll bring lunch from Frances' Deli."

I spent last evening with you and that P.I. bimbo and last night alone in my hotel room. You reneged on your promise to come watch my oral argument this morning, and now you want me to hang around Chicago for two more hours to meet you *for lunch? Not effing likely.*

I didn't answer the text. Instead—planning to take the train to my car at O'Hare and head home—I changed into shorts, a T-shirt, and sneakers. Dominic didn't know my argument had finished earlier than scheduled, and with any luck, I'd be on the interstate when he finally tried calling.

Between bites of the muffin I hadn't gotten to eat before court, I texted Lily: "Not sure if u & Marissa r up yet. Call when u r." Not surprisingly, she didn't respond. I dialed Abby's cell phone and listened with increasing impatience as it rang and rang. She picked up on the tenth ring.

"Sorry, Caroline," she said, breathlessly. "My phone was in the bottom of the diaper bag. Red and I walked the twins to their camp and now we're at the zoo. It's beautiful here. How 'bout there?"

"I'm just getting ready to go outside and see. My case was heard sooner than I expected, so I'll probably be home by midafternoon. How'd the sleepovers go?"

"Fine. The littles had a blast. And you'll be glad to know that when I checked on Lily and Marissa at 11:00, they were already sound asleep."

And you don't think that's the least bit suspicious?

"Oh, Caroline—I need to go. Red's climbing on the railing. See you this afternoon."

A wave of relief hit me when a vacant elevator car arrived to pick me up on the 27th floor—casual attire wasn't the norm in the courthouse and I felt a bit conspicuous. I rode down alone and rushed through the lobby and onto the sidewalk. Though it would be a steamy day, the breeze through the half-block plaza felt glorious. I decided to walk along the lakefront for a mile or so and catch a train north of the Loop. A life-long Midwesterner, Lake Michigan always felt vast to me. As though we had our own ocean.

And it felt like a sin if I missed seeing it whenever I went to Chicago.

I headed to Michigan Avenue. Though less crowded than at rush hour, the sidewalks still teemed with people—mostly tourists with bags of souvenirs or Garrett's popcorn. The line to get into the Art Institute stretched half a block, and I had to dodge through a busload of folks wearing cameras and matching T-shirts while their guide ushered them to the front of the queue.

As I took a selfie in front of the Millennium Park bean—the huge iconic silver sculpture—that I knew the twins would get a kick out of, my cell phone rang. Dominic.

Might as well get this over with. "Hello," I said, coolly.

"Are you out of court?"

"Obviously."

"How did your argument go?"

"Fine."

"I'm really sorry I missed it. I'd been looking forward to seeing you in action."

If it'd been a priority, you would've been there.

"Look, Caroline, you have every right to be angry and I understand why you didn't answer my texts. I really want to see you before you go home, to apologize in person. Please say you'll meet me at the zoo."

I glanced at my watch. "Fine—if you can make it by 11:30. I need to be home for the twins' T-ball game at 5:00."

"Can do," he said, and I could hear the smile in his voice. "Do you have any requests for lunch?"

"Surprise me," I said, and hung up.

I kept walking. Past the glitzy stores on the Magnificent Mile. Through the tunnel under Lake Shore Drive toward Oak Street Beach. And, finally, to the Lakefront Trail. I bought a two-dollar bottle of water from a vendor and sat for a few minutes on the rock ledge, staring toward the horizon. Sailboats flitted among a few yachts—headed, I supposed, for weekend jaunts up to Door County or Mackinac Island.

I wiped the sweat off my brow with the hem of my shirt, readjusted my sneaker socks, and resumed my trek.

When I arrived at the zoo—ten minutes early— Dominic sat waiting, a Frances Deli bag on the bench by his side and a huge bouquet of fresh flowers on his knee. He looked up warily as I approached, then stood and took me into his arms. "Thank you for coming," he said, his voice cracking with emotion.

I started to pull away. "I'm sweating like crazy and must smell something awful."

"Hush," he said, and kissed me. A long, slow kiss that dissolved all but a little of my anger.

He handed me the flowers. "Forgive me?" The cacophony of scents and one look into his hypnotic brown eyes melted my heart.

I blinked back a few tears and nodded. "Let's stroll a bit before we eat, okay? I want to take a few pictures of the polar bears to show the kids."

"Sure," he said, brushing a tear from my cheek with his thumb. "Let me take your bag."

"Have at it," I said, gratefully, as he attached the deli bag to the handle of my suitcase.

We walked to the exhibit in companionable silence. Putting on a show for us, two polar bears frolicked in their pool with a huge, yellow ball. Dominic had me pose in front of the window with my arms extended as though I were playing with them. Luke would be delighted when he saw the pictures. "Thanks," I said. "Now how 'bout some lunch?"

We found a picnic table and he laid out oversized sandwiches, coleslaw, potato pancakes, and two Dr. Brown's cream sodas. "Take your pick—the Reuben or the turkey-avocado club. Or, we can share both of them."

"Let's share," I said, as I opened a bottle of soda.

He took a huge bite of coleslaw, dribbling a bit down his chin. "Sorry," he said, as he wiped it with a napkin, "I guess I was hungrier than I thought. I didn't get around to breakfast. Did you?"

I told him about my ill-fated trip to the coffee shop and the muffin I'd eaten in the courthouse restroom. I told him about the oral argument and that I expected the judges would rule in our favor. Dominic listened with rapt attention—all eyes and ears—and I reveled in it. And he gazed at me longingly while I ate my half of the Reuben sandwich and wrapped the other one to go.

He didn't bring up his mother's situation. Nor did I— until we were in his car, within a few miles of the airport parking lot where he'd drop me off.

"Dominic," I began, "I was angry, hurt, and disappointed when you left last night, but I can understand why you're worried about your mother."

He took his eyes off the road for a split second and glanced at me. I saw gratitude in his eyes—probably because I'd finally broached the subject.

"Did you get things worked out?"

"Some things, I guess," he said. "I went straight to Mom's. I told her it was me who'd gone into her place and snooped and that I'd found the letter from the bank about her being behind in the mortgage. When she got done fuming—which took awhile, believe me—I demanded an explanation. A 'perfect storm' of circumstances is what she said. She needed to install new air conditioning and replace her roof, all at once. And she's been helping Dani out because her ex is behind on child support."

"Are you satisfied with her answers?" I asked.

"Pretty much." He stared ahead, apparently lost in thought. *What is he not telling me?*

I wanted to press him but bit my tongue.

"Did you ask about the ring?"

He nodded. "She says she took it to the jeweler who designed the ring for my dad years ago. He agreed to fix it, but it's taking longer than expected."

"So what happens now?"

"I called my bank this morning. I'm going to take out a line of credit to help Mom get back on track."

Now, I found myself lost in thought. Dominic had worked long hours, many of which he never billed to my attorney, to win me the insurance settlement after David's death. I could afford to loan him some money.

He must have read my mind. He reached over and rested his hand on mine. "Don't even think it."

"What?"

"About loaning me the money."

"But… you've done so much for me."

"Life isn't a score card, Caroline," he said, with a gentle smile. "You and your family are in my heart—and I'm grateful every day for that."

A moment later, we drove into the parking ramp and I directed him to my car. Dominic got out to retrieve my suitcase from his trunk. "Are you heading back to Madison now, too?" I asked.

"Not until tomorrow. Dani and I need to talk a little more this evening."

"I hope it all works out," I said. "Thanks for the lift. And for lunch. And for the flowers."

He pulled me into his arms. "It was the least I could do—after messing up yet another romantic evening."

"There'll be more romantic evenings…" I said, and we kissed goodbye.

Traffic on the interstate moved at a good pace, and I pulled into my driveway at 4:15, content with how the day had turned out.

But my mood almost instantly deflated. No one met me at the door, and, inside, it looked as though a tornado had touched down. Toys, shoes, and piles of clothing were strewn randomly throughout the foyer and living room. "Anybody home?" I called.

No response.

I tripped over Luke's Tonka dump truck, kicked it aside, and headed angrily for the steps. I knocked on Lily's closed door. No answer. I knocked again—louder this time—and tried the handle. It was locked. "Lily, open the door."

I heard someone say, "Shit!" and what sounded like a dresser drawer closing. Then, Lily opened the door a mere three inches. "What are you doing home so early?" she asked, in an accusatory tone, as she peered out through the crack.

I felt my pulse racing in my ears, shoved the door open, and stormed past her into the room, hands on hips. A too-thin, blonde girl—wearing a blaze-orange tank top and cutoff shorts that barely covered her anorexic butt cheeks—stood at the open window with her back to me. A cloud of cigarette smoke hung in the air.

"I'll be asking the questions here, Lily. Are you Marissa?"

The girl turned around slowly, probably trying to decide whether to sucker me with pleasantries or to go on the defensive.

"It's a simple question: Are you Marissa?"

She nodded but didn't make eye contact.

"As Lily well knows, neither locked doors nor smoking are allowed in this house. What's your last name and where do you live?"

A look of defiance crossed Marissa's face.

"It's Baxter. She lives on Mandan Crescent," Lily piped up. "Why do you wanna know?"

"This is the way it's going to be," I said. "Marissa, you'll leave now and walk straight home. I'm calling your mother to tell her what's happened. Lily, you're grounded until further notice. Hand me the cigarettes."

Lily yanked open the dresser drawer, grabbed a pack of Newports, and slung it at me. "I hate you!" she yelled, throwing herself onto her bed. "You're ruining my life."

I stooped to pick up the cigarettes and put them in my back pocket. "Sorry you feel that way. Now let's go, Marissa," I said, grasping the girl's elbow to steer her out the door. She jerked away and stomped ahead down the stairs and out the front door, slamming it behind her.

"Good riddance," I muttered, and sat on the lowest step to regroup.

"What's goin' on, Mommy?" I heard Amy say, from the upstairs landing.

"Nothing you need to be concerned about. Where're Luke, Red, and Abby?"

"In our room. Did you bring us anything from Chicago?"

"No, pumpkin, not this time. I'll be there in a minute to say hello, though."

I went to the kitchen cupboard where Abby and I kept phone numbers, carryout menus, and coupons. Fortunately, she'd jotted Marissa's address and phone number in our battered spiral notebook. I dialed.

"Baxter residence," a woman answered.

"Mrs. Baxter," I began—

"Oh, no," the woman interrupted. "This is the house-keeper. Mrs. Baxter's out of town on business today."

Of course she is. And, of course, she has a housekeeper. "Please take a message," I said. As patiently as I could manage, I explained the reason for my call. "...And I need *you* to call me back if Marissa doesn't arrive home within ten minutes," I concluded. I glanced at my watch as I hung up: 4:30.

I bounded back up the steps—we'd need to hurry to get to the T-ball game on time—and stood in Lily's doorway. "We're leaving in ten minutes for the twins' game. You're coming with us," I said. "No arguments." Then, I noticed about ten bottles of nail polish and several tubes of lip gloss and makeup on the bed. She shifted her position in a not-too-subtle effort to block my view of the cosmetics. "Where did you get all that stuff?"

"What?"

"The makeup and nail polish. Where did you get it?"

"Oh… uh… from Abby. Abby bought it for me. For helping with the kids while you were off in Chicago *again*."

I turned on my heel, intent on finding and confronting my mother-in-law for needlessly indulging my contentious oldest child. She was in the twins' room, rocking Red in time to the soundtrack from *Frozen* and smiling as she watched Amy and Luke making shapes with Play-Doh and cookie cutters at their Little Tikes table. I cringed at the sight of the pesky pieces of colored dough, some of which would inevitably make it to my living room carpet. Abby heard me approach and looked up with a grin. "I know Play-Doh's a mess," she whispered, "but they love it."

Her comment and another look at the whole scene brought me up short. Red, her eyes half-mast, utterly content on Abby's lap. The twins, gloriously absorbed in their play, getting so much enjoyment at the table David had struggled to assemble on Christmas Eve two and a half years ago. *If only he could see them all now! And if only he were here to help me deal with Lily…*

I decided to postpone my talk with Abby about buying Lily the toiletries.

"Okay, T-ballers," I said, making sure my tone was light, "we have ten minutes to get dressed and into the car." I pulled open a couple of dresser drawers and rummaged through the contents. "Abby, do you know where their shirts are?"

She stopped rocking. "I completely forgot about the game. They're not in there?"

"Nope. Kids, help me look for 'em. And for your gloves."

Luke, of course, had to make three more Play-Doh cookies before joining the search. And Amy, of course, found the shirts tossed onto the closet floor—dirty and wrinkled from last week's game. "This one's got ketchup on the front," she wailed. "I'm not wearing it."

"Put on the other one," I said, grabbing the stained shirt and heading for the bathroom to run it under water. "Luke, follow me."

Luke squirmed into the mostly-wet-and-none-too-clean shirt, and I sent him back to find his glove. I glanced down at my own T-shirt and shorts, both wrinkled and sweaty, and dashed to my room to find a clean pair of capris and a fresh shirt. Buttoning the shirt as I went, I yelled to Lily, "If you're not in the car in two minutes, the grounding period'll be doubled."

We managed to find only one baseball glove in the bottom of the toy box. "You'll just have to share," I told Luke and Amy. *Nobody catches the ball anyway.*

By the time we all got into the minivan—a sullen Lily in the way-way back seat, a squirmy toddler in the back flanked by the twins in their booster seats, and Abby riding shotgun—I felt sweat dripping down my back. "I'm hungry," Luke said, as I shifted the car into reverse.

I looked at Abby who stared down at her lap. "They each had a Popsicle and couple of cookies around 2:00," she said, "but nothing healthy since lunchtime. If I'd remembered the game…"

"Never mind. We'll stop at the Micky D's drive-thru on Regent Street," I said, glancing at the littles in the rearview mirror, "but it's milk and apple slices with your Happy Meals, understood? And, Red, you'll have to wait to eat yours 'til we get to the game."

We arrived at the T-ball game just as the opposing team wandered onto the field. When Luke bolted from the car, I noticed more ketchup on the back of his shirt and felt—once again—like a less-than-adequate mom. But later, when another mother sitting near us in the bleachers giggled and told me she had sangria in her Starbucks to-go cup, I felt slightly *less* inadequate.

Throughout the game, Lily uttered not a peep to me. Even Abby noticed. "What's up with her?" she asked, during a lull in the action.

"Long story," I said. "But I'd appreciate it if you could hang around a little longer this evening so we can talk about it."

She fidgeted on the bench. "Sure. Whatever you need."

I wanted nothing more than to sit on the back porch with an ice-cold beer after the interminable game. But Luke and Amy were covered with caked-on dust from the base paths, and Red felt sticky from God knew what. "C'mon kiddos," I said, as we walked in the front door, "straight to my bathroom."

"Can we turn on the whirlpool jets?" Amy asked, with excitement.

"If you don't fight."

I scrubbed Red clean and pulled her out before starting the jets. Luke and Amy managed to soak for ten minutes before sniping at one another—and by then, the water was brown. I drained the tub and declared them clean.

I settled them in front of Nickelodeon with a bowl of popcorn, left Abby in charge, and forced myself to climb the stairs, again, to talk with Lily.

You can do this. Just keep it calm and firmly tell her your concerns. Maybe try negotiating how long she should be grounded? David—help me here, please!

Lily's door had been open when the littles finished bathing. Now, it was closed. I turned the handle and couldn't open it. "What in God's name were you thinking, Lily? Now unlock this door. This instant," I yelled, as I pounded on the door.

"It's *not* locked," she yelled back. "Turn the frickin' doorknob."

I tried again, jiggling the knob this time, and the latch clicked open. I took a deep breath and strode into the room. "I'm sorry I accused you of locking it, Lily. That doesn't excuse your using such disrespectful language in this house. Understood?"

She sat cross-legged on the bed, earbuds in her ears, and nodded sullenly. I motioned for her to remove them.

She jerked them off and threw her phone toward her feet. "What do you want?"

"To talk with you," I said, sitting on the edge of the bed and facing her. "About the cigarettes. And the locked door this afternoon. And what your punishment should be."

"Marissa's the one who was smoking—and who locked the door. I didn't see her lock it, and she didn't know it was against the rules."

"But you had to know she was smoking."

"You never told me *that* was against the rules."

I felt my blood pressure rising—the veins in my temples throbbed, and I feared my head would explode. "Come on, Lily, you can't expect me to believe you thought it was okay for you or your guests to smoke. You're *twelve years old*. It's against the law."

"How would I know that?" she asked, her voice rising to meet mine.

I shook my head, stood up, and began pacing the room. "As I remember," I said, measuring my syllables, "when you were in fourth-grade, you won that writing contest with your essay on the dangers and consequences of smoking. Your dad and I couldn't have been prouder. What do you think he'd say if he heard you rationalizing allowing your friend to smoke in your room?"

She didn't answer, but fat tears began creeping down her cheeks.

"Lily, we need to talk about this."

"I don't have anything to say."

"All right, then. What kind of consequences do you think are in order?"

"*You're* the parent. You decide."

"Fine," I said. "You're grounded for two weeks with no phone privileges." I grabbed her cell phone and left the room before she could witness my tears.

When Red and the twins were down for the night, I reached for that cold beer—a Leinie's Summer Shandy—and found Abby dozing on the couch in the living room. She startled when I walked in. "Sorry," I said. "I know it's been a long day."

"It's okay," she said, rubbing drool from her cheek with the back of her hand. She muted the TV. "I guess this show wasn't as interesting as I thought. What's going on with Lily?"

I slumped into my chair and took a long pull from the bottle. "When I came home this afternoon, she and Marissa were in her room with the door locked, and at least one of them was smoking. Lily said it was Marissa."

The color drained from Abby's face. "Cigarettes?"

I burst out laughing. "I guess things could be worse—they could've been using pot or meth."

She looked aghast. "Don't even joke."

"Abby, I know there's nothing funny about this. It's just nervous laughter. I don't know what's gotten into Lily. And I'm afraid Marissa Baxter's a bad influence. She was insolent when I confronted them—not a bit sorry for what they'd done."

"She's always been polite and courteous to me. And, like I told you last night, her mother seems nice and responsible."

"Her housekeeper answered the phone this afternoon and told me Mrs. Baxter's away on business. Is she gone a lot?"

"I don't know."

"Well, I grounded Lily for two weeks and took away her cell phone. I'll let her off a week early if she agrees to do some specific chores and help you more with the kids."

Abby raised an eyebrow.

"What?" I asked. "Too harsh? Too lenient?"

"No, no… it's probably about right. And I'll keep a closer eye on her, I promise."

"One more thing, Abby," I said, as nonchalantly as I could, "it's really not necessary for you to buy Lily stuff for helping with the kids."

"Stuff?"

"Yeah. She told me you bought her all those bottles of nail polish and makeup as a thank-you for helping with the littles while I was in Chicago. You know she gets a generous allowance—she can buy those things herself."

I thought I saw a tinge of alarm in her eyes. But it passed as quickly as it had appeared.

"Oh… that stuff… yeah, I'm sorry, I forgot. We did go shopping the other day. Just a few trinkets, some nail polish. From now on I'll have her buy that kind of thing herself." She stood and handed me the remote control. "I really am bushed. Goodnight, Caroline."

I switched off the TV and sat in the silent living room sipping my beer, bewildered and alone. I picked up a framed photograph from the end table beside me—a candid shot Glenda had taken of our family at a picnic the summer before David's death. David and I were seated next to one another in canvas sling chairs, a twin on each of his knees and Lily sprawled across my lap. We looked so carefree. *Oh, honey, I miss you so much.*

CHAPTER TEN

The fifteenth of August—moving day for some twenty thousand University of Wisconsin students—and I'd made the mistake of driving down Dayton Street on my way home from work. Stopped for the fourth time behind a double-parked moving truck while scantily clad, sweaty kids unloaded mattresses, desks, bookshelves, and miscellaneous junk, it had taken me twenty minutes to go two blocks. And when I held my clammy hand in front of the dashboard vent and felt warm air blowing at me, I realized my air conditioning had given up the ghost. I rolled down the windows hoping for a breeze, only to be hit with an unmoving wall of humidity and the stench of garbage piled up along the curbs. *Shit, shit, shit!*

The scene on my front porch when I got home half an hour later was no better: damp, sandy beach towels strewn across the railings; plastic buckets and shovels littering the floor; a filthy cooler, half-filled with water and a floating Juicy Juice box, sitting next to the door. *Could I catch a break here, please?*

The cool air inside the house brought a moment of relief. That is, until I kicked off my shoes and felt sand on the hardwood foyer floor. And looked up to see three bathing suits, wet and algae-stained, hanging from the coat tree.

"The kids are on the back porch," Abby yelled from the kitchen. I tossed my purse and briefcase on the dining room table and went to talk with her.

She stood at the stove, her face flushed and glistening with sweat, and brushed the hair from her brow with the back of her hand. "I'm sorry for the mess," she said. "The afternoon turned out to be a disaster. Sit a minute and I'll tell you."

I reached into the fridge for a Leinie's, twisted off the cap, and sank onto a kitchen chair. "What happened?"

"After Red woke up from her nap, I took her and the twins to Vilas Beach. I slathered them all with sunscreen but Red still got burned. Amy cut her foot on a piece of glass on the playground, and Luke got into a tussle with a kid who laughed about it. We just got home a little while ago, and I hosed them off in the back yard. Then I realized we didn't have any aloe lotion to put on Red's sunburn or any antibiotic cream to put on Amy's foot, so I sent Lily over to Mallatt's to get some. She should be back any minute. I thought I'd bake these Papa Murphy's pizzas for dinner if that's okay with you."

It wore me out just listening to her. "Sure. But I'll put 'em in as soon as I say 'hi' to the kids. You go sit and relax."

Kisses and sympathy administered, I finished my beer, swept the sand from the floor, and threw together a bagged Caesar salad while the pizzas baked. Lily stalked into the kitchen just as the timer buzzed. "Thanks for getting the first aid supplies," I said to her, leaning into the oven to extract a pizza.

She tossed the pharmacy bag, some crumpled bills, and a few coins onto the table without a word and headed back toward the front door.

"Hold on, where are you going?"

"Grandma said I could go to the mall with Marissa," she called over her shoulder.

"I don't care if Grandma said it's okay, we need to talk before you go. Come sit down while I put dinner on the table."

I delivered the pizza, salad, and some Hi-C to the back porch—naturally, we were all out of milk—and nonchalantly asked Abby, "Did you tell Lily she could go to the mall with Marissa?"

She looked up from the picnic table in alarm. "Yes. Shouldn't I have? She's been off grounding for two weeks and following all the rules. And she volunteered to go to the drugstore for me."

"Uh... yeah. I just wanted to make sure."

Lily sat slumped at the kitchen table, typing furiously on her phone, and didn't make eye contact when I entered the room. "See?" she asked. "I told you she said it was okay."

I took the chair across from her. "Lily, I worry about you hanging out with Marissa. She seems—I don't know— a little wilder than you. How are you getting to the mall?"

"Bettina's taking us."

"Bettina?"

"Yeah, the Baxters' housekeeper."

"And where are her parents?"

"Her dad lives in Seattle. Her mother's out of town on business. And, Mom, you really don't know Marissa. She's, like, the smartest kid in our class, and she's really nice. Not stuck up or anything, even though her parents make a lot of money."

Maybe the fact that Lily had actually spoken several sentences to me clouded my judgment, but I ignored my trepidations. "Okay. Be home by 9:00."

She gave me half a smile, nodded, and got up to leave.

"And let me give you my debit card so you can buy a few new things for school. Keep it under a hundred dollars, though."

Wow—she actually grinned!

While Amy and Luke splashed in my tub, I patted Red dry with the softest towel in my bathroom closet and reached for the aloe gel. Even after a cool bath, her sunburned shoulders and upper back still felt hot to the touch. "This'll feel good," I said, dabbing on a dollop of the soothing lotion, just as my cell phone rang. I glanced at the screen. Dominic.

"Hey!" I said. "Sorry it took me a few rings to answer. I had aloe goo all over my hands and had to wipe 'em off. How are you?"

"Fine, but I'm sorry I took this case. Looks like I won't get back to Madison for at least another couple days. In fact, I'm working right now. The guy I'm watching is on his own phone and I figured I'd have a minute to call and say 'hi.' I miss you."

"I miss you, too."

"Oh, he just hung up. I'll call tomorrow, okay?"

"I'll look forward to it."

Once the littles were in bed, I texted a wine glass emoji with a question mark to Glenda. She magically appeared at my front door five minutes later, a sweating bottle of Pinot Grigio in hand. "I know this isn't your favorite, but it's too hot for cabernet," she declared, planting a kiss on my cheek and heading for the living room. "And it's too hot to sit outside."

I fetched two glasses and a paper plate full of cold pizza from the kitchen and joined her on the couch. "How was your vacation?" I asked.

"Jackson Hole was wonderful, but I could've skipped the drive to and from. The kids bickered the whole way—I can't wait for Edgewood to start next week so at least Jake'll be busy. But of course, Trey and Sarah are lording it over him 'cause the public schools don't go back 'til almost two weeks later. I'm not sure I agree with this start-after-September-first-law, though it's good for me as a public school employee!"

"Yeah. I'm glad I decided to send the twins to 4K at Edgewood so they can start the same day as Lily. I feel like this house would implode if we went an extra day without some structure."

Glenda swallowed a bite of pizza and washed it down with a generous sip of wine. "Is anything in particular amiss?"

I told her about catching Marissa and Lily with cigarettes behind a locked door.

"Didn't you ever try smoking when you were a teenager?" she asked, with a grin.

"First of all, Lily's not a teenager yet. And, yes, I did—but I had the good sense to do it somewhere other than my own house. But more than that, it's Lily's abominable attitude."

"Is she still upset that you're seeing Dominic?"

"I don't really know. She refuses to talk about it when I ask her directly. And, truth be told, I haven't seen much of him in the past couple weeks. He took on a case in Chicago with the folks he used to work for, and he's been gone a lot."

"Why'd he do that?"

I shrugged. "He told me they offered him top dollar— he had to bail his mom out of some financial troubles and this case'll put him back in the black. But I suspect he also wants to keep a closer eye on his mom's mental health."

"You said she's bipolar?"

"Uh-huh."

"That can really be tough to get under control," she said, topping off our wine glasses. "Hope she's got a good shrink."

"His sister says she does."

I heard footsteps in the foyer and looked up to see Lily. "I didn't hear you come in, honey. C'mon in and say 'hi' to Glenda," I said, glancing at the mantel clock and noting she was ten minutes early.

Much to my surprise, she walked in without a fuss. "Hey, Glen. Hey, Mom. Look what I got on sale at Macy's." She pulled an off-white, American Rag pullover sweater and a pair of Levi's skinny jeans from the shopping bag and held them in front of her.

"Nice," I said, sincerely.

Lily handed me my debit card. "The total was a hundred and five, but I'll pay you the extra."

"That's okay, kiddo."

"Thanks, Mom. Well, I'm gonna head up and read a while. G'night."

We sipped in silence until we heard Lily's bedroom door close. "She didn't seem abominable to me," Glenda said.

"No, she didn't."

CHAPTER ELEVEN

I woke up before my six o'clock alarm on this milestone Wednesday and bounded out of bed with a mélange of feelings. Excitement about the twins starting 4K, for which Amy was beyond ready. Trepidation that Luke might *not* be ready. Sadness that David couldn't be here to share the experience and make the traditional, first-day-of-school pancakes he'd always made for Lily. Giddiness about a long-overdue lunch date with Dominic—who'd finally returned from Chicago.

By 7:15, everyone but Lily sat at the kitchen table in anticipation. Amy wore a new pink sundress she'd tried on a dozen times before and kicked at the table leg with her rhinestone-studded sneakers to make sure their lights still blinked. Luke wore a new T-shirt and shorts, still creased from their Amazon packaging. Abby, hands cupped around her coffee mug, stopped herself at least two times from getting up to help me cook. And Red, still in her PJs, sat in her high chair picking at an orange slice.

I sprinkled a few drops of water onto the pancake griddle, heard the hiss that told me it was hot, and poured out the batter. My attempt to make Mickey Mouse ears failed miserably—I ended up with misshapen blobs—but there was no time to start over. "Lily," I yelled from the kitchen doorway, "hurry up! Breakfast is almost ready."

She appeared just as I dished up the pancakes. "I'm not hungry," she said, and turned to leave.

"But it's pancakes," I said.

"So?"

"We always have a pancake breakfast on the first day of school."

"That was Dad's thing—not yours."

My heart sank. "Lily, that's not true. We've done it since he's been gone."

"Yeah… and it was lame." Lily's phone buzzed. She glanced at the screen. "Marissa's waiting for me on the corner. We're gonna walk together and I don't want to be late."

"You're not leaving 'til we get our first-day-of-school picture," I said, grabbing my phone from the counter. "Amy, Luke, stand over by the fridge. C'mon, Lily—this is important to them." Lily stalked into position behind the twins. I handed Amy the construction paper sign she'd made to commemorate the date, and she held it in front of her. Luke couldn't smile with a mouth stuffed with pancake and Lily glared, but Amy beamed when I muttered, "Say cheese."

The picture taking accomplished, I moved to hug Lily. She pulled away and headed toward the door. "Abby's picking up the twins," I said in defeat. "Text her if you'll be late walking home for any reason. And, Lily—I love you."

She left without a word.

Tears welled in my eyes as I sat to eat. I needed coffee to wash down my first bite of the too-dry pancake and couldn't manage another. But Luke and Amy ate with relish and I took solace in knowing they wouldn't be starving by lunchtime.

I pulled into the school parking lot at 7:55 and glanced around for an open spot. "Mommy, you can just drop us at the door," Amy said. "We remember where our room is."

"No, honey," I said. "I'm sure you do, but just for today I want to walk you in."

They'd done fine at orientation, but I'd pictured a somewhat tearful farewell when I dropped the kids off in their classroom. Luke ran in to say 'hi' to a buddy from camp before I could even plant a kiss on his head. Amy gave me a sophisticated hug and said, "Have a good day, Mommy."

"Thanks, pumpkin. You, too," I said, swallowing the lump in my throat.

I trudged—emotionally exhausted—down the hallway to my office at 8:30. George Cooper waited by the desk of my secretary, Roxanne, bearing a cardboard tray with two cups of coffee and a pastry bag.

"I come bearing gifts, Caroline," he said, with a grin.

"I'm guessing it's more like a bribe, since I see they're from Barrique's." The coffee shop, deli, and wine bar across the street from our office had full-flavor coffee and to-die-for pastries, but most of us settled for in-house coffee and the miscellaneous treats people left in the lunchroom.

"You're right," he said, following me into my office.

I set my briefcase on the chair, glanced at the phone message slips Roxanne had left on my desk, and pushed aside a stack of files to make room for the coffee. George settled himself in one of my visitors' chairs and I took the other. He lifted the lid off his cup, blew on the coffee a few times, and took an appreciative sip. "This is my favorite of their blends."

Uncovering my own cup, I was pleased to see he'd put in double cream. "You remembered how I take it."

He laughed. "You gotta know your mark. Look what else I brought."

I peeked into the pastry bag: cinnamon morning buns. "You had me at coffee," I said, taking one and passing him the bag. "But thanks for the extra treat… and still warm, no less!" We took a few bites, eating over napkins spread on our laps. "You realize you don't actually have to bribe me to give me an assignment, don't you?"

George nodded. "Uh-huh, but this is a little more than a routine assignment. I want you to take on a developing case and help coach a new FBI agent along. The case was brought to us by a Janesville detective by the name of Matt Witte—"

"I've met him. Seems like a good guy."

"Yeah. He uncovered a scam to steal high-end vehicles via identity theft. At least one of the four vehicles he recovered in Janesville was taken by bank fraud in a Chicago suburb, hence the FBI involvement. Now, the Madison FBI office and the Janesville PD are working the case jointly. Matt thinks they're just seeing the tip of an iceberg."

"Who's the new FBI agent?"

"Jimmy McGee. He transferred here from Cleveland last month. He's got a good rep for financial crimes, deciphering documents and following the money, though he isn't your typical 'suit.'"

"Oh?" I replied, wishing for the millionth time that I had the ability to raise an inquisitive eyebrow. I pulled off another piece of morning bun and popped it into my mouth.

"Jimmy's a little rough around the edges; looks more like an undercover street cop and has a tough time holding his tongue. Matt'll balance things out for you, though. He's low-key and seasoned. Knows his way around a courtroom. Could you meet with Jimmy, Matt, and me this afternoon so they can bring us up to speed?"

I glanced at my calendar: *12:30—lunch with Dominic—Liliana's.* "Uh, yeah… Can we make it after 3:00?" I felt a tad guilty leaving myself a three-hour block of time for "lunch," but I hadn't seen Dominic in weeks. It would take me half an hour to get both to and from the restaurant in suburban Fitchburg, and I hoped his schedule would permit a detour to his condo a few blocks away. In anticipation of that detour, I'd worn the blue silk blouse he'd shyly complimented me on before we began seeing one another romantically—he'd said it made my eyes sparkle, but I knew it's low-cut neckline was also flattering. *Will George wonder why I can't meet 'til 3:00?*

"Let's make it 3:30 in the small conference room," George said, without a trace of suspicion. He stood, crumpled his napkin, and threw it in the wastebasket on his way out the door.

In the elevator, heading to my car at noon, I got a text from Dominic: "Would you mind meeting at my house rather than at Liliana's? I don't know what I was thinking when I suggested a restaurant. It would be torture to sit through a meal without being able to touch you. I'll leave the door unlocked."

I felt my face flush and gave a silent prayer of thanks for both the message and the fact that I was alone in the elevator. And, though traffic on Fish Hatchery Road moved smoothly, it felt like an eternity before I pulled into Dominic's driveway.

I opened the front door without knocking and walked in. The antithesis of his mother's apartment, Dominic's spacious condo was the picture of comfort and simplicity. Hardwood floors with geometrically-patterned area rugs in the living and dining rooms. Overstuffed sofa and club chairs with sleek coffee and end tables. Off-white walls adorned with large, framed, black-and-white photographs. And a big-screen TV, now tuned to Sirius Radio's Spectrum station. The aroma of garlic and parsley wafted from the kitchen, but Dominic was nowhere to be seen.

"Hello?"

"Just getting out of the shower," he called, from down the hallway. "Come in."

I gasped at the sight of him standing naked in the doorway between the master bedroom and bath, toweling off his wavy, almost-black hair. *Wow! This amazingly hot guy is waiting for* me! My feet felt rooted to the floor.

He threw the towel on the bathroom floor and walked over to take me in his arms. "Oh, lord, I've missed you."

"Me too—"

He slowly undressed me, each exquisite touch awaking nerves I didn't know I possessed. He must've realized my knees were weak, for he lifted me gently to the bed as though I were a cherished piece of porcelain. "I can't wait," I whispered.

"Sure you can," he said, with a throaty chuckle. He nuzzled my neck, teased my breasts with his tongue, and stroked the inside of my thigh.

"Please—"

"If you insist."

Lying beside him afterward, our fingers entwined, I felt contentment I hadn't known in years. "Thank you," I said.

"My pleasure," he said, then kissed my cheek. "There's more where that came from, but I fear I'll need time and sustenance to recover. How does empanadillas in bed sound to you?"

"Wonderful," I said. When he got up, I pulled back the comforter and climbed between the sheets.

He returned five minutes later with a Fiestaware platter of bite-sized stuffed pastries, two wine glasses, and a bottle of Pinot Grigio. "There're two kinds of empanadillas: tuna and egg or spinach and cheese," he said, handing me the platter. He poured the wine and set the bottle on the dresser, then joined me in bed.

"Did you make these?"

"No. I bought them at a Spanish restaurant before I left Chicago yesterday. I just put them in the oven."

We sat cross-legged, the sheet across our laps, sipping wine and nibbling at our food. I caught a glimpse of us in the mirror atop Dominic's dresser and reached for the sheet to cover my bare breasts. He gently grabbed my wrist. "No, please, I love looking at you like this. You're so beautiful."

After half a glass of wine, three empanadillas, and another round of love-making, my self-consciousness dissipated. I lay back against the pillows and grinned as Dominic got up to pour himself more wine. "Are you sure you have to go back to the office today?"

"Yes, and I don't know what I was thinking when I agreed to a late-afternoon meeting."

From the kitchen, I heard my cell phone ringing—the "William Tell Overture" ringtone I'd assigned to the kids' school. I glanced at the bedside clock: 2:15. "It's Edgewood," I said, as I pushed aside the sheet. "I've gotta take it."

I raced to the phone, fumbling to activate the call before it went to voicemail. "This is Caroline Spencer."

"Mrs. Spencer, it's Elizabeth Walker, the assistant principal at Lily's school. I hate to interrupt your workday, but I've suspended her and need to have you come pick her up."

"Suspended? Lily?"

"I'm afraid so. She and another student were smoking on school grounds during the lunch break. I would have called earlier but it's taken awhile to sort things out."

Dominic walked up behind me and put his robe around my shoulders. I leaned against him for support. "How long is the suspension?" I asked, my voice quivering.

"Until Monday."

"Uh… okay. I'm not in my office so it'll take me about half an hour to get there." I disconnected the call and sat heavily on a kitchen stool.

"I couldn't help overhearing that Lily's been suspended," Dominic said. "What for?"

"Smoking."

He shook his head. "I was praying she'd learned her lesson with the grounding."

"You and me both," I said, bitterly. "It's one thing to leave a lovely tryst to go back to work but another thing entirely to have to pick up your delinquent kid from school."

After a quick wash-up in Dominic's bathroom and a call to tell Abby I'd pick up the twins along with Lily, I set out on my awful errand. And, at a stoplight on Fish Hatchery Road, I called and left a message for George Cooper, saying I might be late for our 3:30 meeting.

The line of cars waiting to get into Edgewood's parking lot sent me into a panic. Not for the first time, I wondered how so many parents were free to pick their kids up when school ended at quarter to three. I created a parking spot at the far edge of the lot and dashed toward the door: I'd collect the twins in their classroom and take them with me to the office.

"Mommy! What are you doing here?" Amy asked, when I appeared in Abby's place.

"Kind of a long story, kiddo," I said, nodding to the teacher and ushering her and Luke into the hallway. "And I really want to hear all about your first day, but it'll have to wait. Okay?"

The assistant principal stood at the counter when we walked into the office. "Luke and Amy, isn't it?" she said to the twins, who nodded absently. "I need you to wait here for a few minutes while your mom comes with me. There are some crayons and paper on the table so you can draw while you're waiting."

I'd met Elizabeth Walker at a couple of PTO functions over the past two years. A compact woman, probably in her forties, with short, low-maintenance hair, she epito-mized efficiency. Today, she wore a simple navy dress with flat shoes, no makeup, and small, gold, hoop earrings. I'd heard she'd been a nun at one time but had never bothered to ask her. She led me behind the counter and into a private office where Lily slumped in a wooden armchair, glancing only briefly at us when we walked in.

I sat in the vacant chair next to Lily. Ms. Walker sat behind her desk. "Lily, a group of fifth-graders saw you and your friend smoking and reported it to the playground monitor, who then witnessed it himself. I'm sure you remember how the younger students see upper-class mem-bers as role models?" She paused while Lily nodded her reluctant assent. "As a consequence, you'll be suspended from school for the rest of this week. That might sound harsh to you, but the principal and I agree it's important to set the tone for the new school year. Your teachers have given me your books and homework assignments, and we'll expect them to be completed when you and your mother report to me at 7:45 Monday morning. Do either of you have any questions?"

"Who was with Lily when she was smoking?" I asked.

"I'm sorry, privacy laws don't allow me to disclose that information, but I'm sure Lily will be straightforward with you about the incident." She stood, clearly dismissing us.

Lily took three books from a stack on the desk, shoved them into her backpack, and zipped it shut—the other three wouldn't fit. I reached for them, but she grabbed them away and headed for the door.

I followed several steps behind. Ms. Walker placed a hand on my shoulder. "Lily's a good kid and an excellent student. I only hope she'll make better behavioral choices as the year progresses."

"Me, too," I said.

Amy looked up from the table where she and Luke sat coloring. The expression on her face told me she was surprised to see her older sister emerging from the vice-principal's office—and that she understood it involved punishment. "What's going on, Mommy?" she asked.

Oh, Lily, why did you have to go and sully your little sister's first day of school?

"We'll talk about it later. Right now, I need to drop you all off at home and get back to work. I have an appointment in half an hour."

When we got to the minivan and Lily opened the door to climb into the rear seat, I opened my mouth to object, but thought better of it. Any efforts to talk with her on the way home would be fraught with danger—I very much feared I'd say or do something hateful. During the ten-minute drive, I managed to learn about the twins' day. Amy had made three new friends and loved her teacher, who was "so nice and so pretty." Luke thought the playground equipment was "so cool," though he'd fallen from the climbing structure and now had "a huge owie" on his elbow. Via the rearview mirror I admired the Superman bandage the nurse had applied.

Abby stood at the front door, wringing her hands, while the twins bounded up the steps. I noticed her looking over their heads at me to assess the situation. Lily lagged five paces behind as I walked in the house.

"Red's in the living room watching a movie," Abby told Amy and Luke. "Go join her and I'll be in in a minute to hear about school." Amy lingered a moment in the foyer, clearly curious about Lily, though one stern look from Abby sent her on her way.

When Lily tried to move past me toward the stairway, I grabbed her elbow and turned toward my mother-in-law. "Abby, as I told you on the phone, Lily's been suspended. Turns out she and a *friend* were caught smoking. Lily, who was it?"

Lily dropped her backpack and armload of books on the floor and followed them with her eyes. "Marissa," she said, almost inaudibly.

"Rest assured that we're gonna have a long talk when I get home from work about your behavior *and* your association with Marissa. In the meantime, hand me your phone, pick up your things, and go get started on your assignments. I'm too angry right now to decide what other consequences to impose."

In slow motion, Lily unzipped her backpack and rummaged through it, finally locating the phone, while Abby and I held our breaths. "Whatever—" she said, slapping the phone into my outstretched hand and striding toward the stairs. If Abby hadn't grabbed my free hand, I'm sure I would have struck my daughter.

I sat on the bottom step, head in hands, shaking with rage. "Thanks, Abby."

"Hey, we've all been there. Looks like she's just getting to the rebellious stage a little earlier than we hoped."

My blissful interlude with Dominic felt like it had happened in the distant past. And clearing my head to confer about a new criminal case seemed like an insurmountable task. It took every ounce of energy I could muster to stand up.

"I'm sorry, I have to leave. I'm gonna be late for a meeting that I can't cancel—but I'll have my phone turned on in case you need me."

Sweat trickled between my breasts when I hurried into the conference room fifteen minutes later and found the meeting had already begun. George waved off my apology and made introductions. "I think you mentioned you've met Matt Witte?" he said, nodding toward the man who stood to greet me.

I didn't recognize him but shook his hand. "I'm sorry, I must've been mistaken." The detective I'd previously met had been clean-shaven with a full head of impeccably-cut blond hair. In fact, he'd reminded me of a Ken doll. This guy was completely bald and had a goatee and mustache.

"You're not mistaken, Caroline—we have met," Matt said, with a gap-toothed grin that I did recognize. He rubbed his head. "And no, I'm not undergoing chemotherapy. I like to switch up my look now and then to keep the bad guys guessing."

I laughed. "Well, it's good to see you again."

"And this is Agent McGee from the FBI," George said. "Jimmy, meet Caroline Spencer. She'll be overseeing the case and handling the prosecution if we take it on."

George had been spot-on when he'd described Jimmy McGee, who shuffled to his feet belatedly and shook my hand a bit too hard. "Nice to meet you, Catherine," he said.

Someone must've told Jimmy it was bad form to come to the U.S. Attorney's office wearing anything less formal than a sport coat, but they'd neglected to school him on taste. His wrinkled brown jacket, circa 1995, looked goofy with faded navy Dockers, a rumpled yellow shirt, and a rep tie. Matt managed to look more professional in a fresh-from-the-dry-cleaners white button-down and jeans.

"It's Caroline," George said, and motioned everyone to take their seats.

"Huh?" Jimmy asked. George ignored the question.

"You called her Catherine, but it's Caroline," Matt said, the corners of his eyes crinkling with glee. He handed me a file folder with a sheet of paper stapled to the front. "Here are the loan documents, and that's a summary on top."

I glanced at the detective's outline as he continued: three luxury vehicles had been purchased in different names at three different locations... But it was all I could do to concentrate on the conversation. My head keep swimming from Dominic's condo to the Edgewood School office to the foyer in my house. Finally, I jabbed my right thumbnail into the palm of my left hand to bring myself back into the conference room.

"Here's what we've got so far," Matt was saying. "About six months ago, a white guy in his thirties named Bobby Marks and an older woman go into a suburban Chicago dealership. They say they're looking to buy a 2011 Mercedes SUV that's on the lot. Marks tells the salesman he can put down nine grand in cash and wants to finance the balance. Says the woman, his mother-in-law, has good credit and the loan will be in her name, but they want both names on the title. And they need the car that afternoon."

"Didn't that strike the salesman as suspicious?" I asked.

"A little," Matt replied. "Nine grand is under the limit requiring them to file a currency transaction report with the IRS, so he figured the money Bobby Marks put down might've been the proceeds of illegal activity. But he wanted to make the sale, and all the info the woman, 'Iris Wellington,' provided on the credit application checked out."

"At least long enough for 'em to drive the car off the lot," Jimmy added. "And to stay under the radar for several months. When the *real* Iris Wellington started getting notices about late payments for a Mercedes she didn't own, she called the FBI."

"And how did the Janesville PD get involved?" I asked.

"One of my snitches works at a detail shop," Matt said. "He told me about some guy he knew who was involved in buying and selling luxury vehicles that didn't seem on the level. We nosed around and found the aforesaid Mercedes in the driveway of a vacant, foreclosed house on Milwaukee Street in Janesville. My snitch's physical description of the suspicious guy matched the car dealer's description of 'Bobby Marks.' We've been watching the house and so far, we haven't seen Marks."

"What else do you know about the suspects?" I asked.

"They're Gypsies," Jimmy said.

"Gypsies?"

Jimmy gave an exaggerated sigh. "I understand that's not the politically correct term," he replied. "That they prefer to be called the *Romani people* or *Rom.* There are probably larger populations on the coasts, but they're here, too," he said. "The Chicago PD has a whole unit devoted to confidence crimes; a lot of those bad guys are Rom."

George Cooper shifted in his seat. "Any idea how Iris Wellington's identity was hijacked?"

Matt picked things up. "At first, she told the agent she didn't have a clue. Then, she remembered that when she had her leaky roof replaced about a year ago, she applied for credit with the contractor. She changed her mind, decided to pay cash, and didn't think any more about it. I surmise that contractor was either 'Bobby Marks' or someone who funneled her credit information to him."

"What about the other cars on this list?" I asked.

"When we went to recover the Mercedes on Milwaukee Street," Matt continued, "we looked through the garage window and saw an Audi and a BMW. We got a search warrant, and a check of the VINs showed both those cars had been stolen, too."

Jimmy glanced at his watch, and I sensed his impatience at the pace of his partner's narration. "A guy matching the description of Bobby Marks bought the Audi from a private party in Florida with a phony cashier's check," he said. "The Beamer was sold on credit by a dealership in Wausau, to someone matching Bobby Marks' description and a woman—younger than 'Iris Wellington.' Turns out the woman used the identity created from a stolen Chicago death certificate."

Jimmy took another, longer look his watch and got up from his chair. "I gotta be back to my office before 5:00." He turned to George. "So, you'll take the case?"

"Caroline and I will read through the rest of the file and let you know," George said, with obvious restraint. "Since Matt knows how our office operates, he'll be the point person." He stood, shook hands with Matt and Jimmy, and left the conference room without another word.

Jimmy shook his head in bewilderment and then he, too, left the room.

I noticed a bemused expression on Matt's face. "Doesn't look like your boss thinks too highly of Special Agent Jimmy McGee," he said.

I grinned but elected not to comment. "Thanks for coming over," I said, as I saw him to the door. "I'll call if I have any questions."

Chapter Twelve

When I pulled into the driveway after work that evening, I could see something was deeply amiss. My three youngest children were arguing in the front yard, Red and Amy versus Luke, apparently over a soccer ball. Abby sat in an Adirondack chair on the front porch, gazing off into space, oblivious to the dispute. When the kids saw me, they ran over to the car to make their cases against one another. Abby finally noticed us, and the look on her face said she wondered how I'd appeared in the driveway and what all the fuss was about.

"Let's go inside and sort this out," I said. Luke grabbed the soccer ball and stormed up the steps. "The soccer ball stays *outside*," I added. He threw the ball off the front porch with the force of a world-class goalie, narrowly missing Red.

"Five-minute time out, Luke," I yelled, following him into the house and then the dining room. Angry tears ran down his face as he slumped onto the vacant chair in the corner, his arms crossed. I felt a moment of sadness for him. *It can't be easy being the only one with a Y-chromosome in a multi-generational household.*

I settled Amy and Red at the picnic table on the screened-in back porch, with juice boxes and a bag of Goldfish crackers, and asked Abby to join me in the kitchen.

She sat in her customary chair, staring down at the table. I grabbed a beer from the fridge for myself, and put a mug of tea in the microwave for her.

"I'm so sorry, Caroline…" Abby began, her eyes glistening with tears.

"For what?" I set the tea on the table and took the chair beside her.

"I shouldn't have let her hang around with Marissa. I guess I just felt sorry for that kid, what with her mother being gone all the time. I didn't realize what a bad influence she was on Lily. You've already got enough to worry about… I'm going to cancel my trip to Dallas this weekend."

"You'll do nothing of the sort. You've been looking forward to it for months, and your other grandkids deserve some time with you."

We sipped in silence for a moment. Abby took a napkin from the table and blotted the end of her nose.

"Before I go talk with Lily, I wanted to ask what you think her consequences should be," I said. "My first reaction is to ground her again, but that didn't have the desired effect last time. I almost think it made things worse—she's been so distant and hateful toward me. David was always so good at knowing how to discipline the kids, though God knows we never had to deal with anything this serious."

Abby hung her head. "I don't know." I sensed there was something she wanted to say, but Abby'd always been one to avoid making waves.

"Okay, I'll just play it by ear. Please let me know if you have any insights or suggestions."

As though moving through Jell-O, I trudged upstairs and found Lily on her bed, curled in a fetal position and hugging Grover. My anger toward her instantly dissipated. *She's just a confused kid.*

I sat beside her. "Honey, please sit up so we can talk."

She faced me and struggled into a cross-legged position but remained silent.

"I'm really at a loss here. Can you tell me what you were thinking—smoking itself seems so out of character for you, but at school?"

"I don't know, Mom," she said, quietly.

"I want you to think hard about it and come up with some answers, and I'm gonna think hard about what your consequences should be. The one thing I do know is that Marissa's no good for you. I don't want you associating with her."

Lily's face—already downcast—fell further. She turned away from me. "But she's the only one who gets me…"

"What do you mean, gets you?"

"Whatever," she said, bitterly. "You've already made up your mind. I don't want to talk about it anymore."

The word "whatever" triggered another frightening flood of anger in me. I got up from the bed, took a deep breath, and moved toward the doorway. "Oh, we *will* talk more about this. But not just now."

I went back downstairs to the kitchen, drained of emotion. Hearing the voices of Abby and the littles from the back porch, I decided to sit in peace and finish the beer I'd opened earlier. But my jumbled thoughts were interrupted by a sound from the adjacent dining room. *Is that snoring? …Oh, my God, I forgot Luke!*

I found him, asleep, where I'd left him.

He looked at me with confusion when I knelt beside him on the floor and took him into my arms. "I am so sorry, honey," I said. "Your time out's been over for a while. I forgot to come get you."

He rubbed his eyes with closed fists and nodded. Then, his face brightened. "Can I have a Popsicle?"

I couldn't help laughing. "Yes, you certainly may have a Popsicle."

Later, when Abby'd gone to her apartment and the littles were asleep—Lily'd retreated to her room after remaining silent throughout dinner, and I expected she'd be there all night—I called Dominic. "What're you doing?"

"Staring at the Brewer game and worrying about you. How are things with Lily?"

"Tense. Can you come over?"

"I was hoping you'd ask."

He arrived twenty minutes later, carrying a chilled bottle of Pinot Grigio and a Tupperware container.

"What's all this?" I said, with a smile.

"The remains of the feast I prepared for lunch. If you're not hungry, you can feed the empanadillas to the kids for a snack tomorrow."

"Thanks. Let me put 'em in the fridge and get us some glasses."

"Tell me about Lily," Dominic said, when we'd settled onto the couch.

Between sips of wine and tears, I recounted the afternoon and evening. "Sometimes, I feel like I'm playing *Whack-A-Mole*," I said. "I start to attack one problem and another pops up. It broke my heart to see Luke sleeping on the dining room floor because I was too busy dealing with Lily's smoking to remember to lift his time out. And I still haven't decided what consequences to impose on her."

He gently stroked a tear from my cheek with his thumb. "Do you think she needs more punishment? The school's already suspended her. Maybe it's better to treat it as a teachable moment."

I felt unaccountably frustrated with his suggestion, which he must've read from the look on my face.

"Sorry," he said, quietly. "I don't have any other ideas."

"Well, I'm gonna need extra help from Lily this weekend when Abby goes to Texas to visit my brother-in-law. At the very least, I'll have her work off a 'fine' of sorts."

We didn't talk for several minutes. I could feel tension in his arm as it rested on my shoulder. "What's troubling you, Dominic?"

He sighed, and when he reached for his wine glass and took a sip, I noticed his hand trembling. "You don't need to hear my problems."

"A relationship's a two-way street. Tell me."

"All right. During dinner with my mother in Chicago one night last week, I asked her again about her ring. She told me the repairs were taking longer than expected because the jeweler had health problems, but she wouldn't look me in the eye when she said it. After you left today, I went through some paperwork and found an extra copy of the picture I took of the ring last year for Mom's new insurance carrier. I'd noted details on the back—the appraised value, the name of the jeweler, and the approximate date my father had purchased it."

I nodded.

"I called the store in Chicago and learned the guy who designed the ring *isn't* having health problems. He's been dead for ten years."

He paused and took another, longer sip of wine. "The ring isn't in for repairs," he said, "and nobody named Marquez has been a customer at the jeweler's in the last thirty years. Mom lied to me, Caroline."

I saw tears welling in his eyes and had to look away.

"I don't know what in God's name is going on…" Dominic stared into his wine glass, and I pondered how to speak my mind.

After a moment, I got up, sat on the coffee table facing him, and placed my hands on his knees. "It's understandable that this whole thing has you discombobulated. Do you think she's taking her medications?"

He nodded.

"Well, your mom's an intelligent, resourceful woman. Hard as it is, if she wants you to stay out of her financial affairs, maybe that's what you need to do."

He waited a beat. "You're probably right."

We gazed at each other—somewhat shyly, I thought—then he gathered me onto his lap for an exquisite kiss. I'm not sure how long we kissed, but I'd pulled his T-shirt over his head and was unbuttoning my shirt when I heard footsteps in the foyer.

I turned to see Lily approaching the living room door-way. "Oh," she said, her voice dripping with vitriol, "I guess you didn't want to talk with me after all." She turned on her heel and went back upstairs.

Intending to go after her, I extricated myself from Dominic's embrace. "Shit, shit, shit!"

He put his hand on my arm. "Let her go. She's just being manipulative."

"How do you know that?" I asked, more sharply than I intended.

"You're right, I don't know that." He reached for his shirt. "I'll get going so you can talk to her. But I've got an idea to run by you."

"What?" I asked, making every effort to keep my voice calm.

"Mom and Dani are bringing her kids up to go to the Wisconsin Dells on Saturday. They've been dying to go to Noah's Ark, and it'll be closed after Labor Day. Why don't you and your kids come along?"

I sighed. "Dani's kids aren't gonna want to hang out with a sullen, twelve-year-old girl and her much-younger sibs."

"Lily is only a year younger than Jordan and three years younger than Briana, and it's pretty hard not to enjoy a water park."

"I don't know…"

"Briana, Jordan, and Lily can keep Luke and Amy entertained. You'll only have Red to keep track of."

I had to admit it sounded like fun. "I'll let you know tomorrow—after I see how things go with Lily."

I swallowed the remnants of my wine for a jolt of calm and headed up to Lily's room. Her door was shut and no light shone from underneath it. Though tempted to postpone the encounter 'til the following day, I knocked lightly and went in, flicking on the light switch. "Okay. Let's talk." She pretended to be asleep. "I'm not buying it, Lily. Five minutes ago, you came downstairs to talk with me. We're going to talk."

She threw back the bedcovers. "Fine."

I sat at the end of the bed and waited her out, knowing silence usually induces even the most recalcitrant people to talk.

A flood of words rushed out. "Marissa doesn't want to give up cigarettes 'cause she's afraid she'll gain weight. When we went outside after lunch, I walked with her to the edge of the school grounds so she could have one. She asked me if I wanted one, and since there wasn't anybody around I, like, thought I'd try it. But I guess there was somebody around—and we got caught… Mom, please don't make me stop being friends with Marissa!"

I looked down in surprise to see her gripping my hand. "Tell me what you meant when you said she's the only one who gets you. You have other friends."

"Yeah, and they all have two parents." Her voice cracked with emotion. "Marissa knows what it's like not to have a dad around. He's got a new wife and a baby in Seattle; Marissa prob'ly won't even see him at Christmas."

I stroked her hand. "I'm sorry for Marissa's problems, Lily, but I can't let her bring you down. So—for at least the next couple weeks—you're not allowed to have contact with or hang around with her outside the classroom."

"That's so harsh, Mom," she said, crying harder now. "Especially now that I'm suspended—all my other friends will think I'm no good."

She's right. I swallowed the lump in my throat. "It might take awhile for you to earn back their trust, but they'll come around. No contact with Marissa, and no phone until further notice. Volleyball practice starts Tuesday; that'll keep you busy a couple afternoons a week. And I'll draw up a schedule so you can earn back your phone privileges by helping more with the littles, especially while Abby's gone this weekend."

I handed her a Kleenex. She blew her nose but didn't say anything.

"In fact, Dominic invited us all to go to Noah's Ark with his sister and her teenaged kids on Saturday. I'll give you credit for keeping an eye on the twins."

She looked skeptical.

"What d'ya say?"

"All right, I guess."

CHAPTER THIRTEEN

"But *why* isn't Lily coming to school today?" Amy asked, as I ushered the twins out the door on Thursday morning.

"Get in the car and buckle up. I'll tell you on the way."

I'd been awake much of the night ruminating about my oldest child, but I hadn't thought about what to tell the twins about their sister's absence from school. I contemplated some options as we loaded the minivan, but David's voice in my head gave me the answer: *The truth.*

"Okay, kiddos," I said, glancing at them in the mirror when we were on our way. "Lily broke the rules at school yesterday, and she was suspended until next week. Do you know what suspended means?"

"Kicked out," Amy replied, proudly. "What for?"

"Yeah, what'd she do?" Luke asked more slowly, his voice quivering.

I instantly realized his concern: would *he* get kicked out? He broke rules, albeit smaller ones, virtually every day.

"It's pretty serious. She was smoking cigarettes."

"Gross!" Amy said. Luke looked relieved—smoking was way beyond his repertoire of bad behavior.

I, too, breathed a sigh of relief when the conversation turned to our upcoming trip to Noah's Ark. They climbed out of the car in front of the school without a look back and ran to meet their friends.

Work provided just the respite I needed from my domestic tribulations. Engrossed in the reports Matt Witte and Jimmy McGee had compiled, I didn't even hear George Cooper when he approached my desk with another case file. "Got a hot one for you," he said. "Late yesterday afternoon, the FBI arrested a guy for robbing a bank on University Avenue, wearing what he claimed was a suicide vest. It's a new M.O. for him, but surveillance video shows he's the same guy who robbed banks in Cross Plains and Dodgeville last week and the week before. His initial appearance is set for 3:00 today. Can you handle it?"

"Of course."

And the day sped by.

I found Abby sitting at the kitchen table when I got home. Staring blankly at the microwave, where a mug of tea brewed, she startled when the timer dinged.

"I'll get it," I said, with a glance over my shoulder and an immediate sense of foreboding. "I can see something's bothering you. Is it Lily?"

"I called your office to tell you about it but they said you were in court. I didn't want to leave a message."

"Tell me about what?"

"You'd better sit down."

I pulled the tea from the microwave, splashing steaming water on my thumb in the process. "Shit!" I managed a deep, calming breath, set the mug on the table in front of Abby, and wilted into my own chair. "Okay, tell me."

"After we went to get the twins from school, I took all the kids over to Mallatt's Pharmacy to pick up my prescription. Lily pitched a fit 'cause she didn't want to go, and since she was so snotty, I decided not to reward her by leaving her home alone."

"Good move."

Abby hung her head. "I wish I *had* let her stay home."

"What happened?" I asked, my voice rising with alarm.

She blew on her tea and took a sip, as if summoning courage. "I saw her put a tube of lip gloss into her pocket."

My shoulders sank with the weight of her disclosure. *Good God, what next?*

"She walked around to another aisle and did the same thing with a Snickers bar." She paused, shaking her head.

"What did you do?"

"I made Amy and Luke hold Red's hand and had them stand right where we were—back near the pharmacist. Then, I took Lily aside and told her to show me what she'd put in her pocket. First, she said, 'What are you talking about?' Then, she said, 'I was gonna pay for 'em.' I told her I knew she was lying because she hadn't brought her wallet and she should hand the stuff over to me. Finally, she did, and I made her walk with me to put the stuff back on the shelves."

"Did any of the employees notice what she'd done?" I asked.

"I don't think so. But I was so shook up, I almost left the store without my prescription. Amy had to remind me."

I patted her hand. "What happened with Lily when you got home? Did you talk to her?"

"No. I didn't know what to say or do, so I just sent her to her room."

"You handled it just fine, Abby."

"What are you gonna do?"

It took every ounce of strength I could summon to lift myself from the chair. "I'm not sure. I'll have to see what Lily has to say."

As I headed toward the kitchen door, I heard Abby clear her throat. "There's one more thing…" I turned and saw her blotting her eyes with a paper napkin.

"I'm guessing you didn't buy those cosmetics I saw her with," I said.

She shook her head. "I should've told you."

"It gave me a few more weeks of blissful ignorance."

I found Lily's door locked, and in a flash, my blood pressure shot up about fifty points. "Open this door now, young lady!" I yelled.

No response.

I reached to the top of the dusty door frame and felt around for the skeleton key I'd put there "just in case." David and I had planned to replace the doorknobs on the kids' rooms with ones that didn't lock—but then we'd planned to do lots of things that had never gotten done. I blinked back a few tears and fumbled around with the key, eventually managing to make the tumblers turn.

Lily lay on her back on the bed, eyes closed, pulling absently on a strand of hair. Loud music escaped from the earbuds connected to her ancient CD player, I suspected so she could say she hadn't heard me yelling to open the door. She jumped as if startled when I slammed the door behind me. The room, typically kept clean, smelled vaguely of unwashed hair. Books and papers littered the floor around her closet.

Where do I begin? Another locked door? Shoplifting? Lying? Dissing her grandmother? I knew I needed to tackle the tough topics first.

"Music off," I said, and waited while she removed the earphones and powered down the player. She swung her legs over the side of the bed, her back to me. I pulled the computer chair from her desk, wheeled it in front of her, and sat, knee to knee. "Look at me, Lily."

She raised her head almost imperceptibly, managing to look no higher than my stomach. *Close enough,* I decided.

"Tell me when you started shoplifting."

Silence.

"Your grandmother saw you put two items into your pocket today at Mallatt's. And, contrary to what you told me several weeks ago, she didn't buy you that pile of cosmetics."

"Marissa took most of those things," she said, shifting her gaze back to her feet. "She does it all the time."

I stifled a sigh and leaned forward to move her chin upward. "Look at me when we're talking, please. And right now, we're talking about you. When did *you* start stealing? And make no mistake, it's *stealing.* It's a crime."

I imagined the wheels in her head turning as she tried to decide how to play this: penitent or confrontational.

Lily shrugged and then hunched her shoulders, seeming to shrink into herself. "I was with Marissa maybe a couple months ago when she took—I mean stole—some stuff at Mallatt's. And I guess I thought I'd, like, try it, too. I took a pack of gum the first time."

"Is Mallatt's the only store you've stolen from?"

My heart sank as she shook her head. "Uh-uh. I've taken a couple things, like those travel bottles of shampoo and stuff, when I was at Target with Grandma."

"Why, Lily?"

A lone tear meandered down her cheek. She brushed it aside as her fingers searched for a strand of hair to pester. "I don't know, Mom. I just don't know. I wasn't thinking, I guess. Or maybe I was, like, trying to be cool or something. I'm sorry."

I'd always thought I could read her, but today I had no clue. Was she truly sorry?

"Lily, I'm at my wit's end. You're suspended from school for smoking so I take away your phone privileges and your freedom to hang out with Marissa. And the very next day you go and shoplift. This is all so unlike you."

Silence.

I stared across the room, my eyes lighting on an object on her bookshelf: a picture frame she'd made at summer camp four or five years ago. It contained a photo of David and Lily, both grinning for the camera. My voice caught, but I told myself David would agree that I should hang tough and spit it out. "The only conclusion I can draw is that Marissa's no good for you. You're grounded entirely— including from volleyball—for two weeks, and Marissa is off-limits for the rest of the semester." *With any luck, she'll move away before then.*

I got up to go but looked back to see Lily hugging her knees, her shoulders heaving with sobs.

I ran back and wrapped her in my arms. "This doesn't change the fact that I love you to the moon and back. You understand that, don't you?"

"Uh-huh."

I sat with her until she stopped crying.

CHAPTER FOURTEEN

We were off bright and early on the steamy, sunny Saturday before Labor Day weekend. Alejandra, Briana, and Jordan rode with Dominic. Dani rode shotgun in my mommy van. Lily had been halfway-upbeat about our trip to the water park, despite understanding she'd be on child-care duty most of the day. Now, she sat in the way-way back seat, reading *The Fault in our Stars* while the younger kids watched *Frozen* on the DVD player for the 700th time.

Dani and I chatted about kids, jobs, and the challenges of single parenthood. "I'm not sure what I would have done if my mother-in-law hadn't moved in after David died," I said.

"I know what you mean. My ex's mother has been a godsend, even though her son's a no-account."

"You've got your mother close by, too," I said, glancing at her.

Dani didn't reply for a moment. "Our mom worked her butt off to support us, but—even during her good periods—she wasn't the warm and fuzzy mother Dominic and I craved. And, to tell you the truth, she's been kind of standoffish with my kids, too."

"Have you ever asked her about it?"

"No way. I was taught to respect her, not question her."

Later that afternoon, while the rest of our entourage traveled down the Lazy River in inner tubes, Alejandra Marquez sat with my over-stimulated, tired toddler and me. We moved to the shade of a huge umbrella. Red, appeased by apple slices and Goldfish crackers for only a nanosecond, sorely tested my patience with her whining, squirming, and crying.

"Red," Alejandra said, "if you come sit with me, I'll sing a Spanish song you might like."

Red dutifully grabbed a fluffy yellow towel from my beach bag and trotted over to Alejandra, who wrapped her in it and settled her on her lap. Alejandra began rocking from side to side, ever so slightly, in the lounge chair. In a soothing, yet clear voice, she sang a lullaby I'd never heard.

I watched in amazement. A relative stranger—and one who Dani had claimed was anything but nurturing—had worked magic on my often-terrible two-year-old. Within minutes, Red nodded off.

"Thank you," I said.

Alejandra bent down to place a gentle kiss on the top of my daughter's head. "I think she'll sleep for a while."

I moved to rise. "I'll lay her on the lounge chair next to me."

"Let her be. It's peaceful having her rest on my lap."

After a few moments, Alejandra looked up, her eyes glistening with tears. "You're the kind of mother I'd always hoped I would be," she said.

Her comment flustered me; I didn't know how to respond.

"You're firm with the children, yet you're not afraid to tease and cajole them," she said. "You touch them with such love and easy affection. I can see why Dominic is taken with you all."

"I'm flattered, but I think you're overrating my maternal abilities. My late husband, David, was the one who could interact with them for hours, enjoying every minute of it."

"Neither my husband nor I had that kind of gift. But I think I would have been a different mother if my first child, Cristina, had lived."

"Oh, I'm so sorry," I mumbled. "Dominic never told me you'd lost a child."

"Under the circumstances, it's not something I spoke about very often with Daniela or Dominic."

What circumstances? I wanted to ask, but bit my tongue.

Alejandra stroked Red's hair, sighed, and began speaking in a quiet but confident voice. "During the summer of my eighteenth year, I went to work at a hotel in Málaga, on the Costa del Sol. I met Dominic's father, Eduardo, there. He was a graduate student in Barcelona, also working in Málaga for the summer. We fell head over heels in love and planned to marry after he got his PhD. When he returned to school in the fall and I returned to my parents' home, we wrote each other daily. By the time I realized I was pregnant, Eduardo's letters had already become less frequent, he claimed because he was so busy with his studies. I struggled for weeks with what to do. When I began to show, my father went through the roof and said if we weren't married within the month, he'd send me to a convent to have the child. I chose not to tell Eduardo—in fact, I stopped writing him altogether—and left for the convent."

She stared off into the distance. "I didn't want to stand in the way of Eduardo's career. You see, he was very meticulous in his planning. He knew precisely when he'd graduate, where he'd apply for work, how much money he'd make, where we'd live.

"When Cristina was six months old, Eduardo found me. He'd been frantic, he said. He swept me off my feet again, and we married and returned to Barcelona, leaving Cristina behind. He said we'd send for her as soon as we were financially stable," Alejandra said ruefully.

Too stunned to comment, I waited for her to continue.

"I told myself the nuns were taking good care of Cristina, and I'm sure they tried. She died of influenza at the age of eighteen months."

"Oh… I am so sorry."

"We were eventually blessed with Daniela and Dominic, and Eduardo was fortunate enough to be able to bring us all to the United States to live. He and I never recaptured the love with which we'd conceived Cristina, though. I had too much guilt: why didn't I stand up to him? And too much resentment: why did he insist I make such an awful choice?"

Alejandra sat in silence, gazing into the kiddie pool with unfocused eyes. "Have you ever been to a psychic?" she finally asked.

Her question startled me. "No," I said slowly, "but since David died, I've been tempted to go. You know—to contact him."

"You believe there are people with psychic abilities, then?"

"I have to confess, I'm skeptical. But I believe we're spiritual beings and I *know* some people are way more perceptive of those spirits than others." I hoped my answer would keep her talking.

Alejandra paused for a moment. I held my breath.

"I met a young woman in Chicago—her name is Barbara—whom I know in my heart is a true psychic."

"Oh?" I asked, in a level, tell-me-only-if-you-want-to-tell-me tone. "Did you see her to try to contact Cristina?"

She didn't answer at first, then glanced at me with a hint of surprise, as though she'd forgotten we were conversing. "Yes," she finally replied, "I wanted to know if Cristina had been able to forgive me.

"My sister, Luz, and I went to the first reading together. Barbara did Luz first. She held her hands and they closed their eyes. I kept my eyes open and watched, and I noticed Barbara started shaking a little bit. Then, Barbara started asking Luz how she was feeling and whether she'd noticed any changes in her eating habits. When Luz said yes, Barbara advised her to see a doctor. She said she had a strong sense that something was amiss. And—as I'm sure Dominic has told you—it turned out she had cancer. We're still hoping the treatments will make everything okay.

"Barbara was very certain of herself. When it came my turn, she knew right away that I'd suffered a great loss in my younger years. And she said that money was the root of my problems, which was precisely the case."

"I'm sorry. I don't understand about the money part of it," I said.

"It was money and prestige that made Eduardo refuse to bring Cristina to Barcelona. He thought he'd be passed over for the professorship—and with it the salary and benefits such as faculty housing—if there were any indiscretions in his background."

"Did you go back to see Barbara again?" I asked, feeling vaguely guilty since I already knew the answer.

Alejandra shifted in her chair. "Would you mind if we moved Red to the other chaise longue?" she asked. "I'm afraid my leg has fallen asleep."

I got up and hurriedly lifted the child from her arms—too hurriedly. Red startled awake, let out a wail, and didn't stop crying until ten minutes later when Dominic walked up with Amy on his shoulders and Luke in tow.

Luke sported an extra-large Band-Aid on his knee but couldn't stifle his grin. "Mom!" he yelled, pointing to the wound. "Look what happened! The lifeguard hadda do first aid."

Dominic opened his mouth—I suspected to apologize and explain—but Amy interrupted, jabbering a mile a minute as he lifted her over his head and to the ground. "Yeah, Mom," she said. "A bigger kid pushed Luke on the steps when we were getting out of the Lazy River and he fell and started bleeding."

I pulled Luke into my lap. "Did it hurt much?"

He collapsed against my chest. "At first it hurt a lot and I cried, but then I got brave. The lifeguard gave us suckers."

I smiled at Dominic, who stood looking down at his feet, waiting his turn to speak. "Don't worry about it," I said. "Better first aid than CPR."

Dominic grinned with relief. "Dani thought it'd make sense for Mom, you, and the littles to head back to Madison now. The twins are exhausted, and that might have contributed to the F-A-L-L on the steps. The older kids will probably be ready to leave in a couple hours. I'll pick up Mom at your house when I drop off Lily. Does that sound okay?"

"Yes," I said, anxious to get Red into the car, where I knew she'd again sleep.

We made our way back to the parking lot and loaded our gear into the cargo hold and my three walking, but near comatose, children into their car seats. They fussed and argued about whose turn it was to pick the DVD and, against my better judgment, I bribed them with M&Ms to be quiet and let me choose. At least the music from *The Lion King* made me smile. After five minutes on the highway, the kids were sound asleep.

I was taken aback when Alejandra resumed our conversation as though there'd been no half-hour interlude.

"I did go back to see Barbara again," she said, looking frankly at me. "Quite often, in fact, though I didn't tell my sister."

"Why? Luz obviously believed the woman had psychic abilities; she knew without being told about the cancer."

Alejandra shrugged. "I thought Luz might find it strange—and a little frivolous. Some of the things Barbara asked me to do *seemed* a little strange, even to me," she acknowledged. "On perhaps my third or fourth visit, she said she wanted to order a specific candle and some rare crystals and have them blessed by her grandmother in Italy. She said it would cost $250 to purchase the items and have them shipped to Chicago. Barbara's credit card reader wasn't working, so I went to an ATM and got cash.

"Ten days later, Barbara called to say the package had arrived. She showed me how to make a sort of shrine, with the crystals surrounding the candle, and instructed me to pray over it every day for Cristina's forgiveness. It may sound silly, but I know it's working; my mood is definitely lifting."

I could feel the hair on the back of my neck rising. *If she's being conned by this woman, Dominic will want to know. Keep her talking,* I told myself.

"Did she want you to do any other unusual things?"

Alejandra considered my question. "No, not really. But she's asked me to make amends in any way I can until Cristina lets her know she's at peace. And that feels very right to me."

I nodded. "Alejandra… that day Dominic and I came to see you and you were so distressed, Dani said you were worried that you wouldn't be able to make something right. Is this what you were talking about?"

She didn't respond.

"I'm sorry. I didn't mean to pry," I said. One glance at the stony expression on her face, and I knew I'd gone too far.

"I'd prefer not to talk about this anymore," she said, without a trace of warmth. "And I implore you not to tell my son about our conversation, which I intended to be in confidence. He's already far too worried—needlessly— about my *personal* affairs."

We made the rest of the sixty-mile trip in agonizing silence.

A half hour after arriving home, with a sullen Alejandra seated in a living room armchair flipping through a magazine and the kids munching on celery with peanut butter in the kitchen, I heard the front screen door slam. I walked into the foyer in time to see Lily storming up the stairs and Dani standing helplessly on the porch. Dominic remained in the car, parked at the curb, with his niece and nephew in the back seat.

"Why on earth are you back so soon?" *And why isn't Dominic coming in?* I thought with alarm.

Dani came in the screen door I held open, shaking her head. "The kids and I were just coming off the Congo Bongo when Dominic came back from talking with you. Lily ran up to him and asked where Luke and Amy were. She completely lost it when he said you and Mom had taken the little ones home."

"Lost it?"

"She started crying and saying, 'How could my mom leave me here with you?' Dom tried to put his arm around her to comfort her but she pushed him away, yelling that she wanted to go home. There didn't seem to be much choice but to leave." Dani's jaw, drawn tight, dropped when she glanced over my shoulder.

I turned around and saw Alejandra in the living room doorway. She stood like the cigar-store Indian I remembered being freaked out by as a kid: arms crossed with a fierce, stony look in her eyes. "Daniela, I think it's time for us to leave," she said, without explanation. "Caroline, please tell the children goodbye."

CHAPTER FIFTEEN

The littles finally asleep, I put on my summer sleepwear—boxer shorts and a cotton tank top—and headed downstairs in hopes of taking refuge in my overstuffed chair. My spirits sank with one look at the disastrous living room. The floor littered with well-worn Matchbox cars, several missing a wheel or a windshield. The coffee table covered in wrinkled pieces of paper, crayons, and small globs of dried-up Play-Doh. A lampshade askew. And the pièce de résistance: a sippy cup, sans lid, containing soured milk and cookie crumbs, sitting on the table next to my chair. I picked up the odiferous cup to carry it to the kitchen and stepped on a LEGO. *Shit! Those frickin' things* hurt*!*

I dumped the milk and crumbs down the drain and reached into the fridge for a beer. Of course, there weren't any. *Can this day get any worse?* I grabbed my phone from the counter, and collapsed onto a chair to text Glenda. I hadn't had time to fill her in about Lily and knew I could use her advice. "Big Lily problem. Really need beer but don't have any. Do u?"

Her reply brought a smile to my face: "Yep. See you in ten."

Fifteen minutes later, my BFF appeared carrying a carton of Spotted Cow and a sleeve of Girl Scout Thin Mint cookies. "How in God's name do you still have any of those left? Weren't they delivered in March?" I asked.

"I stuck 'em in the basement freezer so I wouldn't eat them all before the snow melted and—believe it or not—forgot about 'em. I took a gander in the freezer when I went down for beer. We only had a couple Buds, so I stopped at PDQ and got us something good."

I stood on the kids' step stool and fished two of David's prized beer mugs, embossed with the Navy SEAL logo, out of the cabinet over the fridge. I wiped the dust from them and handed one to Glenda, who raised an eyebrow.

"I think we deserve to drink out of nice glassware," I said, with sigh. "I'm pretty sure David would approve."

She nodded and handed me an ice-cold bottle. "Let's sit on the back porch so I can smoke." I grabbed an ashtray from the cupboard and followed her outside. Wearing cutoff jeans and one of her husband, Hank's, old Oxford cloth shirts with the sleeves rolled up, Glenda looked much the same as when we'd met almost two decades earlier. She grumped about the excess twenty pounds she carried, but her face remained unlined and her blond hair, in a perpetually messy ponytail, retained its youthful luster with no signs of gray.

While not quite as unkempt as my living room, the screened porch bore the signs of children in residence. I kicked aside Luke's Big Wheel and a couple of stuffed animals belonging to the girls, set my beer on the picnic table, and unfolded some canvas sling chairs. They smelled slightly of mildew and the finish had long ago worn off the wooden arms, but the chairs were among the most comfortable we'd ever owned. I settled back and looked out into the mostly-wooded back yard. The ceiling fan spun lazily, blowing still-warm and humid air, which somehow felt soothing on my bare skin.

We drank a few sips in companionable silence. Glenda lit a cigarette, took a deep drag and exhaled with obvious pleasure, then turned to me. "So how awkward was the 'meet the families' outing? On a scale of one to ten—ten being beyond awfully awkward."

"How do you know it was awkward?"

She laughed. "Gimme a break."

"You're right. And I wish I could laugh about it, 'cause it was more like a fifteen or twenty."

I gave her an abbreviated version of the conversation with Alejandra and ensuing weirdness in the car.

"Sounds like she might prove difficult for you. Do you think Dominic'll have the cajónes to stand up to her if need be?"

"Stand up to her?"

"If you two commit to an intimate relationship, he'll have to be willing to put you in front of his mother."

I shrugged and got up to grab more beers. "I guess that'll remain to be seen."

The foam hadn't settled on my mug before Glenda raised the obvious question, "What'd you mean by 'big Lily problem'?"

I took a sip of beer and wiped the foam from my lip with the back of my hand. "I don't know where to begin…"

Glenda munched down two Thin Mints and waited me out.

"To start with, she got suspended from school on Wednesday—midway through her first frickin' day…"

My friend sat forward in her chair. "Lily? You gotta be kidding me."

"I wish I were. She and that Marissa girl got caught smoking at lunchtime. I had to drop what I was doing in the middle of the afternoon and pick her up, and she can't go back to school 'til Monday." I felt vaguely disingenuous not telling my friend *what* I was doing in the middle of the afternoon, but figured it was really beside the point.

"It sounds like *that Marissa girl* is bad news. I trust you've put a halt to their association?"

I nodded. "Oh, yeah. But you haven't heard the rest. On Thursday, Abby took all the kids, Lily included, to Mallatt's while she picked up a prescription. She saw Lily pocket a tube of lip gloss and a candy bar. She made her put 'em back, of course, and told me about it when I got home from work. When I confronted Lily, she admitted she started shoplifting with Marissa a few months ago. Said she wasn't sure why, but maybe 'to be cool or something.' I'm not sure the consequences I imposed are on target, but I grounded her for two weeks and said she can't associate with Marissa 'til the end of the semester."

Glenda tapped her fingernails on the arm of her chair and thought for a moment. "I can see why you're upset— it sounds like Lily's morphed into a different kid—and I don't have any better suggestions. Maybe she's acting out to get your attention, and having her home all the time will give you the opportunity to give her more. I'm assuming she went to Noah's Ark with you today even though she's grounded?"

"Yeah. I couldn't let the twins down by cancelling, and I figured it'd be better to have Lily to help with them. Mostly, I let her come along 'cause I couldn't trust her home alone. But even that was problematic."

"How so?"

I told her about Lily's reaction when Alejandra and I left early with the exhausted littles. "She completely freaked out because I *left her* with Dominic and his family so she could stay longer at a place she's crazy about. He said Lily was practically hysterical. I talked with her about it after dinner tonight. She refused to say more than a few words—only that she was upset because she'd gotten her period and didn't know what to do. I guess she finally asked Dominic's niece, who gave her a tampon, and she was too embarrassed to ask how to use it. She had to figure it out on her own."

Glenda swallowed the last of her beer and set the mug on her chair arm. "Getting the hang of tampons was hard for Sarah; I can see how Lily might have panicked when she found out you weren't there."

"I dunno, Glen. I can't help feeling there was something else behind her hysteria." My fingernail had found the tiny scab behind my right ear that I often picked at when worried; I reached for my now-warm beer to distract my hand.

"What's going on is no big mystery. Lily liked Dominic 'til he graduated from private investigator and family friend to being your lover. She's jealous of the time Dominic spends alone with you. And she's smack dab in the middle of puberty—one of the most confusing, horrendous times in a person's life."

"So?"

"Caroline, I've raised two kids through adolescence. It wasn't easy. They push you away when they need you the most. They expect you to read their minds when they, themselves, don't know what they're thinking. They're like grenades with the pins askew, ready to explode at the slightest provocation. Plus, Lily's got extra baggage, being adopted and losing her dad. Try to understand her feelings, however selfish they might be."

"Are you saying I shouldn't be seeing him?" I asked, startled to hear the panic in my voice. "It's not like I rushed into this."

Glenda reached over and grabbed my forearm. "That's not at *all* what I'm saying. You have every right to move on, and Lily'll have to buck up and deal with it. She'll come around to acceptance, but maybe, right now, counseling would be worth another try. Someone impartial to bounce her thoughts and feelings off of."

"I don't know. The last counselor she saw, after David died, didn't seem to help much."

"Sometimes you have to try a few before you find the right fit. I could give you a couple names."

"I'll think about it."

"Get some sleep and let me know if you want to talk more tomorrow." She stood up, kissed the top of my head, and was gone.

I took our mugs to the kitchen, poured the remaining beer down the drain, and grabbed a cold one from the fridge. I drank from the bottle this time and carefully hand-washed the mugs to preserve the gold logos, my eyes welling up as I looked at them. David had been tough and loyal and principled, and he'd always put me first. Would Dominic?

A band of light shone beneath Lily's door when I went upstairs for bed. Perhaps steeled by my beer consumption, I impulsively decided to have another talk with her. I tapped on the door and entered without invitation, to find her asleep against the pillows, *The Hunger Games* face down on her chest. She startled when I reached to turn off the bedside lamp.

"Didn't mean to scare you, kiddo. I thought you were still awake."

"Well, I wasn't."

I sat on the edge of the bed and took a deep breath, exhaling slowly. "There are a few things I want to talk with you about."

She scrunched up her face and turned her head away. "Are you *drunk*?"

"I've had a couple of beers, though—believe me—I'm far from drunk. If you don't want to talk, that's fine. But I do need you to listen. Okay?"

She shrugged and, thankfully, refrained from a *whatever*.

"I have to be honest, Lily, your behavior lately has me baffled. I can somewhat understand your flying off the handle at Dominic today—the hormonal fluctuations of puberty are awful, and getting your period when you're not expecting it is a bummer. But I can't understand the smoking and shoplifting, and you can't seem to explain them, either. Next week I'm going to schedule an appointment for you to see a counselor, who will hopefully help you come up with some answers."

"No! Please don't make me do that again. That last lady was so lame."

"I can assure you, we'll find someone who is *not* lame. Going to counseling is not negotiable."

Silence.

"One more thing: I know you don't approve of me seeing Dominic—"

"Oh, *Mom*..."

"Please don't deny it; honesty is important in our mother-daughter relationship. I can't tell you how to feel, and I hope your feelings about this will change soon. But, bottom line, this isn't your decision to make. It's been over two years since your dad died. I know *he* would want me to find happiness again—especially with a good guy like Dominic."

Another wordless shrug and she hunkered beneath the covers, head and all.

"G'night, honey. And don't ever forget that I love you."

CHAPTER SIXTEEN

The kids and I had been used to sleeping in on weekends and lollygagging through our mornings. But this Sunday morning, the weekend following Labor Day, was the first day of Sunday school after the summer hiatus. I felt compelled to get us there. David and I had been lapsed church-goers when we met, but we'd both appreciated our religious upbringings and wanted our children to have that foundational experience. Disillusioned with the Catholic Church in which he'd been raised, David had happily joined me in Presbyterian pews. We'd had Lily and the twins baptized and attended Covenant Presbyterian Church—a ten-minute drive from both our former and current home. A relatively modern building with a medium-sized congregation, it still felt homey to me. I loved its friendly people and the spectacular sound of its pipe organ.

The kids' structured Sunday school classes began at 10:00, the same time as an adult education program. Often, I dropped the older three off, skipped the adult class, and took Red with me for coffee. Or, if I wanted to hear a sermon and sing hymns, we'd all go to the 11:00 service; Red went to the nursery and the twins went to the Kaleidoscope education program after the children's message. With all the stress I'd been experiencing lately, I needed a jolt of spirituality, and chose the latter option today. I'd make us a nice breakfast first. Pancakes and scrambled eggs. Sausage links if there were some in the freezer.

In an upbeat mood, I stepped from the shower and went to my closet to select the day's clothes. The breeze through the bedroom screens felt chilly on my bare skin, signaling—I hoped—the onset of fall weather. I picked a pale pink, long-sleeved linen shirt, a new pair of jeans, and wedged sandals to offset the fact that the jeans were two inches too long. *If I go to the trouble to shorten them, they'll surely shrink.* Mascara and lipstick applied, I checked my look in the full-length mirror. *Lookin' fine!* I told myself and said a silent prayer of thanks that the shirt hid my stubborn baby weight.

Abby usually left us on our own on Sunday mornings, often attending Mass at Blessed Sacrament and having breakfast with a friend. So, I became uneasy when I found Red's crib empty and the bathroom stool tipped over in front of it. As I rushed downstairs, the unmistakable clatter of silverware and dishes coming from the kitchen heightened my apprehension.

Engrossed in bowls brimming with Cheerios, Luke and Red didn't hear me come in. Amy looked up from her seat atop the kitchen counter and promptly spilled the orange juice she was pouring from a half-gallon container into the last of three glasses. "Oh, sorry, Mommy. I was just getting us some OJ."

I reached for the dishrag and sopped up the mess, then lifted her down from the counter, stepping on Cheerios as

I deposited her in her chair. "You kids have some explaining to do," I said, looking around at the mess they'd made. Red sat in her high chair with the tray akimbo. Puddles of milk sat beside Luke and Red's bowls, and the front of her pajama top was soaked. My iPad—which I'd put on top of the fridge before bed—had somehow ended up in the middle of the table with so many sticky fingerprints on the screen I could hardly see the cartoon playing on it.

Luke looked up from the screen for a nanosecond. "Huh?"

"First of all, how did the baby get out of her crib?"

"I not a baby," Red declared.

"I stand corrected. Luke, Amy, how did your little sister get out of her crib? You know she's supposed to wait for Abby, Lily, or me."

Amy shifted in her chair and stared at her lap. "Well… she was calling for us… and we thought you would wanna sleep. So, I climbed in and boosted her up, and Luke got the bathroom stool and helped her out."

"And how did the stool get tipped over?"

"Red's heavy," Luke said. "We fell on our butts but didn't cry."

"Well, thank heaven for that. I don't want you to do that ever again. It's dangerous. Understand?"

They all nodded in unison.

"I was going to make pancakes and eggs, but since you've already eaten, I guess I won't bother." I fastened the tray onto the high chair and passed out the juice, then trudged back upstairs to wake Lily.

"Why are you making me go to church?" Lily asked, when I jostled her shoulder and told her to get up. The deep pillow creases in her cheek framed an angry pimple that matched the tone in her voice. "You told me you'd try to respect my feelings, and I'm not feeling like hanging out with you or with God. I just wanna be left alone."

Her vitriol shocked me. Church had been difficult for Lily in the months following her dad's death, bringing back memories of the funeral when, as she'd correctly realized, everyone stared at her in her raw grief. But during sixth-grade, she'd participated enthusiastically at church, both in worship services and youth activities. Furthermore, two days ago, she'd finished her two-week grounding—coming through it without a hitch—and now had phone privileges. *Why this turnaround? What does she have, now, to be so pissed off about?*

"Lily—"

"I'm serious, Mom. I want to be left alone. I have a huge history paper due tomorrow that I need to work on—it'll take me 'til midnight if I don't start on it this morning."

"When was this paper assigned?"

A panicked look crossed her eyes, but she recovered quickly. "While I was suspended. And nobody remembered to tell me about it 'til Thursday."

I didn't believe her for a minute but decided to avoid another confrontation. "Get out of bed and get busy, then. And you're going to church next Sunday, so plan ahead."

We dropped Red off downstairs in the church nursery, and the twins and I took a seat in the next-to-last pew. Though they had coloring pages to occupy them, they fidgeted through the announcements. I felt my muscles tense and began to regret my decision to come to the late service. But midway through the first hymn, "Morning Has Broken"—always a favorite and one I couldn't resist signing loudly—I looked down to see Amy swaying to the rhythm and heard Luke humming along. When the organist finished with a flourish and we sat down, the kids leaned into me, one on each side. The warmth of their bodies mingled with mine, and I felt God's presence. *Oh, how I wish Lily could feel this.*

"Now?" Luke asked when it was time for the children's message. I nodded, and he and his sister trotted up to the front of the sanctuary, listened well enough to make me proud, and followed the teacher to their Kaleidoscope activity. I sat back to drink in the remainder of the service in a decidedly more relaxed state.

When the pastor asked for prayer requests, I thought for a moment about asking the congregation to pray for my oldest child. Instead, I whispered a silent prayer: "Dear God, please guide and comfort my daughter. And please give her new therapist the wisdom, compassion, and skills to be able to reach and help Lily." I believe He heard me.

The service ended with the rousing hymn, "To God Be the Glory," which I knew would be playing in my head for several days. As I shook hands with the pastor, I noticed a few groups of couples, clearly friends both in and outside of church, laughing and talking with one another. I couldn't help feeling left out. When a young couple strode down the corridor in front of me, hand in hand, to pick up their child in the nursery, a lump formed in my throat. Red rescued my mood with an exuberant hug to my leg. Holding her warm, sticky hand as we went to get the twins felt like a healing balm.

Amy sat at a table in the activities room, carefully gluing the last of several sequins onto a Popsicle-stick cross.

Luke ran over to show us his crooked cross—decorated with crayon scribbles instead of bling. "It's beautiful, kiddo. We'll put it on the bookshelf when we get home."

The kids' happy chatter and the warmer-than-predicted sunshine gave me an idea: "Who's up for Michael's Frozen Custard?" I asked, when we were buckled in and pulling out of the parking lot.

"Ice cream for lunch?" Luke asked.

"For dessert," I said, smiling at him in the rearview mirror, "if you eat some real food first."

The wind had picked up by the time we arrived at the iconic Monroe Street restaurant. I couldn't imagine trying to corral all our paper napkins and plastic dinnerware at a picnic table. "Let's see if we can find a spot inside." I needn't have worried; the place was deserted and felt a tad forlorn.

We took a booth in the corner. I grabbed a plastic booster seat for Red, setting it on the bench next to Amy. I reached into my purse for the coloring sheets and package of crayons we'd used at church. "You guys can color while I order, okay?"

In the short time it took me to order two plain cheeseburgers, cheese curds, sweet potato fries, and four cups of water, they managed to break three crayons, color on the table, and get into a fight over who should get the picture of the dancing bear. I returned to find Red tottering precariously as she stood on the booster seat. I caught her and sat her on my knee. "You'll eat on my lap, young lady." I glanced around to see customers situating themselves at two other tables. "And everyone better use their restaurant voices if they want ice cream."

The counter person—with a green streak in her hair and both a nose and eyebrow ring—must've taken pity on me. Rather than call my name to pick up the completed order, she ducked under the counter and brought it out herself. I nodded my thanks and somehow felt all-the-more inadequate. *Why on earth did I think taking three little kids to a restaurant alone was a good idea?*

I broke the last cheese curd into two pieces to settle a minor tussle between Amy and Luke. As I reached into my purse for a baby wipe to de-ketchup Red's face, the vibration of my cell phone startled me. I fumbled to find it and answered the call from home with some trepidation— probably Lily.

"Mom," she said, before I croaked out a hello, "why aren't you answering your calls or texts?"

I made a concerted effort to calm my voice. "I had the phone on silent in church and forgot to turn it back on… and I can't hear the text signals when it's in my purse. What's up?"

"Dominic texted me that he's trying to reach you. How does he even have my number?"

"You gave it to him the day you got your new phone and were showing it off, remember? Back when you still liked Dominic."

"Where *are* you anyway? Church has been over for, like, an hour."

"The kids did so well in church today I decided they deserved Michael's Frozen Custard. We just finished our burgers and sides and are getting ready to order ice cream. Do you want us—"

She'd already hung up. I stared at screen; I had two missed calls and three unopened text messages.

As usual, Dominic's texts were written in complete sentences with perfect spelling and punctuation. No emoticons. The last one read, "I'm leaving Chicago soon and should be back to Madison around 4:00. May I come over for dinner with you and the kids tonight?"

"Not a great idea," I typed, but stopped myself before pushing Send. Without further explanation, that would certainly upset him. I felt a vein in my temple throbbing. It pulsed harder when I looked down to see Red sitting on the floor under the table, reaching for an errant French fry. I grabbed her up, setting off an earsplitting yowl, and perched her on my knee.

I shushed Red, began bouncing her on my leg, and dialed Dominic. "Sorry I missed your texts," I said, when he answered on the second ring. "I had the ringer off for church and didn't hear it vibrating in the bottom of my purse."

"So can I come over for dinner?"

"I don't think that's a good idea. Lily's still not on board about us, and your text seemed to her set her off again. But I'm sure Abby would watch the kids so you and I can go out to dinner."

"Good. What time shall I pick you up?"

"Uh… why don't I just meet you? How does Jac's at 6:00 sound?"

Silence.

"Dominic?"

"Okay. See you then."

CHAPTER SEVENTEEN

Abby and her friend, Bert, greeted us at the door when we got home from our Sunday lunch. Despite her lament that she felt like a giant around him—Bert was three inches shorter than Abby's five feet ten—he seemed like a good fit for her. With a full head of white hair, a mustache to match, and twinkling blue eyes, I couldn't help thinking Santa Claus after Nutrisystem. I'd only met him once, but the kids knew and liked him.

"Hope you got to eat some of the ice cream before it melted all over you," Bert chided the three littles, whose shirts were dribbled with chocolate custard. Amy and Luke giggled. Red, so tired she looked like a somnambulist, stared up at him with a puzzled expression.

"Caroline," Abby said, "we'd like to take the twins over to the zoo while Red naps. Is that okay with you?"

"Be my guest!"

I found a note from Lily on the kitchen table. "Finished my paper. Went to the mall with Brenda and Shelley. Brenda's mom is driving us. Back by 5." My stomach knotted with several emotions: anger that the history paper which kept her from church wasn't so *huge* after all; trepidation at the thought of her at the mall; and relief that she was with two kids I knew and trusted. I reached for the phone to call her but thought better of it. *You've gotta pick your battles and this one ain't worth it.*

After giving Red a quick rinse in the tub, I dressed her in clean clothes and put her in her crib for a nap. I laid down on my own, king-sized bed, intending to do a ten-minute mindfulness exercise on the iPad I kept on my nightstand. I woke up two hours later, completely disoriented, to wailing from the baby monitor.

I found Red standing in her crib, shaking the rails like a crazed penitentiary inmate, the front of her T-shirt soaked in vomit. As I reached to pull the shirt over her head, a wave of anxiety swept over me; her skin felt dangerously hot.

In the kids' bathroom, I wrapped her in a towel and took her temperature—102.6. *Now what? I hate handling this alone!* If David were alive, one of us would've comforted her and cooled her brow with a damp washcloth while the other got instructions from the internet or the on-call nurse. Red squirmed in my arms and retched once more. Grabbing the wastebasket, I held it in front of her and watched helplessly as she threw up again. The acrid smell stung my eyes and set my stomach heaving; I had to swallow back my own vomit.

"It's okay, honey," I told her, when she'd stopped. "Let's clean you up and see what the experts say."

Now where's my damn phone? Probably still in the bottom of my purse in the foyer where I left it. I carried Red downstairs, rummaged through my purse for the ever-elusive phone, and dialed the on-call nurse's number from my list of contacts. With ubër efficiency, the male nurse with whom I spoke asked questions and took note of my answers. No, she wasn't complaining of a headache or stiff neck. No, she wasn't coughing or short of breath. No rash; no blisters. Since her stomach was upset, I could give acetaminophen by suppository and, yes, I had some. Yes, I'd monitor her tonight and take her to the E.R. if her temp went over 103.

Back upstairs, just as I'd finished administering the medication, Red spewed yet another puddle of vomit onto the bathroom floor. *God, help me!*

I heard the front door open. "We're up here," I called down, "and I could use a hand." The twins' running footsteps echoed on the stairway, but they stopped short at the bathroom door.

"Icky!" Amy cried, turning away.

Luke stared in fascination. "It still looks like cheese curds."

Abby appeared a moment later, turning her head away from the stench. "Oh, I'm sorry I forgot my phone… we'd have come right back."

"I didn't try calling. Please take her and the wastebasket while I clean up this mess."

At 5:10 p.m., I looked up from the living room couch where I sat with the three littles watching *SpongeBob* on Nickelodeon, to see Abby in the doorway, her brow furrowed with worry, holding her phone. She passed it to me but stood to listen.

"Caroline, it's Sam Jacobs—"

I didn't stop to question why he'd called Abby's number. "Hey, Sam. I've been meaning to come by to congratulate you on your promotion."

"Thanks, but this isn't a social call. I'm calling from the Madison PD Central Station. We've got your daughter, Lily, here—"

I couldn't make sense of what he was saying. "Lily's with you?"

"She got picked up for shoplifting over at Hilldale. The cops couldn't get ahold of you or her grandmother, so at shift change they brought her downtown and took her to juvie. The shift commander recognized the name and told me about it; I said I'd keep trying to reach you. They agreed not to take her to the living unit if I could reach you by 6:00."

"Thanks, Sam. Would you call and let them know I'll be there in ten?"

But it turns out I wasn't. With mounting frustration, I circumvented countless streets barricaded for the city's Ironman triathlon—its route the most direct way from my house to downtown Madison, its finish line only blocks from where Lily waited. Thousands of spectators lined the streets; there wasn't a parking spot within blocks.

I finally opted to park at my office building on West Washington Avenue and ran the four blocks to the City County Building, crossing twice against a Walk light and inciting a raised middle finger from a driver who slammed on his brakes to avoid me.

Breathless and panting, I rode the dingy elevator up to the juvenile detention center, arriving a half-hour later than promised. "I'm here to pick up my daughter, Lily Spencer," I said to the deputy sheriff, who glanced at me with mild alarm, quickly looking away. I realized I had tears running down my cheeks.

"Uh, yeah… we've been expecting you." He fumbled through his top desk drawer and handed me a packet of Kleenex so battered it looked like it hadn't seen daylight since World War II. Though yellowed and wrinkled, the tissues would do the trick. I nodded my thanks.

The deputy picked up the phone and inclined his head toward a row of gray, metal straight-backed chairs on the opposite wall. "Have a seat. I'll let her know you're here."

A petite Latina wearing an elegant, red silk pantsuit, a Georgia O'Keefe inspired scarf, and a disarming smile, came through the door a few moments later. She reached out to shake my hand. "I'm Estella Rodriguez from intake. Please come with me."

I followed her into a small office with mustard-colored unadorned walls, a plain desk, and a couple of mismatched file cabinets. She sat behind the desk and motioned me to one of two gray, metal chairs. "Mrs. Spencer, I understand you're an attorney and former ADA. Are you familiar with juvenile court procedures?"

"Not really, no."

"All right. I'll explain. Lily was stopped by a Macy's loss prevention officer when she tried to leave the store. He'd been watching her via video camera for about twenty minutes while she tried on jewelry and scarves, and while she sampled perfume and makeup. She'd pocketed an Anne

Klein watch, two pair of sterling silver earrings, and a vial of perfume—and she'd hidden a silk scarf in her backpack. The scarf alone was valued at $40.

"Police officers were summoned. They searched Lily and her backpack and recovered the items. Since they were unable to reach you or Lily's grandmother, and since the officers were going off duty, they brought her downtown and had no choice but to place her in detention."

I tried to picture the scene at Macy's. My stomach knotted as I envisioned Lily furtively putting merchandise into her pockets and backpack. *How* could *she?* And then, as I imagined her—no doubt scared to death and feeling abandoned—being taken to juvenile detention, a towering wave of guilt hit me. *Why did I once again leave my cell phone muffled in the bottom of my purse?*

A few minutes later, another deputy came to the door with Lily in tow. Wearing a wrinkled, pink miniskirt and T-shirt, her eyes swollen and red, she shuffled in and sat in a chair next to mine, avoiding my gaze. She looked as apprehensive as I'd ever seen her. Estella's appearance and demeanor had instantly assured me of her professionalism and kindness, but Lily had no way of knowing my assessment. I scooted my chair a bit closer and took her hand.

"Lily," Estella began, "I'm Ms. Rodriguez from the juvenile court. I'm going to review your case with you and explain what will happen next. If you have any questions, feel free to ask."

Lily nodded.

Estella handed me an electronic tablet. "This is the form releasing Lily to your custody. Please look it over and make sure the address and phone numbers are correct. Then I'll need you to sign it." She handed me a stylus.

I studied the form while Lily looked on, and my heart began to race. "This says *misdemeanor theft*. Shouldn't it be an ordinance violation?"

Estella took the tablet back and clicked on another document. "Often, shoplifting is an ordinance violation, Lily, allowing the issuance of a non-criminal ticket. But the items you reportedly stole had a total value exceeding $250, which makes this a misdemeanor crime."

I took a deep breath. My hand felt heavy as I scrawled my signature onto the device. "Is there anything else?"

"No. I'll go print the documents for you. The initial appearance date is listed. If that day or time won't work for you, call the clerk of court to reschedule. It's a mandatory court appearance."

As Estella left the office, Lily turned to me. "Dad would be so disappointed."

I stifled a sob and kissed her on the head. "Your dad loved you no matter what; he'd have found a way to understand. I will, too."

Estella returned with the forms, we stood to leave, and I shook her hand wordlessly. "Good luck," she said.

We might need more than luck, I thought, as I ushered Lily out the door.

Lily and I rode home in silence. She leaned against the passenger window, her eyes vacant, twirling a lock of hair. The closer we got to home, the faster she twirled. By the time we pulled into the driveway, I noticed some strands in her hand.

I glanced at my watch: 6:30. "Why don't you go up to your room and lay down for a while. I'll see what Abby's got planned for dinner and call you when it's ready."

She blinked back tears and got out of the car. "Thanks, Mom."

I found the rest of the family in the living room. Amy and Luke sat at the coffee table eating PB&Js and carrot slices while watching TV. Abby, with Red sound asleep on her lap, rocked at less than her usual speed, though I could tell it took some restraint. "How is she?" I asked.

"Better. Fever's gone and she hasn't thrown up since you left. I gave her some ginger ale and Ritz crackers about twenty minutes ago and it's stayed down. How did every-thing go?" she nodded toward the twins, signaling she didn't want to say Lily's name in front of them.

"Okay, I guess. She's sorry and very sad. I told her to go rest a bit before dinner."

"'fraid I didn't make any dinner. The twins weren't that hungry, and I couldn't imagine eating. There's enough left-over tuna casserole in the fridge for you and Lily."

"Oh, shit! I completely forgot I was supposed to meet Dominic for dinner half an hour ago."

I reached into my purse for the still-silenced phone. Dominic had left an uncharacteristically terse text message: "Where are you?"

He'd also left a voice message. I didn't bother listening—just dialed his number. "I'm so sorry. I had a couple of family emergencies; I just now realized the time."

"I'm just finishing an old fashioned. I don't mind wait-ing a few more minutes."

"Oh, Dominic," I said, with a deep sigh, "I'm all done in. I don't have the energy to go into it right now, but suffice to say it's been one awful day. I need a rain check. Okay?"

"I miss you. I haven't seen you for two weeks…"

Whose fault is that? It wasn't my idea for you to take a case in Chicago. "I miss you, too. Would it be okay to have lunch tomorrow, when I know I'll be better company?"

"I guess it'll have to be. Text me in the morning, when and where." He disconnected before I could reply.

Chapter Eighteen

"Mom… wake up." Lily was shaking me by the shoulder. "I can't go to school today. I just *can't*," she said, dissolving into tears.

I sat up on one elbow and glanced around. It was still dark outside. Lily handed me her cell phone. "Look at this."

"What is it?" I mumbled.

"A Facebook post—*look* at it!"

I leaned toward the bedside table to find the Walgreens' reading glasses I sometimes wore when my eyes were tired. It took a moment to focus. Around midnight, Marissa Baxter had posted a blurry photograph of Lily being led from Macy's by two police officers. She'd tagged Lily and captioned the picture, "And she thinks she's better than everyone else!!!"

I spoke the first words that popped into mind. "You were with Marissa yesterday? You said you were going with Brenda and Shelley."

"I *did* go with Brenda and Shelley; Marissa was just there. It's, like, a public place. But you're missing the *point*. Now *everyone* will know I'm a thief. I won't have any friends.

You didn't see the looks on Bren and Shelley's faces when the cops came. Why did she have to take the picture? *Why?*"

My 6:00 alarm rang in the middle of her rant. I reached over to shut off the shrill tone. "Lily, I don't know why she did it. I suspect she's trying to get back at you for not being able to associate with her. And I'm sorry, but you're not missing school today. I have to be in court at 9:00 for an important motion hearing, and I need to study my notes before we leave. So you need to figure out how to handle this. We'll talk about it in the car."

I struggled to disentangle myself from the sheets and walked toward my bathroom. Lily hung her head and stalked out.

Standing in the steamy shower, my thoughts turned to the hateful Facebook post, and I found myself scrubbing my legs frantically with the loofa. *Why can't that kid leave Lily alone? Should I call Marissa's mother—or housekeeper—and ask her to take down the post? Am I being callous to send Lily to school?* I felt so abandoned; the one person I trusted to know how to handle this was dead.

Stop second-guessing yourself! I told my reflection in the mirror, while applying mascara to my twitching eyelashes. *You've made a decision, now move on.* Then, as I'd planned, I sat on the chaise longue in my window alcove and boned up on the arguments I'd make in court.

A blessedly calm scene greeted me in the kitchen half an hour later. Amy, Luke, and Abby sat at the table eating scrambled eggs, toast, and orange slices, chatting in "restaurant voices." The twins wore the crisp, new jeans and long-sleeved shirts—Amy's a vivid purple with *Hello*

Kitty on the front, Luke's a striped polo—that I'd bought at Target a few weeks ago.

"G'morning, Mom," Amy said, with a mouth full of eggs. "Don't you *love* this shirt?"

I poured a cup of coffee. "Yes. And I'm so happy to see you all looking bright-eyed this morning."

"Red's still asleep, but her forehead felt cool so I decided to let her be," Abby said, nodding toward the baby monitor on the counter. "And after yesterday, I wasn't sure Lily still had phone privileges but I just texted her with the usual five-minute warning. She said 'okay.'"

I had to appreciate Abby's willingness to embrace technology but felt another bout of indecision at the mention of consequences. "I'm gonna have to think about the phone thing. Let's talk about it tonight."

Dressed in faded black jeans and a nondescript gray hoodie, Lily slunk into the kitchen a moment later. She must've used a whole stick of concealer to cover the redness around her eyes but wore no other makeup. I realized with a pang of alarm that she was trying to appear invisible. She grabbed a Pop-Tart—an indulgence purchased by Abby and Bert—and headed for the car.

"Sit up front with me, please," I said. She complied but didn't bother helping the twins buckle their seat belts, as was our usual routine. *Let it go.*

With the *Frozen* soundtrack turned up to high volume in the back seat, I turned to Lily. "Have you thought about how you'll deal with any comments you might get today?"

She blinked back tears and gripped the shoulder belt 'til her knuckles turned white. "I don't have a clue…"

"Well, there might be some drama, but try to ignore it. Don't feel you need to explain—"

"Dad wouldn't have made me go to school. *He'd* understand—like you said you were gonna."

I felt like she'd kicked me in the stomach. And I realized my suggestion was lame. We didn't speak for the rest of the ride.

By 8:15, I was sitting at my desk with a cup of semi-burnt coffee and a two-day-old blueberry muffin someone had brought into the lunchroom, catching up on interoffice emails. Still unnerved from my morning's Lily encounters, I found some meditation music on my iPhone. I texted Dominic, "How is 11:45 @ Barrique's?" and crossed that off my to-do list.

The Indian flute music, which more than one co-worker had teased me about, worked its placid magic. I hunkered down and finished outlining the argument I'd present at the 9:00 hearing. But my reverie shattered when my iPhone signaled a call from Dominic. *Why didn't he just text? I don't have time to talk.* But, feeling a twinge of guilt for cancelling the previous night's dinner, I decided to pick up.

"Hello, Caroline." I shivered at his formality. "Something has come up; I'm afraid I have to cancel our lunch today."

I wanted to scream. *For God's sake, are we destined to be star-crossed lovers?*

"Caroline? Did you hear me?"

"Uh-huh."

"I'm on my way to Chicago. Emma called last night to let me know she located my mom's ring at a pawn shop.

This morning, we're going to put a case together for the police. You're not going to believe who pawned it."

"I don't have time for guessing games today."

"Barbara. The psychic."

I'll admit, I was intrigued. And more than a little sad for Alejandra. "Are you sure?"

"Ninety percent. Emma's spent several days visiting pawn shops on the North Side, browsing the jewelry cases in hopes it had been taken in for a loan. If it'd been sold outright, the pawn shop would probably have melted it down for the gold and diamonds right away. Anyway, on Saturday morning she hit pay dirt. She went into a shop on Fullerton and saw the ring on display; someone *had* pawned it for a loan."

I glanced at the clock on my desk—a gift from David to celebrate my hiring as a federal prosecutor—and realized I needed to leave. "Look, Dominic, I'm running late for a court hearing. Can we talk another time?" I cringed at how terse my words sounded.

I heard him inhale. "Sure. Let me know when you have the time." He clicked off.

Though my workday had gone well enough, I could barely summon the energy to make my way to the car that evening; an enormous emotional cloud loomed on the horizon.

I arrived home to find the twins playing *Candy Land* at the kitchen table while Abby stood at the sink peeling potatoes. Red sat in her highchair, pushing dry Cheerios around on the tray, occasionally popping one in her mouth. "Hey, kiddos," I said, planting kisses on their heads. "Abby, the house looks great. Thanks for picking up."

She didn't respond, and when she turned to greet me, I noticed her brow creased with worry.

"What's wrong?"

"I didn't know if I should call you or not… When I picked the kids up from school, Lily was crying and wouldn't say why. She ran up to her room the minute we got home, locked the door, and won't come out."

"It's fine, Abby. I'll go deal with it."

My head throbbed while I ran my fingers atop Lily's dusty doorframe, searching for the skeleton key. It fell to the floor just as she opened the door. With snot running down her swollen, blotchy cheeks, she fell sobbing into my arms. "Oh, Mom, it was so awful."

"C'mon, let's go sit in my room and talk." I led her by the hand to my lounge chair and gave her a box of tissues. Long and lean, she snuggled beside me, resting her head on my chest, as she'd done when she was the twins' age. "Okay. Tell me."

She blew her nose and snuffled a few times, then began. "It started in homeroom. I took my usual seat but kept my head down and didn't talk to anybody. Then, this girl, Tiffany, who sits next to me, leaned over and said real loud, 'I saw the picture of you getting arrested on Facebook. When did you get out of jail?' I didn't answer, just kinda looked away. Then, the boy behind me said, 'You were *arrested?* What for?' I tried to ignore him, but Tiffany told him I stole a bunch of stuff from Macy's. By the time the teacher came in, everybody was, like, laughing and talking about it."

I stroked her back and tried to keep my voice calmer than I felt. "What did the teacher do?"

"She asked why I was crying, and I was too upset to say. Tiffany started to tell her, but the teacher stopped her and took me to the office to see the guidance counselor, Ms. Peterson. Mom, I was so embarrassed. She made me tell her all about it, and she looked all judgmental at me. And then I had to meet with the principal."

I should've foreseen this. Why did I make her go to school? "Was the principal helpful?"

Lily shook her head. "Not really. She said it'd be hard today but easier tomorrow. She let me skip first period so I could, like, stop crying. But Shelley and Brenda are in my second period class and they wouldn't even look at me. And, later on in third period, I overhead Marissa telling someone I tried to get her to shoplift. Nobody knows the truth about her but me." She paused and blew her nose again, then began pestering a strand of hair.

"And the rest of the day?"

"Lunch was the worst. I got my tray and went to go sit where I usually do. All the kids got up from the table and moved. What was I supposed to do? I threw away my food and sat in the handicapped bathroom 'til afternoon classes started. Mom, don't make me go back there—I just can't do it."

"Oh, honey, one of the main reasons your dad and I moved to the neighborhood was so you could go to Edgewood. It's a great school and a good fit for you."

"Correction: it *was* a great fit for me. It never will be again."

I hated to admit she might be right. I turned her head toward me and looked her in the eye. "Honey, I need some time to look into other options. I'll call and have you excused from school tomorrow, and we'll take it a step at a time. But I'm not promising you won't have to go back to Edgewood. Understand?"

She nodded. "I'll do anything you say—just please find me another school."

I hugged her tightly. "I'll do what I think is best, honey. Now, go get cleaned up for dinner. Abby's making your favorite: pot roast and mashed potatoes. She's worried sick about you. I'd like us to have a pleasant dinner if we can."

I sat for a moment, my heart aching for Lily and my mind totally muddled. Who to call for advice?

I threw my rumpled work clothes, now stained with Lily's tears, into the pile for the dry-cleaner, pulled on a pair of well-worn yoga pants and one of David's old, button-down shirts, and headed toward the stairway. The tantalizing aroma of Abby's rosemary and thyme-seasoned pot roast beckoned. I realized I hadn't eaten anything since a carton of yogurt at lunchtime; I was famished.

Abby glanced at me as I walked into the kitchen, and reached into the cabinet for a wine glass and bottle of cabernet. "How is she?"

I took a sip before responding, weighing my words and making sure the littles weren't in earshot. "Hurting. Late last night, Marissa posted a picture of her on Facebook, being led out of Macy's by two cops. It was all over school this morning, and it sounds like kids were beyond cruel. She's begging me to enroll her in some other school."

I collapsed onto a chair. "What do you think?"

She wiped her brow with the back of her hand, poured herself a juice glass half-full of wine, and sat across from me. "This cyber bullying—or whatever you call it—is beyond me. I don't remember kids being so evil in the old days. But since it's already on the internet, don't you think the bullying might follow her to a new school, too? I mean, Madison's not that big a place; kids from all over the city are connected with each other."

"Sheesh. I hadn't thought of that."

Abby took another sip of wine and went back to the stove to check the potatoes. "I don't know what to suggest. Maybe Glenda'd have some ideas?"

"Maybe," I said, absently. "I guess let's just try to get through dinner."

Amy wandered in a moment later, Luke and Red trailing behind her. "We're hungry," she said, with a serious tone.

I laughed. "I guess you're the spokeswoman for your brother and little sister?"

Amy looked at me quizzically. Abby smiled and handed her a stack of harvest gold melamine plates she'd gotten at a rummage sale, and a handful of silverware. "Dinner's almost done. You set the dining room table and, Luke, you go knock on Lily's door and give her the five-minute warning."

I pulled Red to my knee. "The dining room?" I asked.

"Change of scenery might lift the mood," Abby replied.

It did. Lily'd managed to stop crying and emerged in fresh clothes. The littles, remarkably oblivious to her emotional trauma, chattered and giggled through the meal and succeeded at making her laugh a time or two. Without my prompting, Lily cleared the table and loaded the dishwasher while Abby and I sipped more wine.

"Want me to give the twinkies their baths?" Lily asked, when she'd finished.

"Me, too!" Red chimed in.

I nodded gratefully. "Yes, please—all three."

Glenda texted me at 8:15, when she knew Red and the twins would be in bed. "I heard about Lily. Need an ear?"

"Yes. Come over. Door's unlocked."

She found me in the darkened living room, hunkered down under a quilt in my chair. A re-run of *The Mary Tyler Moore Show* played on TV, sans audio. She leaned over and hugged me wordlessly, then switched on a table lamp and turned off the TV. Seated cross-legged on the couch, she finally spoke. "Sarah showed me the Facebook post."

I shook my head as the words hit my ears, as though trying to keep them from penetrating my brain. Two years earlier, after a suicide attempt, Glenda's daughter, Sarah, had transferred from Edgewood to public school. Now fourteen, Sarah had a totally new set of friends—but she'd *still* seen the hateful post.

I recounted for my friend the last twenty-four hours. "Lily's adamant that she can't go back to school there," I concluded, "but it looks like Abby's right, that it'll follow her wherever she goes. So what do I do?"

"You told her she could stay home tomorrow?"

"Uh-huh."

"That's a good start. Deb Peterson, the guidance counselor, was helpful to us during Sarah's ordeal. I'd call her and see if she can run interference for Lily. Maybe talk *that Marissa girl* into taking down the post."

"Lily said Ms. Peterson seemed kind of judgmental today."

"Don't take this wrong, Caroline, but Lily was led out of Hilldale by the police. It's hard to keep hints of judgment off your face when you're talking to a kid in a situation like that. I think she'll do better the next time she talks with her."

I nodded mutely.

The bedside clock read 10:05 when I climbed into bed and 10:06 when I began tossing and turning. I missed David. But I also missed Dominic—not my lover Dominic, but the steady male presence he'd been for me, my kids, my niece, and my nephew some two years ago when he'd feared a predator was in our midst. I'd valued his judgment and insight. Could I call on him now?

He never went to bed before midnight; surely I wouldn't wake him up. With shaking fingers, I dialed his cell phone, surprised when it went straight to voicemail. I left a halting message—just saying hello and that I missed him. I asked him to call me.

He didn't.

Chapter Nineteen

I awoke ten minutes before my alarm the next morning, with a clear plan of action. I needed to call my dad.

I hadn't told my parents about my romantic relationship with Dominic or about Lily's emotional and legal issues. My mother had a tendency to become unglued in any emotional situation and—even as a kid—I'd found her advice suspect. My dad was an old-school stoic upon whom I'd always relied for nuts-and-bolts, day-to-day decisions, but matters of the heart were not usually his bailiwick. He *had* been helpful, though, when the complications of my pregnancy with Red had caused me to consider abortion; I knew he'd be willing to help me now.

Though he'd been retired for several years, Dad remained an early riser. I texted and asked him to call, and my phone rang seconds later. "I need your advice about Lily, Dad," I began, my voice cracking. "And it may take a while to explain."

"I just poured myself a fresh cup of coffee and I've got all the time in the world. You know your mother won't be up for hours. What's going on with Lily?"

I told him about everything: her personality changes, her opposition to my relationship with Dominic, her gravitation toward Marissa, the smoking and the shoplifting. Her arrest. About the Facebook post and the bullying and the big question on my mind: should I transfer her to a different school?

"Well, I don't fully understand why you're considering moving her from Edgewood. Sure, she'd have a few days or weeks of discomfort with folks knowing about her shoplifting, but it'd pass—and trying to keep secrets just makes them all the more shameful. Having her stay and work it out might make her stronger in the long run."

"On the other hand, it might break her."

He waited a beat before responding. "Yeah, that's a risk. You said you're letting her stay home today?"

"Uh-huh… I'm going to make some calls this morning— the first one to Edgewood's guidance counselor—to see what options are available. If she stays there, we need a clear plan to counter the bullying."

"What would you think about me driving down? I could be there by late afternoon. This evening we can talk with Lily and make a decision. And I'd be there to help her through the first few days back to school, wherever you decide is best."

"It sounds great, but Mom might have other plans for you."

"Your mom and her friend Helen are leaving tomorrow for some scrapbook convention in the Cities that lasts through the weekend. The list of projects she made for me to do while she's gone can wait."

I sniffed back tears. "I'd appreciate it so much…"

"Tell Abby I promise to stay out of her kitchen and to not disrupt her routine. I'll be there around 2:30."

With a renewed sense of calm, I showered, woke the twins and got them ready for school. Abby walked into the kitchen in time to hear Red yelling into the baby monitor. "I'll get her," she said. "Relax and eat a real breakfast for once."

"Abby, I just called my dad. He's coming this afternoon to help sort things out with Lily."

"Oh, thank God!" she said, leaning against the doorframe. "I was going to suggest you get his advice but didn't want to intrude. Seems like a man's opinion helps sometimes. I don't know why. Maybe they just think differently?"

"I suspect you're right."

When I pulled up to the drop-off zone at the kids' school, I thought briefly of going in to speak with Deb Peterson in person. Three cliques of middle schoolers stood along the walkway, one including Shelley, Brenda, and Marissa—heads together, looking at a smart phone, talking in animated voices. I suspected they were discussing Lily, but couldn't know for sure. My stomach churned as I tried to imagine Lily running that gauntlet, and I realized my doing so on her behalf would make things worse.

"Bye, kiddos," I said, to the twins. "Have a super-duper day."

Yelling their goodbyes, they ran into the school, blissfully unaware of the trials that awaited them eight years down the road, and I drove off to work.

At my desk with the large cup of McDonald's coffee I'd detoured to the drive-thru to pick up, I took out my purple, felt-tipped pen and began jotting notes from Google searches on a legal pad. Phone numbers of possible schools where Lily might transfer. Articles and books about bullying. Articles about shoplifting. The first item on the resulting to-do list: talk with Lily's guidance counselor.

"Ms. Peterson, it's Caroline Spencer—Lily's mom. Did you get the message I left on the attendance recorder about not sending her to school today?"

"I haven't looked at today's attendance list yet, but I can't say I'm surprised. And I planned to call you this morning. I spoke with Lily at some length yesterday about her... uh... her arrest and the Facebook post. It's a difficult situation, especially coming so soon after her suspension." Her tone and the pregnant pause after the word "suspension" put me on high alert.

"Yes, well... Lily is reluctant to return to school at Edgewood and we're looking at other options. My question is, how would you propose to handle the bullying if she were to stay there?"

"You're considering having her remain with us?"

Why would you assume we wouldn't? Are you hoping *she'll transfer?*

I took a sip of coffee before answering. *I can do pregnant pauses better than most.* "Yes, that's one option. I'm reluctant to move her because this cyber bullying could easily follow her to another school. I'd like to know how you might help us nip it in the bud here. I read one article that suggests a group intervention. In this case, you would invite Marissa

Baxter—who posted the photograph—and others who were involved in spreading the comments to meet with Lily and hear her point of view."

"Hmmm. It's certainly worth considering. I'd need to talk with the principals. Maybe involve the other parents. May I call you tomorrow and let you know?"

"Of course. I'll keep Lily out of school at least another day. Please ask her teachers for her assignments and have them ready for Lily's grandmother when she comes to pick up Amy and Luke."

I made a few more calls, becoming increasingly anxious. Blessed Sacrament School had no openings for seventh-graders. Wingra School would need to see transcripts and interview Lily before making a commitment. We could consider schools outside our neighborhood but not without rethinking transportation and finances.

I felt my heart racing and a wave of light-headedness washed over me. *Relax! You can handle this. One baby step at a time.* I turned on my Indian flute music, leaned back in my chair, and closed my eyes, visualizing myself floating on a crystal-clear lake in the sunshine. It worked; I didn't even startle when my phone rang.

Dominic. "Hi, Caroline," he said, in an all-is-well-with-us tone and with no mention of my unreturned call from the night before. "I'm on my way back to Madison for a meeting this afternoon. Could you meet me for an early lunch?"

I glanced at my calendar. "I'm free any time after 11:00. Where?"

"How about Tutto Pasta on State Street? 11:30?"

"Fine. See you there."

I savored the five-block walk from my office to the restaurant, a narrow, triangular-shaped building on the corner of State and Johnson streets. Though it was uncommonly hot and humid for early September, being outside the office cleared my head. I felt confident in the sleeveless red linen dress I'd chosen that morning, and the clunky, multi-colored beaded necklace I wore with it always cheered me up. I arrived before Dominic and waited by the host's station just inside the door 'til he walked in.

"Wow," he said, after a warm hug, "you look—and smell—terrific. Is that a new perfume?"

I felt my cheeks flush, both gratified and embarrassed by his complement. "Thanks. Yes, Abby got it for me at a little boutique when she was in Dallas."

The host seated us at a small corner table in the lower level—hardly private considering the confined space—but we were the only patrons for now. The waiter brought a basket of warm focaccia bread with olive oil and took our orders. Though we'd selected grilled panini for lunch, I couldn't resist dipping a piece of bread and nibbling on it while we waited for the sandwiches.

Should I ask him why he didn't call back last night? No, don't be clingy. "So… yesterday you said you'd located your mother's ring and that it was the psychic who pawned it. How do you know it was her?"

He paused while the waiter brought our iced teas, took a sip, and then spoke with obvious pride. "After Emma saw the ring in the display case, she browsed around for a bit, trying to get a read on which employee might be most likely to give her information."

Waiting for a guy who looked like he might fall for her flirtatious blonde routine.

"Finally, she approached a middle-aged, male clerk and inquired about the ring, explaining that she believed it to be stolen property. The clerk, who turned out to be the weekend manager, agreed to meet Emma yesterday afternoon and bring her a copy of the security video taken on the day the ring was pawned."

I impatiently scooted my chair forward to make room for the couple being seated at the next table. Dominic, too, looked annoyed. He lowered his voice. "Anyway, Emma had to sift through quite a bit of video but finally located the transaction. She pulled some still photos from the video and had them printed. We compared them to the shots she took that day she followed Mom, and we're both convinced it's the person called 'Barbara.'"

Our panini arrived, prosciutto for him and portabella mushroom for me, with side salads. I sheepishly nodded for the waiter to take away the breadbasket, wishing I'd refrained from eating any so I'd have more room for the savory sandwich.

We didn't talk during the first several bites. "I've been hungry for one of these for two weeks," Dominic finally said. "And this one's even better than usual."

"This one is, too." I paused to take a sip of iced tea and to wipe tomato sauce from the corner of my mouth. "So, what's your plan from here? About the ring, I mean."

"Emma's going to take her photos to the pawn shop today to see if the clerk who handled the transaction remembers the woman. And she and a couple of her associates are doing surveillance of the shop during business hours. I think I told you the loan on the ring is up on Thursday?"

I nodded.

"We think it's a pretty good bet that Barbara will come in, to either pick up the ring or renew the loan on it, between now and then. When she shows up, they'll call the police and have her arrested. I'm in town for just a few hours, heading back to Chicago after my meeting. Tomorrow, I'm going over to my mother's to have her sign an affidavit of loss." Dominic glanced around for our waiter and signaled for the check.

I shifted in my chair and set my napkin beside my plate. "What makes you so sure your mom will sign?"

He looked up at me in alarm. "Why wouldn't she sign?"

I shrugged. "Maybe she gave Barbara the ring."

"Why on earth would she do that? Mom treasured that ring."

I didn't like his caustic tone and found myself tempted to end the conversation. While I paused to consider my response, my pinkie fingernail gravitated to that small scab on my scalp and began to worry at it. *Tell. Him. Now!*

"Dominic," I said, and took a quick sip of tea to lubricate my tongue. "There's something you need to know before you meet with your mother." I told him about my conversation with Alejandra at Noah's Ark. All of it. He didn't interrupt, though I feared the vein in his temple might burst.

"And you didn't think this was important enough to tell me at the time?" he asked, when I'd finished. The harsh words, spoken in undisguised fury, bit into my brain; I knew I'd replay them a thousand times. I looked around to see if other patrons in the now-crowded dining area had noticed.

I swallowed a lump in my throat. "Your mom asked me to keep our talk in confidence; I felt it would be a betrayal to tell you."

"Caroline, you know how worried I've been about my mother. This was—and is—critical information."

The phone in the breast pocket of his polo shirt buzzed. He took it out and glanced at the screen. "I need to take this," he said. "What's up, Emma?"

I watched as he listened intently, occasionally interrupting Emma with a one-word comment. I wondered if he'd forgotten I was across the table. He didn't glance up when the waiter put the check folder next to his plate.

When he rang off and looked up from the phone, I realized he was miles away. The stony expression on his face made me shudder.

"We'll discuss this later, Caroline. I have my hands full and right now I have to get to my meeting."

He stood up, shoved two $20 bills into the folder, and left without saying goodbye.

The dining room walls seemed to close in, and the restaurant din grew cacophonous; I had to get out of there. A waiter, bearing a tray laden with food, glared when I jostled him during my rush to the stairway. I got to the front door only a few steps behind Dominic and watched as he turned to walk down State Street. As if in a trance, I followed him.

A few, deep breaths of steamy air, which felt like a soothing Nebulizer for my aching lungs, enabled me to think. *I am sick to death of hearing about that fricking ring and the rest of his mother's drama. And I'm sick of his total lack of interest in what might be going on in* my *world. I need a partner—not this.*

I came to my senses in front of The Soap Opera, a longstanding local shop that sold soaps, lotions, essential oils, and the like. Lured by the array of scents floating from the doorway, I stopped in to browse. I pumped a dollop of thick lavender lotion onto my hands and smoothed it in. I squirted three different perfumes into the air and smelled them, choosing to buy a vial of Hawaiian white ginger. I bought soap bubbles for the littles and new loofas for Abby and Lily. I could've written a testimonial for aromatherapy, as I left the store feeling significantly happier than when I'd gone in.

CHAPTER TWENTY

My phone buzzed as I ambled around the Capitol Square toward my office. It was Roxanne. "Matt Witte's waiting for you in the reception area."

I was momentarily confused. *Did I forget an appointment?*

"He said he was hoping to meet with you."

"I'll be there in five." I took the back entrance to my office, avoiding the reception area, and sat for a few minutes to regroup before calling for Matt to come in.

The detective entered carrying a large plastic bag of Cleary's caramel and cheese popcorn—the combination I found irresistible—a bottle of Gray's root beer with two paper cups, and a battered, brown leather briefcase. I pushed aside a stack of files to make room. He pulled paper napkins from his briefcase, spread them on my desk, and dumped out a mound of popcorn.

Glad that I'd eaten only a small portion of my panini, I poured the root beer and took a sip, then reached for a handful of popcorn. "Oh, my God—it's still warm. And Gray's is my favorite. How'd you know?"

Matt leaned back in one of my visitors' chairs and grinned, calling to mind my younger brother, the prankster. "I'm a trained detective."

"No, really. How did you know?"

"I saw two empty bottles in your wastebasket last time I came to your office."

"Good detecting. Where's Agent McGee today?"

"Quantico. For some high-tech training," he said, with more than a trace of sarcasm. "I hope you don't mind that he's not here. I'd like to get a federal search warrant for the property on Milwaukee Street—where we located the stolen cars—and I'd prefer not to wait until he gets back. I'd like a federal criminal complaint and arrest warrant for Bobby Marks, too."

"Tell me what you've got."

"We've been watching the property on Milwaukee Street but never saw anything suspicious. I figured 'Bobby Marks' had abandoned the place after we seized the vehicles. But I happen to know one of the neighbors—a Barney Fife wannabe—and asked him to let me know if anyone came around. Last week, he called to tell me a woman, in her fifties or sixties, moved in with four kids. She told Barney Fife the kids' mother is sick and she's got temporary guardianship. Said she planned to get them enrolled in school as soon as she got their transcripts from Chicago."

"Did he find any of this suspicious?"

"Nope. Said she seemed like a nice lady, down on her luck, and a little overwhelmed with things. She told him she didn't like to drive, but that her oldest granddaughter had just gotten her license so that'd make things easier. He said they had a rusty, red minivan sitting in the driveway."

Matt reminded me a little of Dominic—both were certainly detailed storytellers. But my phone was on forward and my calendar was clear. I relaxed and listened intently between mouthfuls of popcorn.

"This morning my snitch at the detail shop texted me to say that 'the suspicious guy'—Bobby Marks—was scheduled to pick up a 2012 Cadillac Escalade around 10:00. It was similar in description to one stolen by fraud from a dealership in Eau Claire, so I had the snitch get me the VIN. We ran a check. It's a match."

His phone buzzed. He paused to glance at it and smiled. "Where was I? …Okay, so I drove over to the detail shop and got there just as a rusty, red Caravan pulled up. Managed to take a few good shots of Marks when he got out. He went into the shop and drove out in the Escalade. I followed him to the house on Milwaukee Street. He pulled into the attached garage, got out, and closed the garage door behind him. I called the LT—my lieutenant, I mean—and asked him to set up surveillance on the house so I'd be free to come up here and get the warrants."

"Is the Escalade still in the driveway?"

"As of fifteen minutes ago."

"And you're sure Marks hasn't taken off out a back door?" I asked, as I poured another pile of popcorn onto my desk.

"Yeah."

Matt handed me his iPhone, displaying a photograph of a man in his thirties with dark eyes and a full head of collar-length, wavy dark hair. The top three buttons of his white shirt were undone, revealing a gold necklace with an elaborate, possibly diamond-studded cross. "I emailed a copy of this picture to the cops in Eau Claire, who took it by the dealership. They just got back to me. The salesman says this is definitely the guy who identified himself as Bobby Marks and came in with his 'sister' to buy the Cadillac Escalade. He says they paid $9,500 in cash, and the 'sister' applied for a loan to finance the rest. The salesman described the woman as a blonde in her twenties— obviously not the same woman who used Iris Wellington's ID to buy the Mercedes in Chicago. The blonde used an actual driver's license and credit card stolen from a woman who physically resembles her—we're not sure how that happened."

"Could this be the same woman who went with Marks to buy the BMW in Wausau?"

"The descriptions are pretty similar, so it could be."

"Did you send the photo you took today of Bobby Marks to the cops in Wausau?"

"Yeah. Still waiting to hear from the detective there."

I drained my cup of root beer and studied my notes for a moment. "What about getting a search warrant today but holding off on the criminal charges against Bobby 'til we've got enough on the cohorts to charge them at the same time?"

Matt shook his head. "I have a strong feeling that if we don't nab him now, we might never see him again. He's a traveler."

"Okay. Probable cause for the search warrant's a no brainer; you saw a vehicle known to have been taken by fraud driven to the Milwaukee Street house and parked in the garage by a subject matching the description of the bad guy."

I licked the stickiness of caramel and cheese corn off my fingers, wiped them with a napkin, and began typing into our standard search warrant form. "When do you plan to do the search?"

"My LT will have a team together by 4:00. With any luck, Marks'll sit tight 'til then."

I finished typing the first form, then pulled up the template to draft the criminal complaint. "We've got two potential counts of bank fraud—for buying the Escalade in Eau Claire and the BMW in Wausau with stolen credit. But I don't want to allege that Marks was involved with the Beamer without a positive ID from the dealer. So, let's just go with one count for now."

He shrugged. "Whatever'll get him in custody."

I picked up my office phone and dialed George Cooper. "…yep, I just finished the search warrant request and a one-count complaint for bank fraud," I concluded. "Are you free to review them now? Janesville PD can be ready to execute the warrants at 4:00." I nodded to Matt to let him know George had agreed and hit Send to email the documents.

Five minutes later, as Matt and I polished off the popcorn and root beer, George appeared at my door with a manila folder.

"Looks good," he said. "I had Roxanne send 'em over to Magistrate Brillstein's office electronically, but here's the set for him and Matt to physically sign. Did you call to see if he's available?"

"Uh-huh. He's expecting Matt by 2:15."

George nodded. He handed Matt the papers and was gone.

Matt stood up, brushed a few errant popcorn kernels from his pants, and stooped to retrieve them.

"I'll clean up," I said. "You get yourself over to Brillstein's office and text me when the warrants are signed."

"You got it." He moved toward the door.

"The grand jury meets Thursday; we can get an indictment then and avoid a probable cause hearing relating to his arrest. See if you can get those Wausau detectives moving on ID'ing Bobby before then—I'd rather present more than just the one count."

"I'm on it." He turned and smiled a confident smile that made me glad to be on his team.

"And, Matt…"

"Huh?"

"Thanks for the snacks. And for your great work."

"I aim to please."

On my way to the courthouse for a 4:30 appearance, my cell phone rang. "Hey, Caroline, it's Matt again," he said breathlessly. "Something's come up. About 3:30, the garage door of the Milwaukee Street house opened and Bobby Marks drove away. The surveillance officer called for backup and I was close by. We tailed him to the interstate, heading south toward Illinois. I radioed the Wisconsin State Patrol and they pulled him over for us. I booked him into the Rock County Jail on the federal arrest warrant. Thing is, he was talking on a cell phone when they stopped him. It'd be helpful to know if he alerted anyone at the house. Do you think we can get a warrant to search the phone?"

"Is it a throw-away?"

"No, an iPhone… oh, shit, they're encrypted, so a search warrant wouldn't do us a bit of good."

Part of me was relieved. The last thing I wanted to do tonight was request an emergency search warrant. "I'm assuming he was driving the Escalade?"

"Yeah."

"Good. That gives us a little more ammunition for detention. Did he say anything?"

Matt laughed. "'I want to call my lawyer.'"

"Are you ready to execute the search warrant on the house?"

"Uh-huh. The team's in place; we're going in as soon as I get there."

"Good luck. Call when you're done to let me know how it went. And, whatever happens with the search, the court will schedule an initial appearance for Bobby Marks tomorrow—so you'll have to free yourself up for that."

And, so will I, despite the fact that Lily needs to come first.

CHAPTER TWENTY-ONE

My 4:30 court appearance—a detention hearing for a bank robber who'd been arrested the previous week—lasted an hour. Though I'd prevailed in my motion to keep the robber in jail pending trial, I felt drained when I got back to my office. I'd promised to bring carryout Chinese home for dinner, and placing the online order seemed to take forever. The dashboard clock read 6:15 when I got into the car.

Finding a parking spot on the street near Hong Kong Café was never easy. I poached a spot in the clinic parking lot across the street and ran in. Back at the car, I set the three plastic bags filled with carryout containers on the hood while I fumbled to find the keys I'd thrown into my purse only moments earlier. And, as I should've known would happen, the bag containing a quart of hot-and-sour soup slid off, dislodging the lid. Half of it spilled all over the crab Rangoon.

Ten minutes later, with frazzled nerves and gooey fingers, juggling my briefcase, purse, and the carryout bags, I struggled up the front steps of my house. My heart sang with glee when my dad opened the door. He carefully unburdened me, set my load down, and engulfed me in a bear hug. "It's great to see you, kiddo!"

The three littles appeared behind him, their hair still wet from the bathtub, bearing the streaks of careful combing. All wore fresh PJs and grins. "Did you get those crab thingies?" Amy asked, grinning wider when I nodded.

Red rushed up and hugged my leg—almost bowling me over—shouting, "Mommy!"

"Hey, guys! I'm glad to be home. Where's Lily?"

"Right here," she said, strolling in from the kitchen with a remarkably placid look on her face. "I was just setting the table. We're starved."

We ate on the screened porch, savoring what we knew as Wisconsinites might be one of the last warm nights of the year. The breeze brought the faint scent of honeysuckle from our neighbors' hedge and cooled my brow. The twins chattered happily about their days at school, and at one point, Amy asked to be excused to go get the art projects she and Luke had made. "Those are spectacular," I said, when she returned with two construction-paper creatures. Amy's was quite clearly a dog, Luke's some mysterious species.

"Mommy, when is Lily going back to school?" Amy asked, when she'd resumed her seat.

Lily looked down at her lap and my dad coughed. "That's something Lily, your grandpa, and I are gonna talk about after dinner. I don't want you worrying about it, okay?"

Amy nodded and bit into another one of the "crab thingies."

We finished dinner with fortune cookies. I broke into mine last and read it aloud, "'Big decisions await you.' No kidding?" I glanced at my dad who choked on a sip of beer.

Abby volunteered to change Luke's pajama shirt and put the littles to bed so that Dad, Lily, and I could start our confab—she'd be in when she finished. "Can we sit in the living room?" Lily asked. "I'm getting chilly."

"Sure," Dad said. "Caroline, I'm going to grab another Pabst. Do you want one?"

Oh, how I wanted one. But I needed all my senses operating at full capacity for the argument I expected from Lily. "Not now, thanks."

Lily settled herself, pretzel-legged, on the couch while I took Abby's rocking chair, facing her. My dad wandered in a moment later and sat, shoulder to shoulder, beside Lily.

I leaned toward her and rested my elbows on my knees. "Before I fill you in on the options I've looked into, honey, tell me how you're feeling."

She hung her head. "Like I dug myself into a huge hole and there's no way to get out. I mean, I *know* I did something terrible, and it's my fault. But it's like people keep throwing more dirt on me." She brushed back a tear and dabbed at the end of her nose with the sleeve of her T-shirt. "I untagged myself on the picture Marissa posted, but it didn't do any good; everybody already knows it's me."

Abby came silently into the living room and sat on the ottoman. She fished out a Kleenex from the long sleeve of her blouse and blotted her own nose, her eyes downcast, as though she couldn't bear to see Lily in such pain.

I explained the options I'd researched. "…you could apply to Wingra and hope to be admitted," I concluded, "or stay at Edgewood and work with Ms. Peterson to try to stop the bullying."

Lily blinked several times and took a deep breath. "How 'bout if Abby homeschools me?"

Abby did a double take and laughed nervously. "I graduated from high school almost fifty years ago with a C average. As smart as you are, you'd have to be the one schooling me."

"Sounds like you need a Plan B," Dad said to Lily.

Sobbing now, she choked out her words. "I guess applying to Wingra would be okay."

I paused a moment, scratching that stupid scab. "I'm pretty sure you could get in. My concern is the cat's already out of the bag. Glenda told me Sarah saw the Facebook post and she's not even at your school or in your grade."

Dad didn't flinch. "Your mom's probably right; rumors travel in ways we can't anticipate, especially on the internet. Which goes to show you can't run from your troubles."

Lily wasn't buying it. "But, I just *can't* face the kids at Edgewood again. You don't know how awful it was yesterday."

My dad went on, "Remember that time you and your mom and dad came to visit us at that cabin up north?" She nodded. "Even though you wanted to go swimming, you were afraid the water would be too cold. Your dad said you were torturing yourself and said, 'Sometimes the only thing to do is jump right in.' I remember how proud he was when you jumped off the dock. And how much fun you had that day. We practically had to drag you out of the water to get you to eat lunch."

"So?" she asked, between sniffles.

"I think your dad would want you to go back to Edgewood—after all, one of the reasons you moved here was for the school. And I think he'd be proud of you facing the kids and their comments head on, letting them know you made a mistake and you're not afraid to admit it. After a few days, they'll realize you're still the smart, nice kid you've always been. You'd never have to look over your shoulder and wonder whether someone might find out your 'secret,' because it wouldn't *be* a secret."

Lily turned to me. "Do you really think Dad would want me to stay at Edgewood?"

I realized I'd been holding my breath. I nodded. "Yes, Lily, I do."

She turned to Abby. "Grandma?"

Abby choked out the words, "I think that's exactly what he would want. And I believe he'll be a guardian angel, walking with you in those hallways."

"Okay, but can I stay home just one more day?" She looked at me expectantly.

"Well, yes, but let me tell you why," I said. "I called a DA who handles juvenile matters today and asked how a case like yours is typically resolved. Since you've never been arrested before, if you plead guilty at your initial appearance, she'd recommend deferred prosecution. You'd have to do community service and report to a court social worker, but after a year without any further incidents, the case would be dismissed."

My dad's face broke into a smile. "Sounds like a pretty fair deal," he said. "Can you do it, Lily?"

"I think so," she said, quietly.

Dad's question had startled me, but my heart had sunk at Lily's answer. *You* think *so? How about some confidence?*

"Good answer," he said, calmly. "Shows you know you've got a problem and need to figure out how to deal with it. Hopefully, the social worker they assign will help you."

"The social worker isn't actually a therapist," I said, "so we'll still go with our own psychologist. But the DA—Janice Middlecamp is her name—said we could schedule the court appearance any time. I set it for 1:00 tomorrow. Which is why it's okay that you miss school again. It'll also give me time to talk with your school social worker about doing some sort of group session with you and Marissa, and maybe a few others."

I could see mixed emotions on my daughter's face. I read them as relief at one more day's reprieve from school, apprehension at the thought of the court appearance, and dread at the prospect of a meeting with her new nemesis—especially in the presence of Deb Peterson, who she'd deemed "all judgmental."

"And Lily," I said, measuring my words, "at least until we see the psychologist and get you back into school, no cell phone or internet. Sometimes, the best way to deal with bullies is not to react to them, and you can't react to what you don't know about. Okay?"

She nodded.

"C'mon, I'll walk up with you."

As we headed up the stairs, she held my hand and leaned against my shoulder. "I'm so sorry, Mommy… for being such a disappointment."

"Oh, honey. We *all* make mistakes—it's just part of growing up."

When she opened the door to her room, I drank in the smell of furniture polish and the fresh air that wafted in through the screens. "Wow. Your room looks amazing— just like when you finished redecorating. Great job!"

She shrugged. "Thanks." She handed me her cell phone.

I stopped in the kitchen to grab another Pabst and the last Spotted Cow that Glenda had brought over on Sunday, and rejoined my dad on the living room couch. He stared at the Brewers' baseball game on TV, the volume down so low the announcers seemed to be whispering. I handed him the beer. "You hate the Brewers."

"I know. I'm just watching the crawl to get the Twins' update."

I nodded. "Thanks for the advice on Lily. I hope she'll be strong enough to pull this off."

He popped the tab and took a long pull on the fresh beer. When he spoke, his voice was choked with emotion. "I'll do anything I can to help her through it—and I'll stay as long as it takes."

I bent over to kiss his cheek and leaned back to answer the cell phone that buzzed in my shorts pocket. Matt Witte.

"Hey, Matt. Please tell me some good news," I said, in as airy a tone as I could manage.

"Mission accomplished," he said, clearly amped with adrenaline. "The search went off without a hitch. I think we've hit the mother lode and can't believe Bobby Marks' stupidity! It looks like he intended to live with the woman and kids on Milwaukee Street for a while; he left a boatload of clothes *and* a laptop computer—with the password on a piece of paper sitting next to it."

"You've got to be kidding."

"No, ma'am! And one of our detectives took a cursory look at it and found some hidden files, one of which contains what appears to be stolen ID info. He'll dig deeper when we get the computer back to the office."

"Were the woman and kids there?"

"Uh-huh. And there's more good news: The woman gave her name as Sonia Marks. She has an Illinois ID card in that name, but I'm almost sure she's the woman who used Iris Wellington's identity to buy the Mercedes with Bobby. She's got dark hair and a rather dark complexion, but we found a gray wig and some lighter colored make-up in the bathroom. If you remember, the car dealer described Wellington as an older, white woman with graying hair. And the height and weight match pretty closely."

"That's great. Let's talk tomorrow and see if we've got enough to indict her along with Bobby Marks on Thursday. Speaking of whom, have you gotten anything back from AFIS on his prints?"

"Damn, I forgot all about it. I'll check first thing tomorrow and let you know."

"Okay. And I'll get back to you about his initial court appearance."

"G'night."

I suspected he'd be up all night poring over the seized evidence.

"Work?" my dad asked, when I'd hung up the phone.

"Uh-huh. They executed a search warrant tonight on an interesting fraud case I'm working on. But I'm too drained to get as excited as the lead detective."

"Why don't you go get some sleep? And I'll help Abby with the kids in the a.m."

"Thanks, Dad. I'm not sure how we could've handled this without you."

"No problem," he said, with a grin, proudly using the hip response.

When I got upstairs, I tapped out a text to Dominic: "How r u?" But I didn't send it.

Chapter Twenty-two

My dad drove the twins to school on Wednesday morning, allowing me an extra twenty minutes to eat a leisurely breakfast with Abby and Red—at least as leisurely as breakfast can be with a two-year-old. Red sat in her highchair, splashing her spoon in a bowlful of milk and Cheerios. I swear, she smirked a bit each time some sloshed over the edge and onto the tray. Her appetite for fresh fruit, though, heartened me. "More," she signaled, in sign language— which Lily'd taught to her several months earlier—after popping the last bite of banana into her mouth.

I put down my coffee and got up to slice another banana and a couple of strawberries. "Thank you," she signed.

When I got to work, I found a half-cup of burnt sludge in the coffee maker in the break room. I cursed the co-worker—two suspects in mind—who had neglected to start a new pot. *It's just as well. You're already on edge.* I zapped a mug of water, threw in a green tea bag, and headed back to my office.

The phone rang as I sat down. "Caroline Spencer," I said, without looking at the caller ID.

"It's Julia," my sister-in-law replied. "I just heard about Lily getting arrested. What can I do to help?" My late husband's sister and Abby's daughter, Julia had moved to Madison with her two teenaged children shortly after David's death. Though not as close as we'd once been, I still considered her a good friend. But her seemingly heartfelt offer of assistance troubled me: *Was there a tinge of gloat in her voice? That previously-perfect Lily had joined the ranks of the bad kids? Nah… you're just being overly sensitive.*

"Thanks, but I'm not sure what you could do. We're going to court this afternoon. It looks like she'll get put in a first offenders' program. And we're on a waiting list to get in to see a shrink Glenda recommended."

"That's good. Call if you need me. You remember how much trouble my kids had after the divorce, especially Carlos. His psychiatrist would be great if Lily needs meds."

When Julia hung up, I called the clerk of court to tell them the arrest warrant for Bobby Marks had been executed and that we needed to schedule his initial appearance before the magistrate judge. "How's 3:30?" the deputy clerk asked. "And do you know whether he's hired an attorney?"

"The time's fine with me. No idea about the attorney, though the case agent told me Marks wouldn't make a statement 'til he talked to one."

I grabbed my mug of tea and wandered down to George Cooper's office. "Got a few minutes?" I asked, tapping on the frame of his open door.

"Absolutely. C'mon in and have a seat."

I sat on the ancient red leather sofa—complete with rolled arms and brass tacks—that he'd gotten from his father's law office when he retired. George eased into the adjacent, wingback chair and put his feet up on the coffee table. "What's on your mind?"

"First of all, Bobby Marks was arrested late yesterday afternoon and booked into the Rock County Jail. His initial appearance is set for 3:30 today. And Matt Witte tells me execution of the search warrant went fine. There was a middle-aged woman in the residence at the time; he thinks she's the woman who bought one of the cars—the Mercedes SUV—at that dealership in the Chicago area. He's going to try to pull together enough evidence to indict her along with Bobby tomorrow. We'll see."

"Where's Jimmy McGee in all of this?"

"Quantico, I guess. But Matt seems to have it all under control."

I took a sip of tea, stalling for a moment to decide how to approach my next topic. I'd spent no less than an hour of last night's wakefulness thinking about how to tell George of Lily's arrest.

"You said 'first of all,' leading me to believe there's something else you wanted to talk about. What is it?" he asked.

"Actually, I don't *want* to talk about it, but I think you need to know: Lily was arrested for shoplifting over the weekend."

George took his feet off the table and leaned forward, elbows on knees. "How're you doing with it?"

"I feel ashamed. No mother wants to admit her child's been engaged in criminal behavior. And this was misdemeanor theft, not just pocketing a couple candy bars. People will undoubtedly attribute it to bad parenting."

"Yeah, and it's probably even worse for parents in law enforcement."

I nodded. "Still, hiding the truth from people whose help I'll need to deal with the problem feels wrong. And, as I learned from years of trying to hide my panic attacks, secrecy is just an added burden."

"I know exactly what you mean. When our son got popped for possession of marijuana—and it wasn't just a personal-use quantity—Deidre and I decided not to tell our colleagues. That was a big mistake. We could've used their experience and advice early on. When they eventually found out, they were completely supportive. Every family's got some cross to bear, believe me. Let me know what I can do."

"Thanks. I'm anxious to put this behind us, so I scheduled her court appearance for this afternoon. I'll need to take an hour or two off."

"You got it."

Matt Witte called midmorning. "I'm emailing you Bobby Marks' rap sheet," he said, with unmasked enthusiasm. "He's no newbie. Several arrests and four convictions—all property crimes. But even better news: we searched Sonia Marks' purse and found an ID in the name of Iris Wellington. It's the same one that was presented to the Chicago car dealer to buy the Mercedes."

"Great. That should be enough for us to indict her along with Bobby tomorrow. Did you get my message that Bobby's hearing's at 3:30 today?"

"Yep. See you then."

I hung up and tried to concentrate on my work but couldn't banish Lily from my mind. *Why not head home and take her to lunch before her court appearance? She could clearly use a boost.*

"Where is everybody?" I called, when I walked into my foyer.

Abby emerged from the kitchen, wiping her hands on the dish towel she perpetually wore on her shoulder. "Your dad took Red to the playground about an hour ago. Lily's still up in her room. Sorry—I didn't think she needed to be ready 'til about 12:30."

Awake, but sitting in bed with a paperback book on her lap, Lily looked at me with unseeing eyes. Her long, dark hair was snarled into birds' nests—either from tossing and turning or the work of her fingers. I went to hug her and cringed at her stale morning breath.

"Hey, kiddo. Get up and brush those teeth. I thought we'd go get some lunch before court."

She trudged down the hallway toward the bathroom and returned a few minutes later, wiping her mouth with the back of her hand. Hair still askew, she leaned against the doorframe. "Do we hafta go to lunch?"

My heart sank at her response. I thought we'd turned a corner with our promising conversation last night. "Uh… no. I guess not. But go and get showered so we don't have to rush."

Lily emerged forty-five minutes later looking marginally more presentable than she had in bed. She hadn't washed her hair but had managed to get out most of the tangles.

She wore clean jeans and a long-sleeved, gray T-shirt with stains on the tattered cuffs. *You've gotta pick your battles.* I bit my tongue to stifle my reflexive, "You're not wearing *that?*" response.

The strained silence during our drive downtown weighed heavily on my mind. I felt confident about the court appearance but beyond anxious about the school situation.

I hadn't thought about one thing, though—the likelihood of running into some of my former colleagues in the county courthouse. I didn't recognize any of the security screeners, but four steps past the metal detectors I noticed the district attorney's secretary walking toward us. In an embarrassed panic, I scanned the hallway for a way to avoid her spotting us. No luck.

"Caroline," she said, giving me a warm hug. "What brings you to the old stomping ground? And this can't be Lily—all grown up!"

Be like a politician: when you don't want to answer a question, evade it. I drew Lily into our circle. "Honey, do you remember Clarice? She's the one who had M&Ms on her desk; you always wanted to stop to visit her when your dad brought you to my office."

"Uh, hi," Lily said.

"How've you been?" I asked Clarice. "I'd heard you were getting ready to retire."

She grinned. "Yes. Twenty-seven days and four hours from now, but who's counting?"

"Are you still planning to move to Arizona to be closer to your grandkids?"

"As soon as we can sell the house. We've got a couple prospective buyers already."

"I'm glad I ran into you, then," I said, moving to usher Lily past her. "I'll give you a call and we'll have lunch before you go, okay?"

"I'd love that. See you soon! 'Bye Lily."

Lily looked over at me as we walked away. "Thanks, Mom."

"No biggie," I said, realizing I'd abbreviated our encounter with Clarice more for myself than for Lily. And I knew at once that my discomfort was nowhere near what Lily would feel re-entering the halls of Edgewood School.

In the courtroom, we checked in with the clerk, who directed us toward the assistant district attorney. If the prosecutor had a negative opinion of Lily's attire, she didn't let on. "Hello, Lily," she said, shaking my daughter's hand, "I'm Ms. Middlecamp. Your mom and I talked on the phone earlier. This is just the initial appearance in your shoplifting case, but we can make it the last appearance if that's what you'd like."

Lily nodded and added a respectful, "Yes, ma'am."

"All right, then. If you're willing to admit to the judge that you took the items from Macy's without paying for them, I'll ask her to put you in our first offenders' program. You'll have to obey all laws, do 100 hours of community service, and report to a social worker. If you comply, after a year the shoplifting charge will be dismissed and your record will be clean. Is that what you want to do?"

"Uh-huh."

"Fine. Take a seat and come forward when the clerk calls your case."

The first rows were already occupied, so we sat in a middle row of the gallery. Lily positioned herself several inches away from me, but as the clock ticked toward 1:00, I noticed her moving closer and closer. Like an adolescent boy on his first movie date, I nonchalantly stretched and put my arm across the back of the bench, and when I sensed the time was right, I drew her toward me. She rested her head on my shoulder and cried softly, all the while twirling a lock of hair.

I'd spent years in state and federal courtrooms and had seen far too much heartache in those hallowed halls. It unnerved me to be sitting on the defense side of the aisle—without my righteous indignation and moral high ground. I said a silent prayer that this court appearance would, in fact, be her last. Ever. *Please, God, help her straighten this out.*

The judge, a pudgy, fifty-something woman with freckles and dusty red hair, took the bench at precisely 1:00. She settled herself in the creaky, red-leather chair, opened a file, and called the first case. The emaciated African American boy had run away, apparently for the second or third time, from a group home. Perhaps thirteen years old, he looked far too young to be the repeat offender the judge referred to when she sentenced him to a year at Lincoln Hills reformatory. I stifled a gasp.

Three equally-distressing cases followed: a rail-thin white girl with pockmarked skin charged with selling heroin; an angry looking, brown-skinned boy charged with sexually abusing a neighbor child; and an overweight black girl charged with aggravated battery to a classmate at Madison Memorial High School.

All of the teenagers wore orange jumpsuits, signifying that they'd been held in juvie while awaiting court. And all appeared with the same haggard-looking public defender, who carried an apparently heavy satchel full of file folders.

I glanced at my watch and realized it was almost 2:00. *Will we be done in time to get to my own 3:30 hearing?* Much to the chagrin of a bailiff, I began typing a text to George Cooper, to send in case the delay continued. The bailiff gave me the stink eye, but I continued 'til he signaled for me to put away the phone.

"Lily Spencer for initial appearance," the judge announced, just as I'd finished. Though her voice was kind, the corners of her mouth turned down, making it difficult to read her thoughts. Lily stood and the judge beckoned her forward.

"Make eye contact, even if it's difficult," I whispered to Lily, as she scooted in front of me to make her way to the defense table.

She sat alone, reminding me of the orphaned bunny the twins had found in the back yard the previous summer. My heart ached for her.

"Hello, Lily. Is that your mother seated behind you?"

"Uh-huh."

"She's welcome to join you at the table."

Thank you! I wanted to shout, as I took a seat next to Lily. Instead, I nodded a sedate, lawyer-like greeting.

"Ms. Middlecamp, please state the charge."

Janice Middlecamp rose, recited the charge, and described the deferred prosecution agreement we'd reached. The judge told Lily her rights and asked if she wanted to plead guilty.

Barely audibly, Lily replied, "Yes."

"Have you thought about where you'd like to do your community service?"

"Uh-huh. There's this apple orchard and farm that's close to where I used to live," Lily began, in a quivering voice. "Near Middleton. And it's, like, a charity, run by volunteers. They give apples and vegetables and the money they make to poor people. If that would be okay with you, I mean."

"That sounds like an exceptional idea. Good luck to you, young lady."

Within five minutes, we were signing papers in the social worker's office. Within half an hour, we were in the car heading home. The low-key nature of Lily's court appearance troubled me a bit; surely such a cataclysmic event in my daughter's life warranted more fanfare, if only to impress upon her the seriousness of her behavior. I would've appreciated a stern warning from the frowny-faced judge. Or, a lecture from the just-out-of-college social worker, who looked only slightly older than Lily. Still, as I glanced over at her leaning on the passenger door, with shoulders slumped and vacant eyes, I knew she felt the weight of the day.

"I'm impressed that you'd already thought about where to do your community service," I said. "How'd you hear about that place?"

"Huh?" She hadn't registered a word I'd said.

"I said, I'm proud and impressed that you knew where you wanted to do your community service. Where'd you get the idea?"

"Oh. Our church youth group went there last fall. Remember?"

"No." *Maybe she is crying out for your attention—you don't even remember her youth group outings?*

We pulled into the driveway at 3:00—too close to my 3:30 hearing for comfort. "Sorry, I can't come in, honey. I'm running really late."

Lily shrugged and opened the car door. "It's okay. See ya later." She ran up the steps without looking back.

I dashed from my car to the elevator to my office and grabbed the Marks file. I took the stairs down and fast-walked to the courthouse. My watch read 3:32 when I opened the door to the courtroom, just as Magistrate Judge Brillstein strode to the bench. He looked at me in annoyance when I walked through the bar to join Matt Witte at the counsel table; I should've been in my appointed place five minutes earlier.

A moon-faced man with a receding chin, Stanley Brillstein appeared milquetoast but was anything but. He detested tardiness, continuances, and interruptions. My only consolation was the judge's track record: his conservative bent made it unlikely he'd release Bobby Marks on bail.

Bobby sat at the defense table with an attorney—one I didn't recognize, so certainly not someone appointed by the court. When the clerk asked for the appearances, the attorney identified himself as "Stefan, S-T-E-F-A-N, Adams, Esquire, of Chicago, Illinois." Wearing an undertaker's black suit, he looked a bit like Johnny Depp in *Chocolat* but without the ponytail. Matt and I exchanged brief eye rolls at his pompous manner.

At the judge's request, I recited the charges and potential penalties Bobby Marks faced. I explained that

I intended to present the matter to the grand jury for indictment the following day; thus, we did not need to schedule a probable-cause hearing. Finally, I requested that Marks be detained pending trial based on the risk of flight, and asked for a continuance for the detention hearing.

S-T-E-F-A-N Adams jumped to his feet. "Objection! I came prepared to address the issue of detention today. I have a two-week jury trial starting in Chicago tomorrow."

The judge looked over his reading glasses at me. "Since we already have a pretrial services report in hand, Ms. Spencer, I believe there is sufficient information to hold the hearing today."

The two-page report sat before me on the table, but I hadn't had time to read it. I glanced at Matt, who nodded and whispered, "It's a pretty clear detention case. I made some notes for you." He pushed a legal pad toward me.

"Very well, Your Honor," I said. "But might I have a few minutes to read the report?"

He nodded.

While I read, a middle-aged woman and two children— both talking—walked into the courtroom and sat in the front row, behind Bobby Marks. The youngest, a boy of about six, leaned over the rail and said, "Hi, Uncle Bobby!"

Bobby turned and grinned.

Judge Brillstein leaned forward and bellowed, "We'll have quiet in this courtroom."

I finished reading the report and Matt's notes that summarized the new information he'd learned since we'd talked. At the bottom of the page, he'd written in red ink, "Share ONLY if needed!"

"Thank you, Your Honor," I said. "I'm ready to proceed."

The pretrial services officer's report recommended detention for Marks based on the risk of flight. He had no permanent residence in the area, had prior arrests and four convictions for property crimes, and had served a two-year prison term in California and a thirty-day jail term in Chicago, under different aliases. "The prosecution agrees with the PSO's recommendation. This defendant has no legitimate ties to this district, and he's used multiple aliases. He faces significant penalties if convicted, increasing his incentive for flight."

"Your comments, Mr. Adams," the judge said.

Bobby's attorney stood, buttoned his suit jacket, and nodded knowingly toward his defendant's relatives. "Mr. Marks *does* have a suitable residence here. He recently moved to Janesville to live with his mother and the children of his sister, who is undergoing treatment for a serious illness at the University of Wisconsin Hospital. The children's father is deceased, and—as a skilled construction worker—Mr. Marks is the primary breadwinner for the family. He doesn't use alcohol or drugs but would willingly undergo testing to prove it. Finally, his mother is willing to post the home she owns in Chicago, with an appraised value of $219,000, to ensure his future appearance. His mother is present in the courtroom and will testify to these facts if the Court wishes."

Magistrate Brillstein remained silent, chewing on the end of his pen, and—to my utter amazement—seemed to be considering the defense's proposal. *Don't fall for it!* I wanted to scream. "May I comment, Your Honor?"

He tipped his head in my direction.

"We are not alleging that the defendant poses a physical danger to the community. However, the Court is allowed to consider the nature of the crimes and the weight of the evidence along with the defendant's personal history or characteristics in making its decision."

Magistrate Brillstein sighed and moved his pen in a rotating motion, a clear signal for me to move it along.

"The government's case is a strong one," I continued, "bolstered by evidence seized yesterday during execution of a search warrant at the Janesville residence. A *preliminary* examination of a computer found in the home revealed that the defendant was in possession of social security numbers, credit card numbers, and identifying data from at least fifteen other individuals, three of whom were defrauded when he and female cohorts purchased luxury vehicles in their names. Furthermore, the woman the defendant claims is his mother, and with whom he proposes to reside, possessed a photo ID card, bearing her likeness, in the name of one of those victims. Clearly the defendant has the means to procure or manufacture stolen identification documents, increasing his likelihood of flight."

I paused to take a sip of water from the cup Matt had poured for me. "Further, we believe it would be preposterous and irresponsible for this Court to allow the defendant's mother—if that's who she really is—to post a home as surety when she, too, was involved in the use of someone's stolen identity. Next, let's turn to the defendant's prior—"

"I've heard enough, Ms. Spencer," Judge Brillstein said, holding his hand up like a stop sign. "Your motion for pretrial detention is granted."

Bobby's mother raised her arms and began wailing, "No, no, no… it's lies… all lies!" She turned toward the prosecution table. "A curse on you liars and on you, Mr. Judge!"

Judge Brillstein searched under a pile of papers for the gavel I'd never seen him use and banged it on his desk. "Bailiffs, get this woman out of here before I'm forced to hold her in contempt. The defendant is remanded into the custody of the United States Marshals. Court is adjourned," he said, and hurried out the door behind the bench.

Matt turned and gave me a gentle fist bump. "Good job."

"Except now we're cursed!" I said, with a grin.

Chapter Twenty-three

My cell phone rang during the walk back to my office: Julia. *Twice in one day? What's going on?*

"Hey, Caroline. I wondered if it'd be okay for me to bring pizza and salad over for dinner tonight. The kids and I haven't had a chance to see Mom in a while."

And you want an opportunity to give me some advice about Lily. "Fine with me. Did you make sure Abby doesn't have something planned?"

"I checked. She's good with it. See ya around 5:00."

I wasn't surprised to see Julia's car parked at the curb when I got home. But I nearly came unglued when my dad met me at the front door and led me to the kitchen to find Lily and Marissa sitting at the table, deep in conversation.

"What the—"

Dad held up his hand. "Before you get up in arms, Caroline, you need to know I invited Marissa to come here. I think you should sit down and join us."

I glared at him. "You *invited* her here?"

"This is exactly what you were thinking the school counselor should do—get the girls together to hash it out. Who knows when—or if—she'll get around to it."

But it wouldn't have happened in my house! Too tired to argue, I slid into the chair next to Lily. She gave me a grateful nod.

"Marissa was just telling us why she posted the picture of Lily on Facebook," my dad said. "Why don't you repeat it for Mrs. Spencer, honey?"

Honey?

Marissa's lip quivered and she blinked several times before beginning. "After Lily told me she couldn't hang out with me anymore, I was really, really hurt. I, like, understand why you made her do it, but it still really hurt a lot. I don't really have any other, like, good friends. I don't know why I do things that get me in trouble and I don't mean to. But, like, sometimes I can't, like, stop myself."

I felt my temples throbbing. "Let's get to the Facebook post. How could you do something so hateful?"

My father shot me a withering look, which I returned in kind.

"I did it to get back at her," Marissa said, tears streaming down her face. "It was mean, and I am so, so, so sorry. I took the post off Facebook before I came over here. If Lily can be my friend, I'll never do anything like that again. I promise."

It sounded like blackmail to me.

"What do you think, Lily?" my dad asked.

She looked down at her lap and kicked at the kitchen floor with the toe of her sneaker. "I dunno. Now all the other kids hate me 'cause of what I did."

"What if I told Brenda and Shelley the truth?" Marissa asked, in a whisper. "That I was the one who, like, taught you how to shoplift. And that we're both gonna stop it."

My dad glanced at me, then back to Marissa. "I think it'll be a while before Mrs. Spencer is willing to let Lily hang out with you outside of school," he said. "But maybe if you'd be Lily's ally at school—and could get those two girls to be her allies, too—she could sit with you at lunch and go to afterschool activities with you. And when you both win back her trust, Mrs. Spencer could rethink your being friends outside of school."

The three of them looked at me for my response. I paused to consider what to say. Unconvinced of the merits of this détente, I nevertheless realized how helpful it'd be if Lily didn't have to walk her middle-school hallways alone. "Do you understand what he means about being allies?" I asked the girls.

Lily nodded.

"It means we'd have Lily's back," Marissa said. "Like, if other kids were making fun of her or talking bad about her, we'd stick up for her. And sit with her at lunch and stuff."

"And not try to get her to break the rules," I added, in an acerbic tone.

Marissa's face colored but she mumbled her agreement.

"I'd feel a lot more comfortable about this if we knew Brenda and Shelley were on board," I said.

"They're over at Shelley's right now—it's just around the block," Marissa said. "I could text 'em and have 'em come over."

"Fine." I stood up and stretched my neck and back. "A word, Dad?" I asked, nodding toward the back porch.

"What makes you so sure Marissa'll keep her word?" I hissed when we'd closed the kitchen door behind us. "Maybe she's too screwed up to change and will always be an evil influence on Lily."

He put an arm around me and rested my head on his shoulder, as he might have done when I was a kid. "Oh, honey. You can't always think like a prosecutor. I think she's just a confused twelve-year-old girl with very little family support and few friends. We talked for quite a while before you got home; I don't think she's a bad seed."

"But why should we be responsible for saving her?"

"I'm thinking she and Lily can help save each other," he said quietly. "If it doesn't work, you can always go back to the 'no contact' edict."

I bristled at his suggestion that Lily needed saving—but had to admit he had a point. "Okay, but only if Shelley and Brenda agree to join this posse of allies. At least I know and trust *them*." Hesitant to leave Lily alone with Marissa, I moved toward the door. He put a hand on my shoulder.

"Give them a few minutes." He ushered me to the picnic table bench and sat across from me. "I did some reading on the internet today. About shoplifting. After listening to Lily and Marissa, I'm wondering if there's more going on with them than simple thrill-seeking or acting out."

"Like?"

"Well, at least one researcher believes people get into shoplifting to compensate for loss. Both of those girls have lost their fathers—Lily due to death and Marissa because of divorce and estrangement. I also read that about 5 percent of shoplifters have kleptomania. Maybe Lily's one of 'em."

"I'm not sure if that would be a bad or good thing."

"Seems to me that knowing what you're dealing with is always a good thing. And I read that they've found medications that can be helpful in treating kleptomania."

I shrugged. "Worth looking into, I guess…"

Lily knocked on the back door and opened it a crack. "They're here. Brenda and Shelley."

We resumed our confab, the four girls and I sitting around the kitchen table and my dad leaning against the counter by the sink. He nodded to me as if to say, *It's your rodeo.* I wanted to scream back: *This was your frickin' idea—you lead the charge.*

Marissa beat us to it. "You guys need to know that Lily's not the only one who's been shoplifting," she blurted out. "I'm, like, the one who taught her to do it, and I've stolen way more stuff than her. That's why it was so, so wrong of me to post that picture."

Brenda—always the more outspoken of the two BFFs—looked Marissa straight in the eye. "But why? Your mom gives you everything you ever want."

Marissa hung her head. "A friend in Seattle dared me to do it with her the first time. And after that it was, like, something that just made me feel better. And I guess I thought it would make Lily feel better, too."

Brenda turned to Lily. "Did it?"

Lily found a lock of hair and began twirling it. "Kinda," Lily said, in a timid, little-girl voice. "But sometimes I don't even, like, realize I'm doing it. And I feel awful after."

With Herculean effort, I stayed rooted to my chair. I wanted to take her in my arms, rock her, and make it better.

My dad walked over and put his hands on her shoulders. "Lily went to court today," he said, to Brenda and Shelley. "If she follows the rules for a year and does volunteer work, the judge will dismiss the shoplifting charge and clear her record. The judge believes in her. We're hoping you girls will believe in her, too, and help her through the tough times she might have at school. What do you say?"

Shelley reached over and patted Lily's free hand. "I will."

"Me, too," Brenda said. "And I'm sorry I was so mean the other day."

I swallowed the lump in my throat before I could speak. "You girls are welcome to stay and have pizza with us if you'd like." My heart almost burst with joy when Lily grinned.

After dinner, Julia and I put on sweatshirts and sat on the front porch, sharing a bottle of cabernet. "You're sending Lily back to school tomorrow?" she asked, after I'd filled her in on the arrest, the Facebook post, the subsequent bullying, and the alliance we'd arranged with Marissa, et al.

"Uh-huh. And even though she'll have at least three girls in her corner, I'm still scared to death for her. But Dad and I talked about it. We figured the longer we wait, the harder it'll be. He's here for at least a few more days, to help prop her up if things get tough."

"Your dad is a rock star. I love the way he stepped up when you needed him."

I took a sip of wine. "Unlike my so-called boyfriend who's so preoccupied with his *mommy* that he can't be here for me." The vitriol in my voice surprised me—and apparently Julia, too. She looked at me with a raised eyebrow.

"I thought things were going well."

"The sex—the few times we managed to get together—was phenomenal. But over the past couple of days, I realized that what I need more than a lover is a life partner. Someone I can share my joys and concerns with. Someone who has my back. Dominic was here for the kids and me when he was investigating David's accident, but it doesn't feel like he's here, now. I don't know what's changed."

"Maybe you're not as ready to move on as you thought you were? Or maybe you're unfairly comparing him to David? Or to your dad?"

"Maybe I'm *not* ready. But is it really unfair to compare?"

Julia shrugged and poured herself another glass of wine. "I loved my brother David to the moon and back—he's gonna be a tough act to follow."

I felt my eyes stinging and couldn't reply.

"So are you gonna break up with him?" she asked, after several moments of silence.

"I'm thinking about it."

"You could always try some casual dating instead. Even some no-strings-attached sex, if that'd make your life happier for a while."

"I haven't done the no-strings-attached sex thing since college. I'm not sure it's appropriate for a widow with four kids."

She snorted out a mouthful of wine and used the sleeve of her sweatshirt to rub the spray off the arm of the Adirondack chair. "Why on earth not?" she asked, with a wicked grin.

Chapter Twenty-four

At my desk the next morning, I held my head in both hands and rubbed my throbbing temples with my forefingers. I blamed my fogginess and the dull headache on sleeplessness; I'd been awake half the night trying to decide what to do about Dominic. But too much wine couldn't have helped.

Matt Witte texted me five minutes before our 9:00 meeting. "Want coffee? DD?"

Momentarily puzzled by the "DD," I didn't know how to respond. Then, I remembered the Dunkin' Donuts shop on Park Street, located conveniently on the route from his office to mine. "Yes. Coffee w/ cream and 1 donut," I replied, adding a smiling emoji.

"You're a life saver," I said, a few minutes later, as he set a cardboard tray with two large coffees and a bag of donuts on my desk. "I haven't been able to shake loose the cobwebs, and I need to get the draft of the indictment over to George before 11:00."

I took the lid from my coffee and blew on it a few seconds before taking a sip. Matt had gotten four donuts and a half-dozen cinnamon donut holes. I popped one of the little morsels into my mouth and grinned. "Nothing like a caffeine-and-sugar buzz to get things rolling."

We went over Matt's grand jury testimony and wrote up the indictment that would charge Bobby Marks with conspiracy to commit bank fraud, for helping to buy two, high-end vehicles in Eau Claire and Wausau with stolen identities. He would also be charged with conspiracy to transport two, other stolen vehicles into Wisconsin. We named his mother, Sonia Marks, a/k/a Iris Wellington, as a co-conspirator for her role in purchasing the Mercedes SUV that was eventually recovered in Janesville. And we'd go before the grand jury and seek an amended—or superseding—indictment when we learned the identity of his other cohort.

"I didn't find any prior record on Sonia, but without fingerprints, we can't know for sure," Matt said. "Are you going to get an arrest warrant or summon her to appear on the indictment?"

I shrugged. "What do you recommend?"

"A warrant. And not because she put a curse on us," he said, laughing. "The Milwaukee Street house looked to me like a temporary stopping place—not a permanent residence. I think these folks are used to skipping town in a heartbeat."

"Okay. You got it."

Matt stood up, brushed donut crumbs from his pants, and threw his empty coffee cup into the wastebasket. "I almost forgot—we inventoried the Escalade after Bobby Marks' arrest and found an iPad under the passenger seat. Can you get a search warrant for it?"

"Sure, but won't we have the same problem as with an iPhone. The encryption, I mean?"

He shrugged, heading for the door. "Yeah, but maybe we'll find another Post-it note with the password. See you at the courthouse at 1:45. Text me if anything comes up before then."

I'd given Lily a note to take to school, requesting that she be allowed to use the office phone during her mid-morning study hall. She called a few minutes after Matt left.

"Hi, honey," I said, hoping for good news. "How'd things go this morning?"

Her voice trembled. "It was really, really hard, Mom."

My stomach twisted. "Tell me."

"Well... Marissa, Shelley, and Brenda were great. We met on Monroe Street and they walked with me. But some of the eighth-grade boys were standing on the sidewalk and started laughing and saying stuff like 'How'd you get out of jail?' and 'When did they start letting crooks go to our school?'"

My hand tightened around the telephone receiver; I had to check my impulse to throw it across the room.

"Then, Marissa told 'em to mind their own effing business. The principal heard her and was gonna give her detention. But Brenda and Shelley told the principal what the boys did, and she, like, made them apologize."

"Oh, Lily..."

"After that it got a little better. At least one of the girls is with me in every class, and they've been sticking up for me. I just hope everybody forgets about this."

"They will, kiddo."

"I gotta go, Mom."

"Okay, honey. I love you."

"You too."

I hadn't heard from Dominic for two days, not since he'd stormed out of our lunch at Tutto Pasta. We'd never gone this long without communicating. No calls. No texts. No emails. No Instagram pics of scenes he thought would make me smile.

He finally called that afternoon, twenty minutes before I was scheduled to present the Marks case to the grand jury, two blocks away. I hesitated, then picked up.

"Hello, Caroline. I'm sorry I've been out of touch. How are you and the kids?"

Gee, since we last spoke my oldest child's appeared in juvenile court, she's been bullied on the internet and at school, and I'm a basket case wondering how her day's going. I took a deep breath and tempered my tone. "Okay. My dad got here Tuesday afternoon, and he's been a big help with Lily's situation. Everyone else is hanging in there."

"I'm glad. I've got some good news to share."

"Oh?"

"Barbara's in jail. She went to the pawn shop to pick up Mom's ring shortly after they opened this morning. Emma managed to keep her there until the police arrived to arrest her. They're holding the ring for evidence, but we'll eventually get it back."

Emma is a certifiable Wonder Woman. Is there anything she can't do? "That's great, Dominic. I'm happy for you."

"Thanks."

I glanced at my watch. "I hate to cut this short, but I've got a grand jury appearance in a few minutes. Can we talk later?"

"How about tonight? Dinner at my place?" he asked. I could hear the sexy smile in his voice. "My mother made some incredible crabmeat empanadas and a pan full of flan. I'll pick up a bottle of that Grenache I was telling you about."

My thoughts—caroming around in my brain like a pinball in a machine ready to tilt—were interrupted when my iPhone signaled an incoming text. Matt Witte. "Where r u? We're on in 10 and I have new info u need to know b4 we go in."

"Sorry, Dominic—I really have to go. Is 6:30 okay for dinner?"

"Perfect. I'll see you in a few hours."

I once again rushed breathlessly to the courthouse, only to find that the case ahead of ours was running longer than scheduled. Matt had plenty of time to tell me his news: the car salesmen in Eau Claire and Wausau had both picked Bobby Marks out of photo lineups, certain that he had facilitated the fraudulent purchases at their dealerships. By 5:00, with Matt's skilled testimony, we had our indictment and a warrant for Sonia Marks' arrest.

"Want to head up to Cooper's Tavern for a celebratory beer?" he asked casually, as we left the building.

"I wish I could," I said, truthfully, "but my oldest daughter's in the middle of a crisis. I need to get home to deal with it. Another time?"

"Sure. Hope it all goes well." He headed to the parking ramp, and I headed back to my office.

I needn't have hurried home. Lily'd left a note on the foyer table: "We're all down at Grandma's. Bert is grilling burgers for dinner."

I grabbed a beer from the fridge and went upstairs to change. I stood before my closet mirror trying on the new pair of black, stretchy jeans I'd gotten on sale at Macy's. They fit like Spanx but flattened my slightly protruding stomach and looked pretty darn hot with my slightly snug, red silk sweater and a multi-colored scarf tied around my waist.

What are you doing? This is the kind of outfit you wear when you're trying to seduce someone, not when you're thinking of breaking up with him.

I changed to a faded pair of blue jeans and a long-sleeved T-shirt, added a pair of flip-flops and a dash of lipstick, and headed down to say goodbye to my family.

I'd read Lily's note as upbeat, but as I neared Abby's apartment I wondered if I'd been wrong. Maybe I'd find her in tears and again clamoring to leave Edgewood.

My worries were groundless. Lily and my dad sat at Abby's patio table playing cribbage, a game he'd taught her about a year earlier. Still not adept at counting her hands, Lily relied on him to help, but she managed to be a great strategist. "Hey, Mom," she said, when I approached. "I already won one game and I'm fifteen points ahead in this one!"

I gave Dad a sidelong glance—silently asking if he'd let her win—and he shook his head vehemently. "Your daughter's an ace."

I rested my hand on her shoulder. "How was the rest of your day at school?"

She finished pegging her hand and looked up. "It was actually okay. The janitors had to break into the bathroom 'cause one of the eighth-grade girls locked herself in after her boyfriend broke up with her. And they'd, like, posted all their drama on Facebook… so everybody just started talking about that."

My dad nodded. "It appears her fifteen minutes of infamy's passed." Concentrating on shuffling the cards, Lily paid no attention to his armchair philosophy, but I breathed a sigh of relief.

"Well, enjoy your evening. I'm going to Dominic's for dinner."

"Say 'hi' for me," Dad said, as I walked away.

CHAPTER TWENTY-FIVE

Preoccupied with my thoughts, I almost rear-ended the car in front of me at a stoplight on Fish Hatchery Road. I heard the squeal of brakes and looked in my rearview mirror to see the truck driver behind me flipping me off. *Get your head out of your ass, Caroline. You can decide when you talk with him.*

I pulled into Dominic's driveway ten minutes late, halfway regretting my decision to forgo the sexy clothing. I ran my fingers through my hair, pinched some color into my cheeks, and walked toward the house, feeling anything but desirable.

Wearing cutoff jeans and a chef's apron but no shirt, he greeted me at the front door with his gorgeous, dimply smile, led me into the foyer, and gave me a long, tender kiss. "I've missed you."

Weak-kneed, I almost replied, "Me, too," but I didn't want to lead him on. Fortunately, the kitchen timer rang. Dominic went to turn it off, giving me blessed seconds to gather my wits—no small task as I watched his seductively toned, olive-skinned arms and hands deftly removing a pan from the oven. He reached into a cupboard for glasses and uncorked the wine. I imagined those arms around me, those hands touching me in delicious places.

He motioned for me to sit at the table that was set with black-and-white plates, heavy flatware, and red, linen napkins. "My mother gave me strict instructions about baking the empanadas and made me promise to heat the sauce on the stovetop rather than in the microwave."

I pulled out a chair. "Does she know you're serving them to me?"

He laughed and shook his head. "Call me a rebel, but, no, she doesn't."

Call you a wimp, is more like it.

Bearing a platter heaped with steaming tapas and a dish of poblano cream sauce, Dominic joined me at the table. He raised his glass. "Together, alone—at last," he said, as I tapped mine to it. I lowered my gaze.

The meal smelled and tasted heavenly. The lime, garlic, and scallions melded perfectly with delicate crabmeat, and the cream sauce was like tangy icing on the cake. We ate and sipped in silence for a while.

"Caroline," he finally said, "I'm sorry I got so upset with you on Tuesday. And that my mother pressured you not to tell me about your conversation. It was no easy task for Dani and me to get her to tell us the truth about what was going on."

I swallowed a forkful of food, then wiped the corner of my mouth with a napkin. "So you confronted her?"

He nodded. "We told her we knew she'd seen the psychic, in hopes of connecting with Cristina. And we told her we knew that Barbara took her ring."

"How did she react?"

"She hit the roof. She started screaming in Spanish, calling us ungrateful, ill-mannered children who didn't know how to mind our own business. And she called *you* unspeakable names for betraying her confidence."

Unsure of whether—or how—to respond, I poured us each another glass of wine and waited for him to continue.

"Did you ever see that episode of *The Sopranos* when they did the intervention to try to get Christopher into treatment for heroin addiction?"

Despite myself, I had to laugh. "Uh-huh. It was hysterical—fisticuffs and all."

"Well, our intervention with Mom didn't come to blows, but it was every bit as uncomfortable. I told her that Barbara had pawned the ring and we planned to have her arrested when she went to get it out of hock. At that point, Mom started wailing, 'You can't *do* that. I *gave* her the ring. She's the only one who understands me.'"

"So she *did* give it away?"

Dominic nodded. I could see the pain in his eyes. "Dani managed to maintain a level tone. She told Mom that if, in fact, she'd given the ring to Barbara, she needed to explain why. Finally, she told us. She said Dad had it designed with a large ruby in the center, signifying their love, surrounded by three, half-carat diamonds, signifying their three children. Mom finally admitted to us that Cristina had been conceived before their marriage and died at the convent because she and Dad had been more concerned with his career than the welfare of their child. Barbara'd convinced Mom that the ring—and her relationship with my dad— had been cursed by the love of money. In order for her to find happiness and peace, the curse needed to be removed. Barbara promised to pray over the ring and to have her mentor do so, as well. She told Mom she'd return it once the curse was lifted. Mom willingly handed it over. That's why she's so adamant about not having Barbara arrested."

"Didn't she wonder why it was taking so long?"

He took a sip of wine and stared into the glass for a moment. "Yes. She said that perhaps a month ago, she asked Barbara about it. Barbara said her mentor found the curse too powerful for them to handle alone; they'd ordered special crystals from Spain to use in the rituals. She told Mom they were still waiting for the crystals to arrive."

"Your mom wasn't troubled that Barbara pawned the ring in the interim? That pretty clearly demonstrates fraudulent intent."

He shook his head in disgust. "She implicitly trusts Barbara, who's obviously a savvy and dangerous con woman."

Dominic's phone emitted a ringtone I'd never heard before—the refrain from the Beatles' "I Want to Hold Your Hand." He popped up instantly to retrieve it from the counter. "Hello, Emma. How did it go?"

My last bite of empanada roiled in my stomach. *Frickin' Emma.*

I watched from the corner of my eye as he listened, nodding intently. "I can't thank you enough," he said. "I'll call you later."

He hung up and sank back into his chair. "Sorry for the interruption. As a special favor, Emma asked a detective in the CPD fraud unit to come take a statement from Mom. She sat in on the interview for me. They just finished."

Emma is very adept at getting people to do favors for her.

"The detective thinks the resulting affidavit should support a theft-by-fraud complaint; he promised to push the issue with the prosecutor. Of course, he can't guarantee she'll get any prison time. Especially since the other money Barbara talked Mom out of won't be part of the criminal case."

Unskilled at raising an eyebrow, I adopted my tried-and-true, dumbfounded look.

"Turns out Mom also spent another $20,000 in an effort to lift the curse."

My jaw dropped.

"Insane, huh? Barbara really made Mom feel guilty that she and my father valued money over the life of their child. As penance, Mom emptied her savings account and donated it to her church."

I shifted in my chair. "You're right—they can hardly charge Barbara with fraud for soliciting a donation to a church. Is there anything else to get her on?"

"Mom also admits that she spent about $2,000 in 'reading fees' and $250 for some magic candles."

"As crazy as it sounds, the prosecutor might have a hard time arguing the reading fees and magic candles weren't worth what your mom paid for them. It's difficult to prove a negative."

"That's what the detective said. I wish they could factor in my mother's vulnerability, with her bipolar disorder and all that goes with it."

The timer beeped again. Dominic got up to take the flan out of the oven. "I hope this came out okay. Mom put it together before I left this afternoon and all I had to do was bake it." He laughed nervously. "And not slam on the brakes on the way home—it was packed precisely in the cooler."

"I'm already pretty stuffed; make mine a small piece, please."

I waited 'til he returned to the table to take my first bite. "It's every bit as delicious as it was when your mom made it for us in Chicago," I said, truthfully. But my stomach was just as queasy now as it'd been on that day.

He took a sip of wine and looked at me expectantly. "Dominic—"

"Before you say anything, I want to apologize for how distracted I've been lately."

I reached across the table and rested my hand atop his. "Please. I need to tell you what's on my mind."

He glanced away. "The look on your face says I'm not going to like it…"

I took a deep breath to steady my voice. "Remember the night we had dinner at Lousianne's? When we decided to explore where our romantic relationship might go?"

He nodded.

"Well… my big fear, then, was that I wasn't ready to move on after David's death. As you well know, now, my body's ready for a sexual relationship. But over the past couple of weeks I've realized that I'm not *emotionally* ready for intimacy with you. Or anyone else, for that matter."

"Are you sure it's you and not *Lily* who's not ready?" he asked, still avoiding eye contact.

"I'm sure. You and I both have a lot of baggage to bring to a relationship, and neither of us is ready to partner-up to help with the other's load. I've been feeling abandoned rather than connected, and it's unfair for me to judge you harshly for needing to deal with your own stuff."

"Stuff…" he muttered. Bitterly, I thought.

"You're a wonderful guy and a great friend. It'd make me heartsick to lose you as a friend."

"A *friend*," he said, now with unmistakable bitterness. "I want more than a friend."

My stomach lurched as I pushed my chair away from the table. "I know you do. And I'm sorry I can't be more right now."

I hurried out the front door without looking back.

Driving away from Dominic's, I tried to slow my breathing and discern my feelings. My gut told me I felt both relieved and sad. I'd made a decision, and while I might regret it later, at least I'd moved off square one. Somehow I knew Dominic wouldn't settle for friendship, though. That loss brought tears to my eyes.

Intending to cry it out, I stopped at the curb on a side street. My eyes locked onto a discarded Dairy Queen blizzard cup in the gutter. *You deserve a DQ sundae. Two empanadas and two bites of flan—made by a woman who detests you and served by a man who couldn't bring himself to tell her who'd be eating them—hardly constitute a proper meal.*

With no remorse, I pulled into the drive-thru at the Dairy Queen on Fish Hatchery Road. I ordered a large hot fudge sundae with caramel and pecans, then sat alone in my car under a streetlight, the radio blaring oldies on WOLX, savoring every gooey bite.

I found my dad in the living room on what had been David's end of the couch, sipping from a can of Pabst and watching an ancient re-run of *The Rockford Files*. He looked up when I walked in. "Remember watching re-runs of *Rockford* with me when you were little? Your mom used to harp at me 'cause it wasn't an appropriate kids' show. But you loved it."

I grinned. "I loved sitting with you and annoying Mom—it didn't matter what we were watching."

He chuckled, then turned off the TV. "How was your evening?"

I sank down onto the couch and rested my head on his shoulder. "It was okay, I guess. I broke up with Dominic, but I'm pretty comfortable with my decision."

"Want to talk about it?"

"I think I've been comparing him to David—and to you, for that matter—and he just wasn't measuring up. I took that as a sign that I'm not quite ready for a new, significant relationship."

"Hmm."

I leaned away from him so I could look him in the eye. "What do you mean by 'Hmm'?"

"Nothing."

"Dad, you never say something just for the sake of making noise."

He glanced down at his lap. "I just worry when I think you're selling yourself short. Like we were telling Lily the other day—sometimes you just have to jump in the water and swim."

"Believe me, I did jump in. The water was just too full of weeds."

Chapter Twenty-six

I awoke the next morning to the tantalizing aromas of bacon and coffee. The bedside clock read 5:45. *Am I dreaming in smell-i-vision? Oh… Dad.*

Downstairs, after my shower, I found him stirring a bowl of pancake batter. "You're gonna need a good breakfast to face your day," he said, sheepishly. "And, quite frankly, I was hungry for the kind of breakfast your mom won't let me eat."

"This sounds like blackmail material," I said, pouring myself a cup of coffee. "But you're in luck; it's been so nice having a man's influence around this house that I'll let the opportunity slide."

He grinned. "One or two pancakes?"

I recalled last night's sundae with no small measure of guilt. "One, please. And just two slices of bacon."

He poured one large pancake onto the already-hot griddle and smiled with satisfaction. "How'd you sleep?"

I swallowed a sip of coffee. "Amazingly well. Which, I contend, supports my position that breaking up with Dominic was a good idea."

"Could be." He flipped my pancake with an expert flourish. "Or, possibly, you were just very tired."

"Whatever, Dad," I said, with a chuckle.

Later, at my desk, I reviewed the day's schedule. Matt Witte planned to arrest Sonia Marks at the Janesville residence that morning. If successful, we'd try to schedule an initial appearance before the day's end. I had a lunch date with my former secretary and friend, Rosalee. And at 3:00, Lily and I had an appointment with the psychiatrist Julia had recommended.

When Matt called at 10:00, I could hear defeat in the first two words out of his mouth. "Sonia's split."

"Shit."

"One of the kids, who says his name's Johnny and he's twelve, opened the door and told us Sonia wasn't home. He didn't want to let us in, but we showed him our badges and the warrant and explained we had to verify she wasn't there. We looked around and she wasn't. None of her clothes were there, either—and believe me there'd been plenty. The oldest girl, Ruby, was asleep and two younger kids were watching TV. I asked the little girl where her grandma was and she said, 'She left.'"

"Did you ask when?"

"Yep. She said 'this morning' at the same time that her little brother said 'yesterday.' They looked at each other for a second, and then the girl said, 'Oh, I mean yesterday morning.'"

"The kids are stonewalling?"

"Looks as if. All of 'em said Ruby was taking care of them 'til Sonia returned."

"What'd Ruby have to say?"

"Very little. She wandered in when we were talking to the other three in the living room—apparently unalarmed that we were there asking questions. Said they'd moved here 'a while ago' and weren't enrolled in school yet because their records hadn't come. Said she thought maybe Sonia'd gone to Chicago to get the records but didn't know for sure."

"Are you still at the house?"

"Yeah. Waiting on social services. The kids couldn't—or wouldn't—give us the name of an adult relative to contact. Even though Ruby's old enough to babysit for a while, there's no evidence of an adult presence in the home and the kids are all truant."

"You told 'em you were contacting social services?"

"Yep, and it's kinda spooky. They don't seem at all bothered."

"Maybe they've been through it before?"

"Maybe," he said, with an audible sigh.

I suddenly wanted nothing more than to cheer him up. "Sonia's not that smart. We'll find her."

"I hope you're right."

In truth, I wasn't disappointed about the cops' inability to locate and arrest Sonia Marks. I'd been on an emotional roller coaster for days and didn't feel sharp enough, on this day, to appear in court—especially if Sonia had a good lawyer who'd contest my motion to detain her.

I looked forward to lunch with Rosalee, one of my favorite people but whom I didn't see as frequently as I'd like. Though the sky threatened rain, I decided to walk to meet her at Sardine, a great restaurant on the shore of Lake Monona, about three-quarters of a mile from my office. I needed to justify the dessert I planned to eat. I put on my raincoat, grabbed an umbrella, and set off toward the state Capitol building, intending to cut through it to cross the Square. I always enjoyed the sound of feet echoing across the ornate, mosaic floor and craning my neck to look up at the rotunda's elaborate ceiling, replete with gold leaf and a multitude of niches.

As is often the case, I ran into two former colleagues on the Capitol steps. We stopped to chat for about five minutes. So, at 11:45, when my phone signaled an incoming text from Rosalee and I was still a block from the restaurant, I assumed she wondered if I'd forgotten. Without reading her message, I dictated a quick response, "On my way. Be there in five."

Rosalee met me at the entryway of Sardine, gave me a quick hug, and moved to steer me back out the door. "I think we should eat at Paisan's."

I shook off her grip on my elbow. "You're the one who always says Paisan's is passé. And it'll cost you to park there. C'mon—I made a reservation here for a lakefront table."

"Caroline, you really don't want to go in."

"Why on earth not?"

She let out a deep sigh. "Dominic's in there with another woman—a tall blonde."

"Probably Emma, his co-worker," I said, reaching for the restaurant's door handle.

She grabbed my elbow—more firmly this time. "When I pulled into the parking lot I saw them sitting at a window table. They're holding hands, looking like way more than co-workers."

My heart skipped a beat. "I broke up with him, Rosalee, so I can't very well be upset if he's moved on."

"You broke up with him? When?"

"Earlier this week," I mumbled.

She rolled her eyes. "Pretty quick to be on the move."

If you only knew. "We're here now," I said. "Let's just go in and I'll tell the hostess to seat us away from the window so we don't have to look at them."

Rosalee stood aside to let me open the door. "I think you're making a mistake."

"Maybe," I replied, straightening my shoulders and striding into the restaurant. I stole a glance toward the window tables and noticed the only vacant table was right next to the one where Dominic and Emma—resplendent today in a low-cut, coral-colored sweater—sat, their eyes fixed on one another. "Hello," I said to the hostess, a thin woman with short, square-cut bangs and black glasses. "We have a reservation for a window table under the name Spencer, but we've changed our minds. Could we sit in the back room, please?"

She didn't bother to consult her seating chart. "Normally it'd be no problem, but the back room is reserved for a large party. But, there are two seats at the bar."

I surveyed the bar. Dominic and Emma wouldn't likely notice us some forty feet away, and we'd have to turn our heads if we *wanted* to see them. "The bar's fine," I said. "Thank you."

The bartender approached as soon as we'd settled onto our seats. "Something to drink?"

"Sweet iced tea for me," Rosalee said.

"Give me a moment, please," I said. He went to fetch my friend's tea while I surveyed the drink menu.

She gave me a smug look. "Let me get this straight. You're not upset that Dominic's here with another woman but you're breaking your own rules and drinking at lunchtime?"

"I don't have a *rule* against alcohol at lunch—it's just my standard practice. And, no, I'm not upset."

"If you say so."

"Yes, I do say so. And you know what? I'm gonna have a cocktail—maybe even two—and take the rest of the afternoon off. There's nothing on my calendar, and I'd have to leave early, anyway, for a 3:00 shrink appointment with Lily."

The bartender returned with Rosalee's tea. "I'll have a Provencal, please," I said to him.

"A Provencal?" my friend asked.

"Vodka, lemon, lavender, and sparkling wine," the bartender replied. "One of our bestsellers."

I nodded. "I had one last time I was here—very refreshing—and just what the doctor ordered today."

Rosalee shrugged and took a sip of her tea. "After that magic potion comes, you need to give me the lowdown on why you broke up with that gorgeous man. I thought you and Dominic were perfect for each other."

"I thought so, too," I said, with a sigh. "But as time went on, I realized I'm not ready for all his baggage. His mother's got issues that always need his attention; I feel abandoned every time he leaves to deal with 'em."

She raised an eyebrow.

"What?" I asked.

Rosalee held up index finger in a "wait" gesture while the bartender set my drink in front of me and took our orders—two smoked salmon sandwiches. Then, she turned to me. "You're telling me *Dominic* has too much baggage for *you* because he's got a needy mother? You've got four kids, for God's sake. Talk about baggage."

Not sure whether to laugh or cry at her comment, I choked on the first sip of my cocktail and coughed till my eyes watered. "You don't mince words, do you?" I said, when I'd caught my breath.

My friend shook her head. "Not with you, I don't. When my husband died and left me with two little kids, lots of people were condescendingly nice. They didn't tell me when the kids were acting like jerks, or when my constant complaining about money drove them nuts, or even when I needed to get professional help. Everyone seemed to believe I'd become incapable of dealing with candor. One weekend about a year and a half into my widowhood, my sister came to visit and we had a frank talk. I was mortified when she pointed out how I'd been acting and how I'd allowed the kids to act. I vowed to seek honest opinions from then on. You're like me; I know in your heart of hearts you don't want me to pull any punches."

I took a long sip of my drink then turned to sneak a look at Dominic. Emma's back was toward me, but I could see her leaning forward and stroking his hand. He hung his head and stared at the tablecloth, glancing up briefly when the busboy filled their water glasses and removed their salad plates.

"You're staring," Rosalee said. "Not the best move if you want to avoid being spotted."

"Thanks," I said, shifting my position and reaching again for my glass. "So you think I've made a mistake?"

"You can answer that better than I can."

I sipped in silence for a while, contemplating my response. "Breaking up seemed like the right decision last night."

"This just happened *last night?*"

"Uh-huh. We had dinner at his place and I told him then, though I'd been thinking about it for a while."

She sat taller on her stool to look over my shoulder toward Dominic and Emma. "And he's here with someone else *already?*"

"In fairness, I could tell the first time I met her that she was hot for him. I'm guessing she's the pursuer."

"Still…"

The bartender ambled over and cleared his throat. "Ladies, there's been a mix-up with your order and it won't be out for a bit longer. May I offer you another drink—on the house?" I nodded, drained my glass and pushed it toward him. "Ma'am," he said to Rosalee. "Feel free to order an alcoholic beverage if you'd prefer."

"All right. I'll have what she's having." She looked at me and grinned. "I'm off this afternoon, too."

When the drinks arrived, I raised my glass in a toast. "Here's to candor, and I don't feel like talking about Dominic anymore today."

Rosalee took a sip and giggled. "It's yummy, and it tickles going down."

Twenty minutes later, and only halfway through my sandwich, I felt an urgent need to use the bathroom. "Don't let the waiter take away this incredible food," I told my friend, as I set my linen napkin next to my plate. "I'll be back in a flash." Hands on the bar, I stood for a moment to steady myself, then headed down the stairs to the basement restrooms. I gripped the railing; two drinks on a virtually empty stomach had made me dizzier than I'd foreseen.

As I stood at the ladies' room mirror washing my hands, the door opened and Emma walked in. Hoping she wouldn't notice me, I lowered my head and rinsed my hands for a second time. "Caroline?"

Three syllables of her syrupy-sweet voice made me want to retch, but I forced a smile and turned around to greet her. "Oh my gosh—Emma. What are you doing here?"

"I'm having lunch with Dominic…"

Well, duh!

"…he called me last night and asked me to come help him figure out how to deal with his mother's situation. I suppose you heard we recovered her ring and had Barbara—the Gypsy 'psychic'—arrested?"

"Yes, I heard." I reached for a paper towel and dried my hands.

"I'm going to meet with the prosecutor and see if I can convince him to pursue more serious charges—perhaps for fraud. Mrs. Marquez's bipolar disorder makes her particularly vulnerable, and this whole thing has been incredibly traumatic for her."

Though tempted to remind her she'd initially characterized Barbara as just a "small time charlatan," I bit my tongue. Tossing the paper towel in the wastebasket, I moved toward the door. "Well, good luck."

"Thanks," she said. I thought I detected in her voice a note of disappointment, that I didn't want to prolong our conversation.

Rosalee glanced up from her plate as I teetered back to the bar. "Did you manage to avoid the blonde?"

I shook my head. "Nope. But I acted surprised to see her and didn't make a scene. I consider that a victory." I took a bite of my sandwich, then caught the bartender's eye to signal for another drink. "Are you joining me?" I asked Rosalee.

"No way—one's my limit. And you'll be needing a ride home."

We finished eating while chatting amiably about our mutual friends, our kids, and her grandkids. But the troubled look on Rosalee's face as I described the twins' recent soccer game didn't compute. "What?" I asked.

She put her hand on my arm. "Dominic's headed this way."

I took another sip of my drink. "Shit. Do I have time to get up?"

"Uh-uh."

Dominic walked around to stand beside Rosalee, inclined his head a quarter of an inch in my direction, then put his arm around her and kissed her on the cheek. "When Emma told me Caroline was here, I looked around and saw that you were, too. I can't believe you didn't come over to say 'hi,'" he said to her. "It's been too long since I've seen you."

She shifted on her stool, moving away from his arm. "Yes… Well, when you weren't available to work that case for Frank, he found another investigator and has been trying him out."

"I'm sorry to hear that. I'll call him later today and see if I can't mend the fences. How've you been?"

"Fine." Her icy tone—and the pregnant pause that followed—made me want to slide under the bar. I almost spoke, if only to ease the discomfort.

"Okay, then," Dominic mumbled. "Take care. Both of you." And he walked away.

It took a moment for my heart rate to slow down. "That was beyond awkward. You didn't need to give him the cold shoulder on my account. And telling him Frank found somebody else? That's completely unlike you."

She grinned. "It's also not true. But it rankled me to see him all over that bimbo so soon after you broke up. Let him squirm a little."

We turned around to unabashedly stare as Dominic held Emma's chair for her, offered his arm, and they strolled from the restaurant engrossed in conversation.

CHAPTER TWENTY-SEVEN

Rosalee refused to allow me to walk back to my office when we left Sardine. "You're not going to sober up in the time it takes you to get there—assuming you could even make it without falling flat on your face. You can retrieve your car tomorrow, and if your dad can't take you and Lily to the psychiatrist's appointment, I'll take you myself."

I leaned my head against the passenger-side window and groaned. "What on earth was I thinking having three drinks?"

"You weren't thinking. You were trying to drown your sorrows—which never works. By the way, we're making a stop at Cargo Coffee for a double espresso. I don't want you passing out before I get you home."

The strong brew, and a couple of biscotti to settle my stomach, woke but couldn't sober me. When Rosalee pulled to the curb in front of my house, I cringed to see my dad and mother-in-law lounging in the Adirondack chairs on the porch. Red tromped through puddles on the sidewalk in her yellow rain slicker and flowered, rubber boots.

"Not to worry," Rosalee said. "Abby and Gene will understand, and I'll distract Red while you go take a shower. You've got time."

I lingered a few steps behind and watched in awe as Red came running to her, yelling, "Rose-a-ree!" Rosalee grabbed my daughter under the arms and spun her around in circles, eliciting screams of delight.

"Your mom needs to go upstairs and change, honey," she said, when she set Red down. "Why don't you jump in a couple more puddles while I talk to your grandma and grandpa?"

I nodded my appreciation, waved to Abby and my dad, and trudged into the house.

After a cool shower, two Excedrin tablets, and a twelve-ounce bottle of water, I made my way downstairs. Rosalee had things under control. My dad was already on his way to pick up Lily and he'd swing by to get me before the appointment. She'd stay with Red while Abby picked up the twins. I sat heavily on the arm of her chair. "What must they think of me?"

"They love you and know you're going through a rough patch."

The honk of my dad's car horn from the driveway set my head throbbing, but I stood with reasonable confidence and planted a kiss on Rosalee's head. "I can't thank you enough."

Lily was riding shotgun and I climbed into the back seat, grateful that I didn't have to make much eye contact with her or my dad. He stole some glances at me in the rearview mirror, but I read them as kindly rather than judgmental. "Thanks for driving, Dad."

"You're welcome."

"And, Lily?"

"What?"

"I'm ashamed of myself—having too much to drink at lunch and not being able to take you to the appointment myself." I paused to swallow a few times. "There's no excuse… and I know this is a *really bad* example I'm setting. I'm sorry."

Lily looked over her shoulder and shook her head. "No biggie, Mom."

Somehow, their acceptance made me feel more guilty; I cried silently for much of the ride.

As my watch ticked closer to 3:00, Dad circled the blocks near the psychiatrist's downtown office, unable to find a parking spot. "Go in," he said, double-parking in front of the building. "I'll park in that ramp and meet you in the waiting room after the appointment."

"Okay. It's Dr. Grube, G-R-U-B-E. Third floor." While the driver behind us honked in frustration, Lily and I unbuckled our seat belts, gathered our belongings, and got out of the car. In the lobby, a sign on one of the two elevators declared it out of order; the other was stopped on the sixth floor. "C'mon, honey," I said. "We'd better take the stairs."

Breathless, and with my head throbbing, we walked into the psychiatrist's office at 3:05.

"Relax," the receptionist said, handing us each a clipboard. "He's running a bit behind. You'll have time to fill out these forms."

During the ten-minute wait, my breathing returned to normal and my penmanship became increasingly less scribbled—the doctor would probably be able to read the information on the last few forms. My dad walked into the waiting room just as Dr. Grube came out to escort us to his office. "Larry Grube," he said, shaking hands with each of us. "Pleased to meet you."

We'd spoken by phone when I scheduled the appointment, so I'd expected the Sam Elliott-like accent. And though short and pudgy, Dr. Grube nevertheless reminded me of the actor, with a full head of longish gray hair, thick black brows and mustache, and a twinkle in his eye.

He walked side by side with Lily down the hallway while I teetered behind, touching the wall to steady myself a couple of times. In his office, Dr. Grube motioned Lily and me toward a brown leather couch with well-worn arms and cushions. "Please, take a seat."

It felt heavenly. I sat on one end and Lily took the middle cushion. "Thanks... thanks so much for fitting us in, Dr. Grube," I said. "My sis... sister-in-law says you're the best."

"Well, I don't know about that," he replied. "And, please, call me Larry. You too, Lily."

Lily lowered her chin a quarter of an inch, apparently signaling her assent, but I knew she'd never take that leap.

With what I suspected was feigned nonchalance, Larry glanced through the forms Lily and I'd completed, then tossed them on his desk. "Don't know what I was thinkin' when I made up those questions," he said. "Lily, mind if I ask a few more?"

"It's fine," she said.

"Your mom can stay or go—your choice," he said.

Lily looked at me. "Stay, please."

He nodded at me and turned to Lily. "What's your favorite school subject?"

"English."

"How 'bout your favorite book?"

"Oh, gee. There's so many. I just finished *The Fault in Our Stars*. That was a good one."

"I read it too and cried like a little baby," he said, grinning.

Lily giggled.

"Any subjects harder for you than others?"

"Math," she replied. "I have to study hard to get As in it."

He nodded. "Do any extra stuff like sports or clubs?"

"I play the clarinet and take Spanish. And I play soccer and volleyball."

"Who's your best friend?"

She paused for a moment. "I guess right now it's Brenda. Or maybe Shelley—it's hard to choose."

Another nod. "Why're you sittin' on your hands?"

Lily pulled her hands out from beneath her. "I… I do it so I don't twirl my hair."

Larry pinched the corner of his mustache with two fingers and gave it a twist. "What's wrong with twirling your hair?" he asked, with a smile.

"I dunno. But sometimes I pull at it and end up with little bare spots."

"Ah. I can see that might be worth avoiding. Your mom tells me you've been doin' some shoplifting—another thing I'm guessin' you want to avoid. Why don't you tell me how it started?"

In a quivering voice, she told him how Marissa had shown her how to take toiletries, candy, and other small items, how she'd started stealing by herself, and how—to her shame and horror—she'd gotten caught at Macy's. "I don't want to do it anymore, but sometimes I'm afraid I won't be able to, like, stop myself," she concluded.

"Want to hear something interesting?" Larry asked.

"Yeah…"

"Some doctors at the University of Minnesota did a really cool experiment a couple years back," he said. "They found that people who took a simple amino acid—a supplement you can buy over the counter at health food stores—helped some people stop doing impulsive things. Things like shoplifting. Or twirling or pulling out their hair."

I found myself leaning forward in my seat. "Is it, uh, safe for kids?" I asked.

"It's been used in adolescents without significant side effects—certainly a lot fewer than some of the antidepressant and antianxiety meds that have been tried. If Lily were my daughter, I'd give it a try." He took a prescription pad from his desk, scrawled the full name of the supplement and the recommended dosage, and handed it to me. "And you could try the supplement, too. Might help you keep your fingernails away from that spot on the back of your head."

I laughed out loud—a little *too* loud.

"What are you hoping for Lily to accomplish in treatment?"

Caught off guard by his question, I paused to collect my thoughts while Lily squirmed beside me. "Um… I guess the main thing is to stop shoplifting. But… her moods. Until a few months ago, Lily was always a sunny kid. Lately, she's been sullen, often snotty, and hard to be around. I thought having someone to talk to would, I dunno, help her."

"What about it, Lily? Anything happen awhile back that's been bothering you?"

"Yeah," she blurted out, "Mom started seeing Dominic." She hung her head, perhaps ashamed of her quick and vehement response.

"And you don't like Dominic?" Larry asked.

Her eyes welled with tears. "He's not Dad."

"I see. You must miss your father a lot."

She hung her head. "Yeah."

"Did you see a grief counselor after your dad died?"

"Yeah."

"And?"

"And it was lame. She didn't help me at all."

"I'm sorry to hear that," he said. "Losing a parent is huge, and it can affect you in ways you never thought about. A friend of mine's a grief counselor and I've learned a lot from her. She tells me counseling can sometimes be more useful if a little time's passed since the loved one's death. And she believes adolescents often find it easiest to sort out their feelings with their peers, in a support group setting. She just started a new kids' group a couple weeks back, and I don't think it'd be too late for you to join. Would you be willing to give it a try?"

Lily looked skeptical. "I guess so, but I'd rather just come talk to you."

Larry gave her a self-deprecating smile. "My specialty isn't talk therapy. I prescribe medications to people who need them, and I steer people to other folks I think could help them the most. In your case, I think it'd be the support group. How 'bout you go to some meetings, then come back and let me know what you think?"

"Oka-a-y."

"Great. Do you have any questions before I talk to your mom alone for a bit?"

Lily shook her head. Larry stood up and extended a hand to help her from the couch. "You're a fine young lady, Ms. Lily," he said, as he ushered her to the door. "I'll look forward to seeing you again, and I'm guessing things'll look up for you soon. Tell your grandpa we'll be done in about half an hour."

Half an hour? I can't hold it together that long.

Larry shut the door behind Lily, returned to his seat, and scratched his head. "How do I put this?" he finally asked, in a far more serious tone than he'd used with Lily. Then he waited another beat—which felt like an eternity. "I surmise your father is serving as your designated driver this afternoon?"

I nodded and stared at my shoes.

"I saw you wobbling to my office—"

"How—"

"In the mirror at the end of the hallway. And your speech and glassy eyes confirmed my belief that you're under the influence of alcohol."

Another wave of shame washed over me, and I could hardly speak. "I've already apologized to Lily and Dad... But I need to, uh, apologize to you, too. I thought it'd be out of my system by 3:00, but I guess it's not. Great role model for my screwed up kid, huh?"

"Do you drink to intoxication frequently?"

I shook my head and instantly regretted it—the room began to spin. "No. God, no. I'm usually really responsible."

Larry got up and opened the mini-fridge next to his desk. He handed me a can of Coke, so cold it shocked my fingers.

I fumbled with the pull tab then took a tentative sip.

"Hold it to your head between sips," he said, and paused 'til I'd settled the can against my temple. "Now, why don't you tell me what precipitated your uncharacteristic overindulgence?"

What "precipitated" my "overindulgence"? What happened to the down-home, folksy-talking guy that was here when we walked in?

He waited me out.

"I broke up with Dominic—the guy that Lily mentioned—last night. Today, I saw him holding hands with another woman… at the restaurant where I was having lunch with a friend." *God, you sound like a teenager in some bad soap opera.* "I guess it, uh, upset me more than I thought; I had a couple drinks more than I'd planned."

"Did you break up with Dominic because Lily didn't approve of the relationship?"

Fortunately, the can of Coke stopped me from shaking my head again. "No."

"That's good. Why, then?"

"Because I didn't feel like he was there for me when I needed him," I replied, surprised to hear the quiver in my voice. "Not like David was. Or my dad is."

"I see. How long were you and David married before his death?" he asked, quietly.

Hot tears stung my eyelids and I blinked them back. "Fifteen years."

"And he's been gone two years?"

"Two years and two months."

"Kind of a short time in the scheme of things."

"Uh-huh. But sometimes it feels like forever. And I thought I was ready for a new relationship."

He shrugged. "Maybe you are, maybe you're not. But every relationship is different from those that've gone before, and every relationship poses different challenges. Were you expecting him to be like David?"

"I'm not sure. Maybe."

Larry leaned forward and rested his elbows on his knees. "It's something you might want to explore. You told me on the phone that you've been in psychotherapy before, right?"

"Uh-huh. With Dr. Clarice Brownhill."

He grinned. "She's one of my favorite people—and a mighty fine psychologist. How 'bout you schedule a few sessions to sort this all out with her?"

"Probably a good idea."

"What I said to Lily about loss affecting you in ways you never dreamed about? That goes for you, too. Give Clarice my regards when you see her, please. I'll call my colleague right now and see about Lily joining the kids' group and will let you know her answer by tomorrow. See my assistant on the way out to make an appointment for her, back here, in a couple of months."

As he'd done with Lily, Dr. Grube helped me to my feet. But he went a couple steps further, offering his arm, which I gratefully accepted, to walk me to the waiting room to meet my dad.

CHAPTER TWENTY-EIGHT

What a difference twenty-six hours can make. Rather than tantalizing, the aroma of bacon wafting from the kitchen on Saturday morning set my stomach roiling. Sleep had glued the corners of my eyes shut, and my puffy lids opened only halfway. My head weighed a ton and throbbed when I tried to lift my cheek from the sweat-drenched pillow. I felt every wrinkle in my nightgown, bunched up under my hip. I stared at the sodden Kleenexes strewn on the bed. With Herculean effort, I managed to turn onto my back, where I lay watching the ceiling spin.

What on earth did I do to myself?

I remembered arriving home from the appointment with Dr. Grube, and my dad telling me to take a nap. I remembered rushing to the bathroom to throw up after Luke—coming to wake me for dinner—exuberantly jumped on the bed. "Get up, Mommy!" he'd said. "The pizza's here."

I remembered eating pizza in the living room with my dad and all four kids and managing to consume half a slice. I remembered dozing on the couch while Dad put the littles to bed. I remembered answering the door when

Glenda arrived a while later, carrying a bottle of William Hill Cabernet that she'd gotten on sale at Barrique's. I remembered carrying an afghan and following her to the back porch so she could smoke while we talked. I remembered telling her I couldn't possibly drink another drop as she poured us each a glass of wine. Then I remembered telling her about Dominic and Emma—and taking that first sip.

How stupid can you be? Not one, but two episodes of drinking to intoxication in one frickin' day!

Despite my best intentions to get on with the day, my eyelids closed again. When I awoke, sometime later, to the message signal emanating from the iPhone beneath my pillow, at least the bacon smell had dissipated. Through bleary eyes I looked at the screen. Glenda: "How r u doing? Sorry I pushed wine. D is a jerk. U deserve better. Call if u want. XOXO"

Too groggy to type, I used the microphone feature and dictated my reply: "If you ever again use the phrase 'hair of the dog' in my presence, I swear I'll strangle you." I inserted a smiley-faced emoji wearing sunglasses and pushed Send.

I'd slept through two other texts: At 8:15 Dominic had written, "About your offer to remain friends, I'm available to talk if you'd like." *Not frickin' likely. The "friend" ship has sailed.* And my dad's message at 8:40 read, "Lily is at the apple orchard. Her boss will bring her home. Twins, Red, and I are going to soccer, then to the Milwaukee kids' museum. See you around 4:00. We will bring carryout Chinese for dinner." *Thank God.*

After two large glasses of iced tea, three Excedrin, and a breakfast of scrambled eggs and buttered toast, I could count myself among the living. I rummaged through the junk drawer for a pen and sat at the kitchen table to write a to-do list, but found myself stymied after "go get car." *Well, then, might as well get on with that.*

I donned running shoes and took off down the street, walking 'til I could jog, and jogging until I could finally break into what one might call a run. Every cell in my body screamed with fatigue. *If you did this more often it wouldn't be so hard. And it wouldn't be so hard if you didn't have the mother of all hangovers.*

A mile and a half later, when I arrived at my office's basement parking garage and bent down, hands to knees to catch my breath, my head felt clearer. Clear enough, in fact, that I decided to go in and catch up on some work. All but empty on this Saturday morning, the garage echoed with each squeak of my shoes across the dank pavement. I couldn't help looking around furtively to make sure no one lurked when the elevator door opened for me.

I expected an attorney or two would be in, but even the workaholics must've preferred spending this crisp fall day elsewhere. Probably at the farmers' market—one of the last of the season. The vacant hallways and empty offices amplified my feelings of loneliness and abandonment, and I felt a tinge of panic. Though I rarely turned on the overhead fluorescents, today I hit the wall switch, relieved when harsh lighting bathed the room. I grabbed my laptop and a banker's box full of paperwork from the credenza behind my desk, deciding I'd work at home instead, and hurried the heck out of there.

—

Back home, I was reminded how tedious it can be to pull together a case for prosecution, especially a fraud case, which tends to involve daunting amounts of mind-numbing paperwork. I sat at my dining room table that afternoon, another tall glass of iced tea at my right hand, sorting stacks of paper—documents pertaining to Bobby Marks and his cohorts—from the banker's box. Much of it was irrelevant and would never be used at trial, but needed to be sifted through for evidentiary value.

As I searched in vain for a highlighter among the miscellany at the bottom of my briefcase, I heard the front door open and close. I looked up to see Abby and Bert walk in, holding hands and giggling like a couple of middle-school kids.

"Oh, gee—we didn't know you'd be working in here. Sorry to interrupt." Abby said, her eyes twinkling with happiness.

"You *didn't* interrupt. I'm having trouble focusing." I tossed the cardboard banker's box on the floor. "Have a seat."

Abby sat, but Bert chose to stand behind her with his hands resting on her shoulders. "We just stopped by get Abby's things and to borrow a couple of DVDs," he said. "We're heading over to my place and thought it'd be fun to have our own movie night."

Abby blushed. "You don't mind, do you?"

"Of course I don't mind if you borrow DVDs," I said, knowing full well she referred to her spending the night at Bert's—a first for her.

"Oh... uh..." she said, the color in her cheeks deepening.

"I'm just teasing, Abby. I'm glad the two of you are getting along so well, and I'm happy you're spending the night
at Bert's. You deserve time away from this madhouse."

She stood to go. "Thanks, dear."

"I told you she wouldn't mind," Bert said, as they
headed toward the living room and our movie collection.

Wouldn't you know it—even Abby's got a lover.

The tedium of reviewing copies of the loan applications and documents for the vehicles Bobby Marks and
his partners in crime had purchased threatened my resolve
to get a handle on the evidence. I fidgeted in my chair and
finally took a stack of papers to the living room, placing
each page on the couch next to me once I'd read it. *Finish
this bunch and then you can play a couple games of* Words with
Friends.

As luck would have it, the car dealer in Wausau
who sold them the BMW must've had a high-end copy
machine. The color photocopy of the driver's license
presented by Bobby's partner, in the name of Courtney
Parks, immediately piqued my interest. I stared at the
picture on the license, impressed not only by its clarity
but because the person looked familiar. Shoulder-length
blond hair, pulled back with a headband. Blue eyes. Listed
as five-one, one hundred five pounds. *I know I've seen you
before. But, where?*

I set the driver's license aside and reviewed the other
loan documents. Though the license indicated 'Courtney'
lived in Cicero, the credit application listed her home
address as being on Armitage Avenue in Chicago. *That's
it! Courtney looks very much like the girl who Emma was watching*

at the psychic shop on Armitage. Could she be Barbara? I stared again at the photograph but couldn't be sure.

I could have called Dominic to have him email me a copy of the surveillance photo Emma had taken, but my ego wouldn't allow that. I had no desire to talk with him, especially if I had to mention Emma.

Put aside your personal issues—you're working on a criminal case, for God's sake. You can text him.

I picked up my iPhone, intending to compose and send the message, but noticed I had six pending games of *Words. Work can wait for a few minutes.*

While I struggled to think of a word to play with X, C, J, I, and three Os, it finally came to me: A booking photo had to have been taken when Barbara was arrested at the pawn shop.

I dialed Matt. He picked up on the first ring. "Hey, Caroline."

"I hate to bother you on a Saturday, but I'm studying the Bobby Marks' case and I hope you can help."

"You're not bothering me. I just dropped my niece off at her dorm in Madison and was getting ready to head back to Janesville. Are you at your office? I could swing by."

"No, I'm at home. Would you mind coming here?"

"Not at all."

By the time he arrived fifteen minutes later, I'd eaten an energy bar, changed from my running clothes to clean jeans and a cotton sweater, brushed my teeth, and applied blush and mascara. Matt arrived wearing khaki shorts and a faded Los Pollos Hermanos T-shirt. I'd always intended to buy David one of those shirts when we became fans of *Breaking Bad* but had never gotten to it.

"Love the shirt," I said.

He looked down as though he'd forgotten what he was wearing. "Oh, yeah. One of my favorite TV series, ever."

"Me too, though I never got to see the end... Want a beer?" I asked, leading him into the dining room.

He glanced at the iced-tea glass on the table. "Are you having a beer?"

"Nope—I'm still suffering the effects of yesterday's indulgences. But I'm happy to get you one. Pabst or Spotted Cow?"

"Pabst, please." He took the chair Abby'd sat in earlier and looked up quizzically when I returned with a frosted mug of beer and a bowl of pretzels.

I handed them to him. "If you're working on Saturday, you deserve a real mug and a snack."

He nodded in appreciation and took a sip, then wiped the foam from his mustache. "Tell me what I can do to help."

"You used to be a Chicago cop, right?"

"Uh-huh."

"Do you still have any contacts with the department?"

"A few, though it's been ten years since I moved to Janesville."

"Well... with a name and a booking photo from the Chicago PD, we may be able to identify 'Courtney Parks,' the woman who bought the BMW with Bobby Marks in Wausau."

"I'm listening."

"This is one of those 'small world' stories: My ex-boyfriend's mother, who lives in Chicago, got conned by a psychic scam artist named Barbara, who convinced her to hand over a valuable diamond ring—in order to have a curse lifted. My ex hired a P.I. who got some pretty good pictures of Barbara, and they showed 'em to me at the time." I paused to show Matt the photocopy of the driver's license. "When I looked at this Courtney Parks D/L pic today, I knew I'd seen her somewhere before. It took me awhile to figure out where, but I finally remembered. I'm almost sure Courtney and Barbara are one in the same."

"You said there's a booking photo. Has this so-called psychic been arrested?"

"Uh-huh. The P.I. located the ring at a pawn shop, and they managed to have Barbara arrested when she went to get it out of hock."

"Sounds like some good investigative work."

I chose not to comment, and, thankfully, Matt dropped it. He pulled out his cell phone. "I've got a friend in the records department. If he's working today, he can easily email me the mug shot. What's her last name?"

I couldn't bring myself to look him in the eye. "That's the thing: I wasn't told and never asked."

He popped a pretzel into his mouth and washed it down with a swig of beer. "And I'm guessing since you said he's your 'ex,' that you're not comfortable asking him now?"

"Good detecting, Detective Witte."

He grinned. "Do you know the approximate date of arrest?"

"Whew—that's an easy question. She got popped two days ago. On the eleventh."

If he wondered about the chronology of the arrest and the breakup, he kept it to himself. "Now we're getting somewhere," he said, with a hint of sarcasm. "How many people named Barbara could've been arrested in Chicago that day?"

I shook my head with chagrin. "I have no idea. Maybe a hundred? But we can narrow it down to white women who were charged with possession of stolen property or something along those lines."

"Worth a shot. Let's hope my friend's working and it's a slow crime day in the Windy City."

I went to the kitchen to get him another beer and heard the tail end of the conversation when I came back. "…I understand. Whatever you can. I owe 'ya, buddy."

"Not too promising, huh?" I asked, when he disconnected.

He nodded his thanks for the refilled mug. "No, it's not that. He's in the middle of something else right now, and it might be an hour before he can get back with the list of names that fit our criteria."

I glanced at my watch: 12:45. "An hour's not so bad in the scheme of things."

"Not when there's cold beer available." He took another sip and leaned back against the chair, then inexplicably flushed. "I'm sorry… You probably have other plans for the afternoon and don't need me hanging around. I can call or text you when my friend gets back to me."

"Good heavens, Matt," I said, gesturing to the cluttered table. "You're looking at what I'd intended to do today. My dad's in town from St. Cloud and he took the three little kids on an adventure in Milwaukee. My oldest daughter's out doing some volunteer work. And I'm playing catch-up on this case 'cause I took yesterday afternoon off to get drunk."

He looked surprised at my candor. "If you're sure…"

"I'm sure."

I picked up a stack of pages and handed Matt another one. "I've skimmed these before but now I'm reading for detail. If you don't mind, look at these loan applications and see if anything jumps out at you."

"Look at this," he said, a short time later. "It's a photocopy of Marcia Baxter's driver's license. Remember, it'd been stolen from her and used by Bobby's partner when they bought the Escalade in Eau Claire."

I glanced at the grainy copy. "The picture's pretty useless—I couldn't identify her by it if she walked into this room."

"Yeah, but the physical characteristics are virtually identical to those of 'Courtney Parks.' I'm guessing Bobby had the same woman with him in Eau Claire as he did in Wausau."

"It makes sense," I said.

We studied the documents for about twenty more minutes, commenting now and then about the dearth of new clues, but my mind kept wandering and I must've checked my watch fifty times. Every time I glanced at Matt, he seemed intent on his reading. I noticed his hair had grown to a quarter-inch stubble, reminding me of Luke when we'd had to buzz his head to cut out a wad of bubble gum, and reminding me of the tantrum he'd thrown, and how Abby'd been able to calm him down with the promise of a chocolate-chip cookie.

Finally, I popped up from my chair. "I can't sit here anymore. And I've been rude—not offering you lunch. How 'bout a turkey sandwich?"

He looked up, apparently surprised by my impatience. "That sounds good. And I'd take a glass of that tea."

Relieved to be moving, I conjured up a decent-looking lunch: deli turkey and Swiss cheese sandwiches on thick wheat bread from Greenbush Bakery, complete with dill pickle spears on the side. I rummaged through the cupboard to find an unopened bag of Ruffles, sliced an apple and put it on a plate with a dollop of caramel dip, and cut a fresh lemon to garnish our iced tea. I found clean placemats and cloth napkins in a kitchen drawer and called it done.

When I returned to the dining room, I found Matt standing in front of the bookcase looking at the family portrait taken a few months before David died. I recalled when I'd once asked Matt if he had children, he'd said, somewhat wistfully I thought, that he and his wife had split up "before we ever had that conversation." He turned to me. "What beautiful kids. I thought you said you had four, though."

"We… I do. But Red—her real name's Lucy—was born after my husband died."

"The kids are pretty talented, too," he said, gesturing to the clay art projects that cluttered the shelf. "And I see you've got my favorite game."

"Which one?" I asked, glancing at the stack of board games. "*Candy Land?*"

He laughed. "*Battleship!* My brother and I loved it."

I nodded with a tinge of sadness. "Lily and her dad had epic battles; they'd let me play the winner once in a while."

"Maybe we can play after lunch?"

"That'd be great. I am *so* done with reading discovery materials." I grabbed the well-worn cardboard game box, its corners repaired with Scotch tape, and headed for the kitchen.

When Matt's phone rang in the middle of our third game—I'd just sunk his battleship and had honed in on his submarine—I was surprised to see by the kitchen clock that it was 2:30.

He fished his phone from his pocket and answered. "Hey—don't worry about it. I know how things go," he said. "Four, huh? Can you email 'em to the AUSA? I'll give you the address."

I recited the address as we headed for my laptop in the dining room. Matt stayed on the phone while we waited for the message to reach my inbox. "Did they run 'em through AFIS already? Great, send us her RAP sheet, too. Thanks, man."

With Matt hovering behind me, I clicked on "download all attachments" and held my breath as I pulled up the first picture: Barbara Stanislovski, a heavyset woman who looked nothing like the psychic. "Nope." My heart sank as I viewed the second Barbara, who had multiple facial piercings, a tattoo on her neck, and spikey black hair. "Shit."

Matt patted my back. "Still two to go."

I cautiously clicked on the third attachment, steeling myself for further disappointment. Mug shots are never flattering, but this one was particularly unflattering. It depicted a pale young woman with a blotchy complexion and unkempt hair. "I don't know," I said.

"It's her. Look at that little scar on her chin," he said, with glee. "Hello, UNSUB 2!"

"Who's UNSUB 2?" I turned around and saw Lily standing in the doorway, an amused look on her face.

I grinned at her. "It means 'unidentified subject number two.' Det. Witte and I just identified her. Lily, this is Matt Witte. Matt, my daughter Lily."

He extended his hand. "Pleased to meet you, Lily."

"You, too," she said, with a smile.

"How'd it go at the apple orchard today?" I asked.

"Great. I'll tell you about it later, though. I'm gonna get a snack—I'm starved."

"Okay, honey." I turned back to the computer and scrolled down the open page to find the identifying data Matt's friend had listed. "Look at this—her name's Barbara *Marks.*"

"Marks? Maybe she's related to Sonia and Bobby?"

"She sure doesn't look like either of them."

"Maybe Bobby's wife?"

My inbox signaled another message from the Chicago PD. I opened it and we both read: "AFIS checks are back on all four subjects, and I've listed their assigned FBI#'s. Barbara Stanislovski is the only one with any priors; RAP sheet attached."

"Too bad our Barbara doesn't have a record," I said. "And we still have to get the car dealer to ID her."

"Jimmy McGee and I'll run up to Wausau and Eau Claire on Monday with a photo spread."

I hesitated.

"I know it's risky," Matt said. "But I interviewed the salesmen once already. The Wausau guy, in particular, seemed sharp and observant. Good chance he'll recognize her. And remember, we've got some good latent prints from the BMW that didn't match Bobby Marks'. I'll have them run against Barbara Marks' fingerprint card. I'm betting there'll be a match."

"Okay."

"Now, let's go finish that game."

Lily, Matt, and I spent the rest of the afternoon playing *Battleship*, the loser of each game sitting out the next but serving as the challenger's cheerleader and chief kibitzer. I hadn't laughed so much in weeks, nor had Lily.

We heard Luke's footsteps running through the foyer a nanosecond after the front door opened. "We're home!" he yelled, bounding into the kitchen and hugging me.

"Did you have a good time?"

"Uh-huh." He swiped at his runny nose with the back of his hand, then looked at Matt. "Are you Mom's new boyfriend?"

I felt a wave of embarrassment, but Matt didn't miss a beat. "No. I work with your mom—and we're friends, too."

Apparently satisfied, Luke returned to report our whereabouts to my dad and his sisters. "That wasn't too awkward," Lily said, with a grin, as she made one last move to destroy Matt's battleship. "I win!"

Matt dramatically wiped his brow and got up from the table. "Good game. Clearly, I'm no match for two scheming women."

"Why don't you stay for dinner?" Lily asked. "Grandpa always gets way too much Chinese food."

"Thanks, but I promised my sister I'd have dinner with her. Rain check?"

Like mother-daughter bobblehead dolls, Lily and I both nodded—though not precisely in sync.

Later that evening, I read my after-dinner fortune cookie aloud: "Look no further, for happiness is right in front of you." Lily winked at me.

Chapter Twenty-nine

Running errands in slow-moving traffic on Johnson Street the next afternoon, I noticed a one-story house with a wooden Psychic Reader sign in the yard and a neon OPEN sign flashing in a front window. *Weird. I never noticed this place before.*

Curious, I turned at the next intersection and came around the block to look again. The sign also read Walkin's Welcome. *Maybe I should send the grammar police to make them fix their stupid sign?*

On my third pass, I realized I wanted to go in. The stars were clearly aligned: Dad had taken the littles to see *Dolphin Tale 2*, I had an hour before picking Lily up from a volleyball clinic on the UW campus and taking her to the grief support group, and I'd just withdrawn $200 from the ATM for incidental expenses. *I'm doing this strictly for research purposes,* I told myself. *I won't give them any clues about myself, and I'll see what kind of BS they come up with.*

I parked around the corner—so the "psychic" couldn't run a check on my license plate—and left my phone and purse in the car. My heartbeat raced as I walked up the creaky, faded gray front steps. *There's nothing to be nervous about. It's a scam but not dangerous. They're not gonna kidnap you or anything.*

I pushed the doorbell but didn't hear a chime, so knocked and waited a few moments. No response. *Shut off your frickin' OPEN sign if you're not here!* Just as I turned to head back down the steps, the front door swung inward. "Can I help you?" a heavyset young woman asked.

"Uh… yes. I was wondering if someone could do a reading."

"Certainly. Come in."

The woman, wearing a floor-length purple skirt, a revealing black shirt, and at least fifteen silver bracelets, held the door open. A tortoise-shell hair clip confined most of her long, black hair to a messy topknot, though several wavy strands meandered down her back. I followed her silently into the dimly-lit house, that smelled faintly of sandalwood incense. *Could this be any more stereotypical?*

She led me to the reading room. Burgundy curtains covered all the windows, and two ornately-carved chairs sat on either side of a table, draped in a blue cloth. A large crystal ball sat in the middle of the table. An altar-like set-up against one wall bore several lighted candles, crystals, and elaborate wooden carvings of the moon and stars.

"My name is Katya, and I'll be your reader today. The charge is $50, cash or credit card. A typical session lasts twenty to forty minutes, depending on what you want to know. Does that sound satisfactory?"

"Yes." I reached into the back pocket of my jeans to take out my cash, feeling vulnerable as I shuffled through several bills to locate two twenties and a ten. *She's not gonna rob me, is she? Maybe I should've told someone I was coming in. Should I say I've changed my mind and leave? Stop it—you're being silly!* I handed her the money, and she slipped it into the pocket of her skirt.

"You can hang your jacket over there," she said, gesturing toward a bentwood coat tree. Though hesitant to shed any layers, the stuffy room left me little choice.

She motioned toward one of the chairs and sat down opposite me. "Take a few deep breaths. Then tell me your name."

Had she noticed I'd been holding my breath since I walked in? I did as instructed. "I'm Jane."

"Pleased to meet you, Jane," Katya said, with no hint of suspicion. "I usually have the best results with a crystal ball, but if you'd prefer a Tarot or palm reading, I'm skilled at those, as well."

"The crystal ball is fine."

"All right. Rest your hands lightly on the ball with all your fingers touching it, close your eyes, and let's see what I can see."

My palms and fingertips were clammy with sweat; I worried they might slide off. And it took every ounce of will to keep my eyes closed. After what felt like an hour but was probably only a few minutes, Katya spoke quietly. "Open your eyes slowly and place your hands on the table."

I opened my eyes. Katya was gazing at me with a peaceful look on her face, as though she'd been transported from some other idyllic world. "You have a very strong and positive aura. I'll tell you what I'm seeing, and you let me know if it makes sense. Okay?"

"Um… okay."

"First of all, though I see you surrounded by many people, you often feel very alone. Does that ring true?"

I nodded. *That's probably true of everyone.*

"You're often pulled in several directions, sometimes frustratingly so."

"Uh-huh." *Also, true for everyone.*

"I see that you've experienced a catastrophic loss—a loss more difficult than most people are forced to contend with. I can't tell exactly how long ago it was, but it still affects you virtually every day."

I felt a shiver run down my spine. *That's spot on, but how could she know? Everyone doesn't suffer losses like mine.*

"Was it your spouse?"

I hung my head. "Uh-huh."

"You loved him very much, and now you wonder if you'll ever find happiness with someone else."

I nodded and swallowed the lump in my throat.

"I can tell you that you will, and it will happen sooner than you might expect. I see a man, close to your age." Katya closed her eyes and raised her head toward the ceiling, then opened her eyes and looked at me again. "Please put your hands back on the ball," she said, with some urgency.

My hands trembled as I did so. I closed my eyes, trying to picture myself in a happy relationship with someone whose face I couldn't see.

After a few minutes, she spoke again, more calmly this time. "Look at me, Jane. You don't need to be afraid."

It took me a moment to remember I'd called myself Jane. I met her gaze, though my eyes stung with tears.

"At first I saw just one man, but it was murky. That's why I had you put your hands back on the ball. Now I clearly see *two* men in your life. Although I can't make out their features, I sense one may be darker than the other. Maybe it's his aura, or maybe his coloring."

"Uh… his coloring," I stuttered.

"And you can't stop thinking about him."

"That's right."

"He loves you, but he may not be good for you." Then, shaking her head ruefully, "I can't tell which man you'll choose, but I definitely see happiness for you."

I didn't know what to say.

"Are there other areas in your life you'd like to ask about? Your children, perhaps?"

She knows I have children? I took another deep breath and my skepticism returned. *Well, that could've been a lucky guess. And she can't know how many or whether they're boys or girls.* "Uh… yeah, I guess so. My oldest has been going through a bad time. Will things turn out okay?"

"She'll be fine. Just be patient."

She said she'll *be fine. How could she know my oldest is a girl?*

"The younger ones will be fine, too," Katya said, "though they'll have their ups and downs. They're all smart and active and spirited. I see them all living long, healthy lives."

This woman's for real. She knows I've got at least three kids. I remained silent, questions racing through my head.

"Is there anything else you'd like to ask about?" she asked quietly.

I shook my head.

"Well, as I said, you have a strong and positive aura. We could easily do more work on areas of concern—perhaps help you achieve some clarity in your decision making."

She handed me a business card. "Call if you'd like to set up further appointments."

"Thank you, I will," I said, getting shakily to my feet and reaching for my jacket.

I followed Katya to the front door, where she took me off guard by engulfing me in a hug. "God bless you, Jane."

I zipped up my jacket, hugged my arms to my body against the wind, and walked to my car, puzzling over the experience. Then, reaching for my keys, I realized the key fob—a two-inch, clear plastic frame displaying a photograph of my four kids—had been sticking out of the pocket. Had Katya seen it? Of course, she had. I'd been taken for a fool. And for fifty bucks.

Fuming, I sat in the car replaying the "reading" in my head. *How could you let yourself get sucked in like that? She knows most of the people who come to her are lonely and hurting; she played you just like she plays the most vulnerable. Sure, she put you on a roller coaster of emotions, but you willingly gave her the ticket. "The darker one loves you, but he may not be good for you." What a load of hooey! What an idiotic waste of money, time, and energy.*

How to break the tirade of deprecating self-talk that threatened to wreck my afternoon? Text Glenda.

"U won't believe what I just did," I typed. "Went for psychic reading. So stereotypical, but hate to say I fell for it. Can't wait to tell u about it."

Her reply came within seconds, "Txt me when kids go to bed."

"Dad's still here. Tomorrow nite okay?"
"Yep. CU then."

I took a circuitous route through the university campus, regaining my equilibrium, and arrived at the Natatorium just as Lily came straggling out the door. She wiped her brow with the hem of her sweatshirt, slung her gym bag onto one shoulder, and got into the car with what looked like trepidation.

"Hey, kiddo. How was the clinic?"

She slammed the door and buckled the seat belt with a loud snap. "Hard."

"How so?"

She sighed, as though giving an explanation constituted torture. "The drills were much tougher than we expected and the coaches didn't, like, even let us stop to breathe. My arms are gonna be black and blue from trying to return their killer serves."

I gave her a sidelong glance. "Did you learn anything new?"

She leaned back and put her feet on the dashboard. "I guess a couple things. But I'm really beat and I didn't have time to shower. I don't wanna go to this dumb group meeting all stinky and skanky looking."

"Believe me, you don't stink. Plus, you couldn't look skanky if you tried."

"Whatever. I don't want to go."

I didn't reply.

"Can't I wait 'til next week to start this group?"

"No. You promised Dr. Grube you'd give it a try, and I already confirmed you'd be there today."

"You were drunk during the appointment, remember? He *never* said I needed to start right away."

I gripped the steering wheel so tightly my fingertips went numb. I had no idea how to respond; I simply kept driving.

When we pulled into the parking lot behind the church where the meeting would be held, I turned off the ignition. I knew I should accompany Lily into the building and introduce myself to the counselor, but I couldn't move. Lily didn't move, either; she simply sat staring out the front windshield.

I startled at a knock on my window. A petite, Hispanic woman about my age stood beside the car, smiling and motioning for me to roll down the window.

"You must be Caroline Spencer," she said, extending her hand, as I exited the car. "I'm Larry Grube's colleague, Juanita Quintana." I nodded mutely and shook her hand.

"Lily?" she asked, nodding toward the passenger seat.

"Uh-huh."

"I sense you're in the middle of a tense moment. Why don't I introduce myself to her and take her in? We try to keep the meetings to an hour. Some parents like to wait in the lounge—they enjoy chatting—but if you're not up to that, you can meet Lily back here around 4:00. Okay?"

"Uh-huh," I mumbled. "Thank you."

I watched while this pleasantly-assertive woman opened Lily's door, leaned in, and spoke to her in hushed tones. Moments later, Lily got out of the car, gave me a small wave, and walked in to her first support group meeting.

I got back in the driver's seat and sat there in a catatonic funk, acknowledging none of the people coming and going from the church, 'til Lily returned.

"Sorry for being so mean, Mom," Lily said, sliding into her seat and leaning over to kiss my cheek.

I did a double take. Had she been overcome by an angelic spirit? "How was it?"

"Actually, okay. Juanita is great, and the other kids were pretty cool. I didn't talk—I mean, I hadda tell 'em my name and how long ago Dad died—but Juanita said listening was just fine."

"So you'll go back?"

"Yeah."

CHAPTER THIRTY

I found my dad in the kitchen at 6:30 Monday morning, conjuring up one last pancake and bacon breakfast; he planned to hit the road after dropping the kids at school. Though Abby'd returned the previous evening, relaxed and upbeat after a weekend with Bert, I dreaded Dad's departure.

"Sure you don't want to stay a few more days?" I asked, as he handed me coffee in a mug bearing a faded photograph of seven-year-old Lily smiling to show off the loss of her first tooth.

"I'd love to, kiddo, but your mom's been bugging me to repaint the guest bathroom before her friend comes to visit next weekend."

I felt myself tearing up. "I hope you know how much I appreciate your help. I couldn't have navigated last week's landmines without you."

"Happy to help," he said, turning quickly to the stove to check the pancakes. I realized leaving would be hard for him, too.

"Thing is," I said, reaching into the cupboard for a to-go cup, "I'm gonna need to take this coffee and run. I promised Lauren we'd meet for breakfast before work."

"No problem," he said over his shoulder, spatula in hand. "I'm sure Luke'll be happy to eat your share."

"I need a hug first, though."

He put down the spatula and gave me a quick bear hug. "Love you, kiddo."

"You too," I snuffled and headed for the door. "Drive safely and text me when you get home."

I didn't have a breakfast date with Lauren—simply a strong desire to avoid a tearful farewell with my father. Instead, I swung by Greenbush Bakery on my way to work. Tantalized by the smell of fresh-baked goods, I ordered six apple fritters and a dozen donuts in various flavors—nothing soothes sadness like fried, sugary dough. The tape on the white bakery box didn't remain intact for even a block; I had half a glazed maple donut to tide me over 'til the main event.

"Throw that bagel in the wastebasket," I said to George Cooper ten minutes later, juggling the bakery box, my briefcase, and my coffee mug.

He grinned and sniffed the air. "Gladly! Greenbush apple fritters?"

"Yep."

He slid a stack of files aside to make room for the box and my coffee. I fished a stack of paper napkins from my briefcase. "To what do I owe the pleasure?" he asked.

"There's something I need to run by you before the day gets away. Mind if I sit?"

He gestured toward his sofa and club chairs. "Of course not, but let's be comfortable."

We settled in, me on the couch and George in his favorite chair, and savored the first bites of our fritters.

"What'd you want to talk about?"

I swallowed, then replied, "The Marks case. You remember Bobby's mother, Sonia, was his accomplice in one of the car deals?" George nodded. "Well, Matt Witte and I think we've figured out the identity of the other one. Matt and Jimmy McGee are going Up North today to show the car salesmen a photo spread, but we're pretty sure it's a con woman named Barbara Marks who works out of a storefront psychic shop in Chicago. Another woman named Sonia works there, too—I'm guessing her full name is Sonia Marks."

"So Barbara may be related to your two defendants?"

"Could be." I shifted nervously in my seat before continuing. "The thing I needed to let you know, though, is that I knew of Barbara through my ex-boyfriend."

George motioned for me to go on, and I repeated the story I'd told to Matt on Saturday. "As far as I can tell, my ex's mother isn't a victim in the scheme we're prosecuting," I concluded. "But do you think it'd be a conflict for me to continue with the case?"

He nibbled on the edge of his fritter while he considered my question. "Do you envision having any future contact with Mrs. Marquez?" he finally asked.

By that, I guess you mean, "Are you likely to get back together with her son?" I shook my head, trying to mask my jumbled emotions. "I don't think that's in the Tarot cards."

He laughed. "And Barbara Marks is being charged in Cook County, not federal court for theft of the ring, right?"

"Right."

"Run it by the prosecutor there, and if he or she doesn't see any connection to our case, I think you should stay on it."

I stood up and brushed crumbs from my slacks. "I was hoping you'd say that—I've already put quite a bit of work into it."

"Keep me posted. And thanks for the fritter."

"Want another before I put this box in the break room?"

He shook his head. "Better not."

Matt called early that afternoon: The car salesman in Wausau had picked Barbara Marks out of a photo lineup, identifying her as the individual who'd purchased the BMW. "He didn't miss a beat," Matt said, and I could hear the grin in his voice. "Said he was 100 percent sure."

"That's great."

"The guy at the Eau Claire dealership picked Barbara out, too, though he hesitated initially. I'm not sure he'll be a great witness if the case goes to trial, but his ID is enough for probable cause."

"The grand jury meets again a week from Thursday—can you be there to testify?"

"Just name the time."

"I'll get back to you." *I sure hope the state's attorney in Chicago doesn't give me a reason to pass this case off.*

I stood up, stretched, and dialed the number the clerk of court had given me for Barbara Marks' prosecutor, fully expecting voicemail.

The attorney answered on the first ring. "Jeffrey Gullickson," came the gruff voice.

"This is Caroline Spencer, an AUSA in Madison, Wisconsin," I said. "I'm calling about a woman you're prosecuting named Barbara Marks—"

"Lemme guess," he interrupted, "you want me to up the charges to grand theft or fraud or something."

"Uh… no."

"I've already had more phone calls about this case than most I've prosecuted in the past five years… the detective, some bimbo P.I.…."—I felt ashamed, but couldn't help smiling at this—"The victim's son and daughter… and now you. The victim willingly gave up the diamond ring, for chrissake."

"I'm not trying to get you to modify your charge. I'm calling to see if there's a connection between your case and one we're planning to bring against her here."

"Sorry. Tell me whatcha got."

I told him—leaving out my personal involvement with Alejandra Marquez and her family.

"Nah—I don't see any connection," he said, when I'd finished.

"Your court docket indicates Marks is set for arraignment at 9:00 a.m. on the thirtieth. Assuming our grand jury indicts her, I plan to have U.S. Marshals in the courtroom to arrest her after that appearance."

"Fine by me."

"I'd appreciate a heads-up if your schedule changes." I repeated my name and gave him my number.

"Will do."

Recognizing his response as a probable lie, I fervently hoped the schedule didn't change.

Jimmy McGee called at 3:30. "The lab got back about the prints," he said, without preamble.

Annoyed by the interruption—I'd just decided how to reword a paragraph in the brief I was writing and lost my train of thought when the phone rang—I replied a bit too sharply, "What prints?"

He sighed audibly. "The latents in the Beamer the Markses bought in Wausau."

"Oh, yeah. What'd the lab say?"

"I faxed my friend there a copy of Barbara Marks' print card this morning and asked him to expedite. Three of the latent fingerprints found in the car belonged to her."

Despite my irritation at Jimmy, this *was* good news. "Thanks for asking the lab to rush it. I'll need you to testify at the grand jury on the twenty-fifth, okay?"

"Aye-aye," he said, and hung up.

I finished the brief and stood up, again, to stretch. Only one item remained on the day's to-do list: call Dr. Brownhill. It'd been three days since I'd gone to the appointment with Dr. Grube in an impaired state. I looked back on my drunken meltdown with shame and embarrassment but didn't feel a pressing need for counseling. *You promised him you'd go see her, though.*

I dialed the number and spoke with the Dr. Brownhill's receptionist, Debra. "I'm sorry, Caroline. She's on vacation until the first of October and booked solid that whole month. Do you need to see someone more quickly? I'd be happy to refer you to one of Clarice's associates."

The thought of getting to know another psychologist made me queasy. "Just give me the first available appointment and put me on the cancelation list in case something opens up sooner."

She gave me a date in November. "Let me know if things change and you want that referral."

Chapter Thirty-One

When I called Matt to tell him his grand jury testimony was scheduled for 4:00 on September 25, he replied, "Uh… yeah, that's fine. Hey, would you like to have a drink afterward?"

My stomach did a quick flip-flop as I glanced at my calendar. "I'd like to, but Lily's got a band concert at 7:00, and we have a longstanding tradition of eating a family dinner at Ella's Deli beforehand."

"How 'bout if I tag along? If it wouldn't be an intrusion."

I thought about the fun Lily'd had playing *Battleship* and how she'd invited him to stay for dinner that night. "We'd enjoy your company," I finally said, pleased that he'd persisted in his desire to see me socially.

So it was that I found myself wedged between Matt and Lily at a table for eight in the over-the-top, iconic deli on Madison's east side. Abby and Bert flanked Red, seated in a booster chair. Her head threatened to swivel off her neck, as her eyes followed every animated toy flying overhead or racing around the room. The twins, old hands at Ella's, stared not at the bric-a-brac but at the monster ice cream sundaes the waiter delivered to the table beside us. The cacophony of kids' voices, clanking silverware, and moving toys made adult conversation next to impossible. "Glad you came?" I asked Matt.

He grinned. "Can you think of a better way to celebrate Barbara Marks' indictment?"

I laughed. "As a matter of fact, I can. But I appreciate you being a good sport. Have you ever eaten here?"

"Just ice cream with my niece and nephew."

"The food's great. I'm ordering a corned-beef Reuben. I'll take half home for lunch tomorrow."

"I'll split it with you if you want," he said. "That way, I'll have room for dessert."

I felt touched by his offer to share a sandwich—an almost intimate gesture. Hours earlier, sitting alone in my office, I'd lamented that two weeks had passed since I'd broken up with Dominic. "Excellent idea," I replied. After dinner, we shared an old-fashioned banana split.

Matt and I left to get Lily to school on time for her pre-concert prep, leaving oversight of the littles' carousel riding to Abby and Bert. We reserved half of the front row for our group, who straggled in with sticky fingers and ketchup-stained clothes, just as the concert was about to begin. *School concerts can be as cacophonous as Ella's Deli*, I reflected, as I listened to the high-pitched tones of clarinets and flutes warming up, percussion instruments being fiddled with, chairs scraping, and the general chatter of folks settling into seats.

Like my three youngest kids, I squirmed in my chair. Unlike them, I anticipated the program with dread. Lily had a seven-bar solo, and she was no Benny Goodman. I sighed in relief when, during the program's second piece, she hit every note in her solo with confidence.

Matt said his goodbyes in the parking lot afterward. He gave Lily a high-five and congratulated her on her "outstanding performance." I lingered outside the minivan while my family crawled in. "Thanks for coming," I told him.

"Thanks for asking me. It was fun." He looked down at his feet.

Wanting to ease his discomfort, I leaned toward him and gave him a quick hug. "We'll do something less kid-oriented next time."

I got behind the wheel. "You said he's not your boyfriend," Luke piped up. "But you hugged him."

I watched in the rearview mirror as Amy punched Luke in the arm. "Friends can hug," she said.

"No hitting, Amy. And she's right, Luke. Friends *can* hug."

CHAPTER THIRTY-TWO

I wasn't entirely surprised that Dominic's number popped up on my caller ID on the morning of September 30, the date of Barbara Marks' arraignment in Cook County Circuit Court. We hadn't spoken since that disastrous day at Sardine, and I'd ignored his message about remaining friends. I considered letting the call go to voicemail, but knew I'd have to deal with him sooner or later.

"Caroline Spencer," I said.

"Hello, Caroline," he said, in an all-business tone but without identifying himself. "I went to court for Barbara Marks' arraignment and have questions about what happened afterward."

"Oh?"

"Two deputy U.S. Marshals took her into custody. I couldn't help overhearing that she was being arrested on a warrant out of Madison. Did you know about that?"

"Dominic, I'm going to have to put you on hold while I find out what's going on."

"Call me back as soon as you can," he said, and hung up.

I hadn't heard of Barbara's arrest, and the indictment was still sealed—meaning its existence wasn't public information. I called the U.S. Marshal's Madison office. "Yep," the deputy told me, "they picked her up around 10:30 and booked her into the Metropolitan Correctional Center. Her initial appearance will probably be later this afternoon."

My typical response would have been to return Dominic's call as soon as I had that information, but my anger reared its ugly head. I wrote "Call Dom" several lines down on my to-do list—right after "Renew Library Books." When I finally did call him back, I didn't apologize for the delay.

"The grand jury here returned an indictment against Barbara Marks last week," I told him. "She's charged, along with her brother-in-law, with two counts of bank fraud. They bought luxury vehicles on credit, using stolen identities."

"Are you the prosecutor?"

"Uh-huh."

His tone became twenty degrees colder. "Why didn't you tell me? You had to know I'd be interested."

"The indictment and arrest warrant were sealed. I couldn't talk with you about it until the court clerk unsealed them."

"Even though I called and *told* you she'd been arrested?" he asked, peevishly.

"Even then."

I heard him sigh. "What happens to her now?"

"She's being held at the MCC—the federal jail—in downtown Chicago. She'll appear before a magistrate judge later today or early tomorrow. She could be detained and brought here in custody, or she could be released and given a date to appear voluntarily. Depends on the judge." I didn't tell him I'd recommended detention, though surely that would've made him happier.

"How do I find out the time of her appearance?"

What about this case has got you so flummoxed? You're a P.I., for God's sake. Figure it out. Or ask your new girlfriend to figure it out. But I bit my tongue and gave him the phone number for the Northern District of Illinois' court clerk.

Dominic texted me at 2:00 that afternoon, right after Barbara's appearance: "The magistrate detained her temporarily and said she would have a detention hearing when she gets to Madison. When will that be?"

I waited an hour before replying, "Look on Pacer.gov."

Barbara Marks would be transported to Madison whenever the U.S. Marshals Service could arrange it, depending on their workload and priorities. It could take days for the 120-mile trip to be arranged. I didn't feel compelled to ask them to rush it.

But, as it happened, Barbara and the deputies were already headed to Madison.

In my office the next morning, I flipped over—to October—the wall calendar Lily had given me the previous Christmas. She'd chosen twelve of my favorite pictures and had the spiral-bound calendar printed at Walgreens. David had taken the October photograph three years ago, of Lily and the twins in their Halloween costumes. Lily dressed as Dorothy from the *Wizard of Oz*, beaming but standing precariously in red, high-heeled shoes. Amy grinning in her yellow M&M costume while her brother squirmed beside her in red, my hand firmly on his arm. I swallowed the lump in my throat, determined to have a good day.

My phone rang a moment later; it was our court clerk's office. "The marshals brought Barbara Marks up from Chicago last night, and we need to schedule her arraignment," the clerk said. "Jason Bittner's representing her, and the only time he's free is 10:30."

"Ten-thirty's fine," I told the clerk. *Yippee! Even if Dominic finds out about the hearing, no way will he be able to get here by then.*

Walking back to my office building after Barbara's arraignment later that morning, Matt seemed unaccountably anxious. I couldn't imagine why; the hearing had gone smoothly. "Are you, uh, by any chance free for dinner and a movie Friday night?" he asked, when we reached the front door. "If you're not able to get a sitter on such short notice, I'd completely understand, and we could, uh, make it another time."

"Hold on a sec' while I ask my mother-in-law," I said, and stopped on the sidewalk to make the call. As is often the case, Abby wanted to chat, and the conversation that should've taken a minute dragged on for three or four. Matt stood uncomfortably by while I finished. "She says it's fine." I tried not to grin at the relief on his face.

"Great. How 'bout I pick you up at 6:00?"

"Perfect," I said, "See you then."

I rode the elevator up alone, enjoying the flutter of excitement I felt in my stomach.

Roxanne glanced up from her keyboard when I walked past. "George wants to see you right away. Said he tried your cell but you must've had it off for court."

"Did he say what about?"

"Uh-uh. Just to tell you to come ASAP."

I dropped my briefcase on the desk and headed down the hallway, the flutter of excitement replaced by a wave of heartburn. George wasn't usually an ASAP kind of guy.

I found him at his desk, bent over an egg-salad sandwich. He chewed a large bite and beckoned me in.

"What's up?" I said, as nonchalantly as possible as I settled into one of the straight-backed visitor's chairs.

He paused to swallow and take a sip of Diet Coke. "Listen to this voice message," he said, pushing the speaker button on his phone. I couldn't read his facial expression.

"Mr. Cooper, my name is Domimic Marquez," the message began. "My mother is one of the victims of a defendant your office is prosecuting, Barbara Marks. I just read the minutes of her arraignment and detention hearing online, and I want to register a complaint. Please call me."

I felt color rising in my cheeks. *Dominic had the audacity to call my boss? What in God's name is wrong with him?*

George turned off the speaker. "I looked at the docket entry. I take it he's upset because you withdrew your motion to detain Ms. Marks. Fill me in so I can return his call." He took another bite of sandwich.

I cleared my throat. "Uh… okay. I moved for detention based on the risk of flight. I told the magistrate Ms. Marks had used two separate, stolen identities to commit the offenses charged in the indictment and argued that she could have access to others, which would make it easier to flee. Also, she admitted to the pretrial services officer that she has no permanent residence, neither in Chicago nor in our district."

I shifted in my chair and tried to relax my grip on the wooden arm. "But then, Jason Bittner told the judge there was space for Barbara to be placed at the halfway house as a condition of release, and Jason made some solid arguments. I could've persisted in my motion for detention, but I knew I'd lose. Anyway, I thought placement at Healthy Horizons was a good idea. Do you disagree?"

He wiped his mouth with a soggy napkin. "Not at all. I just wanted to know the facts before I call. Shall I put him on speaker phone?"

I shook my head. "Hell, no. I don't want anything to do with him. I really resent that he called you."

"Well at least stay and listen to what I tell him." He pushed his half-empty bag of sea-salt-and-vinegar potato chips my way. "And finish these, please. I'm trying to cut down."

The tangy taste and satisfying crunch of chips ratcheted down my emotions. I sat back in the chair and munched while he dialed.

"Mr. Marquez, this is George Cooper. I'm glad you called, because I've wanted an opportunity to thank you. I realize you're the investigator who worked so hard to win the insurance settlement for David Spencer's accident. Caroline is one of our best prosecutors and favorite people, and we all felt pretty helpless when her husband was killed. It was heartening to hear how you put that case together and came through for her and the kids."

Oh, George—you're a master!

"Now, tell me your concerns about this Marks situation."

George listened for about five minutes, commenting occasionally. "I'm sorry to hear that. …How long was she hospitalized? …Yes, I understand how upsetting that must be."

He finally said, in a kind but authoritative voice, "I'm sorry, but under the law your mother isn't a victim of the crimes we're prosecuting. She doesn't have a right to address our court on issues like release or detention. And, though the U.S. Attorney's Office in Chicago isn't under any *obligation* to assist you, I'll give you the number of their victim/witness coordinator who might be able to direct you to some local resources to help your mother. Please hang on a moment while I look for the number." He punched the Hold button and began flipping through a battered notebook.

"Good job," I whispered.

He nodded and returned to the phone. "What the f—? He hung up. Do you think I laid it on too thick?"

"You laid it on just right. What hospitalization was he talking about?"

"He said his mother is bipolar and after this Marks woman was arrested at the pawn shop, Mom, distraught that her trusted advisor was a fraud, went into a period of major depression. He said she was in a psychiatric hospital on suicide watch for three days and they're still trying to get her stabilized on medications. I *am* sorry about that, but you heard me telling him she doesn't have any standing in our case."

"What did he want you to do?"

George shook his head. "He wanted me to tell him how to appeal the order of release. I would've thought someone with his background would know more about the legal system."

"Me, too, but his ability to reason seems to falter where his mom's concerned." I finished the chips, threw the empty bag into his wastebasket, and walked toward the door.

"One more thing, Caroline."

I stopped, certain he was going to pull me from the Marks case. "What's that?" I croaked, turning back.

"I have a hunch we haven't heard the last of Dom Quixote. If this case gets too sticky for you, for whatever reason, don't hesitate to ask me to reassign it to somebody else."

"Thanks, George. But I can handle it."

CHAPTER THIRTY-THREE

I rode the elevator to the basement parking garage on Friday afternoon with my friend and co-worker, Lauren. "Any big plans for the weekend?" she asked.

I found myself grateful for the dim lighting, usually a creepy annoyance. Hopefully it masked the flush moving up my neck. "Well… I'm going on a first date tonight and I'm more than a little nervous."

"Who is he?"

"I'll tell you if it works out," I said, beeping my car door open. "I don't want to jinx it!"

She laughed. "You never struck me as superstitious—but whatever. Have a good time!"

Traffic ground to a halt at the malfunctioning, Regent-and-Monroe-Street traffic signal. I waited, drumming frantically on the steering wheel, for three cycles of lights without getting my turn at a green arrow. The dashboard clock read

5:40. I worried I wouldn't have time to greet my kids, shower, and change before Matt arrived to pick me up.

The heavenly aroma of Abby's Bolognese sauce greeted me when I finally made it home. I found her in the kitchen, pulling lasagna noodles from a steaming pot of water, brow glistening with sweat. "I don't know why I do this; it's so much work," she muttered. "But Bert's been pestering me to make it."

I took a clean dish towel from the rack and dabbed at her forehead. "You know it's worth it; my mouth is watering from the smell."

"You and your friend are welcome to stay and eat with us," she said, with a wink.

I laughed. "It's tempting. I'm kinda skittish about this dating thing. Where're the kids?"

Abby spooned a layer of sauce into the lasagna pan. "The twins took their stuff down to my place—we're having a sleepover tonight—and got waylaid by the new Muppets movie that Bert bought for 'em. Lily's upstairs giving Red a mani-pedi."

"Seems like Bert's a keeper," I said, feeling a tinge of jealousy.

Abby smiled but didn't reply.

"Okay, I'm gonna run upstairs and change."

When she saw me in the doorway, Red, reclining on a towel in Lily's beanbag chair with her feet in a basin of water, could hardly contain her glee. "Look at the color I picked," she said, waving her hand.

I walked in, almost gagging on the cloying scent that hung in the air. "Wow! That is a very sparkly pink. I'm guessing you used some perfume, too?"

Lily nodded and gave me a rueful smile. "I saved my allowance for, like, weeks to buy that little bottle of Juicy Couture. She used half of it before I could stop her."

I kissed them both on their heads. "I'll reimburse you, honey. And thanks for keeping Red occupied while Abby makes dinner."

"No problem. So… you're going out with Matt tonight?"

"Uh-huh."

Concentrating on keeping her sister's hand still while she painted, she didn't look up. "Have fun."

"Thanks."

I headed for my bedroom. I didn't have time for a shower, or for much indecision about what to wear. During the prolonged ride home, I'd settled on black jeans and a geometrically patterned tunic. But now, standing in front of my closet, I felt torn. A sexier top? The pink cashmere sweater David had given me for my birthday, three years ago? *Would you mind, David?*

My ruminations were interrupted by the sound of the doorbell and Abby yelling, "I'll get it." I stuck with Plan A; the tunic would have to do. With a spritz of my own perfume, Dolce and Gabbana's Light Blue, and a swipe of lip gloss, I headed downstairs.

Matt sat at the kitchen table, watching with a bemused expression as Abby slipped a finished pan of lasagna into the oven. The sink overflowed with dirty pans, bowls, and utensils. The counter, stove top, and front of her blouse were speckled with red sauce. She blotted her brow and collapsed onto a chair. "Will you have enough energy left to watch the kids tonight?" Matt asked her, as he stood to greet me. "We could make it another night."

She chuckled, but with less than her usual zing. "Don't be silly. Bert and Lily'll be here to help if I fall asleep at the dinner table."

Matt and I said goodbye to Amy and Luke and set off on our date. But a hint of concern niggled. *Abby's not getting any younger. How long can she keep this up?*

The crowd at the Great Dane in the Hilldale mall was larger and louder than usual, making conversation a challenge. We sat at the bar with a small crowd of patrons standing behind us, jockeying for the stools they hoped we'd soon vacate. "I should've realized the place would be packed," Matt said, after his first sip of beer. He'd ordered the Crop Circle Wheat while I chose the Landmark Lite Lager.

"Yeah, Wisconsinites can't resist a Friday night fish fry," I said, with a grin. "But I never mind eating at the bar."

We chatted about work while waiting for our meals of beer-battered haddock, pub fries, and coleslaw, then ate in companionable silence. It didn't feel awkward when our elbows collided, as is wont to happen in close quarters with a righty and a lefty. And I didn't feel compelled to eat daintily or less than my fill. *This is okay*, I told myself.

We left the restaurant five minutes before movie time at the Sundance Theater across the street. Matt had ordered our tickets online and produced the neatly folded, printed pages from his shirt pocket. "Glad we've got reserved seats. They're center row, halfway up. Even if someone tall sits in front of us, we should be good."

Center row—my worst nightmare. Why in God's name did I have that second beer? Claustrophobic in theaters, stadiums, and airplanes, I always chose seats on the aisle. *Why didn't I mention that to him? It's opening weekend for* Gone Girl*—no chance there'll be any vacant seats.*

I excused myself as we entered the theater. In the restroom, I fished through my purse for the last half of the Xanax Glenda had given me months ago. I swallowed it down with a handful of water from the sink, praying it'd keep my panic at bay, and rejoined Matt. After we'd muttered "excuse me" no less than ten times as we struggled to our seats, I prayed even more fervently that I wouldn't need to exit in a hurry.

The suspenseful movie kept my attention focused on the screen and left the patrons buzzing with comments at the end. "What'd you think?" Matt asked, as we slowly made our way down the aisle.

"I hate it when psychopaths win," I said, flexing the muscles in my hands, which I'd apparently been clenching throughout the film. "And what shitty police work—taking her word that Neil Patrick Harris kidnapped her."

He took my elbow and steered me around a trio of slowpokes. "That's the trouble with being in law enforcement; you can't watch a murder mystery without picking it apart."

Happy to be out in fresh, evening air, I nonetheless shivered with the breeze. Matt put his arm around me. "Up for a nightcap at the Dane?"

I thought for a moment, then shook my head. The day had been long and the movie draining. "I don't think I can handle any more crowds."

Matt deftly drove his Mazda Miata through the back streets to my house and pulled to the curb. Before I could gather my purse, he'd come around to open my door. I grinned.

"You'd better not treat me like this in the office or people will definitely wonder."

He extended his elbow to help me from the low seat. "Which brings up a good question. Is this a secret?"

"I don't see why it should be. But on the other hand, I really don't want Jimmy McGee looking at us funny."

He laughed. "I don't think we need to worry. He doesn't notice us half the time."

On the front porch, I took my hand away from his arm to find my house key. "Want to come in?"

"I'd like to, but I'd better pass. I'm scheduled to be on a surveillance detail at 7:00 a.m." He leaned forward and kissed me, a gentle, two-second kiss, and turned to leave. "Thanks for a nice time," he said, as he walked back toward his car.

A half-hour later, I sat in my living room, alone, listening to Stevie Ray Vaughn playing softly on the stereo. While sipping Bailey's Irish Cream over ice, I recounted the evening. *Nice* was a good way to describe it. I liked and trusted Matt. Could I grow to love him?

CHAPTER THIRTY-FOUR

On Monday morning, I got a phone call from Jimmy McGee.

"Uh, hi," he said. "Matt's on the line, too. I've been studying the hidden files we found on Bobby Marks' computer. Looks like mother and son are running a way-bigger scam than buying a few cars with phony credit. We need to subpoena some bank and brokerage records, the sooner the better. Can we come by at 2:00?"

I glanced at my calendar. "Sure."

"Good," Jimmy said, and hung up.

I stared at the receiver, incredulous that he'd disconnected so abruptly. *What had George Cooper said about him? Rough around the edges? More like raised by wolves.*

That afternoon, Jimmy sat at the head of the conference table with three, six-inch stacks of documents arranged in front of him. He glanced up when Matt and I walked in, then went back to his papers. "Good. We can get started," he muttered. "There's a lot to cover."

"Hello to you, too," I said.

Jimmy ignored my caustic tone. "Take a chair on either side of me, okay? I've got copies of the evidence for each of you." We sat, and he pushed a stack to each of us.

"Bear with me, Jimmy," I said, "but I'm an auditory learner. First, I need you to *tell* us a bit about what you intend to show us."

With a sigh, Jimmy leaned back in his chair. "Like I told you on the phone this morning, the hidden files on Bobby's computer contain tons of incriminating information. To start with, the psychic shop on Armitage Avenue in Chicago was trolling for bereaved widows and widowers. I found a professional-looking brochure…" he paused to search for it.

I touched his wrist. "We'll look at it in a bit," I said. "*Tell* us about it."

He let out another sigh. "Well, they have a brochure advertising the services they offer, including 'communing with your departed loved one,'" Jimmy said, using his fingers for air quotes. "And they kept copies of hundreds of online obituaries—mainly married folks in their forties, fifties, and sixties, virtually all of them posted by funeral homes on Chicago's North Side."

He reached for another piece of paper but stopped. "The obits go back awhile. One of them was for a Leonora Winston, who died a couple years ago. It looks like her widowed husband took the Gypsies' bait. Two of the hidden computer files contain copies of Milton Winston's bank and brokerage statements; he's a businessman worth at least five million bucks. Another file contains power of attorney forms, naming Victoria Marks as his financial and medical POA."

"Let me guess," I said. "Victoria Marks is—"

"Sonia Marks' daughter," Jimmy replied. "Bobby's sister. And the mother of the four kids who were living on Milwaukee Street in Janesville. Now, she's also Milton Winston's second wife. I talked to Milton's adult son and daughter, who were already on to Victoria. In fact, they contacted the FBI about three months ago to report that their dad was being scammed. An agent was assigned to take statements from them, but the case hasn't gone anywhere."

"Why's that?" I asked.

"The agent thinks the kids are just pissed that their dad got hooked up with a younger woman and that she'll inherit his money when he dies. Which could happen sooner than later, since he's got Stage 4 cancer. He's being treated at UW Hospital. From what I can see, his accounts are being liquidated at a pretty fast pace; there might not be anything left by the time he dies. That's why we need the subpoenas for documents, ASAP."

"You got it," I said.

Matt lingered as Jimmy packed up his documents and left the conference room. "I had a nice time Friday night—"

"Me, too."

"I was hoping we could get together again this coming weekend. But the lieutenant has assigned us all a bunch of overtime shifts. You read about that murder?"

I nodded.

"Anyway, I'm gonna have to play my schedule by ear for a while."

I shuffled my stack of papers into a neat pile, hoping to project an air of nonchalance. "I understand. No pressure, okay?"

He nodded with gratitude and walked me back to my office on his way out.

A voicemail awaited, from Dr. Brownhill's assistant, Debra. "She's back from vacation and can fit you in this Thursday at noon, if you don't mind her eating lunch during the session."

I checked my calendar and called to let her know I'd take the appointment.

I'd known Dr. Clarice Brownhill for thirteen years. She'd been assigned by the court to evaluate David and me as prospective adoptive parents before Lily's birth. Later, I sought her out for treatment of panic attacks and to help me through the trauma of David's death and the uncertainty of my high-risk pregnancy with Red. It had been about a year since we'd last met, but she'd always said she'd make time to see me if new issues arose.

On Thursday at noon, she greeted me with a loving smile and a warm embrace. Her silver-gray hair, cut in a chin-length bob, was pushed behind her ears to reveal a pair of striking, silver earrings of Native American design. She wore a simple, turquoise linen shift and hand-painted Tom's canvas shoes, which she kicked off to tuck her feet beneath her in her overstuffed club chair. A homemade sandwich—peanut butter and grape jelly on thick, crusty bread—sat on a paper plate on her side table, along with a mug of spiced tea.

"It's good to see you, Caroline, though I'm sorry for whatever brings you here."

"Thanks for fitting me in. I brought dessert," I said, holding a box containing two, red velvet cupcakes from Daisy Café & Cupcakery.

I loved her office. Sunlight streaming through the slats of the wooden window shutters; lush, green plants evoking serenity and life; soft, welcoming furniture; and the fresh flowers on her desk, all set me at ease.

Dr. Brownhill took a bite of her sandwich and a sip of tea, and I opened the carton of yogurt I'd brought. "Debra says you're distressed about a break-up," she said. "Why don't you tell me about the relationship first, and then about the circumstances that ended it?"

I gave it to her in a nutshell, starting with Dominic's and my growing friendship and our "romantic" weekend in Chicago, ending with the terrible scene at Sardine. "At the time, breaking up seemed like the right thing to do. I thought his mother and her mental health issues would always come between us, and I felt so abandoned by him. But then, when I saw him at the restaurant the very next day with that *floozy*, I was so angry, and hurt, and jealous I couldn't see straight. I drank too much and went to an appointment Lily had with your friend Larry Grube—who confronted me about being intoxicated. I was mortified. I mean, why do you think I reacted like that? *I* was the one who broke up with *him*."

"Why do you think you did?"

I shrugged. "Maybe I realized that I'd made a huge mistake? Maybe my expectations of Dominic were too high. What forty-year-old man *doesn't* have baggage? And, lord knows I have plenty myself. If I'm waiting for a flaw-less man who'll intuitively know what I want, and need, and always be there, I'm gonna die alone."

She smiled. "As I remember, you told me it took you and David some time to get in sync."

"Yeah. It's kinda like training a puppy. But once you're over the hump, there's nothing more wonderful than its unconditional love."

Dr. Brownhill laughed heartily. "A good analogy. And lots of people swear off getting another pet when one they've loved dies, claiming it'd be too hard to go through that difficult a loss again. Is that what's going on with you?"

I paused to think. "It could be. Or, maybe I'm just cau-tiously shopping around for the right puppy. I've gone out a few times with a colleague who's fun to be with. There's no real spark, but maybe that'll come."

A master at silence—which sometimes bugged the heck out of me—Dr. Brownhill sipped her tea and waited until I chose to say more.

"I went for a psychic reading a few weeks ago."

"Oh?"

"I was driving down Johnson Street and saw the sign and decided on the spur of the moment to go in. Shortly before we broke up, Dominic's mother got taken for quite a bit of money by a supposed psychic in Chicago. I guess I was curious how that could happen. I believe there are some people who have psychic, or at least extra-perceptive, abilities. But most of the folks who set up these shops are probably just charlatans."

"You were suspicious when you went in?"

I nodded. "The whole place looked so stereotypically corny. But when this woman looked into her crystal ball and told me she saw I'd suffered a huge loss that was still affecting me, I got suckered in. And when she told me she saw two men in my life, I wanted to believe she could tell me which was 'the one.' And that she was telling the truth when she said I'd find happiness." I blinked back tears.

Dr. Brownhill nodded, silently encouraging me to go on.

"Then, she started talking about my kids, although I hadn't told her I had any. She knew the oldest was a girl. I felt like I'd found someone who really knew me and could help me make decisions. But when I got to the car, I realized she'd seen my key fob with a picture of the kids. I felt like such a fool."

"You let yourself be vulnerable."

"Uh-huh. And the betrayal really stung. First by Dominic, then by some fortune-telling con lady."

"You said you'd wanted her to help you make decisions. Why is that?"

"Lately, things've felt so overwhelming. I haven't known which way to turn." I told her about Lily's troubles and how I'd had to ask my dad to come help. "Dad was able to see angles of the situation that I couldn't."

She smiled. "With kids, it sometimes does take a village. Was Larry Grube able to help?"

"He referred Lily to a grief support group. She seems to like it."

Dr. Brownhill broke off a piece of cupcake and nibbled on it. "This is wonderful, but I think I'll save the rest for later. Do you think it would be helpful to schedule another appointment—or two? Recognizing, of course, that I don't have a crystal ball?"

I laughed. "Could you at least get one of those Magic 8 Balls?"

She winked. "Sources say 'yes.' Debra can set you up; a few slots opened up next week."

I wrapped my own, untouched cupcake in the bakery paper and placed it in the bottom of my lunch bag. "Thanks."

As I walked back to my car, kicking at fallen leaves, I felt lighter than I'd felt in weeks.

CHAPTER THIRTY-FIVE

"Mom, I need a ride to the orchard on Saturday morning," Lily told me one evening in late October. "They're having a festival and I need to sell apples from 9:00 to noon."

"What kind of festival?"

"Their fall fundraising festival, with games and food, square dancing, a petting zoo…"

"That sounds like something the littles would enjoy. How 'bout we join you there after your shift?"

"Sure."

"Would you mind if I asked Matt to come along?" Matt's and my schedules hadn't been meshing. Because of his overtime and a week that he'd been in Milwaukee for training, we hadn't found time to be alone since *Gone Girl*. I knew he'd be working again on Saturday night, but maybe he'd enjoy a daytime family outing.

Lily hesitated a moment. "I dunno—he might think it's lame."

"If he thinks it's a lame idea, he can say 'no.'"

"Okay."

I texted Matt and smiled at his quick response, "Sounds great!"

Luke, excited for Saturday's adventure to begin, waited for Matt at the front screen door. I'd opened doors and windows to let in the unseasonably warm, outside air. "He's here," he yelled when Matt parked the Miata at the curb. "And he's got the top down! Can we go for a ride?"

Amy and I joined him at the door. "Sorry, kiddo, there's no place for your booster seats. But I'll bet he'd let you sit in it."

After each of the kids had taken a turn behind the wheel of the Miata, we headed to my mommy van. Matt climbed into the shotgun seat, and we were off to meet Lily in Middleton.

When we arrived shortly before noon, the main parking lot was already full. The Middleton High School football team, decked out in their game jerseys, waved neon orange flags to direct us to a roped-off area in the farm field. Perky cheerleaders sold tickets at the gate. Other volunteers, dressed in overalls, plaid shirts, and straw hats, manned concession stands and game booths. A country band piled out of a panel truck and began unloading their instruments near a makeshift stage. Pumpkins and fall mums decorated the grounds. The air smelled of apples, cinnamon, and fallen leaves.

"Cool!" Amy said, pulling on my hand. "Can we go pet the goats?"

"In a minute. I'd like to buy some apples from Lily before she goes off duty."

I scanned the grounds, but Amy spotted her first, at a stand about fifteen yards away. "There she is!"

I watched my oldest daughter in fascination. Her hair in long pigtails. A red bandana around her neck. A toothy grin on her face as she handed a customer change from the denim apron tied at her waist, exuding confidence and pride.

Lily smiled and waved when she saw our entourage. "I'd like a bushel of honey crisps, please," I said. "But can we set them aside to pick up when we're ready to leave?"

"A whole bushel?" Lily asked.

"Uh-huh. Next week's Halloween. Bobbing for apples—remember?"

She grinned. "We're gonna do it again?"

I nodded and reached for my wallet. "Weather permitting."

We found the festival anything but lame. We sat on bales of straw, eating lunch from the concessions stands. The charcoal-grilled bratwurst, smothered in dark mustard and sauerkraut, was among the best I've ever tasted. The twins insisted they each needed their own caramel apple, and Matt and I happily finished what they were "too full" to polish off themselves.

Red dozed in her umbrella stroller while the band warmed up. Mesmerized by his fingers flashing over the keyboard, Amy couldn't take her eyes off the accordion player. Luke bounced on his feet as he watched the fiddler. Unsure whether he was getting ready to dance or wet his pants, I said, "Luke, let's go find the potty." He grumbled, but came along willingly; we braved the smell of the Porta Potty together.

The band and at least twenty dancers, mostly kids, were in full swing by the time we made our way through the crowd and back to the others. At the first strains of "Turkey in the Straw," Matt stood up and bowed to Lily. "This one's too good to miss."

"I don't know how to square dance," she cried, but with less embarrassment than I'd have expected.

"Look at this crowd; hardly anyone does," he yelled, over the music. "We'll just skip around in circles."

She grabbed his hands, got to her feet, and followed Matt's lead. Moments later, they reached down to pull in Amy and Luke. When the song ended, all four fell giggling to the ground. "That's so fun," Amy cried. "Can we do it again?"

Matt stood up and brushed off the seat of his jeans. "Yep, but this time I'll sit with Red while your mom dances."

We grinned and hopped to several more songs, including "Buffalo Gal," before Red woke up, cranky. "Time to go, kiddos," I said.

"Do we hafta?" Luke asked, his lower lip quivering.

"'fraid so," Matt said. "I've gotta work this evening."

"On a Saturday night?" Lily asked.

"Uh-huh." And he regaled them with stories of his police work during the twenty-minute drive home.

"Can Matt come to our Halloween party?" Amy asked as I pulled into the driveway.

"Of course he can, if he's free," I said.

He shrugged his shoulders, then smiled. "I can be here by 5:00."

Before David's death, Halloween had always been a major holiday in the Spencer household. Every year, we transformed our garage in Middleton into a spook house and held a party for the neighbors in our cul-de-sac. David served hotdogs roasted in the Nesco, alongside plenty of popcorn and chips. There was beer for the adults, soda for the kids. If the weather was warm, we bobbed for apples in a huge Rubbermaid bin. If it was cold, we served hot chocolate, lacing it with peppermint schnapps for the grown-ups. Over the years, word of the party spread, and guests came from well beyond our little neighborhood. When we bought our Madison home, David and I agreed that the massive front porch would make a wonderful spook house and declared that the party tradition would continue. After he died, though, I hadn't been able to bring myself to host it, even with Lily, Abby, and Glenda's help.

Determined this year to get back into the holiday spirit, I'd told our neighbors about the party and invited them to stop by. Several days earlier, we'd decorated the front porch with streamers, spider webs, black lights, paper bats, and plastic cauldrons.

I took Halloween off from work, but got up early in anticipation. Before the evening festivities, I would help chaperone the twins' school party. Dressed as Princess Leia, Lily joined me at the breakfast table, looking as bright-eyed as I felt.

"You're up early," I said. "Can I make you some scrambled eggs?"

"Yes, please. What's the verdict on the weather?"

"Too cold for apple bobbing," I said, reaching into the fridge for the eggs. "I'll cut a bunch of them up and put out caramel dip. It'd take us forever to eat the whole bushel ourselves."

She nodded thoughtfully. "I'm glad you decided to have the party again, Mom."

"Me, too. Seemed like it was time."

Matt arrived at 5:00, dressed as a prisoner in black and white stripes. The plastic ball and chain affixed to his ankle bonked with each step he took up to the porch.

I grinned. "Really?"

He gave me a quick hug. "What? This isn't an appropriate costume to wear to a prosecutor's party?"

Abby and Bert—dressed, she said, as grandparents—had already left to take Amy, Luke, and Red trick-or-treating around the block. I'd placed Lily and Marissa in charge of the hot dogs; Matt and I would pour hot chocolate. Glenda and Hank were among the first guests to arrive. She winked at me as the men shook hands, then hugged Matt. "It's good to meet you. Caroline and the kids have been regaling us with stories of your square-dancing prowess."

He gave her an "Aw, shucks!" look and went to the kitchen to get Hank a beer.

"Tone it down, Glen," Hank muttered. "You don't want to scare him away."

Everything felt just right: the easy camaraderie with friends and family, the laughter of kids hyped up on sugar, even the scratchy feel of the woolen mittens I wore to warm my chilly hands. I chalked up another post-David milestone, and the look on Lily's face told me she did, too.

The party ended at 9:00. Abby and Bert put the littles to bed while Matt and I put away the leftovers. After cleaning up the porch, Lily and her friends headed to Shelley's for a sleepover.

Finally alone, Matt and I sat at the kitchen table with steaming mugs of cocoa and schnapps. He put his feet, sans ball and chain, on the chair opposite his and took a sip. "This isn't half-bad."

I nodded. "Not an everyday drink, but good on a blustery evening."

"Caroline—" he began, and I knew we were beyond small talk. "I'm really glad you asked me to come tonight. I had a lot of fun."

A knot grew in my stomach as I waited for the serious conversation I wasn't ready to have.

"There's something I need to tell you about my week in Milwaukee."

"What?"

"My wife was there, too. Not at the training session but interviewing for a position at St. Luke's Hospital. She just finished her residency at Yale and is thinking of moving back to the Midwest. And we've been, uh, talking about giving it another shot. Our marriage, I mean."

"Your ex-wife's a *doctor*?"

Matt nodded. "A cardiac surgeon, actually. And she's not technically my ex-wife, though we've been legally separated for six years. I hope you're not upset I didn't make that clear."

I shook my head and thought for a moment, trying to identify my feelings. Not betrayal. He'd never said he was divorced and I'd never asked. Not loss. I hadn't invested enough in our personal relationship to mourn its loss. Relief? *That's it!* I hadn't felt the spark of excitement with

Matt that I'd felt with Dominic and David. And I'd pretty much realized it wasn't ever going to happen.

"No, Matt, I'm not upset. You never led me on, and I've enjoyed doing things with you as a friend."

"Me, too. And the thing is, being with you and your kids has made me see how much I want a family. I finally got up the nerve to talk with Hannah about it, and she's in a place right now where she does, too."

I reached over and patted his hand. "I hope things work out for you."

"It won't be weird for us to work together now, will it?"

"I don't see why it would," I answered, truthfully.

Chapter Thirty-six

Jimmy, Matt, and I had spent weeks pulling together information on the Marks family's fleecing of the ailing Milton Winston. We still lacked evidence that would prove to a jury, beyond a reasonable doubt, that their conduct constituted fraud. Milton had clammed up during two attempts to interview him, including one conducted by Matt alone. If Matt couldn't get him to talk, no one could.

The break we needed came in mid-November: Barbara Marks' attorney, Jason Bittner, called to say his client wanted to plead guilty and to cooperate with the prosecution of her in-laws.

"Hallelujah," I said, pacing in front of my window as sleet pelted its panes. "What do you want in return?"

"Immunity from further prosecution, a recommendation for probation, with or without electronic monitoring, and a WitSec placement," he replied.

"Yikes! Immunity's no problem. A recommendation for probation is doable, though you know it wouldn't be binding on the court. But the Witness Security Program?

These folks are aren't Mafiosi or members of a Mexican drug cartel."

"Barbara says Bobby beat a man into a vegetative state over a territorial beef and that he ordered the murder of his own brother, Georgie, who'd threatened to rat him out. I've got our investigator following up on the details, but I believe her."

"I can't guarantee the U.S. Marshals would accept her, or that our office would sponsor a placement; the bar's way too high. We *could* use funds from our own EWAP—Emergency Witness Assistance Program—to help her relocate and get set up someplace else, but there wouldn't be any protective services. Is WitSec a deal breaker?"

"She wants a new start. If you could do that with EWAP, she might agree."

"How 'bout if we make it a condition of her probation that Barbara start off in a halfway house somewhere, like Minneapolis or Des Moines? I think that could be arranged."

"I'll talk with my client and let you know."

He called back within the hour. "She says 'yes.' And let's try for Minneapolis. She doesn't believe the Marks family has connections there."

"You got it. I'll draft the immunity letter. When can we meet?"

"It's gotta be next week. I'm on vacay the whole week of the twenty-fourth."

I laughed. "Deer hunting?"

"It's practically a requirement if you're male and live in Wisconsin. And my wife's going with me for the first weekend."

"She's a braver woman than me!" I checked my calendar. "Will Tuesday at 9:00 work for you?"

"Yep. I'll let Barbara know."

The following Tuesday, Matt and I sat across the conference table from Jason Bittner and his client at the federal defender's office. Barbara wore leggings and a faded red cardigan over a black tube top. I hadn't seen a tube top in years and vaguely wondered where she'd found it.

"Jason tells us you'd like to cooperate in the prosecution of Bobby Marks and his mother," I began. Barbara nodded. "Do you have any reservations about your decision?"

"I'd be a fool not to have some," she said, in a Marilyn Monroe-like, husky whisper. "I'll be cutting ties to the only culture I've ever known and putting myself at risk. But I haven't changed my mind."

"By your culture you mean what, exactly?" Matt asked.

"The Romani culture. You—the *gaje*—refer to us as Gypsies."

"Do you find the term 'Gypsy' offensive?" I asked.

"Some do. I don't."

"How did you come to be associated with Bobby and Sonia Marks?" I asked.

A pained expression crossed her face. "When I was about fourteen, my father gave me in marriage to Sonia's youngest son, Georgie, to settle a family dispute. They paid my father a good bride price because I was pretty and blonde."

In the twentieth century? I couldn't formulate another question.

Jason Bittner leaned forward. "Is it okay if I summarize a few things for you?" he asked. "I think it'll save time."

"Sure," Matt and I said, simultaneously.

"Barbara was born in northern California in about 1990. Her family traveled a lot, under the radar if you will, and she was born at home, without record. When she was around five, social services became involved and got her identification documents in the *nav gajikano*—or non-Gypsy name—of Barbara Costello. Her father's *nav gajikano* was John Costello, apparently Northern Italian. At fourteen, Barbara moved in with Georgie and his mother, when the *unofficial* marriage took place. When she turned eighteen, they got married by a justice of the peace and she legally took the name Barbara Marks."

"Are your parents still alive?" I asked Barbara.

She shrugged. "My mother died when I was a baby. I haven't seen my father since he sold me to Georgie and Sonia."

Her look told me the subject was closed. "How far did you go in school?" I asked.

Another shrug. "I remember going to kindergarten and part of first-grade someplace near Sacramento. Once, when we lived in Kansas City, the welfare people made me go to school—I think fourth-grade. I did maybe another semester in Chicago. My father taught me math so I could help in his business and I always read because I liked it, but I never went to school after I hooked up with Georgie."

"Staff at the halfway house gave her some tests," Jason added, looking at Barbara with an air of fatherly pride. "She reads at a tenth-grade level and has an IQ of 126—pretty darn bright." His client smiled shyly at him; I hoped she wasn't developing a crush.

"Let's talk about the psychic scam," I said. I noticed Barbara winced at the word "scam."

Jason put his hand atop hers for a moment. "My client informs me the psychic business is not entirely fraudulent. I think it's best that we let her explain why. Go ahead, Barbara."

She shifted in her chair, crossed and uncrossed her legs, and then began. "My grandmother was well-known for her ability to read the spirits. As a little girl, I watched and learned from her how to ask the kinds of questions to get people tuned in to the spirits. I can read their energy, positive and negative, and I can often tell what they're thinking." She paused to take a sip of coffee.

"Barbara," I said, "I know two of your… um… clients in Chicago were a Spanish woman named Alejandra and her sister, Luz. Do you remember them?" Jason and Matt looked at me quizzically; my question wasn't based on any of the discovery materials.

Her faced brightened. "Oh, yes. I was so happy to be able to help Luz. She called awhile back to tell me her cancer treatments were helping."

"How did you know Luz had cancer?" I asked.

"I can't really explain it. When I held her hands, they were so cold, and an intense foreboding overcame me. I knew with certainty that she was sick. I told her to see a doctor right away."

"What about Alejandra? Were you able to read her, as well?"

Barbara glanced warily at Jason. "Go ahead," he said. "Clean slate."

"It was different with Alejandra," she said. "She was very guarded at first, and I had to use other techniques to learn what was on her mind."

"You mean cold-reading techniques?" Matt asked.

"Uh-huh," she replied, looking down at the table.

"Please explain what that means," I said.

She sighed. "You start by making a general statement that would apply to almost anyone but could be interpreted differently by different people. Something like, 'I sense sadness in you. Have you suffered a loss?' If the client says no, you fish some more. Perhaps, 'I could be wrong; it might not be the loss of a loved one. Maybe you've lost money, or a job, or something like your pride? Does that make sense?' Our clients *want* to believe we have psychic abilities, and usually they'll say 'yes' and give us the clues we need. It was that way with Alejandra Marquez."

"And you convinced her to give you her anniversary ring to be 'cleansed,'" I said.

"Not to make excuses, but I did what Sonia told me to do. She'd listen to my readings from the back room and give me instructions. Sonia noticed the ring one day when Alejandra came in—it was quite elaborate—and told me to get it from her during the next session. Sonia loved it and wanted to keep it, but we had to pawn the ring to pay the rent."

"Did she send you to renew the loan against it—when you got caught at the pawn shop?"

Barbara nodded.

"And you told Alejandra her money was cursed?" I asked.

Barbara drummed her fingers nervously on the table. "Again, that's one of Sonia's typical ploys—to get the client to give their money to us for cleansing. Sonia was furious when she learned Alejandra had given her savings to her church, instead. I liked Alejandra, and I think she found some peace in coming to me. Um… I really need to use the restroom. Could we take a little break?"

"Of course," Jason said. "I'll show you where it is."

Alone now in the conference room, Matt asked, "Are these sisters you were asking about related to your ex?"

"Uh-huh."

"Do you believe Barbara's claim to have psychic abilities?"

"I don't know," I said, as I stood and stretched. "Her description of Luz's reading fits with what Luz told me. And I believe some people are more perceptive than others; my late husband David was one of them. You must know cops who are great at interviews and surveillance, who seem to know what a person's gonna say or do beforehand."

He nodded.

"I believe we're all spiritual beings, made up of energy… or whatever. Who says some people can't tap into that?"

Jason Bittner poked his head in the door. "You ready for us again?" he asked. I nodded, and he ushered Barbara back to her seat.

Matt led off. "When you went with Bobby to buy the BMW in Wausau, you used an Illinois driver's license and a VISA card in the name of a Courtney Parks, a child who died at the age of two in 1995. Where'd that ID come from?"

Barbara hung her head. "Courtney's mother came to the shop about a year ago and told Sonia she wanted to contact her daughter's spirit. Sonia said it would help if we could see and touch some things that had belonged to the child. A few days later, the mother brought in a whole box of mementos including Courtney's baby book, which happened to have her birth certificate stuck inside the back cover. I distracted her while Sonia took the birth certificate; I used it later to get the driver's license. Sonia applied for credit cards in Courtney's name, too. I used one when I went with Bobby to buy the car."

"Okay," Matt said. "When you bought the Escalade in Eau Claire, you presented the actual driver's license of one Marcia Baxter, a living person from northern Wisconsin. How'd you get it?"

"Bobby gave it to me just before we went into the dealership. He said I didn't need to know how he got it, but later I heard him and his friend telling Sonia about it. They said they'd been in a bar in Eau Claire and saw this woman who looked exactly like me. Bobby said they'd gotten her drunk and his friend lifted Marcia's driver's license and one credit card from her wallet while she was dancing with Bobby. The thing was, we had to use the IDs before she realized they were gone."

We continued Barbara's debriefing later that afternoon, when Jimmy McGee could join us. Dressed in corduroy pants with bagged-out knees and a wrinkled madras shirt—much like one my brother had worn back in eighth-grade—Jimmy came across as unprofessional but also unintimidating. Which is why I was surprised to see wariness in Barbara's eyes. *Maybe she really is psychic and can tell he's not what he appears?*

"Let's move on to the fraud against Milton Winston," I said. "Barbara, we've got documents showing that Sonia, Bobby, and his sister, Victoria Marks, have obtained over one million dollars from him. We need your testimony to show it was taken by fraud. We've given you immunity so you would not be charged in that fraud."

"Bobby didn't have anything to do with it," Barbara replied.

Jimmy almost jumped out of his chair. "The hidden files on his computer show otherwise."

"On the laptop found at the house in Janesville?" she asked.

"Yes," he said. "On his laptop."

Barbara straightened her back and looked him in the eye. "Any hidden files on that computer belonged to Sonia, not Bobby. She doesn't think he's very smart and never trusted him to do anything more than a few car and roofing scams. She purposely kept him *out* of the plan to get money from Milton."

"You're telling us Sonia Marks was savvy enough to use hidden files?" Jimmy asked.

Barbara nodded. "One time in Chicago, Sonia was grumbling about Bobby being an idiot and having to have his password written down. Ruby, Victoria's sixteen-year-old daughter, who's like a computer genius, showed her how to hide files so they'd be safe."

Jimmy shook his head in disbelief.

"Let's move on," I said. "How was Milton Winston chosen as a victim?"

"He came into the shop a couple years ago and said he wanted to contact his dead wife. He really liked Sonia and kept coming back for more readings. Sonia had Victoria come in during one of his appointments and pose as a young widow who was trying to reach her deceased husband. Sonia pretended it was just a fluke when she introduced Victoria to Milton, saying something about how their meeting was meant to be."

"But Victoria isn't actually a widow," Matt said.

"Right," Barbara replied. "She's married to a guy named Stevo and has four kids by him, though he's living with another woman in California right now."

"Did Milton know about her other kids?"

"No. And later, Sonia moved the kids to Janesville so it would be easier to keep them a secret."

"Tell us about Milton's relationship with Victoria," I said.

"Well… Sonia told Victoria not to rush things, so at first they were just friends. Then after a few weeks, Victoria told him she was being evicted and Milton insisted she stay with him at his three-story brownstone in Lincoln Park. She kept it platonic at first, but within a couple months he'd proposed and given her a three-karat diamond ring."

"Which is what started the rift between Milton and his grown kids," Jimmy said. "And made them argue for a pre-nup. Too bad he didn't listen to 'em."

Barbara nodded, then continued. "Sonia told Victoria she had to get pregnant. But it turned out Milton couldn't father a child. Sonia had to devise a way to make him think he had."

We'd already learned that Milton and Victoria had an infant son, but *this* was evidence of fraudulent intent. "Milton isn't the biological father?" I asked.

Barbara didn't flinch. "A midwife injected Victoria with sperm from a sperm bank. A couple nights later, Sonia gave her some pills to put into Milton's Scotch. The next morning, Victoria made him believe they'd actually made love and it'd been wonderful. He bought it."

Jimmy chuckled and I gave him my best stink eye. "Okay," I said. "How 'bout we talk about their move to Wisconsin?"

"When Victoria was about six-months pregnant, Milton found out he had a rare kind of cancer. Stage 4. His kids had arranged for him to see a specialist at Northwestern Hospital, in Chicago. Sonia was worried his kids might get more controlling because he was sick, so during one of his readings she made him believe he should try another doctor. I'm not sure if she suggested Madison or if Milton decided that on his own, but he began receiving treatment at the UW Hospital's Carbone Cancer Center shortly after that. Victoria and the kids moved here just after the baby was born."

Jimmy, fists clenched on the table, leaned toward Barbara and spoke. "And, during Milton's period of isolation for a stem-cell transplant, *your* charming sister-in-law and the kids up and left him. She sold the multi-million dollar Chicago house and liquidated the brokerage and bank accounts Milton had so *generously* placed in joint tenancy. Estranged from his grown kids because of her, he's now sick and alone and left with nothing! Are you aware he's living on Medicaid in a shit-hole of a nursing home between in-patient chemotherapy treatments?"

Barbara shook her head but didn't reply.

I touched his hand, signaling to let me take over. "Where are Victoria and the baby now?"

Barbara whispered, "I wish I knew. I feel bad for Milton; he was always nice to me. And it's a shame that Victoria isolated him from his other kids."

We'd learned that, because of privacy laws, Milton's adult children had been unable to get information on his condition from UW Hospital. His new wife was the only person authorized to communicate with his doctors. And, despite her absence, Milton had stubbornly refused to modify his privacy instructions.

Jimmy sighed audibly. "What about Sonia? Do you know where she is?"

"No, but I'm betting she's with Victoria and the baby."

"And Sonia and Victoria simply abandoned Victoria's four other kids to foster care to save their own skins?" Jimmy asked.

Again, Barbara chose not to reply.

Jason Bittner turned to me. "My client is anxious to plead guilty and get on with her new life."

"She'll have to testify at the grand jury when we present the indictment against Sonia and Victoria for defrauding Milton Winston. And, she'll have to testify at Bobby's trial." I motioned for Jimmy and Matt to lean in so I could whisper to them. "The grand jury's meeting on Thursday. Can we be ready to present in two days?" Both nodded.

I turned to Barbara. "We can schedule you to testify this Thursday and you could plead guilty the Monday after Thanksgiving."

"You okay with that, Barbara?" Jason asked his client. She nodded.

We'd finished by 5:00 but I was too keyed-up to head right home. "Want to get a beer?" I asked Matt and Jimmy, on the way out of Jason Bittner's office. They nodded in unison. "Does the Old Fashioned sound okay? It's noisy enough that no one will hear us talking shop."

Two more nods.

"I'll buy the first pitcher," Jimmy said, when we were seated at a slightly-tilted table. "As long as it's the house brew."

"Fine by me," I said.

"Jimmy, the big spender," Matt said. "That's the cheapest beer on the menu."

"Not so," Jimmy shot back. "Schlitz and Pabst are cheaper. And I happen to prefer the house brew."

"Boys, boys, boys," I said, as the waitress approached. "Let's not make a scene."

The fresh-from-the-tap beer tasted pretty darn great in a chilled glass, and we all took a moment to sip in peace.

"Jimmy," I said, "you're the most familiar with all the Milton Winston documents. Do we have *anything* incriminating against Bobby Marks?"

"Just the files hidden on his computer. I'm not sure I believe Barbara that those are Sonia Marks' files."

"Why couldn't they be?" I asked. "And try to answer without being a sexist."

Matt laughed.

"Sexism aside," Jimmy said, all-business, "Sonia's in her late fifties and was apparently raised in the Romani culture, where women traditionally weren't educated. Sixteen-year-old Ruby, the alleged computer whiz who taught Sonia these tricks, hasn't attended school with any regularity. Where would *she* have gotten the skills to do it? I still believe Bobby's the mastermind. I think a jury would, too."

"Maybe. But without Barbara's testimony, we'd have a tough time proving fraud. She's the one who can testify about how Milton and Victoria met, that Victoria wasn't really a childless widow, and that the baby was the product of artificial insemination—about which Milton was duped. Without Barbara, defense counsel could claim Milton Winston simply fell for, and spent lavishly, on an exotic younger woman whom he willingly married. Milton won't talk and he could be dead before we ever get to trial. So, if Barbara says Bobby Marks had nothing to do with the scheme, that's the story we're stuck with."

"I agree," Matt said.

I took another sip of beer and thought a moment. "Okay, so the plan is this: with Barbara's testimony on Thursday, we indict Sonia and Victoria Marks for scamming Milton Winston. Barbara won't get sentenced until after she testifies at Bobby's trial. I'll recommend three years' probation with six months in a halfway house, and we'll bring her back to testify against Sonia and Victoria when we find and arrest 'em."

Jimmy drained his beer, wiped his mouth with the back of his hand, and shook his head. "I'd like to postpone

Barbara's grand jury testimony 'til I take one more run at our evidence."

"We've gone over it until we're bleary eyed," Matt said, slamming his beer down on the wobbly table. "The only thing we haven't gotten a look at is Bobby's iPad."

"Bobby's iPad?" I asked.

"Remember? We found it under the seat when we impounded the Escalade," Matt said. "You got us the search warrant, but the FBI lab can't get into it. It's locked with an alpha-numeric password which we don't have."

"Shit," I said.

"I doubt it'd contain much of evidentiary value, anyway," Matt said. "It's probably full of games and pictures."

"I'm not so sure," Jimmy said. "Bobby isn't savvy enough to remember his laptop password without having it written down, yet there's password protection rather than a simple four-digit code on his tablet?"

"Maybe the pictures are kiddie porn and he asked Ruby the whiz kid to lock 'em up," Matt said, with a rueful smile.

When the next pitcher arrived, I glanced at my watch. I threw a twenty-dollar bill on the table. "This one's on me, but I can't stay. As we know, Social Services doesn't take kindly to mothers leaving their kids to fend for themselves."

I couldn't help smiling. I enjoyed working with two such competent—yet very different—guys. I was happy to count them among my friends. I waved goodbye as a waiter returned with a new pitcher of house brew.

Outside the restaurant, I could see my breath in the frigid November air. I fished a pair of gloves from the bottom of my purse and fumbled to put them on. I turned to the west, facing State Street and the UW-Madison campus. Lured by a brilliantly clear, star-studded evening sky, my eyes drifted upward. Atop the Wisconsin state Capitol, the gilded statue of a woman, depicting the state's motto, "Forward," stood out prominently. As I stopped for a moment, a shooting star arched overhead. *What to wish? Hurry—think of something!* I closed my eyes and wished that I, too, could move forward, past my grief over David, past my hurt and anger over Dominic, and into a fulfilling relationship with a man I loved.

A gust of wind sent a crumpled Starbucks cup skipping across the sidewalk in front of me, and my mystical moment passed. I picked up my pace. Abby and Bert had a date at 6:30, and I promised I'd be home. *Maybe I should've wished for all four kids to be in good spirits this evening?*

CHAPTER THIRTY-SEVEN

Barbara Marks' plea hearing was scheduled for 9:00 on the first Monday in December. I'd arranged to meet her and Jason Bittner at 8:30 in the second-floor conference room, to have them review and sign the written plea agreement.

On my way to the courthouse, bundled in my North Face down coat and the thick woolen mittens that Glenda had knit for me, I cursed the biting north wind. I cursed *myself* for failing to wear the coat's detachable hood and for choosing heels. Though the sidewalks were clear of ice and snow, I couldn't walk fast enough to prevent my ears from going numb with cold. I fumbled for my key card and entered through the side door, surprised to see Matt waiting there.

I stuffed my mittens into my coat pocket and gave him my briefcase, freeing up my hands to warm my ears. "What're you doing here so early?"

"Just being anal," he replied, with a half-smile. "I figured I'd sit in the second-floor lobby and read the newspaper 'til you got here. But there are some folks up there already and I thought you might want a heads-up."

"Who?"

"I'm guessing it's your ex and his mom. What's he look like?"

My heart lurched. I'd fleetingly thought that Dominic might show up at the hearing but had dismissed the idea. After all, George had made it clear that his mother had no standing in Barbara's case. "Tall, dark. Like a frickin' Spanish movie star," I replied. "His mom's in her sixties. Average height, attractive woman with gray hair."

He looked down at his shoes. "It's them. And there's a pretty-attractive blonde woman with 'em."

"It's his girlfriend, the P.I. And you can say it—she's hot."

"She is. What do you want to do?"

I want to go home and crawl into bed with a cup of hot chocolate and a good book. "Let's take the elevator up to third floor and come back down to two via the far stairway. Hopefully we can get in to our meeting without them noticing us."

Matt nodded, handed me back my briefcase, and followed me to the elevator. "I'm sorry," I said, as the door closed behind us. "That was a crazy-assed juvenile idea." I punched the button for the second floor, and when we arrived, I kept my head down and walked straight into the conference room.

Though our business with Barbara and Jason could have been accomplished in fifteen minutes, I dragged it out mercilessly, explaining every point two and three times. Even Barbara seemed puzzled by my antics. "I understand completely, Ms. Spencer, and I'm ready to sign the document."

At 8:55, the four of us walked into the courtroom. Dominic, his mother, and Emma were seated in the first row, directly behind the prosecution table. He sat between the two women, Emma leaning against him possessively. *Shit, shit, shit!*

Barbara recognized Dominic's mother, did a double take, then went toward her, murmuring, "I'm so sorry, Alejandra. For everything."

Before Alejandra could reply, Dominic bolted to his feet. "I'll thank you not to speak with her," he bellowed. "You've done enough damage already."

Jason took Barbara's arm, led her to the defense table, and motioned for me to join them. "Who is that?" he asked.

Barbara hung her head. "The woman whose ring I pawned in the Cook County case. I don't know the man; maybe he's her lawyer."

"Not another word to either of them," Jason hissed. "Understood?"

"Yes," she replied, but I sensed she didn't like his admonishment. She turned to me. "Ms. Spencer, I forgot to thank you for scheduling this hearing so quickly. I'm anxious to move on to my new life. I promise you I'll make the most of it." Then, to my complete surprise, she hugged me.

"You're welcome," I said, patting her back awkwardly. Over her shoulder, I saw Dominic glaring. His eyes—to which I'd once been so drawn—locked fiercely onto mine. It took every ounce of resolve for me to walk to the table in front of him. I collapsed into the chair beside Matt, feeling those eyes boring into my back.

I sat a moment, collecting my wits. When I reached into my briefcase for the case file, a red square of construction paper fluttered out and landed on the floor near my feet. Matt picked it up and handed it to me. It was a note from Amy in blue crayon: "Hav a gud Da." She'd drawn a grinning sun in one upper corner. I swallowed the lump in my throat and smiled for the first time since I'd walked into the courthouse.

The routine of most plea hearings is mind-numbing, but this one was different. Hugh Coburn, an imposing and often-intimidating figure, at six foot five with ramrod-straight posture and a booming voice, spoke more like a grandfather than a conservative judge when he questioned Barbara. And I saw an unmistakable hint of compassion in his sky-blue eyes when he listened to her responses.

"Do you believe you fully understand the terms of the plea agreement, Ms. Marks?"

"Well, Your Honor," Barbara said, in her husky whisper, "I don't have much formal education. In fact, I never finished high school. Some of the legal terms were difficult for me. But the lawyers went over everything with me several times, and I trust them. So, yes, I think I fully understand it."

The judge waited a beat before he turned to me. "Ms. Spencer, please summarize the plea agreement for the record."

Still unnerved to have Dominic and Emma in the courtroom, I took a sip of water, cleared my throat, and stumbled through my proffer. "…The government and defendant agree to jointly recommend a sentence of three years' probation," I concluded.

"Probation? Really?" I heard Emma mutter.

Judge Coburn's eyes turned a steely blue. He honed in on her over his reading glasses. "I insist on quiet in this courtroom. Any further outbursts and I'll hold you in contempt."

I wanted to jump up and cheer.

"Now, Ms. Marks, I need to ask you another series of questions," the judge said. For five, long minutes he took her through the standard colloquy. Finally, he said, "Please tell me about the crime. What did you do?"

All eyes in the room were on Barbara. She pushed back her chair and began to stand. The judge interrupted, "You may stay seated."

Barbara sank down, leaned toward the microphone, and said, "Thank you, sir. I'm more nervous than I thought."

"Take your time," he said.

"Well... I went to a car dealership in Wausau with Bobby Marks and applied for a loan to buy a used BMW. I had a driver's license with my picture on it and a credit card in the name of Courtney Parks. I got the loan and we took the car but never made any payments on it. Eventually, it got confiscated in Janesville."

"How did you get the license in Courtney Parks' name?" Judge Coburn asked.

"Bobby's mother, Sonia, gave me Courtney's birth certificate and told me how to use it to apply for a license."

"And you knew it was illegal to use someone else's identity to apply for the car loan?"

"Yes, sir. I did."

The judge didn't need to ask any more questions; Barbara had said enough for him to accept her guilty plea. But he seemed mesmerized by her and I sensed he couldn't stop himself. "How are you related to Bobby and Sonia Marks?" he inquired. "I'm assuming you're related."

"When I was fourteen, my father arranged for me to marry Sonia's son, Georgie."

"Where did this happen?" the judge asked, unable to mask his incredulity.

"We lived in Kansas City at the time," she said. "It's common in my culture—the Gypsy, or Romani, culture—for girls to marry young. My husband, Georgie, was Bobby's brother."

"Was?"

"He died a couple years ago."

"I'm sorry for your loss," Judge Coburn said, shaking his head. He paused a moment, then seemed to realize he needn't go further. "All right. I find there is a factual basis for your plea of guilty."

The judge turned to the matter of scheduling. "Your Honor," I said, "due to the unusual circumstances outlined in a sealed memorandum, the parties are jointly recommending that sentencing be scheduled for January 14." Typically, the hearing would've been significantly later.

"So ordered," he intoned.

The hearing adjourned, Barbara and Jason left to meet with the probation officer who'd been assigned to write the presentence report.

I lingered at the prosecution table with Matt until I felt certain Dominic, his mother, and Emma would've had time to leave the building. But when I walked out of the courtroom, I saw them huddled fifteen feet away.

Alejandra and Dominic stood with their backs to me. "How can you *not* feel sorry for her?" I heard her ask him, in a frantic voice. "She's had a horrible life. These people are the only family she's ever known."

"Mom," he said, with clear irritation, "she's a crook, plain and simple. She almost took you for all your money."

Emma, wearing a slinky, purple, wraparound dress, put her hand on his arm. The gesture made my blood boil. She nodded in my direction. "Here she is."

Dominic turned around, attractive as ever in his impeccably-tailored, olive-green suit, crisp white shirt, and patterned charcoal tie. A few locks of thick hair, a little longer than when I'd last seen him, fell across his forehead. *Quit looking at him like that. This encounter's not gonna be pretty.*

"I need to ask you a few questions, Caroline."

"About?" I asked, making no move in their direction.

"Barbara Marks."

"There's nothing I can tell you that's not already in the court record, which is available online," I replied. I began to walk past him toward the elevator.

"Why on earth did you agree to recommend probation?" he asked, in a voice loud enough that everyone in the lobby could clearly hear. "You *know* how she victimized my mother—with whom you had a personal relationship. A woman who spent time with you and your children."

I spun around. "Don't you *dare* bring our personal relationship into this, Dominic. It has nothing to do with this case."

I glanced toward Matt, standing beside me. Then, to my horror, I noticed a reporter for the *Wisconsin State Journal*, his notebook and pen at the ready, a few steps away. *Shit! What must this look like to the media? How do I handle it?*

I took a deep breath and spoke in an assertive, yet quieter, tone. "The personal relationship I had with you and your mother, of which my supervisors are fully aware, has been over for some time. If I were to share anything other than public information about Ms. Marks with you—even though your mother was the victim in her Cook County case—I would be in violation of the law. What were you hoping to accomplish here today?"

He paused, seeming taken aback by my question. "I was hoping my mother could find some closure," he said, slowly.

"Closure." The ubiquitous word made me cringe. "It seems she got it," I said. "I heard Barbara Marks apologize. And I heard your mother say that she feels sorry for Barbara. What more do you want?"

"How about justice? Learning that you've made some secret deal with her that can't be discussed in open court certainly doesn't sound like justice to me."

My hands were shaking; I had to ball them into fists before I could reply. "Everything I've done in this case has been within the law. Now, if you'll excuse me, I need to get back to my office."

I strode to the elevator with Matt, and waited an interminable thirty seconds for the door to slide open. "Hang out here and see if the reporter talks to Dominic, okay?" I whispered to him. "Text me later."

He nodded and stood nonchalantly against the wall.

On the first floor, I ran to the restroom. I hurried into a stall, threw my coat and briefcase on the floor, and shut the door, leaning against it. Breathing heavily, probably hyperventilating. The bright-white tiles and overhead fluorescents reminded me of an interrogation chamber. A faint hum in one of the light fixtures added to the ringing already in my ears, threatening to push me over the edge. My head swam, my peripheral vision clouded. I slid down to the floor, back against the stall door, steadying myself with my hands on the cool, ceramic floor. *Oh, God, the last thing I can deal with right now is a panic attack.*

It passed, as panic attacks do, but left me, fifteen-minutes later, exhausted, tearful, and reviewing in my mind the scene outside the courtroom.

I couldn't stop picturing Dominic—attractive beyond words in that well-cut suit with Emma hanging on his arm. My jealousy alarmed me. *Stop it! The only emotion you should be feeling right now is anger. He called your boss and tried to get him involved in this stupid drama. He and that bimbo dragged his mother up here for a hearing that was none of their concern. Then, he had the gall to air your personal business and challenge your judgment and ethics in front of a newspaper reporter. He's a two-timing snake and unworthy of your love… Love? You* can't *still love him. For God's sake, move on!*

Back in my office, I turned on my cell phone. I read Matt's text: "Your ex refused to talk with the reporter. End of story."

But, of course, it wasn't. Sitting at my desk later that morning, replaying the awful scene in my mind for the tenth time, I cringed at a knock on the closed door.

"Caroline?" came my boss's familiar voice.

"Can it wait, George?"

"'fraid not."

I sighed. "C'mon in."

He sat on the arm of a chair across from me. "I heard about the dustup outside the courtroom."

Elbows on my desk, I cradled my head in my hands.

"Harry told me when I went over for a ten o'clock motion hearing. Said he was locking up the courtroom at the time and saw the whole thing." Harry, a busybody court security officer, never missed an opportunity to fan the flames of gossip. I hadn't even noticed him in the vicinity of my confrontation with Dominic. "He said there was a reporter there," George added.

"Yeah. But after I left, Matt Witte stayed and kept an eye on things. Matt said Dominic refused to comment. So, hopefully, there'll be no story in the paper."

George stood up. "Still, I'd better let the boss know. I can't let you handle Barbara Marks' sentencing. I'm not sure whether you should handle Bobby's trial, either."

My heart sank. "But George—"

He raised his hand in a "stop" gesture. "You'll have a chance to make your case before we decide, I promise."

He closed the door on his way out, and I burst into tears, yet again.

Chapter Thirty-eight

Lily met me at the front door that evening. I'd regrouped from the blowup with Dominic, but still felt emotionally drained. "Grandma asked me to watch the kids so you can go downstairs. She's got something to tell you."

I kissed her on the cheek. "And hello to you, too," I said. "Do you know what it's about?"

She shook her head.

I noticed Luke standing against the living room door-frame. He ran the back of his hand across his nose, leaving a trail of snot on his upper lip. "Can we come, too?"

"She said just Mom," Lily replied sharply, then turned to me. "Don't you think it's weird that she wants to talk to you alone?" The look of alarm on her face sent a jolt of anxiety to the pit of my stomach.

I shrugged out of my coat and hung it on the coat tree. "I'm sure it's nothing earthshattering," I said, with confidence I didn't feel. "Lily, please wipe his face and get the littles a healthy snack—carrots or an apple and some milk. I'll order a pizza when I come back up."

I trudged downstairs to Abby's apartment, my head spinning with awful scenarios. Abby had some significant health issues—diabetes and colitis. Could she be having complications? Or something worse? As a regular reader of obituaries, I knew of so many seemingly-healthy people who'd died in their sixties and seventies. I prayed silently as I went, *Please, God, let her be okay. These kids can't withstand another loss, and neither can I.*

I walked warily into her kitchen and saw a bottle of champagne chilling in an ice bucket. When Abby and Bert walked in from the living room, beaming with obvious pleasure, my anxiety lifted.

"Oh, my gosh," I said, "I was worried you had bad news."

"Nope," Bert said, with an eye-twinkling smile. He moved three, stemmed glasses from the counter to the table and held two chairs out for Abby and me, motioning for us to sit. "Please join us in a toast, Caroline."

"Happy to," I said, as I eased onto my chair, "if you tell me what we're toasting."

Abby, blushing like a schoolgirl, stood next to Bert and held out her left hand. "He asked me to marry him." The diamond ring on her finger sparkled.

"And she said 'yes!'" Bert added, as the cork popped out and champagne spilled onto the floor. He took a step backward, waited for the fizzing to cease, and then poured.

I stood and hugged Abby. "That's absolutely wonderful! I'm so happy for you."

Bert solemnly handed us our glasses and raised his own. "To you, my love!"

She blinked back tears. "Oh, Bert…"

I reached for some paper towels, mopped the spill off the floor, and sat back down. "Who've you told?"

"Our kids," she said. "Rita's cool to the idea, but Julia and Tony are delighted. Bert's kids are, too."

"What about Lily and the littles?"

"We decided to wait until we talked to you," she said. "Uh… Bert thinks they'll have lots of questions and we wanted your input first."

"Why?" I asked, turning to Bert. "The kids adore you. I can't imagine them being anything but excited."

"Well…" he said. "My apartment's too small for the two of us and Abby's really is, too. We'll need find something more suitable. Of course, it'll be as close to this area as we can find."

The thought of Abby no longer living in her basement apartment sent waves of sadness and panic though me. Her presence was a safety net I wasn't ready to give up. "That sounds like a good plan," I mumbled.

Bert squeezed Abby's hand and they exchanged a quick, unreadable glance. My gut told me there was more. "You still want to be the kids' nanny, don't you?" I asked, mortified at the desperation in my voice and terrified to hear her answer.

Abby hung her head, and I saw a lone tear making its way down her cheek.

"Well, that's the thing," Bert said. "We'd like to be able to do some traveling—before we're too old."

"We still want to help whenever we can, and I can't bear to be away from these kids for too long," Abby said, wiping her nose with a tissue she'd pulled from her sleeve.

I placed my hands on my knees to steady them and inhaled slowly. "Hey," I said in the most upbeat tone I could muster, "you deserve to enjoy your retirement. We'll find someone to take over the day-to-day stuff, and you can be a normal grandmother."

"See, honey," Bert said. "I told you it'd be okay."

Abby looked at me with some skepticism as she stuffed the tissue back up her sleeve.

"We should call the kids down and tell 'em," I said. "Lily was afraid you had bad news."

Bert nodded and set three more wine glasses, a sippy cup for Red, and a liter of 7-Up on the table, while Abby telephoned upstairs. They must've been sitting in my kitchen, perhaps listening at the basement door, for a nanosecond after she hung up we heard footsteps on the stairs.

"What's goin' on?" Luke asked, charging in.

"Chillax," Bert said with a smile, clearly proud of his mastery of the vernacular. When Lily followed her siblings into the room, he put his arm around his fiancée and repeated the news.

The twins solemnly held their glasses of soda, spilling nary a drop. In response to my stern look of warning, Red accepted the less-classy sippy cup without complaint, and we all toasted Abby and Bert. Amid the anticipation of Christmas with a soon-to-be new grandpa, questions about living quarters and nanny duties didn't arise.

I struggled to hide my despair.

I'd naively thought I'd have time to adjust to the idea of Abby's departure from our household. But when I came home from work two days later, Bert met me at the door.

"Abby and the kids are down in her apartment," he said, in a conspiratorial tone. "I wanted to run something by you. Can we talk in the living room?"

I hung my coat on the coat tree. "Sure."

Chilled from the brief walk from my car, I tucked my legs up under me on the chair and pulled an afghan around my shoulders. "What's up?"

"You know those Viking River Cruises they advertise on *Downton Abbey*?"

I nodded.

"Abby's always talking about how she'd love to go on one."

"I've heard they're awesome."

"Well, today I was talking with our travel agent about a honeymoon trip. He told me he's had a cancellation for one of those cruises and can give us a great deal. It's the twelve-day Cities of Lights tour and it looks amazing." His eyes shone like Luke's did when he described his favorite trucks. "We could get married on the boat, which means we could quit listening to Abby's daughter, Rita, telling us what we *simply have to do* for our wedding. The only drawback is that since we'll be in Texas for Christmas, we'd have to leave right from there to get to Paris by the twenty-seventh."

"The twenty-seventh? Of *December*? Three weeks from now?"

Bert's face fell. A wave of guilt washed over me for deflating his mood. "I know it's not much notice..." he mumbled. "It just seemed so perfect."

I threw aside the afghan, forced myself to smile, and went to sit beside him on the couch. "It *is* perfect," I said, taking his hand. "I'm afraid I'm just still in denial about Abby leaving us. But it's time I get my head wrapped around it. Of course, you should go."

His look of relief warmed my heart.

"Are you going to surprise Abby or tell her now?"

He grinned. "I can't wait to tell her!"

Abby, happy as I'd ever seen her, pulled pans of lasagna and tiramisu from the freezer for a celebratory dinner. "I refuse to eat Papa Murphy's pizza on an occasion like this," she declared. And after getting the littles to bed, I watched as she and Bert sat at my dining room table with Lily helping them apply online for expedited passports. I envied the way they teased one another, the tender way they looked at one another, their gentle strokes of affection. My stomach ached with longing for that kind of interaction.

"Would you guys mind keeping an ear open for the littles so I can go visit Glenda for a bit?" I asked.

"Stay as long as you want," Bert said. "That tiramisu Abby made will keep me alert for hours."

I went up to my room, grabbed a sweatshirt, and texted Glenda, "U free 4 me to come over?"

Glenda's daughter, Sarah, responded, "Moms @ Jakes game & forgot her phone. Back around 10."

"Ok. I'll catch her tomorrow," I wrote back. I collapsed onto my chaise longue and burst into tears. *How can I feel so alone in a house full of people?*

CHAPTER THIRTY-NINE

The following morning, I sat alone at the kitchen table with a tepid cup of coffee, too bogged down in inertia to freshen it, lost in thought. Abby and Red had gone to take the twins to school. Lily and I had her follow-up appointment with Dr. Grube at 8:00. The notion of seeing him again mortified me. *Will he ever look at me as anything other than a drunken mess?*

I didn't hear her walk in, but the grin on Lily's face reached all the way to her eyes. It immediately brightened my mood.

"Good to see you smiling, kiddo."

For a nanosecond, a puzzled look replaced the smile. "Yeah. I guess I am feeling happy," she said.

"About anything in particular?"

"Well… Shelley invited me to a party at her house Friday night. Don't worry, her parents are gonna be home and they're okay with you calling them to check. Anyway, there's this cool boy in my Spanish class and he's going, too. He texted me today and said he'd, like, see me there."

"So he's cool, huh?" I said, glancing at her from the corner of my eye.

She nodded.

"Is he also nice?"

Lily giggled. "Yes. And a good student. Not a trouble-maker. You'd like him."

I poured new coffee into a to-go mug and followed her out the door.

The psychiatrist came to greet us in the waiting area. "Great to see you both," he said, as he shook our hands. "Lily, would you like to talk privately with me before your mom joins us?"

I tried to keep my face bland.

"Nah. She can come in now."

"Okay," he said. "C'mon in."

I took the same spot on the sofa I'd sat in during the first appointment. With an air of composure, Lily picked a chair closer to Dr. Grube and rested her hands on her lap.

He leaned forward, elbow on his knee. "You look a darn sight more relaxed than the last time I saw you," he said to her. "What's been goin' on with you?"

She paused, as if wondering where to begin. "Um… things are good. I haven't stolen anything, and I finished my community service hours for the court."

He nodded appreciatively. "And you've been going to the support group?"

"Yeah."

"What do you think of it?"

"At first, it was awkward. I mostly just listened, but then one of the girls who's really nice asked me some questions to, like, get me involved. Now, I like it."

"How many kids in the group?" Larry asked.

Lily stopped to count on her fingers. I imagined her picturing each new acquaintance in her mind. In the process, she began to smile. "Ten. Six girls and four boys."

"Does Juanita Quintana lead the discussion?" he asked.

"She gets us going," Lily said. "Asks, you know, if there's anything someone wants to discuss, or if anyone wants to read something they've written in their journal. If not, she makes a suggestion about what we could talk about. Then, she sits back and lets us talk."

"What do you like best about the group?"

Lily responded without pause. "We all kind of understand what the others are going through. If you cry or something, nobody thinks you're weird. We can be ourselves. And I thought sharing stuff from our journals would be hard, but it's really cool."

Larry smiled and turned to me. "Have you noticed any change in Lily's behavior or mood since we last met?"

Go ahead! Admit to him you've been so preoccupied with work and with Abby's upcoming departure and with your own loneliness that you haven't paid her much attention. And that you didn't know she liked the support group because there she could "be herself." And that you had no clue she was even keeping a journal.

"She definitely seems happier," I mumbled.

Dr. Grube waited for me to elaborate, but I didn't know what more to say.

"Alrighty then," he said, standing and extending his hand to Lily. "It was a pleasure to meet with you, young lady. I'll be here in the unlikely event you need my help in the future."

She giggled and shook his hand. "Thanks."

"There's a few things I want to talk to your mom about privately, if that's okay."

"No problem," she said, walking confidently to the door.

I felt a knot in my stomach. I'd been hoping to avoid another one-on-one talk with him, but it was clear I'd hoped in vain.

He returned to his chair and looked me in the eye. "Is there something else you wanted to tell me about Lily? Your answer was on the sketchy side."

I glanced over his shoulder at the wall calendar, which he hadn't flipped since September, unable to meet his gaze. "I'm ashamed to say it, but I haven't been paying her as much attention as I should've. You know the old saying about the squeaky wheel?" He nodded. "Well, Lily hasn't been squeaking lately."

Larry let out a guffaw. "That's *good* news! And you're too hard on yourself. A single mother with four kids has gotta prioritize; listening for squeaks ain't a bad way to do it."

I gave him a half smile. "Ya think?"

"I think. Have you seen Clarice Brownhill lately?"

"Just before Thanksgiving, when things were pretty calm. But all hell's broken loose since then, and I'm not scheduled again 'til a week from today."

"Could you define hell breaking loose?"

"First off, my ex showed up at one of my court hearings—with his new bimbo on his arm—and opened up wounds I thought were healing. I went home that night to learn that my mother-in-law, who's my nanny, cook, and in-house support system, is engaged and plans to move out and travel. And two days later, I learned that's happening much faster than originally planned—less than two weeks from now." I glanced down at my hands, now balled into fists.

Larry shook his head. "I'm guessing you're feeling pretty abandoned."

"Yes, Captain Obvious. …Oh, shit! That was incredibly rude. I'm sorry."

"I've got tough skin," he said, with a wink. "And sometimes my efforts to clarify my patients' feelings are painfully lame."

I took a few deep breaths and managed to unclench my fists.

"Good job," Larry said, nodding toward my hands. "Are you sleeping okay?"

"With the help of Tylenol P.M."

"How much are you drinking in a typical week?"

"A couple beers or glasses of wine, two or three days a week. Oh, wait. One Saturday, I had three glasses. No hard liquor since the day I met you, though."

He nodded. "Do need me to prescribe something for depression or anxiety?"

"Uh-uh. I took antidepressants and anti-anxiety meds several years ago for panic disorder, but I'm not there now. At least not yet."

"Good. You can have Clarice call me if that changes."

"Thanks. I'll keep that in mind."

Lily, staring at her phone and smiling from ear to ear, didn't see us walk back into the waiting area. "Let's watch," Larry whispered, "I think she's about to LOL."

For the first time in what felt like forever, I laughed out loud.

CHAPTER FORTY

Abby and Bert's expedited passports arrived on the same Saturday morning that Two Men and a Truck came to pick up her furniture. Lily leaned against me as we stood in Abby's living room watching the moving men carrying her sofa through the patio door. "This all seems kinda like a dream, doesn't it?" she asked. "It feels like only yesterday that they got engaged."

I squeezed her shoulder. "For the record, it was almost three weeks ago that they announced their engagement."

She swallowed a couple times and her voice cracked, "Why did they hafta be in such a rush?"

Carrying a laundry basket full of folded sheets and towels, Abby walked in. She cleared her throat. "Uh… I couldn't help overhearing—"

Lily hung her head. "I'm sorry, Grandma. Things are just happening so quick. It's, like, hard to get used to the idea of you not living here."

Abby set the basket on an end table and hugged Lily to her chest. "Oh, honey, I'm sorry for y'all that our plans fell into place so fast. I would've been happy to postpone the move and the wedding a little while, but Bert kept saying, 'What are we waiting for? We're not gettin' any younger, dear.' Truth be told, I think men have a harder time being alone than women do. But I'm not sure that slowing it all down would've made it any easier for you. It's kinda like taking off a Band-Aid; it's better to just do it."

She grabbed a towel from her basket and wiped a tear off my daughter's cheek. "You're gonna love the house we rented, Lily. It's got plenty of room for sleepovers. And with this apartment empty, you could move your room down here. Amy and Luke can't sleep in the same room forever, you know."

Lily looked up at me with a glimmer of happiness in her eyes. "Could I, Mom?"

The baby monitor clipped to the waistband of my jeans squawked before I could formulate an answer. "Red's awake and doesn't sound happy," I said. "We'll talk about it after things quiet down a bit."

I trudged up the two, seemingly endless flights of stairs wondering if I could handle Lily sleeping so far from the rest of us. *What if there's a fire? Or someone breaks in? Or she just has a bad dream?* I found Red standing in her crib, her face full of snot and tears, her sagging diaper leaking its load of sloppy poop. I picked her up and held her at arm's length, carrying her straight to the bathtub. "It's okay, kiddo. We'll have you cleaned up in no time."

By the time I'd bathed and changed her, corralled the soiled clothes, bedding, and towels, and returned to Abby's apartment with Red in tow, the movers were closing the door to the truck. Abby stood at the patio door watching, a dazed look on her face. Lily and the twins sat on the living room floor, their dejected expressions in complete contrast to the pile of brightly-wrapped Christmas packages stacked in the corner behind them. "Look, Mommy," Luke said, in a near-monotone, "they left the presents."

I threw Abby a quizzical glance.

"Uh… I was going to take the presents to our new place and have you all come over to open them before Bert and I leave for Texas. But Luke got pretty upset at that idea. He wanted to put them under the… uh, the tree here."

I could see her quandary. As yet, we *had* no Christmas tree. In fact, our only holiday decorations were the paper stockings the twins had cut out and colored at school, now sliding precariously down the face of the refrigerator under overloaded magnets.

I'd moved "get Xmas tree" lower on my to-do list several times already. Finding childcare and household help and the myriad tasks associated with preparing for Bobby Marks' trial had taken precedence. Abby'd managed to hem up the costumes the kids would need for this afternoon's dress rehearsal of the church Christmas program; that chore would've put me over the edge.

"Well, I'd better get going," Abby said, with a hitch to her voice, heading for the stairs. "Bert'll want me there to tell the guys where to put things." Without making eye contact, she blew kisses and was gone.

The hollow feeling in my stomach threatened to overtake me. I glanced at my watch. "Hey, kiddos, it's almost lunchtime. Why don't we stop at Culver's for lunch and then get our tree at Bruce Company? We'll have time to get it in the stand and at least get the lights on it before your rehearsal."

Luke's face lit up. Whether at the idea of a hamburger, fries, and frozen custard or the tree, I'm not sure, but his smile was infectious. We threw on our jackets and took a canvas bag full of mittens, hats, and scarves to keep us toasty during the tree-selection process, usually a prolonged affair. It'd been so hard for me the past two years, but I'd refused to let David's absence put a damper on the kids' enthusiasm for finding *just the right tree*, no matter how long it took. But I'd had the indefatigable Abby along riding shotgun on those occasions.

Today, Lily buckled Red and Amy into their car seats then climbed into the front passenger seat. "You know," she said, before I'd even pulled out of the driveway, "Grandma's idea about moving my room downstairs makes sense. And we could, like, turn her living room into a playroom for all the kids' toys so our upstairs living room wouldn't look like a tornado hit it all the time."

I gave her a "hush" signal with my hand, but it was too late. "What's Lily talking about, Mommy?" Amy asked. "Is she gonna have Grandma's old room? Can I have her room? It's not fair that Luke and I hafta share."

"Whoa, Nelly! Hold your horses! I have some concerns about Lily sleeping two floors down from the rest of us. And about you playing downstairs without supervision."

"But, Mom," Lily said, exasperation overtaking her voice, "we've got burglar alarms all over the house. It's just as safe for me to be downstairs as up. And we could get an intercom system. Shelley's family just got one, and it's really cool. There's, like, cameras in every room so her parents can see what's going on. Her mom can call the kids to dinner without yelling and stuff."

I cringed. "Sounds creepy."

Lily giggled. "They don't have 'em in the bathrooms, or anything. But, seriously, we could put one in Grandma's old living room so you could keep an eye on the kids when you're upstairs making dinner, or whatever."

You'd better hope I find someone else to make dinner for us or we'll be living on mac 'n' cheese.

"Can we put the Christmas tree down there?" Luke piped up.

"Yeah, let's!" Amy yelled.

If putting the tree in what was Abby's apartment will ease the sting of her departure, it's fine with me. "Okay to the Christmas tree," I said. "I'll think about the bedrooms."

Two hours later, with the perfect tree roped to the top of the minivan, I pulled across the frozen, but bare, back lawn to park in front of the basement patio door. "Hurry up, Lily," Luke yelled, as she struggled to punch in the code for the door lock. "I gotta go potty."

"Hang on! My fingers are frozen," she shot back. "There, I got it."

I released Red from her car seat and all four kids rushed into the house. *Frickin' Jack Frost,* I thought, as my nose dripped from the biting wind. I stood on the door frame of the minivan and pulled at the rope. The two teenaged boys who'd tied the tree on must've gotten Eagle Scout badges in knot tying. No way was I going to get this thing undone alone.

I went inside, blew on my fingers, and texted Glenda: "Can u spare Hank or Trey to help me get this f*ing tree off the car? By the basement door."

"There in 5," came the reply.

Hank, Glenda, and a gangly golden retriever appeared at the door a few minutes later. "Who's this?" I asked, nodding toward the dog, who wandered in and began sniffing the pile of presents.

"Sparky," Glenda said. "His owner got remarried and trophy wife claims she's allergic. We're keeping him 'til we can find him a new home."

"Don't even think it, Glen," I said.

"What?"

I shook my head dismissively and went to help Hank. He'd wisely decided to cut the ropes, liberating the tree from its bondage. "Is the stand ready?" he asked, leaning the now-vertical tree against the van.

"Sorry; I didn't even think of that. C'mon in and grab yourself a beer while I find it."

I dragged the tree stand and two boxes of lights and ornaments out from the crawl space beneath the basement stairway, emerging with cobwebs and dust in my hair and itching with the heebie jeebies. "Lily! Come carry these boxes, please."

Hank, ever unflappable, kneeled on the floor, adjusting the tree 'til Glenda declared it straight. He stood up, hitched up his jeans, and grabbed his beer from atop an ornament box. "You kids picked a great tree; maybe the best one I've ever seen."

Preoccupied with petting Sparky, the littles looked up at Hank as if he was speaking a foreign language.

Lily plugged a string of lights into a wall socket and smiled with satisfaction when they lit up. "It *is* a good one," she said. "Dad would be proud."

I laid a hand on her shoulder. "Yes, he would."

Glenda, Lily, and I wound three strands of lights around the tree while Hank chatted with the twins. "No, Sparky's as big as he's gonna get. …Sit, Sparky. …He'll shake your hand if you ask. …Yeah, he barks sometimes, but only when people come to the door."

We stood back to admire our work. The smell of pine and the glitter of colorful lights gave the room a festive feel—that I couldn't have imagined when Abby and the movers left that morning. "The kids have play rehearsal at 4:00," I said to Glenda, "but why don't you and your kids come for pizza this evening? We can bring down some lawn chairs and a card table and christen the new family room."

"Sounds great," Glenda said. "Sarah'll be so glad; she's grounded and getting pretty sick of spending time alone with her family."

I turned to Lily. "Maybe Sarah could give you some ideas on how to decorate your new room."

She beamed. "You mean it, Mom? I can have my room down here?"

I nodded. "But not until we get the intercom installed."

Lily hugged me and ran upstairs to call her friends.

Chapter Forty-one

I dropped the three older kids off at the church and went to Target for soda, beer, and dessert. Red had gone home with Glenda and Hank to take a much-needed nap.

As is often the case in big-box stores, I found myself drawn down aisles I hadn't planned to visit. A fifty-inch, flat screen TV caught my eye. *If I get this today, Hank can unload it and hook it up to Abby's cable outlet when he comes for dinner. It'll be a Christmas present. Maybe the kids'll quit mooning over Sparky if they've got a bright, shiny TV to distract them.*

Darkness had fallen by the time play practice ended, and the kids didn't notice the box in the back of the mini-van. When we pulled up in front of the Fosters' to collect Red, Luke verbalized what they'd all been thinking, "Can Sparky come, too?"

"Yeah, Mom, please?" Lily and Amy said, in unison.

"Maybe they'll bring him when they come for dinner. He'd be in the way while we're decorating the tree."

Lily found Christmas music on Spotify and played it through the Bluetooth speaker she'd bought with her baby-sitting money. We giggled and sang loudly and off-key to

"Deck the Halls," "Joy to the World," and Alvin and the Chipmunks' "Rudolph, the Red-Nosed Reindeer," while we hung the ornaments. "This is so fun," Amy said, as I lifted her up to place the star atop the tree.

"Look at this one!" Luke cried, holding up a Thomas the Train ornament.

"Dad bought that one for you when you were two," Lily said.

Please! Let's not focus on our loss. But Luke merely nodded and placed Thomas on the tree. Lily reached into the box for a crystal angel as though nothing unusual had just transpired.

I breathed a sigh of relief when the Fosters, sans Trey, who was working and would deliver our pizza and salad, came for dinner without Sparky. My kids' crestfallen looks at his absence gave me pause. *Maybe they do need another living being in this house. One who can give and receive affection.* I shoved those thoughts away. *You've got enough on your plate without adding a dog to the mix.*

"I've got a surprise for you kids," I said, after we'd pushed aside the empty pizza boxes.

"Doggie?" Red asked.

I saw Glenda and Hank exchange knowing smiles and laughed nervously. "No, honey. Not a doggie. A new TV for this room. I'm hoping Uncle Hank and Jake can figure out how to hook it up."

"We'd be happy to, wouldn't we Jake?" Hank said.

Far handier than David had ever been, Hank had the new set assembled, connected, and receiving Netflix before I'd gotten Red and the twins into their PJs. We dragged sleeping bags downstairs and unrolled them in front of *Finding Nemo*. Lily and Sarah retreated to the bedroom, where they'd inflated the queen-sized airbed we used for guests, and were hunting on Pinterest for decorating tips.

"Well, Jake," Hank said, "our work here is done. What say we go home and watch some hockey?"

Glenda, sitting cross-legged on the floor, reached her hand up toward me. "And what say you and I go upstairs and catch up?"

I pulled her to her feet. "Head on up. I'll set the alarm on this door and be there in a couple minutes. There's half a case of William Hill cabernet in the pantry."

"Ooh—you got the good stuff!"

"It's the holidays."

I found a note from Glenda on the kitchen table. "On back porch having a cig. DON'T JUDGE ME!"

"Are you bat shit crazy?" I asked, cracking the back door open an inch to talk with her. "It's freezing out here."

"Uh-huh. Light the fireplace, okay? I'll be in in a minute."

I grabbed the open wine bottle, some cocktail napkins, and the glass she'd left on the counter and headed for my living room. The whoosh of the gas logs as I turned the fuel knob took me aback, as always, but made me glad I'd had the wood burner replaced after David's death. I adjusted the flames and retreated to my chair.

A wave of cold, fresh air followed Glenda into the room, almost masking the smell of cigarette smoke on the jacket she threw over the couch before she sat down. She fiddled with her ponytail for a moment, took a long sip of wine, and leaned back against the cushions. "What's new? It's been too long since we've talked."

"I'm barely keeping my head above water," I said. "I'm swamped at work, getting ready for a trial that I'm not even sure my boss is gonna let me handle. In my spare time, I've been looking for daycare and babysitters and household help. Abby and Bert really threw a monkey wrench into things with their faster-than-a-speeding-bullet wedding."

"Yeah, Jake told me they were engaged. Next thing I heard, she was moving out and eloping on some boat in Europe. He thinks it's the height of cool."

I felt the unmistakable sting of tears behind my eyelids and didn't dare speak for fear they would gather in full force.

"Oh, kiddo, you're gonna cry, aren't you?"

Her question set the tears loose. I slid the napkin out from under my wine glass and used it to blow my nose. "I told you Dominic started seeing that P.I. from Chicago…"

"Uh-huh. As I recall, you described her as a 'gorgeous, statuesque blonde of child-bearing years.'"

I couldn't help but smile. "Perhaps a tad melodramatic. Anyway, the woman psychic who conned Dominic's mother was in court here a couple weeks ago. Dominic, his mother, *and* Emma showed up to watch. He approached me after the hearing and made a huge scene in front of God and everyone, including a newspaper reporter. I had to tell him off. It was just so ugly. My boss got wind of it, took me off the psychic's case, and may even take me off the trial I've been prepping for months because the psychic's scheduled to be a witness. …I thought I was getting over Dominic, but his being there just reopened wounds."

"What's harder to handle: that he's seeing someone else or that you might get the trial taken away from you?"

I shrugged. "I don't know. They're both so hard. But work keeps me from dwelling on being unattached, and this is a case I really want to try."

She picked at a hangnail. "Was it hard when you and Matt stopped seeing each other?"

"Uh-uh. He's a great guy and a good friend. But I was kidding myself if I thought it'd go further."

We didn't speak for a while, the silence broken by the tapping of her foot against the coffee table. "Go smoke another cigarette while I check on the kids," I finally said. "Your fidgeting is making me crazy."

I found Red and the twins nestled in their sleeping bags while the final credits to *Nemo* rolled over the TV screen. Only Luke remained conscious, but barely. Lily and Sarah, glued to their smartphones, nodded when I tapped at the doorframe. "Lily, keep an ear out for the kiddos, please. I don't want to bother taking them upstairs. I'll bring down some bedding later and you and I can sleep on the airbed."

Glenda was warming her hands in front of the fireplace when I got back to the living room. I refilled our wine glasses and sat down.

"Did you find someone to stand in for Abby?"

I took a long, slow sip before answering. "A village."

My friend raised an eyebrow.

"My folks are coming tomorrow, for two weeks…"

"Two weeks?"

I sighed. "I'd hoped to take time off over the holidays, but I'll need to work at least a few days 'cause my boss wants me to bring him up to speed on my trial."

"Sorry for interrupting. Tell me about the other villagers."

"Well, Red's gonna start at St. Mary's Childcare Center when the other kids go back to school after Christmas break. I hired Madeline, a nursing student at Edgewood College, to pick the kids up from school and daycare and watch 'em here in the afternoons 'til I get home. And a woman from my church, Grace, is gonna come on Mondays to make our meals for the week and clean the house. She'll cover for Madeline when there's early dismissal from school, or whatever. That's the plan for now."

"I sure hope you guys like Grace's cooking, and that Abby doesn't throw a fit when she comes back from her honeymoon to find someone's taken over her bailiwick," Glenda said, with a grin.

"Thanks, Glen; I really needed a few more things to worry about." But I had to laugh at the thought of a cat-fight in our kitchen.

I drained my glass. "More wine?" I asked.

"No, thanks. Busy day tomorrow and I don't need a headache."

I awoke around midnight, disoriented by the strange surroundings, the odd feel to the airbed, and the sound of Lily's gentle snoring. Luke stood next to me, tapping my shoulder. "Mom!"

"Did you have a bad dream?" I asked, scooting over and pulling him beside me.

"Uh-uh. I want to tell you something."

"What's that?"

"I won't be scared in my own room if Sparky comes to live with us."

"Is that so?"

He nodded and drifted off to sleep. *I can't believe I'm thinking this, but I might be more comfortable with a watchdog living with us, too. I'll talk with Hank about it tomorrow.*

CHAPTER FORTY-TWO

At 7:30 Monday morning, three days before Christmas, I met my friend Linda for breakfast at Barrique's. She'd called a few weeks earlier, as she'd done every December since David died.

"We need to get together and catch up," she'd said, acting as both the bereavement counselor she was by profession and the friend she'd been since childhood. During most of our adult years, we'd managed to see one another every few months, always picking up easily where we'd left off.

Already seated at a table when I walked in, warming her hands around a mug of coffee, she stood to greet me with a loving hug. "It seems like forever since I've seen you."

"I know," I said. "I've been trying to remember when it was."

"Last summer. You were getting ready to go on a romantic getaway with your new guy. Dominic, right?"

"Yikes! That was eons ago." I unwound my scarf, took off my gloves, and hung my coat over the back of a chair.

"I do remember that it's my turn to buy. I'm gonna have a breakfast croissant. What would you like?"

"The same, please."

I placed our order at the counter and then returned to the table with my coffee. "Yeah, the guy's name was… uh, is Dominic. It was hot for a while, but I broke up with him in September. I've wondered since then if I might've been hasty, but it's too late now."

Linda stirred her coffee and took a sip. "Why'd you break up with him?"

"At first I told myself it was because he had too much baggage—the largest piece being his mother with bipolar disorder. But I think it was really because I started comparing how he carried baggage to how David had. Dominic didn't measure up. I felt abandoned every time he wasn't there when I needed him."

She smiled. "Sometimes in our grief over losing someone, we forget his faults. I didn't know him well, but I suspect David wasn't perfect."

The barista called my name and I went to pick up our order. "No, David wasn't perfect," I said, as I sat back down and put my napkin on my lap. "But we fit together, like our pheromones and our souls matched or something."

Linda finished chewing a bite of croissant. "Do you believe there's only one person in the world you're meant to be with?"

I shook my head. "No, but I don't think just *anyone* will do. You remember that Dominic was the investigator who tracked down the guy who caused David's accident?" She nodded. "And he became a good friend to me and the kids during the whole process?" Another nod. "Well… after my shroud of grief finally lifted and I actually saw his eyes, it was like I melted into them. I thought Dominic was someone I *could* spend my life with."

"I'm guessing you got scared."

"Scared?"

"That you might have chosen wrong, or that David wouldn't approve. Or that Dominic might die and you'd have to grieve another loss."

"You're right. I was afraid of *all* of those things."

She didn't speak for a moment. "A few minutes ago you said your decision to break up with Dominic might've been hasty, but that it was too late. What'd you mean?"

"He started seeing another woman almost immediately. She's young, and hot, and smart, and unabashedly in love with him. She could give him kids of his own…" I couldn't continue.

Linda reached over and took my hand. "Oh, Caroline, I'm sorry. We're so vulnerable when we're grieving—to fear, hurt, insecurity, loneliness."

"Will I *ever* be done grieving?"

She stroked my hand with her thumb. "Do you really want to be? I mean, wouldn't that depreciate the love you felt for David?"

I shrugged. "Maybe the better question is, will I ever be able to move on to an intimate relationship with another man?"

"I'm confident you will."

I pushed aside my plate. "Okay. Then *how* do I do it?"

"It's different for everyone, but a couple widows I've known firmly believe you've got to make room for a new man. Get rid of your late husband's favorite chair so you don't see new guy sitting in it. Park on one side of the garage so there's room for another car. Leave some dresser drawers empty so new guy has a place to put his stuff. Visualize yourself happily interacting with another man. Most importantly, recognize that new guy *isn't* David, but that your heart has the capacity to love him, too."

I reflected on what she'd said. "You know, I actually found myself feeling more upbeat listening to your suggestions. And I have room in my garage for another car; Abby moved out on Saturday."

"Really? How come?"

"She's getting married and retiring from being the kids' nanny."

"Wow—that's going to be a huge adjustment. How are the kids doing with it?"

"Surprisingly, okay," I said, with a smile. "'Course it might help that I caved in to their suggestion that we adopt a dog. And that they're all going to have their own rooms now."

I glanced at my watch. "I wish I could stay longer—I need to hear what's going on in your life. But I've got to meet with two case agents and my boss in fifteen minutes."

Linda picked up her iPhone and checked her calendar. "Can we do this again next Monday?"

"Absolutely."

I texted George: "@ Barriques. Will bring coffee & pastries."

His reply came as I stood at the counter: "Good, but JSYK, bribery won't work." Despite my trepidation about the meeting, I couldn't help smiling. While George loved acronyms, he detested ubiquitous ones like FYI and often made up his own. JSYK was George-speak for "just so you know."

Half an hour later, pastry crumbs littering the conference table, George and I sat across from Matt and Jimmy and got down to business. Jimmy, in particular, wore a puzzled expression. "As Caroline may have told you," George said, "I've been considering taking her off the Bobby Marks trial and handling it myself. The boss wasn't pleased to hear about the oh-so-public questions raised after Barbara Marks' plea hearing and wants to make sure our office's impartiality can't be second guessed."

"That's crazy—" Jimmy began.

George raised his hand. "Not your call, and I've made my decision. I've gone over the list of witnesses and scanned their statements, but I'll need you two to free up your calendars 'til the trial to help me prep them. And just so you know, the judge denied my motion for a continuance."

I felt as though I'd been punched in the gut. I hadn't known he'd decided to take the case. Or, that he'd filed a motion to delay the trial.

Matt looked down at his lap. "I'm available."

Jimmy stood up, fished his phone from the back pocket of his faded corduroys, and checked his calendar. "Not me. I'm in Glynco the seventh through the ninth, and I can't reschedule."

George's jaw muscles tightened and he drummed his fingers on the table. "Then I guess we'll start reviewing your reports right now," he said, sharply. "Caroline and Matt, you can head out."

I stood, unsure my legs would hold. As I reached for my file, I knocked over my half-empty coffee cup, splashing the contents onto a stack of papers in front of George. "Oh, shit… I'm sorry."

Matt grabbed a fistful of napkins and blotted the mess. "No harm," he said, touching my elbow to move me toward the door. "Call if you need anything, George."

In the hallway, I leaned against the wall. "I never thought he'd do it. You were there for the confrontation with my ex, Matt. Does this seem like a necessary response?"

"I dunno, Caroline. It seems pretty unlikely that your ex would confront you again, even if he came to watch the trial. After all, Barbara'll be on the side of the good guys, this time."

"Yeah. And if George was gonna take over the case, why'd he wait so long? The trial starts in three weeks. I'm well on the way to being prepared."

He shrugged. "Maybe he's been waiting for you to convince him you should keep it?"

At 2:00, I buzzed George's secretary. "Is he in?"

"Uh-huh."

"Alone?"

"Yep. Agent McGee left half an hour ago."

"Thanks. I'll be right over. Please don't tell him I'm coming."

I walked with purpose to George's office. His door stood open and he sat at his computer. I ignored the scowl on his face and tapped on the door frame. "Sorry to barge in, but I really can't let you take me off the Marks case."

He looked up in irritation. "Clearly, you've been spending too much time with Agent Lack-of-Social-Skills. I'm in the middle of a DOJ report that's due this afternoon, and the last nincompoop who bothered me forgot to shut the door. Put your argument in an email. I'll get back to you."

Feeling chastised but excited, I went back to my desk and got to work on my message. I apologized for the public confrontation with Dominic and assured George it wouldn't happen again. I reported on the hours of witness preparation I'd already done with Matt and Jimmy. I concluded, "While Agent LOSS's demeanor may be off-putting at times, we've established a good working relationship. He will be a critical witness in the trial against Bobby Marks, and I'm confident I can elicit his best testimony." I proofread the message and hit Send.

I'd answered two more emails, shut down my computer, and was almost out the door, when my phone rang. George. "You had me at 'Agent LOSS,'" he said, with a chuckle. "Go get 'em!"

Chapter Forty-three

Lily, Sparky trotting placidly by her side, rounded the corner a half-block away as I pulled into the garage that evening.

I waited on the driveway for them. "He's great on a leash, isn't he?"

Lily took a dog biscuit from her pocket. "Sit, Sparky." The dog obeyed, and she gave him his treat. "Yeah, he's the *best*. So much better behaved than any of my friends' dogs. Even Grandma likes him."

"Speaking of whom—how'd it go today?" My mother's patience with little kids often left something to be desired.

"Good 'til she got a migraine. She's napping now and says Grandpa should take us out for dinner."

"Did Red nap?"

"Uh-huh. For three hours!"

I thought for a moment, warming to the idea of dinner out. "That's perfect. We can have dinner and then go furniture shopping."

Lily grinned. "Can I get a new bed and let Amy have my old one?"

"Seems fair, you being the oldest. And I was wondering if you might like to have your dad's leather armchair in your room." I couldn't discard the chair entirely; on countless occasions since her dad's death, I'd found Lily curled up in it, often clutching her stuffed dog, Grover.

"Are you kidding?" she shrieked, eyes glistening. "I'd love it. It'd look great in that space next to the bookcase."

We found my dad sitting cross-legged on the new family room floor, Red on his lap, playing *Uno* with the twins. "Do we have any blue cards in our hand?" he asked his partner. She shook her head. "Okay, draw one, and let's hope it's blue or a five." Red reached for the draw pile, picking up and promptly dropping three cards. "Well, that's one way to play it," Dad said, with a grin.

I kissed the kids on their heads. "Hate to interrupt, but Lily and I have a plan. Rocky Rococo's for pizza and salad, then Steinhafel's for furniture. Who's in?"

The kids threw down their cards and bounded up. I extended a hand to my dad. "Furniture sounds like an excellent idea," he said. 'Don't know how I would've gotten up if you hadn't appeared,"

"Won't Grandma want to come, too?" Amy asked. "She loves to shop!"

Yes, but her taste in furniture leans toward aesthetics rather than comfort. "She's not feeling well, honey. We'll take pictures of the stuff we pick and show 'em to her when we get home."

"We can't bring it home with us today?" Luke asked.

"It'll be delivered later," Dad said.

There were very few patrons in the restaurant on a frontage road south of the busy Madison Beltline. I shunned the already-prepared individual slices sitting for-lornly under heat lamps in their cardboard boxes. "We'll take a medium deep-dish pizza, half cheese and half pep-peroni," I told the counter clerk, "a pitcher of water, and six, one-trip bowls for the salad bar."

"Can't we have pop?" Luke asked.

"Nope. I'll buy you each a carton of milk, if you want."

He shook his head and wandered over to snatch a crouton from the salad bar.

The kids chattered about furniture throughout dinner. "I'm surprised they're so opinionated," my dad said, after Amy declared we needed a leather sectional couch, prefer-ably brown.

I wiped a glob of pizza sauce off Red's cheek. "Glenda and Hank have a sectional, which Amy thinks is the height of cool. She's heard me say a million times that leather is the only way to go with little kids. I'm not sure why she wants brown."

"Guess no one shops for furniture three days before Christmas," my dad said, as we walked into the massive, all-but-deserted store, half a mile from the restaurant. Armed with the floor plan of Abby's apartment, to ensure we chose pieces that would fit, he headed directly toward the leather section.

Great! The littles can run around and be loud without bothering anyone but the clerks. Who'll get a good commission for our visit.

Two hours later, long after I'd tired of cries of "Mommy, look at this," "This one's softer," "I like the blue better," and "Luke's jumping on that bed," we'd made our selections for the new family room: a sumptuous, brown leather sectional and side chair, a square coffee table, two end tables, and two lamps. Added to that were two over-stuffed club chairs with coordinating throw pillows for the living room and a new bed and desk for Lily's room. Amy would use Lily's old bed, and Red would use Amy's when we got around to moving her out of the crib.

"We forgot pictures for the walls," Amy said, on our way out the door.

"There's not a lot of wall space in the new family room," I said, "but I'd like to frame and hang some of you kids' artwork. You can paint or draw some more over Christmas vacation if you want."

Red, half asleep in my dad's arms, lifted her head a quarter of an inch. "Yay!"

"I'd call this a successful evening," my dad said, as he piloted the minivan out of the parking lot.

CHAPTER FORTY-FOUR

The Christmas and New Year's holidays passed with relative ease, though David's permanent absence and Abby's temporary one ached when we acknowledged them.

My dad's calming presence and Sparky's unabashed affection were like balm to our wounded souls. Our new furniture, looking fresh and smelling delicious, arrived on the Saturday after New Year's and distracted us from my parents' impending departure. The intercom system, tweaked into near-perfect performance by a geeky installer, allayed most of my fears about unsupervised children. And, I had to admit, we all liked the additional living space.

My dad insisted on staying until Red started daycare, and I didn't argue. On that Monday, which I'd worried about for weeks, my feisty toddler charged into the classroom, her red curls bobbing with each step. She never looked back; the teacher gave us a thumbs-up. "We should've known she'd be fine," Dad said, as we both blinked back tears.

—

At home, we adjusted to the new normal. At work, though, as Bobby Marks' trial approached, my nerves became more and more frazzled. I wasn't concerned about winning a conviction; it was a slam-dunk case. But the antics of Stefan Adams, Esquire, threatened to drive me insane. I'd twice cleared my calendar to meet with him about a possible plea agreement, only to have him call at the eleventh hour to say his client had changed his mind. I'd responded to at least five, half-baked motions and found countering his nonsensical arguments more difficult than I'd imagined.

Adams had filed one reasonable motion, asking the judge to prohibit use of the terms *Gypsy*, *Rom*, or *Romani people* during the trial. I didn't oppose it. In fact, since I wanted to eliminate any grounds for a mistrial, I supported the ban on potentially prejudicial language. Despite my agreement, though, Adams continued to argue his case. Finally, the judge interrupted. "Counselor, we're all on the same page already. Please stop arguing!"

Some of Adams' proposed jury instructions were irrelevant and downright laughable. He included the instruction about an insanity defense, when Bobby's sanity had never been at issue. The judge smothered a chuckle when he denied that request.

The trial began on the second Monday in January. I'd enlisted Grace to come at 6:30 a.m. and to take the kids to school and daycare so I could get a jumpstart on the day. I stepped from the shower to hear the doorbell ringing and Red wailing in her crib. Dripping wet, swaddled in a bath sheet, I grabbed Red then went to answer the door.

Grace stood on the front porch. "I know you said to come right in, but I didn't feel comfortable doing that." She entered and hung her faux fur jacket on the coat tree. "Here, let me take Lucy and get her dressed."

My youngest would have none of it. "Not Lucy. *Red*," she screamed, squirming away from Grace's outstretched arms and causing my towel to come undone. I set her on the floor so abruptly she fell on her bottom as I scrambled to cover myself.

"You know your real name is Lucy, and you may not yell at Grace," I said, ten decibels louder than common courtesy allows. "Now go with her and get dressed."

Red snuffled and toddled upstairs, Grace trailing behind.

Midway through applying my eyeliner—no easy task—I startled when Grace knocked on the bathroom doorjamb. The pencil went askew, causing a perpendicular line beneath my eye. *Shit!* I thought as I reached for a tissue to erase the mistake.

"I'm sorry to bother you," she said, "but is Luke allowed to choose his own clothes?"

I silently counted to three. "Yes—even if the pieces don't match."

She tipped her head to one side—judgmentally, I thought. "Okaaay."

Finally made-up and dressed, I headed to the kitchen, where the littles sat quietly eating scrambled eggs and jelly toast. I blew them kisses and poured myself a cup of coffee. "I didn't know how strong you liked it," Grace said, "so I erred on the side of caution."

Brown-tinted water is cautious? "It's fine. I don't want to be jittery during trial."

"What kind of trial is it?"

"A criminal case," I replied, hoping to forestall her questioning, "involving stolen identities."

"Really? That whole idea makes me so nervous… I shred every piece of mail I get and check my credit card balance every day—"

I dumped out my coffee. "Sorry, I can't chat, Grace. My ride'll be out front in a sec. 'Bye kiddos." I blew more kisses and left.

"Good luck!" Grace called, to my back.

"Where's the Miata?" I asked Matt, as I ducked my head against the wind and climbed into his Jeep.

"Didn't want to blow off the road," he said. "Plus, I figured it'd be easier to load the files in here."

Despite the bitter cold and subzero wind-chill, by the time we'd carried the three file boxes and our briefcases into the card-keyed entryway of the courthouse, I'd worked up a sweat. A security officer greeted us as we shrugged off our outerwear. "You guys should be on the cover of a fashion magazine," he said. "Lookin' shaaarp!"

"This is my lucky suit," Matt replied, fingering the lapel of his charcoal-gray jacket.

"And this is mine," I said with a smile, "though I feel rumpled already."

My smile vanished as we crossed the lobby and I saw Dominic approaching the line for the metal detector. "Is your ex made of money or something?" Matt asked. "How can he make a living, spending so much time watching our court proceedings?"

"Good questions," I replied, in a measured tone. "He's really got a bug up his ass about Barbara Marks. At least he didn't bring his mother along today."

"Or the blonde," Matt said, with a grin. "And, thankfully, we'll be situated before he gets through security."

I couldn't help noticing when Dominic, dressed in a pink, button-down shirt and navy slacks, took his seat behind the defense table. *Why in God's name does he always have to look gorgeous?* But by the time Judge Coburn called in our potential jurors, I'd successfully put him out of my mind. My senses of observation, on high alert, were directed at the folks who would be selected to judge Bobby Marks.

Bobby, who'd sported a full beard during our last pre-trial conference, had arrived clean-shaven. Dressed in a cheap, navy suit with sleeves a couple of inches too long, he fidgeted in the chair next to Stefan Adams, his eyes darting between the prospective jurors. I saw at least two of them squirm to avoid his gaze. I leaned over and whispered to Matt, "Bobby's making 'em nervous; good for us."

Matt and I listened intently while Judge Coburn questioned the potential jurors, and we agreed on those we should challenge. I liked the look of the jury and its two alternates.

I called Matt as my first witness. He explained how he'd developed Bobby Marks as a suspect. I saw Bobby write a furious note to his lawyer on one occasion, but Adams refrained from objecting to my questions. Matt answered with confidence and brevity—always a plus—and made easy eye contact with the jury. Adams asked a few softball questions and wisely kept his cross-examination short.

My next witness, Tyler Cromley, the man who'd sold the Audi to Bobby Marks in Sarasota, tripped up the step to the stand. His hand trembled as he took the oath. "Sorry," he said, when he took his seat.

Chillax, I wanted to tell him but instead tried a calming smile. As I guided him to describe his sale of the vehicle, he became more confident: A man identifying himself as Bobby Marks had called about the For Sale sign posted on the car. Marks had arrived at Cromley's home in a cab, had test-driven the Audi with Cromley, and had readily agreed to the asking price, to be paid in cash or a cashier's check. Marks had returned by bus that afternoon, presented the check, and sped away in the vehicle. When Cromley took the check to his bank the following day, he'd learned it was bogus and called the police.

"Do you see the individual who bought the car from you in the courtroom today?" I asked, in conclusion.

Cromley pointed to Bobby Marks. "The guy in the navy blue suit, sitting next to the lawyer."

Stefan Adams strode across the courtroom, stopping abruptly about six inches from the witness stand. "Mr. Cromley, isn't it correct that the purported sale to my client took place more than a year ago?"

"Yes, sir."

"How long did you spend with the man who bought the car?"

"Probably half an hour."

Adams leaned in even closer. "And you're claiming you can identify him with certainty, all these months later?"

Cromley moved to within inches of the microphone and responded, in a clear voice, "I recognize the birthmark by his left ear. When he bought the car, his hair was longer and in a ponytail—"

"Objection," Adams yelled. "Beyond the scope of my question."

The judge shook his head. "Overruled. Go ahead, Mr. Cromley."

"His hair was in a ponytail. My wife said to me, 'He shouldn't wear a ponytail; it draws attention to that birthmark. Did you notice it looks just like the state of Idaho?' When he came back with the check, I realized she was right; it did look like Idaho. You can see it on his cheek today."

Adams slunk away and muttered, "No further questions."

When we dismissed the witness, and broke for lunch, Stefan Adams made a beeline for the door. He didn't even glance at Bobby as the marshals led him from the courtroom.

Matt and I stood at the prosecution table, backs to the gallery. "Why don't I pick up a couple sandwiches and we can eat here in the conference room?" he asked, twisting around as if to stretch his back.

"Is he gone?"

Matt laughed. "Yes, your ex is gone, but I don't want to risk another scene in the lobby. I told George I'd run interference and keep the two of you separated."

"Seriously?"

"Yes. Now, head into the conference room through the side door. I'll call for carryout from the Old Fashioned and be back in a flash. What do you want?"

I reached into my briefcase and took some bills from my wallet. "A burger with cheddar. No onions, please."

He waved away my money. "You can get lunch tomorrow."

Our afternoon witnesses testified flawlessly, and Stefan Adams' questions on cross-examination failed to undermine their accounts. At 5:00, confident and calm, I packed my briefcase. After Matt texted, "Coast clear!" I joined him in the parking lot for the one-block ride to my office. An hour later, he drove me home.

Madeline met me at the door. "Sorry, I can't chat or I'll be late for my evening class. Tuna casserole's in the oven on warm. The fruit salad's in the fridge."

"Kiddos, dinner's ready," I said, into the intercom.

Amy ran into the kitchen just as I opened the oven. I slammed the door shut and turned to hug her. "Slow down! I don't want you to get burned. Where're the rest of 'em?"

"I'm here," Lily said, wandering in and taking her seat. "Luke's going potty. Red fell asleep on the couch."

"We'll let her sleep," I said.

I donned oven mitts and reached in for the casserole, only to burn my fingers where one of the mitts had worn thin. "Shit!" I yelled, shifting and almost dropping the Pyrex pan. The casserole landed on the trivet with a thud, just as Luke walked in.

"You said a naughty word."

I leaned down and planted a kiss on his head. "I did and I'm sorry. Did you wash your hands?"

"Uh-huh."

I didn't believe him, but let it slide. When everyone was seated, I said, "Before we eat, let's all say something we're thankful for. Lily?"

"We had band tryouts today and I made second chair," she said.

"Congratulations! How 'bout you, Amy?"

"Um… I'm thankful Red fell asleep. She was bothering us."

"Okay." I looked over to see Luke stuffing a forkful of casserole in his mouth. "Hold it, young man. We're saying what we're thankful for *before* we eat."

He spit the food onto his plate. "I don't want it anyway," he yelled. "It's yucky."

"Five-minute time out," I said, pointing to the dining room. He climbed down from his chair, pushing it hard against the wall, and stomped out of the room. The girls looked at me expectantly as I massaged my temples.

"What are *you* thankful for, Mom?" Amy asked, in a goody-two-shoes voice.

"Yeah, Mom," Lily said. "Are you thankful you only have one boy?"

"Well, yes," I said, with half a smile, "there's that. And I'm thankful your grandmother will be back soon. Hopefully, she'll come over and make us a non-yucky tuna casserole once in a while."

I remembered Luke seven minutes later, and called him to join us. He scrambled up onto my lap and leaned his head onto my chest. "Sorry, Mommy."

My heart melted. "Apology accepted," I said. "Now, can you think of something you're thankful for?"

"My scooter."

"Good. Now scoot into your own chair, and I'll zap you a spoonful of casserole with some butter."

He finished that helping and two more. *Thank God for little victories.*

Chapter Forty-Five

When the trial resumed Tuesday morning, I called Barbara Marks as my last witness. She wore the same, beige dress she'd worn to her plea hearing: a simple, short-sleeved shift adorned with a single strand of brown beads. She wore no makeup but for a trace of pale-pink lipstick. *My God, she looks like she's about sixteen years old,* I thought, as she walked tentatively toward the stand.

When Barbara responded almost inaudibly to my first question, Judge Coburn leaned toward her. "Ms. Marks," he said, "you'll need to speak louder so everyone—especially the jurors and the court reporter—can hear."

I had some trepidation about her testimony. During trial prep, I'd asked her to avoid talking about Gypsy customs and the psychic shop; I worried that being nervous might cause her to slip. I caught her eye and held her gaze for a moment, then forged ahead. "How did you come to know Bobby Marks?"

I couldn't have been prouder of her response: "There were some issues with my own family, and when I was fourteen, his mom, Sonia, took me in. Later, I got married to Bobby's younger brother, Georgie. So, I guess it's correct to say he's my brother-in-law."

"Did you and Georgie ever live apart from Sonia and Bobby?"

"No. We weren't able to save enough money for our own place. And then, when Georgie got sent to prison, I just stayed on with them."

I nodded and asked the next question on my list: "How did you come to possess identification in the name of Courtney Parks?"

Barbara looked down at her feet. "Sonia Marks gave me Courtney's birth certificate and some W-2 forms she'd made up with Courtney's name and social security number. I used them to get an Illinois ID card. Later, I used the ID to get a driver's license. Sonia applied for two credit cards in Courtney Parks' name, and she gave them to me to use."

Barbara calmly testified how, posing as Courtney Parks, she'd gone with Bobby to Wausau to buy the BMW. How he'd negotiated the sale price. How he'd put down the cash deposit. How she'd applied for and signed the loan documents. She further testified that Bobby had given her the driver's license and a credit card belonging to her doppelganger, Marcia Baxter. And that, posing as Marcia, she'd gone with Bobby to Eau Claire where they'd repeated the process to buy the Cadillac Escalade.

"Who decided which vehicles to buy?" I asked.

"Bobby'd look online for cars and dealerships that looked promising, and research blue book values. Then he and Sonia would decide."

I took a sip of water and checked my legal pad to make sure I'd covered all my points. "Thank you, Ms. Marks," I said. "No further questions, Your Honor."

When Stefan Adams leapt out of his chair and approached her, Barbara looked impossibly, deer-in-the-headlights, vulnerable. She made no eye contact with him while she answered his litany of innocuous questions, glancing instead at me, the floor, or the judge. *Hang in there, kiddo,* I wanted to tell her. *This'll all be over soon.*

"Mrs. Marks," Adams said, striding closer the witness stand, "you testified that my client provided the cash down payment when you went to buy the BMW. But, isn't it true that *you* handed the money to the salesperson?"

"Uh… yes. I handed it to him, but Bobby had given it to me to put in my purse before we drove to Wausau. He said it made too big a bump in his coat pocket."

"Do you know where my client got that cash?"

Barbara paused, as though picturing the scene in her mind. "From Sonia's safe in the dining room. We were living in Chicago then. She asked how much he needed, opened the safe, and took out a stack of bills. She handed it to him, and he told me to put it in my purse."

"Do you know where Sonia Marks got the money?" Adams asked.

"Not specifically," Barbara said, shifting in the chair. "She handled all of the finances for the family."

"Did you carry the cash used to buy the Escalade in Eau Claire in your purse, too?"

"No. Bobby had a briefcase that day. On the drive up there, he took the driver's license and credit card out of the briefcase—"

Adams held up his hand in a "stop" gesture. "Thank you, Mrs. Marks. That'll be all."

"Redirect, Ms. Spencer?" the judge asked.

"No, Your Honor," I said. "And the prosecution rests."

Barbara Marks hurried from the stand, giving me a huge smile as she walked past.

Stefan Adams brushed an errant lock of hair back from his forehead. He cleared his throat and gave the jury a tight smile. "I'll keep my opening statement brief. The government's case is a road full of holes, which, when patched, will lead away from my client and instead toward his co-defendants. Bobby Marks is a hard-working man, engaged in two legitimate businesses: roofing repair and buying and selling high-end used cars. He has a host of satisfied customers. When we rest our case, you'll have no choice but to find him not guilty."

Adams' first witness, Gary Swearingen, testified that he owned a two-flat on Chicago's North Side and had hired Bobby Marks to repair its roof. More importantly, he testified that Bobby was busily at work on the roof at the time Tyler Cromley sold his BMW in Sarasota. Adams introduced two photographs showing Marks working on the date in question, with a date-and-time stamp prominently displayed in the corner.

When Adams finished, I approached the witness for cross-examination. I'd seen Swearingen's name on Adams' list of defense witnesses but hadn't known what kind of story he'd concoct. "Mr. Swearingen, do you have any other documentation showing when the defendant fixed your roof? A contract or an invoice showing the dates of his services? A cancelled check?"

"Uh… no. We had a verbal agreement and I paid him in cash."

"I see. Now do you personally own the camera with which you took the photographs entered into evidence?"

"Yes, ma'am. I bought it about a week before Bobby fixed my roof, to take pictures of my new grandbaby. When he was up there working, I took a few shots to try it out."

"Who set the date and time function on the camera?"

"The store clerk at the camera shop on Clybourn."

"Are you aware, sir, that a camera's date and time settings can easily be changed?"

"I swear I didn't change it."

"Might someone else have had access to the camera?"

"I guess, but—"

"Thank you, Mr. Swearingen. Nothing further."

"Redirect, Mr. Adams?" the judge asked.

Bobby Marks leaned toward his lawyer, apparently suggesting some additional questions. Adams—wisely, I thought—shook him off. "No, Your Honor."

Adams called another Chicagoan who testified he'd purchased four used cars from Bobby Marks over the previous decade and raved about his integrity. I didn't bother to cross-examine him.

Bobby Marks walked with a swagger to take the stand as Stefan Adams' final witness, winking at the court clerk as he swore to tell the truth. "He's got some cajones!" I wrote on my legal pad and passed it to Matt. "More like sh** for brains," he scrawled back.

Bobby testified that, at their requests, he'd gone with his mother to buy the Mercedes SUV in suburban Chicago and with his sister-in-law, Barbara, to buy the vehicles at the two dealerships in Wisconsin.

"Mr. Marks," Adams continued, "when your mother bought the Mercedes, were you aware she was using the name 'Iris Wellington?'"

"No. I assumed she was using her real name. I went out onto the lot to look at other cars while she filled out the loan application and signed the title papers."

"And when you went with Barbara to buy the other vehicles, did you know she wasn't using her real name?"

"Absolutely not. My only role was to look at the vehicles and bargain for the prices. The women carried the money and did all the paperwork."

"Did you know your mother and sister-in-law weren't making payments on the car loans?"

"No, sir. Not until I was arrested and questioned by the police."

"And finally, sir," Adams asked, with a flourish, "did you purchase the Audi from Mr. Cromley in Sarasota?"

"I did not."

"No further questions."

I'd been watching the jurors during Bobby's testimony: One had openly scowled. Another had rolled her eyes. A third had covered his mouth with his hand, but had been unable to hide the smile in his eyes. I guessed that they viewed Marks as a lying buffoon, unworthy of cross-examination. Still, I wanted to highlight a few points.

"Mr. Marks," I said, "the salesman at the Chicago dealership testified that you introduced yourself and your 'mother-in-law' to him before negotiating to buy the Mercedes SUV. Did you tell him her name?"

"No."

"Why did you introduce her as your *mother-in-law* rather than as your mother, if you didn't know fraud was involved?"

Bobby looked flustered. "He must've misheard me… about me calling her my mother-in-law, I mean."

I smiled toward the jury box. "Let's turn, then, Mr. Marks, to the Audi sold in Sarasota. The vehicle was recovered on Milwaukee Street in Janesville along with the Mercedes and the BMW, both of which you admit to being involved in buying. Are you telling this court you had *nothing* to do with the purchase of the Audi?"

Bobby sat straighter in the witness chair. "That's correct."

"How do you explain the fact that all three cars were recovered at the same location in Wisconsin, 1,300 miles from where the Audi was taken?"

"Someone must've framed me."

"No further questions, Your Honor," I said, trying hard to maintain a deadpan expression.

"No re-direct, Judge," Stefan Adams said. "The defense rests."

"We'll resume with closing arguments at 1:00," Judge Coburn said.

CHAPTER FORTY-SIX

I opened the door to the courtroom that afternoon to see Lily's seventh-grade social studies class filling the first three, center rows. When Lily's teacher had asked if she could bring the class to observe a court proceeding, I'd suggested that the closing arguments of a trial might be interesting. She'd chosen the Marks case.

Lily sat next to the teacher, right behind the prosecution table.

I set my briefcase on the table before turning to the class. I extended my hand to the teacher, Ms. Wallingford, and winked at Lily. "I'm glad you could come."

"Could you summarize what we're going to see?" Ms. Wallingford asked.

"Sure. The defendant, Bobby Marks, has been in jail waiting for this trial. He's charged with conspiracy to commit bank fraud, for helping to buy two luxury vehicles with stolen identities, and with transporting two other stolen vehicles into Wisconsin. The U.S. Marshals will bring him in in a few minutes. The judge will come in, and then he'll call in the jury. The witnesses have all testified, and now it's time for closing arguments. I'll go first, followed by Bobby's lawyer. I can give a short argument in rebuttal if I want but won't decide until I hear what the other attorney has got to say. The judge will read a bunch of pretty boring instructions to the jury before they go into the deliberation room. Then we wait."

"Can we stay to see what they decide?" asked a skinny, pimply-faced boy.

I laughed. "You can hang around as long as the building's open, but they might not reach a verdict today. Sometimes they deliberate into the evening, and sometimes they come back the next day to finish up."

The boy raised his hand again. I glanced over his shoulder to see Dominic taking his seat behind the defense table as the marshals escorted Bobby in. "I need to be seated now," I said, "but we can meet for more questions after the judge dismisses us. Maybe we can have a little contest to see who can guess how long the jury will be out."

I'd gotten used to Dominic's presence in the courtroom and by now found it only a minor irritant. But I did find myself nervous about performing in front of Lily and her classmates. *Relax! You're smart and eloquent, and you know this case better than anyone.* After one furtive scratch behind my ear and a sip of water, I stood and approached the jury.

"Ladies and gentlemen, thank you for the close attention you've paid to these proceedings, and in particular to the witnesses' testimony. You've heard some conflicting evidence, and your task now is to rule out what is not true. In some cases, that might be difficult. In this case, I think you'll find it straightforward. My job is to prove beyond a *reasonable* doubt that Bobby Marks committed the crimes charged in the indictment. I'm not required to prove it beyond *any* doubt, and you are certainly not required to set aside your common sense and reason when you examine the evidence.

"The indictment alleges that the defendant, Bobby Marks, his mother, Sonia Marks, and his sister-in-law, Barbara Marks, devised a scheme to possess two stolen vehicles which had crossed state lines. They also schemed to obtain two other vehicles in Wisconsin by bank fraud…"

Without using any notes, I outlined the elements of the offenses and the testimony we'd presented to prove them. Ten of the jurors maintained eye contact with me as I spoke. The 'non-lookers,' as I termed them, didn't worry me, though. One nodded her head as if in agreement with me, and the other focused on her lap as she had throughout the trial.

"The four witnesses who sold the cars in question," I told the jury, "—three salespeople at dealerships and one a private party—all identified the defendant as the individual who initiated the purchases. Three of the vehicles were recovered on Milwaukee Street in Janesville, a property where Bobby Marks and his mother later resided. And Bobby Marks was seen driving away from that property in the fourth stolen vehicle, in which he was later arrested.

"Now, Bobby Marks tells us he was unaware that his mother and sister-in-law had used stolen identities to purchase the vehicles. That testimony is contradicted by other witnesses. Why did he tell the Mercedes salesman his *mother-in-law* would be financing the balance of the purchase price if his *mother* was using her real name to buy the car? And you'll recall that Barbara Marks testified it was Bobby who gave her Marcia Baxter's driver's license and credit card to use in the purchase of the Escalade.

"Finally, Bobby Marks' supposed alibi for the Sarasota purchase is contradicted by Tyler Cromley's credible testimony. Mr. Cromley identified Bobby Marks as the buyer of the Audi based on an unusual birthmark, which we can see for ourselves on his face today."

I walked back to counsel table, checked my notes, and concluded, "The *credible* evidence ties Bobby Marks to all four vehicles, demonstrating beyond a reasonable doubt that Bobby Marks knowingly and intentionally participated in this scheme to possess two stolen vehicles that had crossed state lines, and to take two other vehicles by bank fraud. I'm confident you will return a verdict of guilty as to all four counts in the indictment. Thank you."

I took three calming breaths to counteract the adrenaline I'd used to make my focused presentation. Matt patted my hand and gave me a thumbs-up under the table.

"May I have a moment to confer with my client?" Stefan Adams asked. He waited for the judge's permission, then bent his head toward Bobby. Though Bobby gestured somewhat erratically with his hands, neither he nor Adams raised their voice above a whisper.

After what felt like an eternity, Adams rose, faced the jury, and began his closing argument. "I have to tell you," he said, without greetings or niceties, "I expected more from this prosecutor's office. I believe they chose to indict the defendants simply because they're Gypsies—"

My head shot up. "Objection! Assumes facts not in evidence."

"Sustained," Judge Coburn barked. "Counsel, please approach."

I wanted to run up to the bench but measured my pace and waited while Adams said something to his client and then joined us.

"*Mister* Adams," the judge said, sotto voce, "I granted your *Motion in Limine* prohibiting any mention of the defendant's ethnicity during this trial. The government played by the rules. You just blatantly violated them. You're not getting a mistrial. Finish your argument without further hijinks and let's get this case to the jury."

We resumed our spots at counsel tables, Adams looking not-one-bit contrite.

"The jury will disregard defense counsel's last statement," Judge Coburn said.

"Ladies and gentlemen, I apologize for getting off track," Adams said. He took a sip of water and picked up his legal pad. "The prosecutor brought in a lot of witnesses to show us how these four cars were obtained. My client admits he was with his co-defendants during the purchase of three of them, but we maintain he was unaware of the illegality of the transactions. Bobby Marks' sister-in-law and mother were the masterminds of this so-called scheme. The government failed to fully investigate and to find the person who went to Florida, posing as Bobby Marks, and bought the fourth vehicle. Someone who knew about my client's birthmark, which would be simple to create with a little makeup."

Adams put down his pad and walked to the jury box. "Bobby Marks is a hard-working roofing contractor and buyer and seller of used cars. His more-sophisticated relatives duped him into helping them buy the vehicles in question. He did not *knowingly and intentionally* engage in illegal behavior. You must find him not guilty."

"Rebuttal, Ms. Spencer?" the judge asked.

I leaned over and whispered to Matt, "Is it worth it?" He shook his head. "No, Your Honor."

Judge Coburn read the agreed-upon jury instructions with the expression and finesse of a Shakespearean actor, so eloquently that Lily's classmates might even have found them interesting. If the jurors had paid attention, I expected that they'd have to find Bobby Marks guilty. The twelve jurors and two alternates filed out of the courtroom, and we were adjourned.

I turned around to speak to Lily's teacher and saw Dominic standing in the aisle. We locked eyes for an instant before he walked out. *What was that?*

"Uh… Ms. Wallingford, there's an assembly room across the hall. I'll meet you there in five."

At 2:45, I laid my cell phone on the podium in the assembly room. I had to be accessible in case the judge called us back to the courtroom. Lily's class quickly found chairs and turned them in my direction.

"What questions do you have?" I asked. Six hands shot into the air. I pointed toward a pudgy boy with a mustard stain on the front of his white, school uniform shirt. I doubted he got picked first in gym class.

A flush moved up his neck, and he looked down at his lap. "Can we do that contest now? To guess when the jury will be done deciding?" A chorus of "yeahs" backed him up.

I laughed. "Sure. Lily, there are some pads of paper over there. Everyone, write your name and the time you predict on a piece of paper. The judge probably won't let the jury stay past 7:00. So, if your guess is later than that, make it sometime tomorrow. I'll call Ms. Wallingford when I know the actual time."

The kids chattered while they wrote down their predictions. Some, including Lily, brimmed with confidence while others were more hesitant to commit. Lily folded her paper and collected the ballots, mouthing to me, "I'm gonna win!"

She's come so far since that awful day at juvie. I gotta call Dad and thank him again for encouraging her to stay at Edgewood.

Ms. Wallingford clapped her hands. "Okay, let's have some substantive questions. Arturo?"

"Have you ever lost a trial?" he asked.

I smiled. "Not as a federal prosecutor. But I did lose a couple during the years I was an assistant Dane County DA."

Several more kids raised their hands. I nodded to Lily's friend, Marissa. "Mr. Marks' lawyer said you prosecuted him because he was a Gypsy," she said. "*Is* he a Gypsy?"

"He's Rom—of Romani descent. It's an ethnic group that originated in India. Some people them call Gypsies. Because of the negative stereotype sometimes associated with the group, both sides agreed not to introduce Marks' ethnic identity during trial. We asked our witnesses to avoid using the term Gypsy. It wasn't relevant to guilt or innocence and might have prejudiced the jury. I usually don't object to what's said during a closing argument, but today I had to let the jury know Bobby's lawyer wasn't playing by the rules. And it's simply not true that we prosecuted him because of his ethnicity."

A black boy, wearing thick, wire-framed glasses, waved his hand and began speaking before I even acknowledged him. "You mean you *tell* the witnesses what to say?"

"It's not sinister," I said, with a grin. "When we decide to call a witness, we tell them ahead of time what questions we plan to ask. We tell them to respond truthfully, to confine each answer to the question, and suggest that they not swear or use slang. And, in this case, not to use a term some people find offensive and prejudicial."

During the seventh or eighth question, my phone rang. I glanced down and saw the court clerk's phone number. *It can't be the jury already!* I hadn't told the class that in one of the two trials I'd lost, the jury had come back in about an hour. Nor that their not-guilty verdict had been a complete shock.

I held up a finger. "Excuse me, I need to take this call."

I listened for a few moments, hung up, and forced a smile. "Well… We can declare a winner. The jury reached a verdict five minutes ago."

The conference room erupted into cheers and jeers. "Who guessed the closest, Ms. Wallingford?" one student asked.

She fished the papers out of her purse and flipped through them. "Arturo, who guessed 4:00," she replied. Arturo stood up and took a bow. "Ms. Spencer, the bus is scheduled to pick us up at 4:30. Will the verdict be read by then?"

"The marshals will have Marks in court in about ten minutes, but the clerk hasn't been able to reach his lawyer. If they can, and if he's close by, you may be able to see it."

They gave me a standing ovation while Lily beamed with pride. I fervently hoped she'd still be beaming when she heard the verdict.

Lily's class sat in the back of the courtroom in case they had to leave before the proceedings ended. Dominic, probably unaware the jury'd reached a verdict, was nowhere to be seen. I strode to the prosecution table to join Matt, trying to project more confidence than I felt. Bobby Marks sat alone at the defense table, and the court clerk looked nervously at the clock. "Mr. Adams said he'd be here by now," she said.

The door behind the judge's bench opened, and the clerk intoned, "All rise," just as Bobby's lawyer rushed in, brushing back his long hair with one hand and mopping his brow with the other.

Judge Coburn glared at Adams. "I don't appreciate the lengths my clerks had to go to locate you." Without further comment, he called in the jurors. "Madam Foreperson, have you reached a verdict?" the judge asked.

"We have, Your Honor."

The court clerk received a document, stood, and read it in a trembling voice. "As to count one, we, the jury, find Defendant Bobby Marks guilty." I breathed more easily, and she gained more confidence as she read the verdicts for the three remaining counts—all guilty.

Matt leaned over and whispered, "Congratulations."

I heard Lily's class moving as quietly as seventh-graders can move and turned briefly to see them grinning as they left the room. Judge Coburn waited patiently through the exodus before dismissing the jury and informing Bobby Marks of his appeal rights.

"Oh, we intend to appeal," Adams said, full of bluster.

I imagined the judge saying to himself, "Whatever."

———

Back in my office after the trial, George popped his head in. "Way to go, Caroline! We haven't had such a quick guilty verdict in years."

"Do I get a raise?"

He laughed. "No. Just verbal accolades."

My phone beeped as George left, signaling an email in my inbox. Dominic. The subject line read, "I thought you should know…" I clicked on it:

"You did a wonderful job in trial. I understand now why you made the plea agreement with Barbara. She was a credible witness and probably as much a victim of Bobby and Sonia Marks as my mother was of her. I'll check online to learn the jury's verdict. Best, Dominic."

My emotions swirled: elation at Dominic's praise, vindication about my judgment of Barbara, and sadness at the finality of the message; he'd sooner look at a computer than call me to hear the verdict.

I wonder if he'll be at Barbara's sentencing tomorrow? George hadn't relented about his decision to handle the sentencing hearing himself, though I'd assured him I'd avoid any interaction with Dominic if he showed up. *Maybe he'd reconsider if he knew Dominic had been in court throughout Bobby's trial, and we'd both kept our cools? Stop it, Caroline. You're just trying to think of another excuse to see him, and that's not good for you.*

CHAPTER FORTY-SEVEN

Matt called the next morning, after Barbara's sentencing hearing concluded. "Just as you recommended: three years' probation with six months in a halfway house in Minneapolis. She's meeting now with the probation officer."

"Thanks. And, uh, Matt—"

"Yeah, your ex was there. He came alone. But something weird happened. After we left the courtroom I saw him in the hallway talking with Jason Bittner. What's he doing talking with the *defense* attorney for his mom's nemesis?"

"No clue."

Matt's question nagged at me all day. But by the time I left the office, my determination to forget about it had paid off.

In early February, on a tip from the landlord of the storefront psychic shop on Armitage Avenue in Chicago, the U.S. Marshals located Sonia Marks. They chose not to arrest her immediately, instead establishing surveillance.

Within days, Sonia'd led them to a posh apartment building in Lincoln Park, where they arrested her and her daughter, Victoria. I got word of the arrest on a Monday morning and felt a wave of relief; we could get finally get the case on the docket.

I left a message for Matt and called Jimmy to share the news. "I've got some good news, too," Jimmy said. "Milton Winston just called me and wants to talk."

"Do you think he heard about Victoria's arrest?"

"He didn't say so."

"When and where do you want to meet with him?"

"He said his cancer's in remission and he's able to get around. I suggested we meet at your office. Next Tuesday morning would work for him."

I checked my calendar. "Tuesday's fine. Say 10:00?"

"Okay, I'll let him know. I hate to wait 'til then but don't want to press him. We'll have a slam-dunk case against those two charlatans if he's willing to testify and to submit to a paternity test on the baby."

I had to agree.

I called Barbara Marks' probation officer in Minneapolis, getting his voicemail. "Bob, this is Caroline Spencer with the U.S. Attorney's office in Madison," I said. "Give me a call, please. Barbara Marks' cohorts have been apprehended and we'll be gearing up for her appearance at a possible trial."

My phone rang later that morning. But it wasn't Bob.

"Hello, Caroline. It's Dominic."

I wasn't about to let his call wreck my mood. "Wow," I said neutrally. "Word travels fast. We just unsealed the indictment and arrest warrants this morning."

"What?"

It took me a moment to regroup. "You're not calling about Sonia Marks?"

"No."

"Oh. I just assumed you'd heard that Sonia and her daughter, Victoria, were apprehended in a new case I'm prosecuting."

"That's good. Congratulations."

"Thanks."

"Listen, I called to ask you if we could get together to talk. In person. Maybe over lunch or dinner?"

Willing myself to remain noncommittal, I glanced at my calendar. "Lunch tomorrow would work."

"May I swing by and pick you up outside your office building at noon?"

"Okay. See you then."

What's this about? And why do we have to talk in person? Oh, shit; he and Emma probably decided to get married and he feels like he needs to tell me face to face. Or maybe…

I startled when my phone rang again.

This time it was Barbara Marks' probation officer. "I've got bad news," he said. "She absconded from the halfway house on Friday; never returned from work that evening. They contacted her employer this morning and learned she hadn't been there at all on Friday, so she's been on the lam for three days. I'll fax you a violation report this morning. I assume your court will issue an arrest warrant?"

"You can bet on it," I said, with defeat.

"Does this bollix up your case against her pals?"

"Big time."

"Well, Martin, her counselor at the halfway house thinks Barbara pulled a fast one on all of us. That she never really came clean about her involvement with her gang of thieves, and that she had money stashed somewhere."

My stomach sank. "What makes him think so?"

"He said at first it was just a gut feeling. About a week ago, she started getting more evasive and seemed to have nicer stuff than she could afford. He wasn't completely surprised she split." He waited a beat for my reaction, but I couldn't think of anything to say.

The only good thing about the news was that it kept me from ruminating about Dominic.

I broke the news to Matt when he returned my call.

"Shit," he said. "I thought she was ready for a new life."

"Me, too. I guess we'll just have to dig deeper to shore up our case against Sonia and Victoria."

"I'll start going through the file again today. Maybe re-contact some of the other witnesses to see if they can remember anything new."

"I sure hope you can come up with something or our case is in the toilet."

CHAPTER FORTY-EIGHT

Matt waited in the reception area when I arrived at work on Tuesday. "I was gonna call, but took a chance that you might be free this morning," he said. "I've got something you need to see."

"Please tell me it's something I *want* to see," I said, as we walked toward my office.

I sat at my desk and lifted the lid from my to-go coffee mug. "If I'd known you were coming, I would've gotten you a cup, too."

"I've had enough already." His hands trembled as he took a manila file from his briefcase. "Here's a page from one of the hidden files on Bobby Marks' computer. Look at the line I've highlighted; the text in the middle is a different font than the rest. I think it's a password. I'm hoping it'll unlock Bobby's iPad."

"Where's the iPad now?"

"Right here," he said, pulling from his briefcase a sealed plastic bag containing the tablet. It'll be weeks before the crime lab can get to it, so my friend over there suggests we turn it on and try the password. The data won't automatically erase unless we try, unsuccessfully, ten times. I want your permission to do it."

I cringed. "Okaaaay." I read him the password, character by character, and watched as he deliberately entered each one.

His face fell. "Oh, shit."

I shrugged. "It was worth a try."

"No, it worked," he said and passed the tablet to me. "But look."

The home screen displayed a picture of Barbara and Bobby Marks, entwined naked on a bed. "I can't believe she and *Bobby* were an item," I said. "What else did Barbara lie about?"

"I'm guessing we'll know more when we look through this thing."

I called our IT guy to come make copies of the iPad's data, and Matt and I spent the morning poring over what was clearly *Barbara's* iPad—not Bobby's. We found emails she'd sent to her sister-in-law, Victoria, with instructions for the artificial insemination. We found a file named Possibilities that contained several electronic obituaries, including one for Milton Winston's late wife.

Attached to an email from Barbara, we found the multicolored flyer advertising the psychic services available at the storefront on Armitage Avenue. Among the offerings were: Tarot and Palm Readings, Psychic Cleansing, Attracting Sole Mates, and Communing With Your Departed Loved Ones. *Sounds like maybe I should go there.*

"So, Barbara's the one who designed that brochure," Matt said.

"She could've used a little help with spelling, though," I said, with a chuckle. "Who really wants a S-O-L-E mate?"

"I'm glad she's got a flaw or two; it'll make it easier to catch her."

Matt and I were still engrossed in Barbara's emails, photos, and documents, him on my laptop and me on my desktop computer, when my phone rang.

"Caroline Spencer," I said without glancing at the caller ID.

"It's Dominic. I'm waiting outside. Are you still free for lunch?"

"Oh, jeez. There've been some new developments in a big case and time got away from me. I'll be down in five." I hung up and turned to Matt. "I forgot I was s'posed to meet someone for lunch. You can keep working here if you want. I'll be back in an hour."

He barely looked up from the screen. "Okay."

When I'd reached into my closet that morning to pick out clothes for work—and for my lunch with Dominic— my hand had come to rest on that blue silk blouse I knew he liked. I'd donned it today with a spirit of vindictiveness. *Let me give you a little reminder of what you'll be missing.* But by the time I got to work I'd wished I'd made another choice; my rancor made me feel tarnished rather than pretty.

Now, I grabbed my purse, made a quick stop in the restroom, and dashed for the stairwell. I didn't have the patience to wait for an elevator and needed to burn off a little adrenaline before seeing Dominic. *How could I have forgotten?*

Out of breath from rushing down seven flights of stairs, I yanked open the passenger door of his Buick and sat down heavily. "I'm sorry to keep you waiting," I said, wiping my brow.

"Relax. It's no big deal." He smiled, but I thought I detected a note of disappointment. "Do you have time to go to Jac's?"

"Sure." In truth, I'd have preferred a McDonald's fillet-o-fish at my desk with Matt to an awkward lunch with my ex-boyfriend. Even at one of my favorite bistros.

"How've you been?" he asked, as he pulled into traffic.

I thought for a moment. *You could tell him he was right about Barbara from the get-go.* "Fine," I replied, instead. "A lot's changed. Lily's doing well. And I hired new household help 'cause Abby and Bert got married and are living over on Midvale."

"That's great about Lily," he said, glancing at me from the corner of his eye. "And I'm happy for Abby."

I nodded but chose silence over more small talk. Thankfully, Dominic took the hint.

We took a corner table at Jac's and I stared at the menu without seeing it. I couldn't imagine anything sitting well in my agitated stomach. When the waiter arrived, I ordered what had always been my favorite sandwich and hoped for the best.

After the waiter brought our drinks, Dominic explained why he'd invited me. "I've applied to be an investigator for the federal defender's office," he said, eyes on his coffee. "And Jason Bittner thinks I've got a good shot at it. It would mean working on some cases with you, so I thought I should get your take on whether we could handle that..."

"The federal defender's office in Madison?"

He nodded. "Where else?"

"I guess I thought maybe Chicago."

"No, I like Madison."

I took a few sips of my iced tea, waiting for him to elaborate. He didn't.

"Dominic," I said with exasperation, "You've made it perfectly clear our relationship is over. So, there'd be no conflict of interest if we were to work on opposing sides of the same cases."

He set down his cup, apparently with more force than he'd intended, spilling coffee onto the table. "What do you mean, *I've* made it perfectly clear? You're the one who broke it off."

"After you demonstrated, on multiple occasions, that your mother would always come before me. And you took up with Emma the very next day. Or that very evening, for all I know."

"Why do you think I ran to Emma? I was *devastated* when you broke up with me. She'd been begging me to get back together for a while—"

The waiter interrupted to deliver our food—a walnut burger for me and a smoked salmon BLT for him—which we both promptly pushed away. "*Back* together?" I asked.

Dominic cleared his throat. "Yes, we dated briefly a few years ago, when she and her husband were separated."

"And you didn't think that might be relevant when you introduced us?"

He shook his head. "I don't know, Caroline. I only know I was completely surprised and beyond hurt when you called it quits. I turned to someone whom I knew loved me and would make me feel better."

Tears stung my eyes. "Someone who's drop-dead gorgeous and young enough to give you kids of your own…"

"That was never on my mind."

I looked straight at him. "Did you go to her that same night, when I told you we were through?"

He nodded.

I stood and grabbed my coat from the wall hook. "There's nothing more to say, Dominic. Take the job if they offer it. I'll Uber back to my office."

"I broke up with Emma a month ago," he said quietly. *Too late!*

I buttoned my coat and hurried out the door, focused on nothing more than getting away. Snow flurries swirled around me and my boots slipped on the rutted sidewalk as I headed east on Monroe Street. I ducked into the Laurel Tavern and pulled out my cell phone to summon a ride. I didn't respond to the text message from Dominic that awaited me: "There's so much more I want to say. Please, let's talk."

Yeah, we'll talk—when hell freezes over.

Uber dropped me off at my office's parking garage. I texted Matt: "Something's come up. Won't be back in today. Stay as long as you want, but shut down computers when you leave, ok?" I phoned George and told him I needed the afternoon off, then got in my car and went home.

I poured lavender bath salts into the tub and soaked 'til my tears dried, ate a PB&J, and called Madeline off pick-up-the-kids duty. I delighted in the surprised looks on the twins' faces when they saw me behind the wheel of the minivan. "Mommy!" Luke cried, bounding into the back seat. "Wait'll you hear what we did in gym class." Amy handed me a finger painting to hang on the fridge. And even Lily, understandably aloof in the presence of her peers, grinned when she opened the door.

"Abby and Bert are coming for dinner," I told my brood. "And—best news yet—Abby's bringing lasagna!"

It felt like old times, sitting at the table, satiated by good food and wine, with loving voices filling the dining room. Lily supervised the twins as they cleared the table. Red sat on Abby's lap, their heads tilted together, listening to her sing "Tura-lura-lural" in a soft voice.

Bert reached into his shirt pocket and handed me an envelope. "I almost forgot; my daughter got you those circus tickets we talked about. Front row to this Sunday's matinee. I had her get six, so Lily can take a friend if she wants."

"Thanks, Bert. What do I owe you?"

"Nothing. Call it our Valentine's Day present."

I grinned. "So Abby won't be bringing any cookies or candy over this weekend, right?"

Abby looked up. "We'll see about that."

CHAPTER FORTY-NINE

When I collected Red from the church nursery on Sunday, she clung to my leg. "She seems crabby," the teacher reported, "and I noticed her tugging at her ear."

I knelt down and put my hand on Red's forehead. *Yikes—she's warm!* "Red, does your ear hurt?"

"I wanna go to the circus," she whined.

"Let's get you home and then we'll see." The matinee would start at 1:00. With any luck, a quick nap and a dose of Tylenol would fix her up.

At 11:30, I conceded no such luck. I dialed Abby. "Any chance you and Bert could take the three older kids to the circus? Red's got a fever and, I suspect, an ear infection. I think we need to go to Urgent Care."

"Bert's playing in a euchre tournament this afternoon. I'll be there in a few minutes, though, to take Red to the clinic. You go the circus."

I'd never gone to a circus. When I was a kid, my mother had had an aversion to them. And I could think of many things I'd prefer to do on a sub-zero, February day. But the twins couldn't stop talking about what they'd see, and Lily and Shelley planned to meet some other friends there.

I'd paid for preferred parking in the massive Dane County Coliseum lot, and the five of us sprinted through the cold toward the door. I searched through my purse for the tickets, while the twins impatiently stomped their frozen feet.

"Lily, Shelley," I said, when we'd made it through the turnstiles, "you two stick together and meet us at our seats at intermission It's section 110."

Lily blew me a kiss and they headed toward the far entrance to join their friends in general admission. I took the twins to the nearest concession stand and stood in line for a large bag of peanuts, hopefully forestalling the inevitable requests for cotton candy. I thought Luke's head would swivel off his shoulders as we walked through the arena, his wide eyes taking in all the sights and sounds. Amy clutched my hand and inched closer as the walkways became more congested. She relaxed when we found our seats, focusing on the handsome ringmaster in his sparkling gold tuxedo.

The pungent smell of elephants, horses, and tigers filled the air. Heat from the center ring's spotlights radiated our way. Another patron, making his way to his seat, tripped on my foot and spilled soda on my sleeve. Five minutes later, the six-year-old behind me dropped a glob of cotton candy on my hair. *I never thought I'd say this, Mom, but I see your point about circuses.* I felt as though I was trapped in an overcrowded snow globe—the kind with glitter rather than snowflakes.

When the show began in earnest, though, I found myself as enthralled as the kids. I held my breath as the trapeze artists and high-wire walkers, in bold makeup and garish, sequined costumes, performed like larger-than-life superheroes. I watched with glee as the clowns made Luke giggle 'til he cried. And my heart almost burst with gratitude as Amy raved about the trained dogs. "I wanna teach Sparky to do that!" she cried. "Can we, Mom?"

At intermission, while Amy and Luke pored over the pictures in their full-color program, I stood up to stretch. From a distance I recognized Lily and Shelley walking in our direction, occasionally turning to speak with a man behind them. My senses went on high alert. *There may be pedophiles lurking in the wings, girls. Get away from that guy!* He kept coming. I reached for my phone to text Lily a warning, then realized who the man was. Dominic. Wearing a shy smile and carrying a massive bouquet of pink roses.

"Look who we found, Mom," Lily said, as they reached our seats. "He'd like a convo. Shelley and I'll watch the kids while you go chat."

Dominic offered his arm. "This way, please."

I didn't know how to react; the absurdity of the whole scene left me dumbfounded. I wordlessly took his elbow and allowed him to escort me to the lobby.

"What are you doing here?" I asked, when he'd found us a deserted alcove.

"I went by your house and Abby told me where you were. Red's got strep throat, by the way, but had her first dose of antibiotic and is resting comfortably."

"Thanks. Still—"

He put his finger to my lips. "If you remember, I texted you on Tuesday that we needed to talk. You never responded. Since you didn't say 'no,' I concluded you might be convinced to say 'yes.' I'm here to convince you."

My heart began beating at twice its normal speed, and I felt a flush moving up my throat. *Keep it calm.* I managed to utter one syllable: "Oh."

He handed me the flowers. "I love you, Caroline. I've loved you since the day we met. I did a stupid, stupid thing after you told me you wanted to break up. Please forgive me."

"I want to…"

He let out a long, slow breath.

"But I still have so many questions…" I said.

"I'll willingly answer them. Can we talk now?"

I shook my head. "I can't miss this outing with my kids."

"May I call you later?"

I nodded, then turned toward the arena. "We've got an extra seat if you want to see the show."

"I'd like that."

We got back to our section a few minutes before the show resumed. Dominic sat beside Luke, who greeted him enthusiastically. "Hey, Dominic," he said, pointing to a picture in the program, "this guy's gonna be shot out of a cannon pretty soon." Lily nudged me and winked. The second half, every bit as mesmerizing as the first, ended in a cacophonous grand finale, with all the performers parading around the arena in glorious garb.

Upset by the jostling crowd, Amy began crying during the twenty-minute trek to the entrance. Dominic calmly lifted her above the fray, carrying her on his shoulders. Lily put Luke's precious program in her oversized purse, and he held tightly to her hand and mine 'til we made it to the car. "Thanks," I said, as Dominic helped strap Amy into her booster seat.

"You're welcome." He turned to go.

"Dominic—"

"Yes?"

"If you want, you could come over around 8:30 tonight. We could talk then."

He smiled. "I'll be there."

The littles were asleep upstairs and Lily'd retreated to her room downstairs when I heard Dominic tapping softly at the front door. Sparky, curled up next to my feet, looked up as if to ask, "Are we expecting someone?" I patted his head. "No need to bark; it's a friend." Nevertheless, he trotted alongside me to open the door.

I shivered as a burst of cold air entered with Dominic. He hung his jacket on the coat tree, and I welcomed his tentative warm hug. "Who's this?" he asked, nodding at the dog.

"Sparky. Supposedly one of Hank Foster's rescues. But I suspect he and Glenda scoured the area for the perfect dog, and secretly bought him just for us. He's really lifted the mood around here since Abby moved out."

He leaned over and scratched Sparky's ears. "That must've been a huge change."

"Yeah. Especially 'cause Abby and Bert were gone for almost a month with Christmas in Texas and their long, wedding cruise. It's been a little easier now that they're back in town and we can see them every few days." I realized we were still standing, awkwardly, in the foyer. "Would you like a drink?"

"A beer if you've got one."

"Of course. Go on into the living room. I'll be in in a sec."

I reached into the fridge for two Spotted Cows, grabbed the bottle opener from the drawer, and joined him. He sat in one of the new chairs, positioned where David's chair had been, adjacent to the couch. He looked up anxiously when I walked in. "I like the new furniture."

"Thanks," I said, handing him the beers and the opener. "We made Abby's old living room into a family room and moved some stuff around. Lily's room's down there now, too."

I sat on the couch closest to him, watching with a wave of affection while he fumbled to open the beers. "I'm nervous, Caroline. I *so* want this to go well."

"I know," I said, and took a long pull from the beer he handed me. "You're pretty much up to speed on life in the Spencer household. How's your mom? And Luz and Dani?"

"Luz is great. The chemo and radiation seemed to have done the trick. For now, at least. Dani's kids are giving her fits, but their dad has stepped up to the plate." He shook his head. "On a less upbeat note, my mother is having a rough time. It's as though she's in mourning over the loss of her psychic advisor. I'm hoping she'll connect with the new therapist Dani found, whom she'll see this week."

"Y'know, Dominic, I feel badly that I wasn't more understanding about your mom. I can't imagine what it's like to deal with someone who's got serious mental health problems."

"It's okay. I was *way* too wrapped up in it all. Since that awful scene after Barbara Marks' plea hearing, I've been seeing a counselor who's encouraging me to detach somewhat from the pathology. To recognize that the situation's out of my control and that getting well is up to my mom."

I looked down at my lap. "Interesting you should mention that. 'Cause one of the things I wanted to ask you was why you brought Emma and your mom that day."

"Mom couldn't wrap her head around the fact that the woman she saw as a godsend had conned her. Emma thought it might be helpful for her to see, and hear, your judge pronounce Barbara guilty. She drove Mom up here and I met them at the courthouse. As you saw, the plan pretty much backfired. And then, in frustration and feeling really hurt, I initiated that ugly confrontation with you." He shook his head as if trying to eradicate the memory. "I hadn't realized how difficult it would be to see you."

As we sipped in silence for several minutes, I remembered Emma possessively touching his arm that day. I relived the anguish I'd felt, sitting on the restroom floor after our hateful exchange.

"Did you love her?" I finally asked.

He waited a beat, as though weighing his words. "I was flattered that Emma loved me. And, to be honest, I tried to make it work. But, as I told you this afternoon, I love you. I can't settle for someone I don't love."

"You said you broke up with her a month ago. Why'd you wait 'til now to tell me?"

He pondered the question. "I made the mistake of running from an intimate relationship with you straight into the arms of another woman, to feed my sexual desires and mend my damaged ego. I couldn't allow myself to do it again. I needed time to reflect, to depressurize, and to make sure I was doing the right thing."

"Are you sure now?"

His voice cracked when he answered, "Absolutely. If you'll give me another chance, I'll be the happiest man on earth."

I wanted to say 'yes.' But a nagging fear made me glance away. I didn't want to see the desire in his eyes, that would draw me in again if I let them.

"I can't give you an answer now, Dominic. I need to think about it."

He rose slowly from the chair, as though he'd aged twenty years since our conversation began. "I understand. I'll wait to hear from you."

Rooted to the couch, I watched while Sparky followed Dominic out of the room. I heard the soft swish as he took his down jacket from the coat tree, and the sound of its zipper as he readied himself for the cold. The sound of the latch as he closed the door behind him. The sound of Sparky's nails on the hardwood foyer floor as he returned to my side.

Tossing and turning amid my tangled bedclothes, I weighed every conceivable angle of the decision I needed to make. *What had Lily called me all those months ago? A human frickin' lie detector? I wish! I was absolutely sure I'd read Barbara Marks correctly, and she took me for a fool. And Dominic saw through her from the beginning? Now, I can't decide whether to trust* him.

I ruminated about it the whole next day—Presidents' Day, when federal employees had a holiday and the rest of the world worked. I'd signed up to volunteer in the twins' classroom. "Ms. Spencer," a freckle-faced four-year-old said with exasperation as she pulled on my sleeve, "I asked if you couldn't please help me mix the red and yellow finger paints. Didn't you hear me?"

"Sorry, honey. My mind must've been wandering."

"Teacher says we're s'posed to be *mindful* of what we're doing."

"Your teacher's very wise," I replied. *But good luck with that, kiddo, when you've got more to worry about than what color finger paint you should use!*

My go-to person for advice, Glenda, was out of town visiting her ailing mother. And knowing how much my dad liked Dominic, I couldn't ask for an unbiased opinion from him. But Abby, who'd graciously babysat for the still-infectious Red while I went to school with the twins, had good common sense.

"Do you mind if I run something by you?" I asked her, when I walked into the kitchen that afternoon. "I need an opinion from someone I trust."

She sat at the table with her ever-present mug of tea. "I'm listening."

"Dominic corralled me at the circus yesterday. He wants us to get back together."

Abby smiled. "I figured as much; he didn't leave the flowers for me."

I acknowledged, out loud, to Abby that his hot and heavy relationship with Emma, commencing the very night

I broke up with him, scared me to death. "I just don't know if I can trust him."

"Oh, Caroline, you've just got to listen to your gut."

"Yeah, well… my gut's led me astray lately."

"Maybe your ears were plugged?"

I laughed. "Maybe."

CHAPTER FIFTY

Matt called me first thing Tuesday morning. "Bad news," he said. "I spent all of yesterday afternoon cataloging the files on Barbara's iPad. It's clear that she called the shots at the psychic shop on Armitage, and orchestrated the scheme to defraud Milton Winston."

I hung my head. "You're sure?"

"Yep, which makes her grand jury testimony against Sonia and Victoria useless. Let's hope our meeting with Winston this morning goes well. We're still on for 10:00, right?"

I flipped open my date book. "Yep. See you then."

I pulled the Winston file out of my drawer. I re-read our indictment against Sonia and Victoria Marks and the statements we'd taken from Barbara Marks. I re-read Barbara's grand jury testimony. Matt was right. Without Milton Winston's cooperation, we had no case. *Let's hope he's seen the light.*

Milton Winston didn't look anything like the victim I'd pictured. About six feet tall with graying, sandy brown hair and vivid green eyes, he was thin but not cancer-patient thin. He walked with a spring in his step. I knew from our file he was sixty-eight years old and that he'd been smart enough to build a small manufacturing company into a multi-million-dollar business. I didn't expect him to be holding a baby, and with such ease and obvious pleasure.

"I'd like to set the record straight so we can get Victoria home to this little guy," Milton said, after introductions were made.

My heart sank. "Mr. Winston, we've indicted Victoria and Sonia Marks for defrauding you," I said, with measured tone. "We don't need your consent to prosecute." *But we sure as hell need your help.*

"I understand that, but there's been no fraud. Aside from the funds Victoria used, with my permission during my hospitalization, my assets are intact. I brought along the paperwork today to prove it."

I glanced at Jimmy's face, beet red with brows knitted in fury. "Do you realize you were duped into believing that baby is your biological child?" he asked. "Are you willing to submit to paternity testing?"

Winston smiled and stroked the now-sleeping baby's back. "There's no need for paternity testing. Victoria told me the truth about her pregnancy, and I appreciate her attempt to preserve my male ego. This child was born to our marital union, and I consider him my son. End of story."

I listened to his words *and* my gut, which told me our case was in the toilet.

"I've admittedly been very generous with Victoria," Milton said, "but everything I've given her has been given freely and out of love."

———

I arrived five minutes late and tearful for my one o'clock appointment with Dr. Brownhill that afternoon. "Wouldn't you know it? The one day I really need my full hour and I can't get here on time."

"Relax. My two o'clock canceled; we have time. Can I make you a cup of chamomile tea?"

"That'd be wonderful."

She filled a mug with water from an electric pot, selected a tea bag from a wicker basket, and dropped it in. "Let it steep a few moments."

I warmed my hands around the mug and inhaled its steam. "It even smells relaxing."

Dr. Brownhill sat in her chair and crossed her legs, revealing a pair of SmartWool socks in the same shade of pink as her cashmere sweater. As usual, her attire cheered me. "What's distressing you?" she asked.

I told her about Dominic, concluding "…I don't know whether to trust him. I thought I had the ability to read people, but I've been proven wrong. In a big way."

She raised an inquisitive eyebrow.

"I think I mentioned to you before that Dominic's mother had been conned by a psychic in Chicago? And that I prosecuted her here for involvement in a car-theft scheme?" Dr. Brownhill nodded. "Well, she—Barbara's her name—agreed to testify for us in a much bigger fraud scheme in which her family members swindled a widower out of more than a million dollars. I believed Barbara'd herself been victimized by the family and that she sincerely intended to turn her life around. She got probation in exchange for her testimony. But it was all a lie. Turns out *she'd* been the mastermind. She absconded from supervision, probably with some of the widower's money. I feel so stupid. Hell, I even believed Barbara might have some psychic abilities."

"What happens to the fraud case?"

"That's why I was late getting here. The case agents and I were meeting with my boss to decide. We could've made the case without Barbara's testimony, but the victim claims he's not a victim. They lured him in to the psychic shop, had the sister-in-law seduce him into marriage, duped him into believing he'd fathered her child, and stole half his money. And even though he knows all that, he says loves her and is *happy* with what she did. He refuses to testify against her. So… after putting all that time and energy into the case, we had to dismiss the indictment."

"I can see why you'd be disappointed to have your case fall apart," Dr. Brownhill said, leaning forward. "But surely you're not comparing yourself to the widower who's been duped?"

I paused to consider her question. "No. I realize I'm not *that* gullible. Or that vulnerable. I guess I just told you about it to illustrate how people sometimes choose to believe what they want to believe, regardless of the facts."

"Okay. Let's get back to the question of Dominic. Tell me again the *facts* about him hurting you."

"Fine," I said, a tad petulantly. "Last summer we decided to embark on a romantic relationship. From the beginning, he was preoccupied with his mother's situation. He got his former colleague—and former lover, it turns out—involved in the investigation, which rankled me. I realized I couldn't count on him and broke up with him. The very same night, he starts seeing her. Now, he says he's sorry and claims the only reason he hooked up with her was because I'd hurt him."

She waited a beat. "Do you believe you hurt him?"

I pictured in my mind the look on his face the evening I'd called it quits. "Yes, I believe I hurt him."

My answer echoed in the silence that followed. I fiddled with the tea bag. Finally, I hung my head and spoke what my gut told me. "Yet Dominic, with no guarantee I wouldn't hurt him again, invited me back into his life. Because he loves me."

I left Dr. Brownhill's office debating whether I should text or call Dominic. *Don't you want to hear his voice?*

I stopped on the sidewalk in front of her building to dig my phone out from the bottom of my purse. I took off my mitten and dialed the number, holding my breath as the call went through.

He picked up on the first ring. "Hello, Caroline."

"Would you like to come over for dinner?"

"That depends—"

"I need to take things more slowly this time, but I want to give our relationship another chance."

"¡Dios mío! I've been hoping to hear those words."

"I should warn you that our new cook and housekeeper, Grace, isn't as skilled a cook as Abby. But she's made us a tater tot casserole that looks promising."

Dominic laughed. "I'll eat gruel if I can share it with you and your kids."

My stomach fluttered as I walked to the foyer. Dominic, too, looked nervous when I answered the door. He came bearing gifts: a bottle of wine and a box of to-die-for, Gail Ambrosius chocolates. "You didn't have to bring presents," I said, looking down at my feet.

Luke, unfazed by the importance of the occasion, came barreling into the foyer, breaking the tension. "Hey, Dominic," he said, grabbing him by the hand. "You gotta come see our family room. Where Grandma Abby's apartment used to be." Dominic glanced at me for the "okay."

I nodded. "But dinner'll be on the table in fifteen minutes, Luke. Don't start a new game or movie."

As I poured milk for the kids, I glanced at the video screen on the wall. Our intercom system included cameras in the family room, living room, and the little kids' rooms, so I could see and hear whether they might be getting into mischief. I rarely turned on the audio, though, preferring to give them some semblance of privacy. Now, I could see that Dominic sat cross-legged on the floor with Sparky licking his cheek. Red and Amy, meanwhile, paraded their Barbie dolls across the coffee table and Luke ran a Matchbox truck over a ramp beside them.

I switched on the audio. "Hello from the kitchen, everyone! Dinner's ready. Amy, please knock gently on Lily's door and tell her it's time to eat."

Dominic, my four kids, and the dog made their way to the kitchen. "Wash your hands and sit down, please. Would you like a beer, Dominic?"

"If you don't mind, I'll have some of the wine I brought. The guy at the liquor store assured me it would complement your casserole."

I laughed and handed him the bottle and a corkscrew. "Then, I'll have some, too."

Grace's casserole passed muster; Luke ate two servings without ketchup. And the lively dinner conversation eased my anxiety. When we'd pushed our plates aside, Dominic stood up. "I brought a few things for you guys," he told the kids. "Let me get them."

He returned with three gift bags, handing the first one to Lily. She pushed aside the purple tissue paper and took out a leather-covered journal with gold-edged pages. "It's beautiful!"

He handed the second bag to Red. "This is for you, Amy, and Luke to share."

Grinning with pride at being the designated gift-opener, Red pulled out a DVD, the newest *SpongeBob*. "Cool!" Luke yelled. "Can we go watch it now?"

"Once we've cleared the table and loaded the dishwasher," I said.

"Who's that one for?" Amy asked, pointing to the third bag.

"Sparky," Dominic replied, pulling out a long-handled contraption that would toss a tennis ball for fetching. "I thought we'd all have fun using it with him. Maybe we can bundle up and go try it in the back yard."

"I don't know about that," I said. It'd been a frigid, dull winter with little snowfall. The outdoors held no attraction for me. "Maybe when it warms up about twenty degrees."

I thought I saw a trace of disappointment in Dominic's eyes and immediately felt guilty. *To hell with guilt; this relationship will have to be built on honesty.*

"Do you mind if I go do homework?" Lily asked. "I've got an English test tomorrow."

"Go ahead," I said. "I'll load the dishwasher."

Dominic, Red, and I sat at the table while Amy carried the plates and glasses, one at a time, to the sink and Luke ferried the silverware over by the handful. "Be careful," Amy said, when he dropped the serving spoon, leaving a glob of casserole on the floor. "And wipe that up!"

I sure hope she doesn't get that bossy tone from me, I thought, leaning over to swipe up the spill with my paper napkin.

Luke turned to me. "Can we go now?"

"Sure," I said, and got up to release Red from her highchair. "We'll be down in a little bit."

I brought the box of chocolates and bottle of wine to the table. "Let's enjoy these in peace." I opened the box while Dominic refilled our glasses.

I nibbled at the dark chocolate-covered caramel, grinning as the rich flavors hit my taste buds. "It's like an amnesiac; one bite and you forget all the cares of the day."

"Rough day?"

"Uh-huh."

"Want to tell me about it?"

My defenses were down. I told him how Barbara had hoodwinked us, how she'd gone AWOL from the halfway house, and how we'd had to dismiss the fraud case against Victoria and Sonia. "You were right about her all along."

He met my gaze. "I hope you know that doesn't give me any pleasure."

"I know. I just feel like such a fool."

He reached over and touched my hand. "Caroline, your vulnerability means you're human. Like the rest of us. As I told you before, when Barbara got on the witness stand at the trial, I believed every word she said."

I nodded.

We sipped our wine in silence for a few minutes.

"The federal defender's office called this morning to offer me the job," he finally said.

My heart lurched. "Oh?"

"I turned it down."

"Before or after my call?"

"Before," he said, with a smile. "Hope springs eternal."

We both jumped when Luke yelled through the intercom, "Mom!"

"What, honey?"

"Sparky *really* wants to try his toy. Can we?"

I looked at Dominic and mouthed, "Happy?"

He grinned. "Luke, how about you and I take him out? I'll bring down our jackets."

I followed him downstairs and shivered when they opened the patio door and a blast of cold air invaded the family room. I grabbed a comforter and snuggled with Amy and Red on the couch, watching Sparky frolic outside with Dominic and Luke. "They're cray-cray," Amy said.

I laughed. "I agree, they're crazy. But it'll do Luke good to burn off some energy." *And, if this works out, it'll do Luke good to have a man around the house.*

Even their Y-chromosomes wouldn't allow Dominic, Luke, and Sparky to spend too long outdoors. Fifteen minutes later, Sparky joined Luke on the floor in front of the TV. "Can I get under that quilt?" Dominic asked the rest of us.

Red nodded. "I wanna sit on your lap."

"Great idea," he said, situating himself on the couch next to me, settling my youngest on his lap. I tucked the comforter around our shoulders as Luke cued up the video.

Ten minutes into the movie, Amy and Red moved off the couch and onto the floor. Dominic tucked us back in, then turned to look at me. "Sorry about Sparky's ball-tossing thingy," he whispered. "I wasn't considering the weather."

I took his hand as if it were the most natural thing in the world. "It's okay. We had fun watching you three out there, freezing your butts off. And Luke loved every minute of it."

He leaned over and kissed my cheek. "Thanks for giving us another try. I've got a good feeling about it."

"Me, too."

ACKNOWLEDGMENTS

Throughout the creation of this novel, I was fortunate to have the assistance of several former colleagues, all of whom I am proud to call my friends. My heartfelt thanks to: Corinne Hollar, attorney and tireless reader-critic, who read every draft and whose suggestions were invaluable; John Vaudreuil, United States Attorney for the Western District of Wisconsin, who advised me on the technicalities of my fictional prosecution; Martin Altstadt, retired Janesville Police Detective, for his knowledge of police procedures and con artists; Linda Colletti, bereavement counselor, who helped me with Caroline and Lily's struggles with grief; Dr. Jean M. McCabe, psychologist, for her expertise with bipolar disorder; Helen Healy Raatz, Asset Protection Associate for a major retailer, who filled me in on shoplifting, arrests, and prosecution; and Jane Erickson, reader and librarian, for her continued support. Any factual errors are mine, not theirs.

Thanks to Karyn Saemann, my editor at Inkspots, Inc., for her insight, instruction, patience, and common sense.

And, I'll be eternally grateful to my husband, Nick Spinelli, for his constant love and encouragement.

www.ingramcontent.com/pod-product-compliance
Lightning Source LLC
Chambersburg PA
CBHW030645120726
47905CB00001B/60